SHE OPENED THE FRIDGE. A HALF-FINISHED BOTTLE OF SAUTERNES STOOD BY THE MILK BOTTLE. TOM WOULD NEVER DRINK SWEET WHITE WINE.

She remembered the Bruce Springsteen record left on the sofa. He never sat on the sofa. She remembered he had been changing the sheets on the bed when she returned home from Greece. He never changed the sheets. He had had a bloody woman there while she'd been away!

Rage struck her with such force that the glass in her hand jerked upwards and some of the liquid spilt stickily on to her hand. The bastard! ... There was always some female simpering and wriggling around Tom ...

MAUREEN O'DONOGHUE

THE TRUTH
IN THE MIRROR

A SIGNET BOOK

SIGNET

Published by the Penguin Group
Penguin Books Ltd, 27 Wrights Lane, London w8 5TZ, England
Penguin Books USA Inc., 375 Hudson Street, New York, New York 10014, USA
Penguin Books Australia Ltd, Ringwood, Victoria, Australia
Penguin Books Canada Ltd, 10 Alcorn Avenue, Toronto, Ontario, Canada M4V 3B2
Penguin Books (NZ) Ltd, 182–190 Wairau Road, Auckland 10, New Zealand

Penguin Books Ltd, Registered Offices: Harmondsworth, Middlesex, England

First published by Viking 1993
Published in Signet 1994
1 3 5 7 9 10 8 6 4 2

Printed in England by Clays Ltd, St Ives plc

To my friends,
Annie, Catherine, Jo,
Maggie, Mary, Maureen,
Natalie, Salma, Sharon and Sylvia;
Brian, Graham, Ken, Michael and Cyril.

PART ONE

Chapter One

'I DON'T love you! It's time you knew I've been conning you for months. I've never loved you!'

'Then why did you marry me?' Bridget asked the question with automatic weariness.

'Because you trapped me into it.'

'That's a lie!' She was stung into angry response. 'You spent months and months trying to talk me into getting married. I didn't want to rock the boat. I was perfectly happy living with you. You were the one who went on and on about marrying. I can remember the exact words which finally persuaded me to agree. You said, "I want us to marry, because then we'll be exclusive."'

'I don't remember any of that.'

'Well, all our friends knew how terrified I was of marrying again. I was in floods of tears on the morning of the wedding and everyone who stayed overnight practically had to drag me to the Register Office, and then I cried during the whole ceremony. You may recall that.'

'No.'

There was a silence, and they did not look at each other. After travelling all night from Athens to Devon, Bridget was exhausted.

'I didn't want to come back, you know,' she said.

'That's quite obvious.' Tom studied his nails, his face closed and impassive.

'You don't love me.'

'I can't stand the restriction any longer. Our life

together has been appalling, I've hated every minute of it. I've never had any happiness with you and I want my freedom. I've always been a nomad.'

He moved pointlessly across the bedroom to stare at the closed curtains.

'You don't love me.'

'No.'

Why hadn't she stayed in Greece, she thought? Those impersonal telephone conversations had made it clear that he was not missing her, nor she him. It had been such a relief to escape his impatience and irritability, to lie in the sun, to change her mind about where to eat, to move on impulse from Paros to Mykonos to Rhodes, to be cheated out of that ten pounds by the taxi driver with the rigged meter, to dither and vacillate, all without his constant whinging. Why on earth had she not stayed there?

The big four-poster was sheltering and safe, the goose-down duvet and pillows wrapping her in warmth. Paintings by her daughter and her friends hung familiar on the walls. Her pots and bottles of make-up littered the dressing-table untidily, just as she had left them. The pottery mouse in a bed, the ebony trinket bowl, silver-framed photographs – each small gift was in its usual place where she could easily see it and be reminded of someone she loved. She had returned because this was home.

'Well, Tom, there's nothing as dead as a dead feeling,' she said, resignedly. 'So you'd better go and be a nomad.'

They looked at each other for the first time. She hoped he would go quickly and without the banging doors and shouting that usually accompanied their frequent rows, ending with one or other packing bags and moving out for twenty-four hours.

'Well, go on.'

He left the room and went downstairs. When he returned, he was carrying a small overnight bag. He pulled a few shirts, socks and some underwear from his chest of drawers and a suit from his wardrobe and crammed them into it. Then he stood in jeans and T-shirt, looking lost, like a child.

She suppressed the tiny stab of sentiment immediately. 'Go on,' she insisted, quietly. In fact, strangely, they had not raised their voices once.

He turned. There were tears in his eyes. 'I'm sorry,' he said, and walked out of the room.

Bridget heard the car start, roll gently to the gates, pause as he checked the road beyond for oncoming traffic and then accelerate away. He was gone.

Leaning back on the pillows, she let a thick down of depression smother her like a quilt. He would be back. They always went back to each other. This was his punishment for her week in Greece; she should have guessed how he would react, instead of foolishly expecting a welcome home.

The curtains were drawn from when she had first climbed into bed expecting to sleep off the journey. He had gone to the pub, as usual. Nothing had changed. She lay in the green twilight gazing blankly ahead, unaware of passing time. Sleep had not come and did not come. Vague thoughts drifted like small, dark clouds.

A quarrel had started it, of course, but not a very fierce one, rather bickering over the telephone between home and office, after he had spent some money, intended to pay bills, upon himself.

'I've had enough of this,' she had snapped. 'You're always doing exactly what you please, regardless of me. I'm buggering off for a week.'

'You're always threatening that sort of thing,' he had responded, unimpressed. 'And you know you won't do it.'

She had replaced the receiver, lifted it again and dialled a couple of travel agents. Thank God for credit cards.

'I'm booked on the nine o'clock flight from Luton to Athens,' she had informed him, minutes later.

Later still, driving past his office, she had stopped for a token kiss, almost for luck, before hitting the motorway at a speed which carried her to the airport with an hour to spare.

Bridget had not thought there was much seriously wrong between her and Tom that a short, sharp shock would not put right. They had been together for six years and married for three. They were a clever, entertaining couple, achievers, he as a journalist and she as a scriptwriter. Their relationship had always been volatile, a crossfire of intense adoration and flamboyant rows. Their friends had ceased to take any notice of their dramatic separations and reconciliations, as they so obviously enjoyed each other's company and were so well-matched. Her time with him had been the happiest of her life. She knew they were happy. They loved each other, and their current unrest had really been caused by Tom's problems at work.

Closing her eyes, she listened to the sparrows squabbling on the roof outside. Just like us, she thought, ruefully. Other middle-aged couples seemed to be able to potter along undramatically, putting up with each other's irritating ways. Tom and she should be able to behave like that. It was time they both grew up. Yet, in her heart, she knew they never would.

Quinky, their black cat, jumped on to the bed and she stroked him, comforted by the crescendo of his purr and his paws trampling ecstatically over her stomach. Thinking back, she knew she should have been more patient, more understanding.

The local newspaper group had been taken over by a multinational, which had appointed a new board of directors and a new editorial director. Her husband, who had left a high-flying Fleet Street career to join her and run the local newspaper, was unhappy with the sweeping changes proposed, to go tabloid and double the advertising rates; he had been right.

In a matter of months, the comfortably profitable and popular little publication was struggling. Tom, forced to carry out the series of catastrophic management decisions and helplessly facing the vociferous daily protests of the town, had begun to spend most of his evenings downing pints of beer and roaring in the pub, returning home only to eat a meal and fall asleep. He had stopped bothering with the garden and the numerous plans they had made for the house. He became cantankerous and critical, answering her mildest remark with unconcealed annoyance. Conversation between them had virtually ceased.

After six months of this, Bridget had had enough. She felt bored and stale, although she knew she was going to feel even more bored, as well as lonely, in Greece. The sun would not be as seductive without him, meals would be dull and eaten uncomfortably whilst reading a book as protection against her isolation in restaurants crowded with jolly twosomes. There would be no one with whom to share the bastions of Rhodes, or count the black-garbed grandmothers herding goats on the hills, or splash in the warm, clear water. She was not a woman who struck up easy conversations with strangers and drinking alone was no fun. She would miss him dreadfully.

At the end of the first part of her journey of rebellion, she had found herself writing in the diary she always kept when travelling:

> If Tom had been dropped in to dinner by helicopter, we'd have had a lovely time, but if he'd had to endure the last disorganized, expensive and exhausting thirty-six hours with me, he'd have turned it into a nightmare, groaning over every disaster, instead of it being something I've managed, with considerable philosophy, to enjoy.

The week had passed far too quickly. Bridget had found herself relaxed and happy, peacefully visiting little monasteries, enchanted with the wood full of millions of red and zebra-striped butterflies on Paros; hypnotized by slow, low flights in the tiny Dornier 228 over the shoals of islands, mountains folding into the sea, deserted sandy coves, isolated cottages surrounded by stonewalled fields, villages and fishing ports set in a sea like silver-blue, finely grained leather.

People had talked to her without her having to make any effort and, to her surprise, they apparently found her entertaining. They had not seemed to think her stupid or boring and, one evening, as a young couple burst out laughing at some remark she had made, Bridget realized, at last, that there was something deeply wrong between Tom and her; that she did not want to return to the life they had been leading.

Sitting motionless in the big bed now, she became aware of large tears running down her face and neck. The short escape had been such an adventure. She had begun to feel almost girlish again there, but here, within only a few hours, she was already bogged down and tired.

Erin and Rake, the two dogs, were barking downstairs. They would not have had a walk this morning. Bridget dragged herself up unwillingly and caught sight of her naked body in the full-length looking-glass, the haggard, lined face and drooping shoulders and pendulous breasts above rolls of stomach and massive, flabby thighs. Even the light filtered to dusk by the curtains could not veil her ugliness and the kimono she pulled on only emphasized it. She had been slim and pretty when they met. She should never have let this happen to herself.

It was cold and windy outside, but the flowerbed bordering the drive was luminous with spikes of delphiniums and hollyhocks and old roses, blues and crimsons and purples like a stained-glass window.

The medieval cottages of the village clung tightly to each other as they had for the last four centuries, their thick walls protecting one generation after another of families older than those of any blue-blooded line. The faces she passed in the car were as known and unchanged as the homes in which they lived. No one had ever painted portraits of their forefathers, but theirs were the same features which had stamped their ancestors who had walked these same streets. Bridget felt a surge of affection for the place and its people.

As she released the dogs, they hurtled down the stone bank on to the beach.

This was not one of those smooth sweeps of sand for girls in bikinis and paddling toddlers. Pebbles littered the strand and low rocks tumbled on to it from far out to sea, breaking up the flow of the incoming tide and trapping the spray. Lines of rotting posts marked where once there had been a thriving small port; but the sea had long since receded from the edge of the village leaving marshland and untidy stony rubble.

9

Erin and her young pup, Rake, had gone off chasing one seagull after another with yelping optimism, bounding through the water and leaping boulders until now they were far beyond shouting range. Bridget turned up the collar of her jacket and stomped gloomily after them. Forced marches in crocodile formation at weekends and compulsory sport every afternoon at school had left her with a deep resistance to exercise and taking the dogs out was a duty she usually left to Tom. But at least the effort kept her from thinking and, as the dogs headed slowly back to her at last, she was slightly surprised to find she was feeling less despondent.

That evening she played Brahms symphonies over and over at full volume on the record player. She sank into the mighty crescendoes and sweeps of Von Karajan's conducting, letting her emotions be manipulated by the soaring and the falling, the violence and sweetness for hour after hour. It was so long since she had listened to any classical music, although it had once been as constant around her as air. But Tom had introduced her to pop and played nothing else, and she quite liked that, too, though not in the same way.

Bridget was not hungry, so it was easy to diet. She was always dieting anyway; well, at least until the past six months, when she had stopped caring and had been surprised and quite grateful that Tom had not seemed to mind either.

He was such a beautiful man, elegant and golden, with wide shoulders and slim hips and round, deliciously tight and sexy buttocks and long, shapely legs any woman would have killed for; a racehorse of a man. She had

10

lusted after him from the second she saw him, and yet . . .
She whipped up the butterscotch-flavoured diet drink
crossly, refusing to continue along that line. What was
the point? That was the way he was and she accepted it,
because she loved him.

Two days had passed since he had walked out and she
had heard nothing. It did not usually take so long for
them to contact each other after a quarrel and she could
not reach him at the office because it was Sunday.

She opened the fridge. A half-finished bottle of Sauternes
stood by the milk bottle. Tom would never drink sweet
white wine. She remembered the Bruce Springsteen record
left on the sofa. He never sat on the sofa. She remembered
he had been changing the sheets on the bed when she
returned home from Greece. He never changed the sheets.
He had had a bloody woman there while she'd been away!

Rage struck her with such force that the glass in her
hand jerked upwards and some of the liquid spilt stickily
on to her hand. The bastard! It must have been that slut,
Cathy, who cleaned for her. Bridget was always catching
them giggling and flirting together, Tom leaning against
the car bonnet, grinning, the girl simpering in the doorway. There was always some female simpering and
wriggling around Tom. The bastard!

At that moment the phone rang.

As though in echo to her own mind, Cathy's breathless
baby voice asked, 'Did you have a nice holiday?'

Bridget drew in a silent breath and felt her free hand
clench.

'Yes, thank you,' she answered coolly.

'I wondered if I'm to come in tomorrow? Only my
Mum's going into Exeter and I thought I'd go, too, if you
don't want me.'

Clotted cream couldn't be more sickly. The slut!

'No, Cathy, I don't want you.' She paused. 'In fact, I was going to tell you I shan't be needing you here any more. Tom and I are cutting back.'

She poured the sweet wine down the kitchen sink, moithering to herself feverishly, rehearsing how she would confront him, accuse him. The bastard! The bastard! He had done it to spite her – and not for the first time.

She paced around the sunlit house and garden unseeing, becoming more and more agitated until she found she was panting, as much from inner dislocation as from the climb to the top of the cherry walk where she sat down under a tree. She must not lose control, she told herself, looking down at her trembling fingers. Hanging around doing nothing for hour after hour letting herself be churned up by her own fantasies served no purpose. She must stay calm.

At midday the following day he finally telephoned.

'How are you?'

'Fine.' She was wary.

There was a silence, which he waited for her to break, since she was by far the more articulate of the two, but this time she did not.

'I suppose we ought to talk,' he offered eventually.

'I suppose so.' She hesitated and then, 'You said you didn't love me.'

'There are things I love about you.' It was a guarded answer and a little chill ran through her.

'I've got a job on this evening, but I could come out tomorrow.'

'No,' she decided immediately. 'I don't think you should come here. We'll only shout at each other.'

'Where then?'

'Somewhere neutral. A pub.'

'I'll ring you tomorrow and we'll fix it,' he said.

'OK. Goodbye.' She was brisk now.

'Goodbye.'

As the receiver clicked, she burst into noisy sobs of anger and bewilderment. Downstairs, the dogs started barking as she bawled, which only made her cry the louder in great, self-indulgent wails.

Her eyes cried themselves dry. The cream sheets lay folded on the ironing board outside the bathroom, washed and waiting to be ironed. Pain flickered through her again at the thought of Cathy lying giggling in her side of the bed. That girl would have giggled all the time. She always did. Bridget decided never to sleep in those sheets again.

She undressed and stood on the scales to discover she was six pounds lighter. This cheered her up. Throwing on a dressing-gown, she went downstairs, surveyed the accumulated mess of ten days without distaste and picked up the telephone again.

'Pat? Are you busy? I wonder if you could help me out? Cathy hasn't appeared again.'

Pat arrived, chattering non-stop. She was a small, wizened woman in her late fifties, brightly and frenziedly overactive from the frustration of thirty-five years' marriage to Bob, a taciturn man, who spent all his time in their garage putting together bits of wood. Their small business had failed and they needed money, but Bob was worried that Pat might earn more than he did if she went cleaning other people's houses. However, on the frequent occasions that Bridget was let down by Cathy and needed help ... well, as his wife said, everyone knew these

writer people were useless at organizing their own lives
. . . so he usually gave his monosyllabic consent.

As she sat at her word processor, Bridget could hear
Pat all over the house, like a chipmunk. It did not matter
whether her endless questions and conversation were
answered or not; in fact, she rarely seemed to hear
answers, the flow of high-pitched words twittered on,
regardless, in soprano above the motorized snarls of
vacuum cleaner, washing machine and tumble drier.

Bridget stared at the dialogue she had written before
going away and brooded over what it must be like to live
with Bob, a man whose lack of response would have
dampened the enthusiasm of women far tougher than Pat
seemed to be.

Yet Pat involved herself in all the committees and
events of the active village with sharp-eyed eagerness and
she nurtured her riverside garden with a competitive
passion which carried off enough prizes at the annual
horticultural show to make her the object of envy.

There was a screech from above and, glad of the
interruption, Bridget hurried into the hall.

'What's happened?' she called. 'Are you all right?'

Pat's normally sallow face appeared flushed over the
banisters.

'A beetle! There's a beetle up here!' she shrilled, trip-
ping down the stairs. 'I don't mind mice, not even rats,
and I don't mind spiders, although Bob won't go near a
spider, but beetles!'

She arrived panting at the bottom and said, triumphantly, 'Do you know, I once had a miscarriage over a
beetle.'

The trouble with Pat's stories was that she never
stopped long enough to reveal the circumstances, but

simply whirred on to the next subject leaving only tantalizing scraps behind. She was also fascinated by biology, about which she had remarkable beliefs. Her lungs were always bubbling, she was allergic to everything and no one's flushes were hotter than hers.

'Of course, I've only got half the number of veins in my right leg that I've got in my left one,' she had informed Bridget once.

'Really, Pat?' Bridget had responded with expectant interest. 'Were you born like that?'

'Oh no.' The reply was faintly pitying at such ignorance. 'The doctor took most of them away some years ago.'

When she had gone, the house seemed empty for the first time. Outside, the garden was already covered in weeds from a fortnight's neglect.

Bridget loved gardening and, soon after Tom had moved into the overgrown two acres, they had drawn up a plan for old rose beds and a flower-covered pergola and the raised round stone pool on the rim of which they would sit trailing their hands through the water under the leaves of the waterlilies. Now there were to be shaded paths between tall, fragrant bushes, and beech hedge, fresh and salad green in spring and covered with potato crisps of leaves in winter, and steep terraces of rhododendrons, azaleas and camellias and a lawn, just bumpy enough to turn croquet into real war.

When she had finished work, Bridget found deep satisfaction in grubbing about in the soil for an hour or so each day. Her tired, but still racing, brain would slow and then stop thinking altogether as she tugged out weeds and dug holes for delicate young plants, aware only of the smell and texture of the earth.

Now, she turned away from the window and the garden. Her daughter and her mother always plunged into orgies of housework and gardening at the first sign of domestic crisis, working off their discontent on carpets and washing, pummelling dough, cooking and freezing gargantuan meals, hacking and chopping hedges, edges and branches into ruthless symmetry until they felt better. But, without Tom, Bridget's surroundings held no appeal. Her safe, secure womb of a home became just a house, any house. It was as though it had lost its soul. The same had happened after her first marriage ended: more than two years had passed before she had felt able to garden again.

That night she drugged herself once more with music, Casals playing Schumann and Mendelssohn and Couperin's *Song of the Birds*, profound, vibrating notes which eased her mind.

In the morning, she rose only to feed the dogs and let them into the garden, then went back to bed to wait for his call. Fear lurked in the corners of the room. None of their quarrels had ever lasted so long, or been conducted with such remoteness. She was used to screaming like the traditional fishwife and rattling off volleys of insults which drove him mad.

Then he would shout back, stomp off to the pub and return later to bang on the locked bedroom door. Finally, they would make up through sheer exhaustion, and peace would reign for another week or two.

She phoned her daughter.

'Honestly, Mummy, you two!'

'It's different this time,' she murmured, miserably.

'Look, you had a super time in Greece without him and he's been a pig all year. Are you really missing him?'

Bridget thought. 'No,' she confessed. She was not missing his actual presence. The house was more tranquil without him. 'But I love him.'

'I know you do, but he's a dildo.'

'Deirdre!'

'Well, he is. He's always been completely selfish and most of the time he just swallows you up.'

'I thought you'd grown to like him,' Bridget said weakly, thinking at the same time that she had been forty before she had even heard of a dildo.

'There are things I like about him.' God! Her daughter sounded just like Tom. 'But he never reveals himself, you know, and he makes no effort at all to do anything that doesn't suit him.'

Bridget was defensive. 'He's worked terribly hard on the house and garden.'

'Because he wants to,' her daughter replied, firmly. 'He doesn't appreciate you and life won't end without him, you know.'

'Oh, but it will, it will,' Bridget thought to herself. She could not bear life without Tom.

She phoned Zoe, expecting her secretary to say she was in a meeting, or away at a sales conference, or abroad on some campaign, but she was put straight through.

'Tom's left me,' Bridget told her.

'Oh, don't worry, babe, he'll be back,' her blonde, high-powered friend responded. 'I must dash, I'm late for a meeting.'

It was true that when someone said, 'Don't worry', what they really meant was 'Don't worry *me*.'

They had met while working for the same London advertising agency years ago. Bridget remembered how it had almost been necessary to schedule time to see her own family, and there had certainly been none to spare for other people's sob stories. She had left to write her plays, but Zoe was now a director of the company.

She wanted to go on calling friends, to talk compulsively through her apprehension, but they had heard it all before and, besides, he might be trying to get through to her. Although she knew he was not.

She closed the curtains and waited, immobilized with tension and, later, lay down and napped a stiff sleep, to wake hunched under the bedclothes with freezing hands and feet and shivering with nerves. It was five o'clock. He would be leaving the office soon and she did not know where he was staying. She had to talk to him.

'Hello.'

'Who's that?'

'You know perfectly well who it is.'

'No I don't. If you don't identify yourself, you could be anyone.'

'You were going to ring.'

'I've been busy.'

'We were going to meet and talk tonight.'

'Well, can we make it tomorrow? I'm working tonight.'

'I suppose so.'

She put down the phone and was suddenly overcome with fury. How dare he keep her waiting all day! He had done it on purpose, to torment her. How dare he pretend not to know her voice! She was not going through tomorrow in the same way.

She rang the number again. 'No, we can't make it tomorrow. It isn't convenient for me. You said we would meet tonight,' she blurted out.

'I didn't make any definite arrangement and I can't come tonight.'

'You promised to see me tonight and you can damn well cancel your bloody job.'

'No.' The phone went dead.

Scalding temper flooded through her so rapidly she felt bloated with heat. She was so enraged, she was sightless. Pounding the receiver buttons with shaking hands, she re-dialled.

'If you don't keep your word and meet me tonight, I shall come down there and smash every window in that sodding office and then wreck every stick of furniture inside,' she shrieked.

'Then you'll be arrested.'

'I don't give a fuck!'

'All right! All right! I'll meet you at eight o'clock at the Dog and Fox. Now, for Christ's sake get off the line and leave me alone!'

Her wrath vanished within minutes, to be replaced by despair. It would be hopeless to try and talk now. They would get nowhere. What had happened to them? She felt confused and impotent.

Sophie answered calmly, as always. 'What is it, Bridget?'

Bridget burst into tears.

Sophie was an immensely elegant and stylish woman, who looked about Bridget's own age, but had to be about seventy. She had been her marriage guidance counsellor through her first marriage, though all her experience had not been enough to overcome the insurmountable problems of a husband who was an alcoholic. Bridget regarded her with an awed admiration which was almost child-like. She felt privileged that they had become friends. Sophie was so wise and, although she always felt guilty for imposing, she was unable to resist consulting her over every major trauma in her life. Sophie met all her dilemmas with measured and reassuring thoughtfulness.

'Well, it does sound as though it would not be a good idea to meet him tonight,' she agreed. 'Why don't you explain quietly how you feel to him and suggest you meet another evening?'

'He's left the office by now and I don't know where he's staying.'

'Then perhaps you could turn up at eight and just say you think it would be better to see each other another time and then leave before you get involved.'

'I don't think that would work. He wouldn't let it work.'

'Then just don't appear and ring the office tomorrow to explain why.'

'That seems the best I can do.'

He might have gone for a drink with the other reporters in the pub opposite the office. Bridget rang there.

'Tom O'Dare? I'll call him,' said the barman. 'Who shall I say it is?'

'Mrs Anderson about the council tomorrow,' she answered, quickly.

'Hello, Tom O'Dare here.' He sounded puzzled.

'It's me. I didn't want to embarrass you by giving my name,' she said.

He laughed in quite a friendly way.

'Tom, I don't think we should meet tonight after all.'

'Why not?'

'I just don't think it would work now that we've had another row.'

'I expect it'll be all right.'

'No. We would only fall out again.'

'I'll ring you tomorrow then.'

'Don't say that if you're not going to. I can't stand it.'

'Well, if I say I'm going to ring, don't believe me.' He sounded rattled. 'I don't know what I'm going to do to-morrow.'

'I'd rather you said nothing.' She could feel her control slipping away and her voice beginning to tremble.

'OK. I'll say nothing.' He ended the conversation abruptly.

He was playing with her. He had always had a cruel streak. He loved flirting with women, leading them on with implied promises, yet remaining just out of reach until they made complete fools of themselves, when he would walk away with a little smile. In the early days of their relationship, he had teased her by blowing hot and cold, so that she never knew where she stood, or what he wanted, or what was expected of her. A friend had once commented that his attraction for her was his elusiveness and she believed that. Most men were neither clever, nor unpredictable, enough to hold her interest. She had met her match in Tom. Yet, she was a straightforward woman, inexperienced. Her first marriage had lasted nearly twenty years and her first husband had been an honest man. They had not manipulated each other and she had had no idea of how to handle such games; but she had learnt since she had known Tom and she recognized the game now. This time she was not going to play.

Chapter Two

OVER the next few days Bridget sat hunched on the sofa, drinking endless cups of coffee and looking back, clutching at the dreams on which she had built the last six years of her life. Her body moved around the house, but she did not notice her surroundings. Her mind was in the past and in another country.

She had visited Portugal for the first time with her daughter, who had manoeuvred her about with military precision in an attempt to force her recovery from the failure of her first marriage.

After the last celibate years of that liaison, all Bridget wanted was a screw, but she would have been better off holidaying with her great-grandmother, for Deirdre, long hair pinned severely into a bun and with an expression of steadfast antipathy on her face, kept the legion of interested waiters, barmen and boatmen firmly at bay. A woman of her mother's age was not supposed to have a libido, even if she did look about thirty and everyone mistook them for sisters.

They had rented a two-bedroomed apartment in Lagos and, two days before they were due to leave for England, they had lunched in a taverna near the beach. After they had eaten and Bridget was about to step back into the sunlight, a man in a dusty pink T-shirt and faded jeans passed her in the doorway. The shock of electricity stabbed her in the stomach like a scalpel. She twisted round and, to her amazement, saw the man walk up to her daughter.

'Hello, Deirdre,' he said.

As he turned, she had seen his features for the first time, tall and deeply tanned, with hair bleached by the sun, not a spare ounce of flesh on his body and a lean face etched by experience. Bridget was already obsessively in love. She hovered politely, but insistently, beside them. Her daughter spoke to him briefly and then herded her out.

'Why on earth didn't you introduce me to that gorgeous man?' Bridget had asked her furiously.

'You're not meeting Tom O'Dare. He's most unsuitable,' retorted Deirdre with insufferable primness. She and her boyfriend, Barney, had met him while camping the previous year. 'He's always drunk *and* he's a journalist.'

'Well, I was a journalist once.'

'Exactly.'

Bridget had lain on the beach and felt that electric volt again and again. She knew the exact shape of his head, the breadth of his shoulders, the length of his arms and legs. She could not speak, she could not think, she could hardly breathe.

Six years later, as she blundered round the garden, or fed the dogs, or gazed blindly at the paintings on the wall or simply curled in foetal position in the womb of the great tester bed, Bridget locked on to that moment when she had first passed Tom O'Dare in the doorway, without even being able to see his face against the sun. In the heart of her home in the depths of rural England, that second before they had met was as acute as it had been then. Her nerves thrilled just as exquisitely and that same sick sensation of fever overwhelmed her at the memory.

Her daughter had pushed her on to a bus which had

taken them to some obscure village above the town for dinner that evening. They were sitting in the vine-covered courtyard and about to order when Bridget had glanced into the obscurity of the bar and seen him again.

'That man is there. Tom O'Dare. I want you to introduce me.' She spoke with urgency.

'No,' said her daughter stubbornly.

'Look, Deirdre, I'm a grown woman and I'm free for the first time in years and I want you to introduce me to Tom O'Dare.'

'Mummy, he's another drunk, like Daddy. You can't meet him.'

'I don't care! I don't care! Introduce me,' she demanded, implacably, flinching at the tears gathering in her daughter's eyes.

'No.'

Bridget stood up and walked into the bar. She sat on a bar stool and boldly caught the eye of the proprietor.

'A Bloody Mary?' she ordered, hoping he understood.

Tom O'Dare was with a group of people in the corner. Deirdre, moving more slowly than Shakespeare's schoolboy, came and sat beside her, and the man turned.

'Oh, hello again,' he said, and joined them.

Bridget ordered a coffee for her daughter and, barely glancing at him, asked, 'Would you like a drink?'

'I'm broke. I can't buy you one back,' he replied bluntly.

'It doesn't matter. I'm not broke.'

He had a beer. The tumblerful of Bloody Mary was half vodka and fierce with pepper and tabasco. She sat, letting them talk, and decided she'd never tasted better. Warmth from two years in the sun radiated from him, she felt it down her side. Perhaps he had not even noticed her, but that did not matter. There was all the time in the world now.

Even Deirdre had been forced to laugh at his tales of travelling disasters, of being chased by the bulls at Pamplona and of losing his only pair of jeans in a bet in Italy and of actually being banned from a beer tent at the Munich Beer Festival, an unheard-of occurrence.

Bridget had bought several more rounds. He was noisy and boastful, bitter about a girlfriend who had left him some years before. She was reserved by nature and, had she not been so besotted, she would have retreated from him. She noticed that his nails were bitten down to the quick.

'Do you write much here?' she wondered.

'Not much.'

Then she knew. She had met men and women like him before, people who had run away from their problems to the sun and somehow become trapped by the debilitating simplicity of survival and been unable to return home. She had done it herself, escaping once with Deirdre from Sam to Madeira for two whole years. She could have stayed for ever, giving the occasional English lesson and facing nothing worse than paying a few escudos a night for their rooms in the pension. It had been the hardest thing in the world to board that boat for London and reality again.

'Have you eaten?' she asked.

'Not recently.'

She had expected the answer. He was very broke indeed.

'We have eggs and ratatouille at the apartment. Do you want some?'

If he noticed Deirdre's agonized expression as he followed them to the bus stop, he ignored it.

There was a bottle of brandy in the kitchen. Bridget did not know why she had bought it, as neither she nor her daughter drank brandy, but she opened it and put it in front of him. 'Help yourself.'

He shook his head.

'Wine then?'

She had thrown the omelettes together and the three of them had sat, mainly listening to him. A series of unbelievable coincidences had begun to emerge. It turned out that, years before, Bridget and Tom O'Dare had worked on the same newspaper, he on the news desk and she on the diary column; they had lived in the same Mayfair street; he had met her ex-husband while at university; he had spent months reporting the court proceedings of a particularly sordid scandal only a couple of miles from her house in Devon. It was as though, for twenty years, they had been leading parallel lives only a hand's breadth apart.

Deirdre had given up the unequal struggle at last and gone to bed. Tom and Bridget had stayed talking at the table about mutual friends and colleagues, stories they had worked on, countries they had visited, of Venice and Florence. She was cool and entertaining. She did not betray herself.

It was the early hours of the morning when she went into her bedroom and took the blanket off the second bed.

'You can sleep on the sofa,' she had said, handing it to him.

In the bathroom, she had showered with care and taken too long over brushing her teeth. No sound had come from the sitting-room and she had not known what to do. She put on her nightdress and went slowly back to her room and sat on the bed.

Bridget was not pretty, but she was attractive. Her fine brown hair was threaded with strands of red and there was an infusion of sympathy behind the intelligence in her grey eyes. She gave an impression of toughness and vulnerability which drew men to her, although she had desired very few and this, together with slightly puritanical views, had left her surprisingly untutored about the opposite sex and its ways.

After being incarcerated in a succession of girls' boarding schools from the age of five to seventeen, she had found a year at home with her widowed mother intolerable and had run away to marry the first man she met: Sam, ten years older, an alcoholic, out-of-work actor. Their daughter had been born six months later, a fact which both mothers-in-law tried to pass off as a premature birth, to the sly amusement of their friends.

The marriage had been physically destroyed within twelve months by Sam's violence, but had lasted another eighteen years. During that time, Bridget had had one wild affair while they were separated. Then, after returning home at the age of thirty, she had simply stopped thinking about sex altogether and her previously overheated body had complied.

This remarkably comfortable state was exploded by the final break-up with Sam. Within weeks, she had become slinky, dramatically changing her hairstyle and spending hours on the sunbed at the local beauty salon and money she did not have on silk lingerie. An amazing number of men had appeared at her door armed with bottles of wine, invitations to dinner and smirks on their faces. They were all married to her friends and all insultingly unacceptable.

Bridget's body had refused to behave any longer, her

27

eyes had grown larger, her mouth pouted, her breasts bounced, her nipples rose at the slightest hint of a breeze, her hips swayed, her stomach muscles were permanently tightened, her crotch ached. Now, Tom O'Dare was lying in the next room and she had to have him.

She waited, but he did not come. If she waited any longer, he would probably be asleep. Then she remembered she had only given him a blanket. The sitting-room, as she pushed the door ajar, was in darkness.

'Would you like a pillow?' she whispered.

'No thanks, there's a cushion here.' He answered in normal tones, which she imagined would waken her daughter.

She closed the door and almost ran back to her bedroom.

He would be gone from her life in the morning. A man she would never see again. A lifetime of believing that the man must make the first move froze her to the spot. But she had to have him.

She had crept back to his door, opened it and tiptoed blindly into the centre of the blackness.

'Would you . . . like some company?' Her voice had sounded as high pitched as a child's. Aghast at her own brazenness, she wanted to rush away.

'Why not?' It was a casual answer, neither inviting nor rejecting.

She crept forward again and knelt on the floor by the sofa, shaking as though drowning in ice.

'I'm very cold,' she tried to explain, terrified by now by her own behaviour.

'I'm a warm person,' he said and put a lazy arm around her.

They were to laugh about that often, such an irresistible, laid-back response.

The bed would be better, they decided, and she had led the way, walking as though on fire. They had climbed in simultaneously, side by side – and failed in their first attempt to make love.

He rolled off and drew her against him. The finest French velvet could not have been softer than his skin. He smelt male and smoky. Bridget, starved for so long of physical contact, lay ecstatically with her cheek in the hollow of his shoulder.

'Don't worry,' she said.

'I'm not,' he replied, in the same unruffled voice.

'I mean –' she had chosen her words carefully '– I don't mind. I'm happy just being here.'

'That's sweet.' For the first time, he sounded a little surprised.

They had dozed lightly, every nerve ending in her body aware of him. Yet she was completely relaxed, utterly happy. It would not have mattered if he had not made love to her at all, but after an hour – or was it two? – he did. The earth did not move. Gently, two strangers explored each other and, with exquisite tenderness, the adamantine winter of Bridget's years in isolation thawed at last.

'I feel replete,' he murmured, and fell asleep.

Early the next morning, she had opened her eyes to find him staring at the ceiling. Putting her arm over his chest, she had snuggled up. He did not stir; not even his gaze flickered. She lay quite still for a moment.

Of course, she should have expected this, she thought. He had had a quick screw with a stray woman and now wanted to be on his way. She went to the bathroom and, on the way back, looked into her daughter's room.

Deirdre was also awake and looking despondent, her long, dark hair falling over her shoulders as she sat up.

'Are you all right?' she asked her mother.

'I'm not sure, but I think so.' Bridget had no regrets.

Taking the blanket from the sofa she had returned to her bedroom to climb into the spare bed.

'What are you doing over there?' Tom O'Dare asked.

'You seemed to want to be on your own,' she answered.

'No. Why should you think that?'

'When I put my arm round you, you rejected me,' she replied, without rancour.

'No. Come back here.'

This time, the earth did move.

For the first time since her arrival in Portugal, it rained, not softly as in England, but in an almost solid sheet of water, accompanied by animal bellows of thunder and lightning which illuminated the entire sky. The fishermen had pulled their boats far up on to the sand in front of the apartment; the sea was writhing and purple and scattered with ermine tails of froth.

When he sat down at the table for breakfast, she had assumed the weather was preventing him from leaving. Mercifully, Deirdre looked more cheerful and had brought in the coffee, then disappeared back to the kitchen to take charge of some stale rolls and more eggs. Bridget knew she might as well tell him now.

'Well, isn't she smashing?'

'Who?'

'My daughter, of course.'

An extraordinary look had passed over his face as a previous idea was visibly rejected and replaced by another.

'Oh,' he said. 'Oh.'

30

'You didn't know,' she smiled.

'That was the last thing I thought.' He seemed very sheepish.

'What did you think then?' She wondered if he were embarrassed, or even upset by the revelation of her age.

'Well, you seemed so ... affectionate ... touching, kissing each other goodnight, you know ...' He ruffled his hair and grimaced. 'I thought you were lesbians.'

Bridget shrieked with laughter. 'For God's sake, don't tell her.'

Had she been more worldly wise, she would have known of every man's ambition to seduce a lesbian, but she only knew about every woman's fantasies about seducing a priest.

Later in the morning, they had braved the weather for the bar on the beach, to sit wetly over innumerable coffees and sticky liqueurs and beer. They had talked about Bridget's plays, which had made little money, and about the film script, for which she had finally gained a Hollywood contract. She knew she would never see him again and all day she wondered why he did not leave. Then she remembered those aimless days in Madeira and realized he probably had nothing else to do.

'Will you send me one of your plays?' he asked.

'Maybe. Where should I send it?'

'I don't know.' He was drifting. His plans, if he had any, were fluid. 'I'll give you a friend's address in England.'

'And what if you don't go back to England? I'll have wasted a manuscript.'

'I'd go back now, if I weren't skint,' he confessed.

She scrutinized him carefully. He looked tired and unhappy and homeless.

'If you don't go back soon, it'll be too late.' She spoke very seriously.

He inhaled on the cheap cigarette. 'I know. I just don't know how.'

'You could be repatriated.' She turned to her daughter. 'We were repatriated once, weren't we?'

The girl shot her an offended glance and stayed silent. Tom looked mystified. For a man who had travelled the world reporting wars and every kind of disaster, he was remarkably ignorant.

'You go to the British Embassy, tell them you have no money and they give you enough to cover the cheapest way home, probably by train from Portugal. When you arrive in England, they take your passport from you and don't return it until you've repaid the money,' Bridget explained.

He said nothing. She waited and then added, 'I'll give you the money to get to Lisbon.'

Deirdre gave an audibly angry sigh and Bridget opened her purse. Tom took the money.

Around teatime he left, insisting that she walk with him to the bus stop by pretending he did not know the way.

'I'll be in England before you.' He kissed her briefly and smiled down at her. 'I'll see you in England next week.'

'Oh, yes,' she said, and did not believe a word of it.

He had boarded the bus. She knew she would never see him again.

'You're mad!' her daughter had raged. 'How much did you give him?'

'Not much.'

'You won't see him or the money again.'

'I know.' She thought she felt perfectly tranquil.

But he would not release her mind. She relived every second they had spent together, went over every word of their conversations. All night she had lain with her heart on his heart and clung to the overwhelming joy which had filled her at the touch of his skin.

'Do you think . . .?' she began a dozen times the next day.

'Maybe, he might . . .?' A dozen times more.

'What do you think?' she pressed her daughter over and over. 'Tell me, honestly, what you think.'

'I think he's a piss-head like Daddy,' Deirdre had replied, remorselessly.

'No.' Bridget was certain. 'If he'd been an alcoholic, he would have drunk that brandy, but he never touched a drop.'

'Well, you're well rid of him. I can't wait to get you on the plane and away from here.'

'Don't you think . . . he just might . . .?'

'Mummy, he's a man who threw up a successful and highly paid career at a moment's notice, who's roamed round Europe for two years, who's spent every penny he had and is probably only left with the clothes he stands up in. He's the last man in the world for you. Be reasonable. Forget him.'

Reasonably, Bridget hugged her pillow in bed and imagined his caresses again. On the flight home, she had stared over the brilliant white cloudscape and watched as the sun was left behind and seen nothing.

Zoe and her husband, David, with whom they stayed in London, were disconcerted by her abstraction and looked questioningly at Deirdre, who sullenly dragged her mother round endless shops and sights in an effort to distract her. But by then Bridget was hopelessly addicted to Tom.

Three days later, jumpy and itchy as a flea-ridden cat, she had driven back to Devon at a suicidal speed which reduced the journey by a whole hour. As they had entered the house, the telephone was ringing.

'How are you?' he drawled.

'Where are you?' She was gasping with shock.

'I'm at Victoria Station. London.'

He must have appeared an unprepossessing figure in dated clothes among the *habitués* of Fleet Street, but ex-colleagues found him shifts on news desks and he had hitchhiked to Devon on his first free day.

Bridget, with the image of beachcomber firmly in her head, had found him waiting on the pavement in the small nearby town wearing a jacket, slacks, shirt and tie. He looked so incredibly handsome, she nearly fainted.

She remembered, as though it had happened that morning, his walking into the wide hall of the house and looking up the sweep of the staircase to the high ceiling.

'Is this all yours?' he had asked.

'Well, the building society's,' she had replied, blushing with pride at his reaction to the lovely old house, which gave meaning to her life's work and effort and which, in truth, was the place she loved more than any human being except her daughter.

Moving as though not touching the ground, she had shown him the drawing-room and the Edwardian conservatory full of geraniums and a rampant vine, the winter sitting-room, her study, the bedrooms, the big farm kitchen with its pantries and utility rooms.

Then they had gone into the garden. How quickly it

was turning back to wilderness. After only half a year of inattention, brambles and bindweed were racing up the shrubs. Oat-grass like gold filigree and slender weeping brome and spires of meadow fescue had grown to full height and paint splashes of wild poppies spotted the kitchen garden. The roses, unpruned the previous winter, flung their branches over the nettles. It had never been a regimented garden, with clean-cut edges and neat lawns. A certain disorder suited Bridget's nature; she had been happy to let daisies and scarlet pimpernel spread, and woolly mulleins and lamb's tails self-seed where they would, and ivy cover the walls. Even now, the garden was beautiful.

She had had three dogs then; Hattie, the oldest, who had not left her side for the past eleven years, had deserted her for the first time, instantly besotted with this man, following him around with liquid adoration in her eyes as though unable to believe her luck. Her flattery was so irresistible to him that within hours he had openly fallen in love with her.

By the end of the day, Tom was part of the house and the house seemed part of him.

That had been the first of many such visits in which she chattered and fed him and played him music and took him to local pubs and lived in a state of enraptured terror.

He was so offhand, sometimes telephoning every night, sometimes leaving days between each call; allowing her to drive him everywhere when he turned up, letting her wait on him, never committing himself, never telling her he loved her.

He played Radio One at full blast first thing in the morning, when she was accustomed to waking with extreme caution. She was a superb cook, but he ate whatever she put before him without comment, seeming to enjoy a white-bread chip butty and cold baked beans as much as *boeuf en croute*. He hinted at London girls. He drove her wild.

They quarrelled frequently. She was so wary of making a fool of herself that she refused to introduce him to any of her friends. Rent left him with little money; sometimes he would arrive, having spent hours waiting for lifts from one truck after another, to find she was going out to dinner, or a party, and he would be left in the house alone. She threw him out regularly, and once followed him all the way back to London to apologize.

But often, after evenings spent closer than bugs, exchanging adoring looks, holding hands, kissing, giving each other all the signals, he would not make love to her at all, or he would finally take her after she had given up hope and was angry. When they did make love it was peremptory, with a minimum of foreplay, and was over quickly. Her thirst for him was rarely slaked and she was left frustrated.

'Why should a man like that be interested in a woman of your age?' The landlady of her local, her only confidante, had confirmed her worst suspicions with barely suppressed glee. 'I know his type. He's like my first husband, always womanizing, and you just turned up when he was on his uppers.'

Why indeed should a man as attractive as Tom O'Dare have wanted her? And, yet, he dug up and restored the neglected garden, repaired the fence, painted the outbuildings and then began on the interior of the house. After living with Sam, who would not have recognized a hammer if she'd hit him over the head with one, Bridget was gratefully bewildered.

Tom never made a decision, suggested what they should do, where they would go, or what might lie in the future.

'I don't know what you think, what you feel!' she yelled.

'I'm here, aren't I?' he would reply coldly and clam up.

It did not occur to her that Tom O'Dare felt restricted by the fact that he had nothing to offer, no money, no status, no regular employment; nor that, having been badly betrayed by the last woman in his life, he was as frightened as she of making another mistake.

All Bridget knew was that he did not speak of love, or talk of their living together, or discuss anything long-term. She could not believe in him. It was unthinkable that the miracle which had happened to her in Portugal had also happened to him.

Her marriage to Sam had broken up only six months earlier. Still far too close to it and neurotically disturbed by its ending, she read aspects of Tom's conduct as indications that he was like her first husband and was convinced that she was heading in the same disastrous direction as before by being so in love with him. So, without being conscious of it, she set him test after test. At times, she behaved like a slave and, at others, with frantic irrationality.

Tom reaped all the pent-up rage and despair she had built up over the years spent with Sam and, being a guarded and undemonstrative man, was unable to reas-sure her, or even to fight with her. He simply shut off and stared blankly ahead, just as he had on that first morning in Lagos. His lack of reaction made her even more capricious. Yet, he always forgave and he always came back.

37

Then, one night after they had drunk a lot and he had turned his back when she wanted to make love, she had flounced off to another bedroom. He did not come to fetch her back and she lay seething with rage. At last, marching back into her own room, she had found him asleep and snoring.

She switched on the radio, turning the volume up full blast, switched on all the lights, threw a jug of cold water over him and ran out. He returned bawling to consciousness, staggered after her, reeling in confusion and dripping wet as he barged into the spare room, shouting for the first time in his life. The words were incoherent and awkward. Unable to pronounce his 'r's, he sounded like a child rounding on his mother. Bridget had burst into howls of uncontrollable laughter, and he had slapped her across the face. They had stared at each other in horrified silence, then he burst into tears.

Love and guilt overwhelmed her. She dashed to him, putting her arms around him, rocking him as they sobbed, helplessly, together.

'I'm sorry. I'm sorry.'

He was trembling alarmingly. 'I've never raised my voice before. I've never hit any woman before.'

She knew. It was one of the characteristics she loved most about him. Sam had been so aggressive.

They had gone up on the moor the following day and walked beside a winding stream in one of its secret valleys, through light dappled by the overhanging trees. They had sat beside the water and were very quiet. She knew he was never going to ask. It had to come from her.

'Would you like to live here . . . with me?'

Tom had moved in with two small suitcases and, finally, met her friends and, almost at once, found a job

38

on a country newspaper at the other end of the county. Because they could not afford a second car, he rode a motorbike over a hundred miles a day through endless, narrow, rural roads in all weathers in order to spend each night with her. In winter, he would arrive, white-faced and frozen, able only to eat supper and fall into an exhausted sleep. In the snows, they would put chains on the old car and she would drive him to and fro. He never complained. Just as he dismissed all difficulties as irrelevant, so he endured discomfort in the same unconcerned way.

'No worries,' he would say, in a broad Australian accent and that was the end of it.

They still fought. They were clever and catty to each other. Tom learnt to shout very well. He survived her tantrums. She came to terms with his inexplicable moods. He philosophically accepted her organizing habits. She continued to be jealous of his flirtations with every pretty woman, but grew to understand that it was only a game of promises on his part, which he had no intention of fulfilling.

She never stopped being amazed that he had come into her life. Every time she saw him, her pulse leapt. Her divorce from Sam came through. She worked hard, completed her film script and was rewarded with the contract for another, and a TV series. He found another job in the nearest town as editor of the local newspaper. He rendered and painted up the old house. They planned the garden together, he and the home she loved so much had become part of each other. They spent every minute possible together. They were happy.

After two years, she had been convinced, at last, that there really had been a miracle in Portugal. Tom O'Dare loved her, and shortly after that he began to talk of marriage. Bridget had thought it was a joke. Tom O'Dare did not make decisions. When she had realized he was serious, all her old insecurity returned.

'I don't want to marry again, ever.'

He left the subject. He returned to it again.

'Why marry? We're perfectly happy as we are. I like us living together,' she had replied.

He waited, then tried again.

'Oh Tom, it's not worth rocking the boat. Everything might be spoilt.'

'No. It'll be better.'

She had not been convinced. There were always stories of people who had lived together for years and then split up almost as soon as they eventually married. He did not tell her that was precisely what had happened with his second wife.

He went on trying.

'Give me one good reason,' she had demanded.

It was then that he said, 'If we marry, we'll be exclusive.'

Exclusive. That was a word she understood. Marriage was exclusive. He really wanted them to be exclusive. Still petrified, she committed herself.

Bridget's first wedding had been a squalid affair, marred by subterfuge, an impatient registrar and the fact that she had eaten shrimps for lunch and was allergic to shellfish. Tom's first wedding had been the full church performance, which he had regretted long before the ceremony was over, and his second marriage had been brief. They decided to invite only good friends, ignore most of their relations and their mothers (whom they both disliked), and do everything exactly as they wanted, regardless of convention.

The invitations, engraved with an art-deco design of a couple drinking champagne surrounded by flowers and butterflies, were to a wedding and a party. Bridget, determined to do all the catering, cooked like a woman possessed, pâtés and mousses, salads and vol-au-vents, quiches and savoury tarts. Boned ducks and eggs and mushrooms and smoked salmon horns were stuffed and the glazed salmon was such a work of art that it was to be photographed as often as the bride. She bought a cream silk dress and a huge hat covered in blowsy roses. Their friends bought them a fragile white and gold Wedgwood dinner service.

Tom had stayed in the local pub with his best man on the night before the ceremony and in the morning Bridget awoke alone in her bed in tears and refused to go ahead.

'I can't. I can't.'

'But he's a marvellous man and he's absolutely besotted with you, babe,' Zoe persuaded her. 'Anyone can see that.'

'Have a cup of coffee, Mummy. You'll feel better soon.' Her daughter, now married herself, was already dressed.

'You don't like him. You know you don't,' Bridget had wailed.

'He makes you happy, so I like him,' Deirdre replied. 'Marry him.'

The old house was pine-scented with conifer branches woven through the banisters of the staircase and tied with red ribbons; Deirdre had crammed every room with flowers – bronze and yellow and burgundy Japanese chrysanthemums in great glazed urns like paintings by Marianne North – baskets of gourds, arrangements of variegated hostas and feathery fennel and trails of scarlet leaves from the vine and terracotta jugs filled with branches of cotoneaster berries, all gathered from the garden and freely massed by Bridget in celebration of her autumn wedding.

The new car was decorated with ribbons. Deirdre pushed her into it, drove them to the Register Office, and gave her a hearty shove towards Tom, who was already waiting at the desk.

By the time it came to her turn to repeat the vow, she was crying so much that she could only whisper, 'I call upon these persons here present to witness that I . . . Bridget Siobhan Flynn . . .'

Minutes of speechlessness passed and the guests held their breath.

'. . . do take thee . . . Thomas Joseph O'Dare . . . to be . . . my lawful wedded husband.'

They were man and wife. They were married. She turned to him and saw the look of supreme happiness on his face. They had made no mistake.

Then came the photographs and food, the champagne and toasts, balloons, jokes, telegrams and good wishes, and everyone danced all night.

It was, without a shadow of doubt, the most glorious day of her life.

Chapter Three

THE divorce documents arrived.

'You've only just married him,' John, her solicitor, who had been at the wedding, protested when she telephoned her instructions.

'Then unmarry me as fast as possible,' she retorted. 'Anyway, three years is not "newly wed". Just tell me how quickly it can be done and on what grounds.'

'About three months,' he sighed. 'And a judge recently commented that a divorce these days is granted if you don't like the colour of your husband's Y-fronts.'

Despite the half-finished bottle of Sauternes, the Bruce Springsteen record on the sofa and the clean sheets on the bed, she could not actually prove Tom's adultery with giggling Cathy, so she decided on 'unreasonable behaviour' instead.

Sitting at her desk, she brooded over the way he had not contacted her again and that renewed her determination not to play his game. Resentful of all the tears she had shed, she unfolded the official form and quickly answered questions one to nine.

She grimaced over the sentence 'The petitioner's prayer is for dissolution of the marriage' – an earnest prayer, indeed. Then she methodically repeated all she had written on the four copies of the petition, re-used her solicitor's envelope, stuffed them inside, sealed it and considered the walk to the letter-box. Instead she filed the lot in her file marked DIVORCE, along with the decree absolute and all the correspondence relating to her divorce from Sam.

This is becoming a habit, she thought to herself, but she felt much better.

Picking up the telephone, she got through to Tom in the office and told him he could have his freedom in three months.

'Great,' he replied, in a voice heavy with sarcasm.

And she dropped into depression all over again.

The dogs gave her reproachful looks for having been left without company or walks for so long. She fed them and wandered aimlessly round the house. It was like a mountain riddled with caves, clammy and empty. She had to get out.

The woods behind the house were clammy and empty, too, but to the dogs, with their keen noses, they were full of the most exciting company. She envied them as they yelped after rabbits and squirrels, pried into fox earths and badger sets and feathered to and fro across the tracks of riders and deer. An enervating lethargy went with her depression, which made every movement hard work. The branches of the trees circled overhead as she trudged dutifully upwards and finally reached the bench at the top of this long high ridge which sliced far into the moor.

The roofs of her house lay below: the slate eighteenth-century valley roof; the pantiled roof over the kitchen and pantries, where a much older thatched cottage had once stood, and the 'new' roof of the small wing which had been added a hundred years ago. Her home stood there so solidly, rooted into the hillside as though it had grown there from the soil. She had wanted a life like this house, secure and unshakeable and permanent. That was what she had searched for through her mother and Sam and Tom, but she had found only transience and uncertainty.

Had the six years spent with her really been so insupportable for Tom? This last one had certainly been rocky, but she remembered only happiness before that. Even their Sunday-morning sex, in which she made all the approaches and he performed the act, left her feeling peaceful and protected by the closeness of their contact.

They had never used any method of contraception and she had converted the desire for orgasm into pleasure at his climax within her, knowing that his sperm would live on and, during that time, she would belong totally to him. He had even made her pregnant two years earlier, and grinned with macho self-congratulation at the news, although neither of them wanted children. In any case, at her age the pregnancy was unlikely to go the full term, but in the few weeks it lasted, she, too, had been pleased, although she would never have admitted it. Her sisters in the fight for liberation would have totally disapproved of such primitive reactions, but there was no denying them.

Her brain and not her body was the big attraction for Tom. It was the kind of relationship half the educated women in the western world claimed as their ambition and Bridget had little complaint.

'I've never met a woman who was any competition,' he had told her once. 'Your mind electrifies me.'

They relished their ferocious arguments about politics, he from the right and she from the left; she for women's rights, he the chauvinist, she the ardent campaigner against nuclear weapons, he in favour of the deterrent; farming; Greenham Common women; the poll tax, National Health Service. They never agreed to differ. That would have been no fun and one or other always played

45

the part of devil's advocate, just for the hell of it. Their loquacious years together had moved her fractionally to the right and him quite considerably to the left. Now, they were both almost Liberal Democrats.

He had developed a passionate interest in the country-side which they shared and now he was as soppy about animals as she. They treated their dogs and goats like undisciplined surrogate children. They loathed hunting and all forms of physical cruelty.

He admired her writing with embarrassing outspoken-ness, always promoting her work and introducing her to strangers with enormous pride. For her part, having once been described by a despairing editor as the worst reporter he had ever employed, who could only be relied upon to miss the point of every story, she was awed by Tom's ability to gain the confidence of strangers and ferret out the news.

Above all, their sense of humour was identical. They giggled over *Private Eye*, silly press stories, the foibles of other people and each other all the time.

On returning home from her walk, Bridget took out the albums of photographs from the cupboard and studied all those of them together, cutting the wedding cake, huddled in the rainswept ruins of the Cornish Celtic village on their honeymoon, on the boat to Puffin Island, spending Christmas with her daughter and son-in-law, in the garden, on the beach, drinking in taverns, with groups of clearly drunk friends, out with the dogs, then the ones of Tom on the ride-on mower, Tom up a ladder, Tom cheating at croquet, Tom with a pint, Tom playing cricket. He looked so happy in every one.

Yet, towards the end of the previous year, their content-ment had evaporated. The giggling and the laughter had stopped. It was not merely that he had become irascible. It was almost as though he had wanted to avoid her. If she had suggested lunching together, he had produced excuses, whereas, before, he had always been delighted when she came into town. He had begun seeking every opportunity to be out of the house, losing interest in the garden, working an hour or so later than usual and staying in the pub longer. Tom and Bridget had both become stale and bored with each other.

Now, she wondered miserably if it had all been her fault. Sometimes, he had dropped hints and she had not listened.

'You never come out with me. I always walk the dogs on my own. You won't come to the pub any more.'

'I'm too busy to go walking and I'm fed up with sitting at bars.'

'Well, I want to be able to show my wife off round the village.'

She had laughed incredulously. 'Round the village! Don't be absurd!'

And he had said nothing more. She should have listened.

Although it was a hot day and she could have been sunbathing in the garden, she lit the log fire in the winter sitting-room and sat huddled over it fretting over what she had done wrong. Five days had gone by without a word between them. Her friends, during her agitated phone calls to them, had all told her not to worry.

'He'll be back,' they had said.

'You know men,' they had said.

No she didn't. Perhaps that was the problem. She did not know men. There had been no father or brother to watch during her childhood, no male teachers in the single-sex girls' schools she had attended. There had only been Sam, who did not seem at all like the mass of nine-to-five males she observed from the sidelines. Then, during their separation after her return from Madeira, there had been that love affair with Sean, which had been intense, but too brief to teach her anything more than the meaning of great sex.

The telephone, which had become more of a crowd of friends than a mere machine, rang again. Hubert, Tom's uncle, was theatrical and gay, friend of Isherwood, Coward, Auden *et al*.

'Darling, I thought Thomas should know that Madam's finally gone gaga,' he drawled down the line from London.

Bridget's shoulders slumped. Madam was Tom's mother.

'She's wandering around with a broomstick called George,' he continued. 'George has a car and is about to take her to Lloret de Mar. What's worse is that she's handing out money to half London. There will have to be a family committee meeting.'

Bridget told him Tom had left her.

'Oh God, not another marriage *hors de combat*,' he commented, laconically. 'Whatever is the matter with the boy? After all, he's not inadequate.'

There was no answer to this. She gave him Tom's office number.

As soon as she put the receiver down, Bridget's protective instincts rose with animal force. It had always been her firm belief that Tom's mother was to blame for most of his problems. She had never met the woman, but her name had only to be mentioned for him to be reduced to the abject misery of a child who always fails to please. Now, when Tom really needed to concentrate on his life and true feelings, this family crisis could not have come at a worse time.

One of the bonds between the two of them was that they shared mothers who might have been twins, bitter widows who had resolutely withheld all affection and approval from them as children. The continual criticism of these two women had left them both deeply scarred with guilt and insecurity.

They had both been packed off to boarding schools at the age of five, institutions for which they had remained blatantly unsuited. Each had tried to cope in different ways, Tom by shrugging off all mortifications and deprivations with a false laugh and the pretence that nothing mattered, and by excelling academically and at sport; Bridget by excelling academically and by unswerving rebellion. Superficially, Tom had been the more successful.

Bridget's breaking of rules and bounds, running away and uncontrollable tantrums had only incurred twelve years of punishments. She had been locked in, denied privileges and sometimes food, sent to bed early, forced to weed the whole of one school kitchen garden during every free minute for an entire summer, placed in official 'coventry', refused parental visits for the three weekends permitted each term and denied promotion to prefect, or even sub-prefect. She had also been expelled several times.

Even now, although she was over forty, the memory of her days at school made her face stiffen as she stood up to turn one of the burning logs and throw another on to it. The complete lack of privacy, even when taking a bath, had been an agony for an intrinsically reserved girl, the rigorous inspections of all her possessions, the impossibility of keeping even a secret toy had left her obsessive about her house and its contents. Other women changed their furniture around regularly and repainted rooms in different colours. Bridget's home remained exactly the same year after year, solid and inviolable. She could see herself growing old and dying in this place and leaving behind a museum, a house held in a time warp.

Tom's achievements had never satisfied his mother. He had always been told he could have done better, always failed in her eyes. His mother did not touch him either in anger or in love. Tom had grown up unable to formulate his emotions.

Bridget's mother had maintained a disposition of unrelenting disappointment, demonstrated by the refusal to speak to her daughter at all for days after the arrival of each school report. Bridget's mother had been vivacious and outgoing, always the 'life and soul of the party'. When they went out together, she would tug at her daughter's clothes and push at her hair and eye her with accusatory disapproval for being so unattractive. Bridget had grown up to be a lumpy and pathologically shy girl, who had still not managed to acquire much self-confidence.

That these had been two ordinary women, who had achieved nothing more spectacular than holding very ordinary jobs and were in no position to sneer at the successes of their children, did not occur to Tom or Bridget.

She had to smile, when other people were aghast at the idea of hating a mother. Where had the belief come from that only good and loving women gave birth to children?

Tom and she knew differently; but, as she had once read somewhere, 'You never stop whoring after your mother until you die.' Now, it looked as though Tom would have to go whoring again. Bridget knew what that would do to him. She had seen him weep when the old witch had actually addressed a few civil words to him over the telephone, and weep again when she had ignored his carefully chosen birthday present. She felt gentled with pity.

'Let me know if I can help,' she said to him, when she rang him at the office. 'You know I'll do all I can.'

'I know you will,' he replied, with a trace of affection.

'If you want me to come with you and wait, I'd be glad to.'

'I've arranged to meet Hubert and my sister tomorrow evening and I'll see how it goes,' he answered. 'I'll let you know.'

It was the sort of occasion to send him right off the rails, she thought the next evening, as she restlessly switched from one radio programme to another. Even Mozart did not calm her as she waited for Tom's call. It did not come and she, who had always slept like the dead for eight hours a night, took yet another sleeping pill and stayed awake.

In the morning, she took a tranquillizer. Surprisingly, it worked very well. When Pat came jigging through the front door, she found herself placidly telling her that she and Tom had parted.

'Yes, I had a premonition. I have them, you know,' Pat shrieked over the noise of the washing machine.

She would.

'Of course, it's not my place to say, but your husband's never liked me.'

'Oh, I think you're mistaken. He's never suggested such a thing to me, Pat.'

'He's always treated me with contempt.'

Bridget was genuinely upset. 'I'm sure that's not true, Pat. He would never do that.'

The other woman just shook her head. Bridget thought about what she had said and then understood. Pat was plain and lined, past the menopause. Pat was sexless. Tom's boyish grins and bedroom eyes were directed only at possible conquests. He had probably completely ignored Pat. He would never even have seen her as a woman, but rather as a scurrying creature who cleaned up after him occasionally. Bridget felt ashamed and very angry.

She changed the subject. 'I've taken off fourteen pounds, a whole stone.'

It was a mistake to mention anything about the body. Pat, skinny as a grasshopper, stopped the vacuum cleaner and rubbed her invisible stomach.

'I've been putting on weight something awful. In fact,' she said, conspiratorially, 'I'm wondering if I'm pregnant.'

Bridget gritted her teeth for a moment, before blurting out, 'You can't be. Not at your age.'

'It's in the Guinness Book of Records,' Pat retorted and the machine started up with an affirmative bellow.

Bridget fled to her study, wishing Tom had been there to share this with her. He had probably stayed on with his sister, she decided. But still he did not phone. She took another sleeping pill that night.

By the next day, she was thoroughly frightened. When confronted by anything unpleasant or difficult Tom simply packed his bags and left. Walking away from the situation, he called it. The complication of his mother's senility and his disintegrating relationship with Bridget might very well have proved too much for him. Perhaps he had already thrown up his job and disappeared.

It was Sunday. Unable to bear the tension any longer, she telephoned his sister.

'We went to mother's doctor together and then he drove me to mother's house, but he said he couldn't handle seeing her.' Dorothy said. 'Isn't he home?'

Bridget gave her the news.

'I'm sick of this. All his life I've had one woman after another weeping her heart out to me over him and I've always supported him, but now I've had enough.' Dorothy was livid. 'Well, he's my brother, but he's rotten to the core. If I were you, Bridget, I'd forget him. Put him right out of your mind and get on with your life. Oh, and watch your money,' she added.

Dorothy, a gaunt-faced and unhappy woman, had never liked her brother and the venom in her voice was shocking. With a sister and a mother like that, Bridget thought, what chance had Tom had? She was sure that money did not concern him. He had lived without it for long enough in Portugal. The last thing he would do would be to try to rip her off.

She knew he had been staying in a pub somewhere since leaving home, but she had no address. Swallowing her pride, she rang one of his male colleagues and was given the telephone number.

The landlord confirmed her worst suspicions. Mr O'Dare had checked out two days earlier.

She picked up a cushion and paced up and down the drawing-room, tearing at a little hole in the material with her fingernail so that curled white feathers floated upwards like bubbles and added to the dust which covered the neglected surfaces of the furniture. He could be in another country, checked into some small pension near a beach, already established in the local bar. She remembered how he had almost let himself be trapped in Portugal. This time, Bridget knew, he would never return.

But the angels must have been looking down on her for it was then that an astonishing thing happened. A stranger rang from London to say he had found Tom's wallet in Notting Hill, containing money, his credit cards and, thank God, his passport. If she was Tom's wife, could he forward them to her?

'People like you don't exist nowadays,' she gasped, almost in tears of relief. Tom could not get far with no money. Even selling the car would take time. The stranger even refused to take a reward.

Tom was back at his desk the next day.

'Where on earth have you been?' she stormed.

'Watching cricket,' he replied icily.

'Well, I was worried sick about you. I thought you'd done one of your runners.'

'Why should I do that?'

'You know the effect your mother has on you.'

'I didn't even see her.'

'How was I to know that? You'd checked out of that pub and, if some man hadn't found your wallet and rung me, I wouldn't have known you were even in the country.'

'You're overreacting as usual.' He was acid. 'And where I go has nothing to do with you any more.'

'I'm your wife.'

'And I've left you,' he shouted. 'You've made it quite

clear that you don't want me to come out there to discuss anything and I've had enough of fucking impersonal telephone conversations. Don't ring. Just don't ring!'

A jumble of panic-stricken thoughts invaded her mind as she was left alone again. It was real. He did not want her any more. He hated her. It was really all over. It was finally all over. There was nothing she could do. Rocking and crying with bewilderment in bed, she wanted to die.

The front door clicked. She started up and ran to look over the landing banisters, thinking he might have changed his mind and decided on impulse to come home, to sit beside her and talk to her, but it was only a pile of brown envelopes. The sheets were grubby as she crawled back into bed.

Each evening, when he had returned from work, she had been so pleased, even lately, when all he did was look into her study to say, 'See you later,' and go straight out again. Watching him shave, watching him dress every morning, had fascinated her; the sight of him walking about the bedroom at night filled her with delight. She could not take her eyes off the bulge under those ridiculous little briefs.

That he had come into her life at all remained a constant source of amazement. There would be nothing for her without him. It was all very well for her daughter and her friends to talk of the satisfaction she must get from writing her plays, that she was now comfortably off, owning her own house and with the prospect of being rich, and, despite her age, a good catch, that she did not need him. They were wrong. Nothing had any meaning without Tom.

Sue ran a catering business in the nearby town and was

always up to her eyes in weddings, parties and dinners. She was a pretty woman despite the smudges of fatigue under her brown eyes and had come from London to live in the village not long after Bridget. They were the same age and had shared a youth of long hair and kaftans, the Beatles and the birth of rock, and disastrously early marriages, Sue to a fanatically jealous womanizer and Bridget to Sam. They had both left their first husbands at about the same time. Sue had remained single.

'Can I come over?' Bridget whimpered to this friend halfway through the evening.

It was only a short walk through narrow, picturesque streets crowded with summer visitors. The sounds of people enjoying themselves carried through the open doors of the restaurants and pubs. Some of the shops were still open, selling souvenirs made in Taiwan, boxes of local fudge and cartons of clotted cream to trippers, whose summer money was the lifeblood of the village in its empty winter. Bridget did not really notice any of them.

Sue was already in bed, watching television with the curtains drawn.

'You don't mind, do you?' she asked, switching off the box. 'Have a coffee. On second thoughts, have something stronger. You look awful.'

She fetched the coffee and a bottle of brandy. 'Don't speak. Take a good slug of that first.'

Bridget, who knew very well she could not hold brandy, drank the triple measure down in one gulp, like medicine.

'Have a fag.'

Bridget lit her first cigarette for fifteen years and chain-smoked a whole packet over the next three hours without even feeling dizzy. Sue poured the brandy, Bridget talked, then rambled and then all the feelings of rejection and anger and fear and confusion and torment exploded. She howled and keened her pain in the darkened room, drinking the brandy, hugging herself in agony, wailing and sobbing.

When, at last, it was all out and she was too drunk to walk, Sue drove her home and put her to bed. The room spun. Bridget's stomach churned and she fell on to the floor, just in time to grab the chamber pot and be violently sick, vomiting over and over again, long after there was nothing left to bring up. Then she lost consciousness.

Her brain was clear and sharp and there was not an ache in her body when she awoke. It was five a.m. The sky was dawn blue and the rays of the sun were already spraying the hill. She knew she had to see Tom.

He was right. Without meeting and talking, there was no hope for them. If they could tell each other their thoughts and feelings, they might discover where they had gone wrong. They might be able to put it all together again, the way it was. It was a slender chance, but the only one left.

Her naked body in the looking glass looked much better. She had lost three inches round the bust, four inches round the waist and two inches round the hips. Her double chin had vanished; her eyes, no longer obscured by puffy cheeks, were larger. She bathed, washed her hair and made up her face with great care. The designer skirt and top she had been wearing on the day they met still hung in the wardrobe. The outfit was perennial. Wearing it, she did not look much different from six years before.

'Whatever happens, Bridget, don't cry in front of him,

don't plead with him,' Sue had warned. 'When we were married, I spent a whole night once crying and begging Phil to come back to me and he just became colder and colder. Men hate that sort of thing. They simply can't handle it.'

She would not cry and she certainly would not plead, she promised herself as she started up the car.

It was only half past six when she arrived in the town and found the pub where she knew he had returned to stay. It was a cheap, run-down place, forbiddingly shuttered. There was not even a bell on the solid wooden door and, in any case, she could hardly wake them all up at this hour.

She drove to the riverside and parked. The water flowed serenely past the park on the opposite bank, a pair of swans were carried along like balls of angora, the morning was quiet, the little country town hardly stirring from sleep. The church clock chimed. A milk float went by and, a little while later, an early van, then the first worker and a man with his dog. Bridget just waited, calmly, almost happy. She was going to see Tom. In a strange way, at that time, the outcome did not really matter.

Another hour passed. More walkers appeared as well as men on bicycles, hurrying towards the factories. A single-decker bus passed, empty except for the driver. Ducks and ducklings disappeared and surfaced on the water.

At eight o'clock she moved the car into a side street and got out to walk. The pub's paintwork was dingy and peeling and the building was barricaded securely against the after-hours drunks of this seedy corner of the town. It was a place where travelling salesmen and middle-aged, unmarried men stayed. Bridget wondered how the residents managed to obtain entry at all.

An alleyway ran up the side and, walking through it, she found herself in a yard where a woman was hanging out washing.

'Good morning. I'd like to see Mr O'Dare,' she said. 'I'm his wife.'

Life held no more surprises for this woman. She had seen and heard everything. She led Bridget up the narrow stairs and along a corridor with a worn carpet and walls stained mustard by smoke rising from the bars below, pointed to a door and left without a word.

Bridget knocked.

'Who is it?' Tom's voice asked, sleepily.

She did not answer.

She heard the bed creak and the sound of movement as he pulled on some trousers. Then the door opened.

His expression did not change when he saw her.

'What do you want?' he asked.

'Can I come in?'

He turned back into the room sullenly, leaving the door ajar.

As she followed, he sat, leaning against the bedhead, with his feet on the rumpled covers. He looked tired, almost ill.

'What do you want?' he repeated.

'You said the impersonal telephone conversations were useless and you're right,' she answered, quietly. 'I thought it would be better if we talked, face to face.'

'There's nothing to say. It's over.' His face was closed, blank.

'Tom, I'm perplexed, completely baffled. I can't understand what's happened. You must explain to me.'

'We've grown apart,' he said, slowly. 'I haven't been happy for a long time.'

'I know. Neither of us has been happy since the job went wrong. But the job's OK now, isn't it?'

'It's better,' he admitted.

'So what else went wrong?' She sat on the edge of the bed, looking at him as he began to pick at his nails.

Then he lifted his head and stared at her. 'Look, I've always been a cunt. I can't stand being tied down. I've always stuck things out for a few years, then got fed up and moved on. I want to move on now.'

'You're not a cunt, Tom,' she said vehemently. 'You've always been told you are and you've always believed it. That's half the trouble. But *I*'ve never believed it.'

'You're mad.' He gave a twisted smile.

'You came into my life, picked me up, dusted me down, cared for me. You worked until you dropped on my garden, you restored my house, created a home. You looked after me.'

'I only did what you wanted. You made all the decisions.'

'Tom, you loved me. I know you did.' She still spoke quietly. It was not difficult. It was like handling a nervous animal, one which had been badly beaten.

'I don't love you now. I've stopped loving you.'

'Love doesn't just stop for no reason,' she pointed out. 'There has to be a reason.'

They sat in silence for minutes.

'Tom,' she began again, with great gentleness, 'however we finish up, whether you come back to me or not, I have to know what happened. Don't you see, if I don't understand, I can't come to terms with it. You must help me.'

Still he did not speak.

'I haven't come here to make a scene. I haven't come to shout and scream or cry. I haven't come here to quarrel with you. It doesn't matter what you say, as long as you explain a little, anything.'

He swung off the far side of the bed and went to the wash-basin. As the water ran from the tap, she gazed at his back, that neat head, the light hair turning grey, those straight, wide shoulders and tapering back, the small bottom and long legs, his dear, familiar figure.

He washed and shaved and she sat without speaking, enjoying the process as always.

When he had finished, he put on his shirt and tie.

'I love you, Tom,' she said, at last. 'I love you with all my heart.'

'I know you do.'

He came to sit on the bed again, incongruously bare-footed, long, bony feet like her own. In the early days, when she had been shy and he had not yet learnt to touch her from pure affection, they had slept back to back with the soles of their feet pressed together. Hers had always been cold, but his were always warm. He was a warm person.

'We must be straight with each other. There's no point in hiding anything now,' she persuaded. 'We've simply got to level with each other.'

'Whatever I say is going to hurt you more than you have been already,' he said slowly and drew out a cigarette.

'Can I have one?' she asked.

He lit it for her without surprise and she inhaled deeply.

'The only way I can be hurt any more is by never really

61

knowing what went wrong. I can't go through the rest of my life not knowing what I did, what happened to us. I can't face that,' she said. 'Please, Tom, please be honest with me. Whatever you have to say must be said.'

She held her breath and forced herself to remain absolutely still. This was it.

'I'm having an affair,' he said. 'I've been having an affair since last November.'

Chapter Four

BRIDGET felt a massive surge of affection for him. It was a completely unexpected reaction, but so over-whelmed her that she could have taken him in her arms and comforted him. He was so manifestly unhappy.

'So that's it,' he said, without looking at her. 'That's the end of us.'

Slowly, she released a breath full of smoke, and asked, 'Why should it be the end of us?'

'I'm having an affair. Didn't you hear me? I'm having an affair.'

She thought calmly, refusing to hurry and then said, 'I'm not saying it's over, Tom. Lots of marriages survive an affair. Ours might survive, too. I don't know how I feel about it at the moment. To be honest, it's not what I expected. I don't know when you found the time. You were always home before eight o'clock, so I am taken by surprise and I don't know what I feel, or how I'm going to feel later, when it's had time to sink in and, until I do know, I'm not saying it's over.'

He had expected her to burst into tears, or round on him in fury. She had always been so jealous. He turned towards her and his face relaxed, at last.

'Is she important?'

'I don't know. I think so.'

Bridget's heart drooped a little, but the sensation of relief remained. At least, she knew the truth now, she knew where she was.

'Well, Tom, if you believe we're finished, that will have to be your decision, but, at the moment, it's not the end for me. That may not be the position tomorrow, or next week, or next month, but that's the way it is now.'

If Tom was amazed, he was not half as amazed as she was herself. After a lifetime of being ruled by her own impulses and neuroses, this unruffled response to the biggest crisis she had ever faced was staggering. Yet, it was genuine. Neither shock, nor distress, disturbed her.

She smiled at him. 'I'm glad to see you anyway.'

'You can't be.'

'I am,' she assured him. 'Whatever happens, we'll remain mates. I don't believe in falling out with my exes.'

He smiled back, widely, knowing she still kept in close touch with Sam, despite all that had happened in that marriage.

'I'd better go now,' she said, and went to the door.

'No, don't go yet,' he said, unexpectedly. 'Wait for me and I'll walk you to the office.'

She sat down again and watched as he put on his socks and shoes and combed his hair.

'You know it really is good to see you,' she said, fondly. 'I've missed having you around.'

'You're looking good,' he offered, in return. 'Very good indeed.'

They walked over the bridge together and up the High Street. She kept her head high and shoulders back.

'I could do with a coffee,' he said. 'Would you like one?'

'Why not?'

They both remembered that reply and smiled, again.

In the café, he told her he had not slept with the woman and she raised her eyebrows in mild disbelief.

64

'Well, only a couple of times,' he admitted. 'It's not physical.'

That made it worse, she thought, knowing Tom's indifference to sex. She wondered about her rival. Only two possible candidates came immediately to mind: Diana, a stylish and intelligent woman of about her own age, wealthy and very pleasant – Tom had once said she fancied him. She would be dangerous; then there was Jane, an office typist, slightly older than herself, who had been chasing him for years with hard luck stories about a husband who did not understand her. Bridget and Tom had nicknamed her Old Panstick, because her make-up was as thick as papier mâché. Bridget dismissed her from the running. It was probably some twenty-year-old flibbertigibbet, anyway, but she would certainly have to find out, and quickly.

'I'm not telling you who it is.' He read her thoughts.

'I didn't expect you to, and I don't want to know, anyway,' she lied.

He had found a flat and was moving in the next day, he told her. As most of his clothes were still at home, he suggested coming to collect them that evening.

'I'll wash your shirts and pack for you,' she offered.

He looked embarrassed. 'You don't have to do that.'

'I'd like to.'

As they walked to his office, he took her hand.

'See you tonight, then.'

'Would you like some supper?'

'Yes, please.'

As she left town, the reaction hit her and she began to shake. By the time she arrived at Pat's bungalow, she was ashen and weak. Pat's husband disappeared, immediately, and Pat poured her a cup of tea and talked about anything but the obvious, then accepted a lift to the house.

'We don't say much, but that doesn't mean me and Bob don't feel,' said Pat, awkwardly. 'Someone's got to look after you.'

Bridget felt pathetically touched. 'The trouble is, the person who should be doing that isn't here.'

'Then you'll just have to put up with me.' Pat was matter-of-fact.

'He's got another woman.'

'I had a premonition.' Her voice held an unconscious hint of satisfaction.

Oh God.

The house had to sparkle with gleaming furniture and polished floors. Reminders of their life together – records they enjoyed, the Victorian epergne they had bought together, the folding hunting tot she had given him – should be left around, casually on display. There had to be vases of flowers everywhere. Each room had to be warm and invitingly comfortable and persuasively familiar. She could rely on the dogs to give him an ecstatic welcome.

'I want him to see what he's losing,' she told Pat, who gave her a glance of disapproval.

If Pat had her way, Mr O'Dare would be shown the door in no uncertain manner.

'If he came here when you were out, I wouldn't let him in, you know,' she said, stoutly.

'No, don't ever shut him out. This is his home,' Bridget pointed out, at once.

Pat tightened her lips and flung Tom's shirts into the washing machine.

Bridget picked runner beans and uncovered enough courgettes from under the weeds, pulled onions and car-rots, dug up some new potatoes and hurried to the butcher, where she spent a small fortune on fillet steak. Nothing which looked too elaborate, just an ordinary supper, she thought to herself, as the Sabatier knife sliced and chopped as though through butter. Criminally, she turned the meat into stew, liberally adding red wine and herbs.

When his shirts were folded, she packed his underwear, socks and sweaters. In the pocket of one of his jackets, she found a card. 'Who loves ya more than me, baby?' it blared. She wrote 'BRIDGET DOES' firmly across the scrawled kisses and dropped it on top of the clothes in the suitcase.

Going to her study, she took down four of the many books she had given to him. In *Arlott on Cricket*, she wrote, 'To my angel, with all my love, Bridget'; in *Bradman*, she wrote, 'Love, love and more love from Bridget'; in *Walter Hammond*, she wrote, 'To my darling Tom, love always, Bridget'; and the message in *The Joy of Cricket* was, 'To Tom, who gives me joy, Bridget'. Then she wrapped the presents.

The Tuesday of the week she had spent in Greece had been Tom's birthday. She had not telephoned on his birthday, nor even sent a card, but the presents had already been bought, four framed old cricketing cartoons, a carving in wood of an Irish Setter, bits and bobs. Now, she wrapped them in paper covered in hearts and flowers and placed them in the bottom of the second case. Then she took the prettiest proof snapshot of them both at their wedding, wrote 'Tom and Bridget. True happiness' on the back and placed it beside the card. Not only would he see them, but any mistress worth her salt was bound to search his possessions and see them, too.

There was no time to visit the hairdresser, but she

washed her hair and bathed for the second time that day, sprayed herself stiflingly with Je Reviens scent and examined her wardrobe. She decided on a black, flared skirt and black top, very slimming, and fastened on a jade necklace and long jade ear-rings. She sat on the sofa and tried to appear natural.

Bridget, married so young and for so long cocooned by this state, had been taken aback upon her first emergence into the world of singles. She had never noticed the number of unattached women. The instant effect Tom had had on her, he also had on them. Perhaps it was a super abundance of pheromone, but they homed in on him like bees to nectar, a situation he certainly did nothing to deter.

Other women phoned him with thinly veiled invitations. They just happened to be passing the office when he emerged. They lurked in waiting in bars, literally pushing in between them and elbowing her aside, batting their eyelashes, displaying cleavages if they had any, intimately touching his arm, taking his hand. One had even jumped out of a window and over a garden wall, on discovering they had been invited to her neighbours for dinner. Their desperation was almost macabre. Tom would grin his heartstopping grin, twinkle over his pints of beer, tell his exaggerated tales, put on his macho act and encourage every one.

Bridget had always preferred the company of women to men, women were more open about themselves, more interesting, had far fewer hang-ups about their egos. They were more supportive, more understanding, but after meeting Tom she learnt, regretfully and for the first time in her life, to view any female under retirement age with apprehension. At least he never flirted with her friends.

'You don't shit on your own doorstep,' was his unsatisfactory comment.

Yet, it had obviously been impossible to keep an eye
on him every minute of every day and, now, in spite of
all her vigilance and the fact that he had always arrived
home at a reasonable time, or told her exactly where he
would be, another woman had hit the jackpot.

The doorbell sounded.

'Why did you ring?' she queried, letting him in like a
visitor.

He shrugged, awkwardly. 'I don't live here.'

'It's always your home.'

Right on cue, the dogs leapt all over him, yelping with
pleasure, as he walked into the kitchen.

'Do you want to eat now?' she asked. 'Supper's ready.'

The stew tasted as though made in heaven. They sat
opposite each other without saying much and tried to eat
it, without success, then they mutually abandoned their
plates and went into the drawing-room.

'The garden's going to pieces,' she commented.

'I was going to talk to you about that,' he said,
eagerly. 'I'd like to come out on Saturdays and help you
with it.'

'That's very sweet of you, but why?'

'It's my responsibility. You can't be expected to keep
up this place on your own and I'm not going to shirk my
responsibilities, you know.'

'I would be very grateful, Tom,' she acknowledged.
'I've been worried about how to manage.'

'Well, you don't have to worry about that. I'll do it.
I've nothing to do at weekends, anyway.'

'Your friend spends those with her husband, I suppose,'
she surmised.

He nodded.

'I'm waiting for the shit to hit the fan there.' He looked rueful. 'In fact, when you turned up this morning, I thought it might be him.'

'No wonder you seemed so wary. Is she nice?'

'Very. Very nice.'

'Children?'

'Yes.'

'Are they young?'

'No. Almost left home.'

So she was no chicken. Which were the most dangerous, dolly birds or discontented older women? There wasn't much in it.

Tom was looking around. The windows were open to the summer's day and the room smelt of roses. She saw him gaze at the view from their land which he had had painted for her one Christmas. The ancient hedge of the paddock cut across the corner and, beyond that, the artist had brushed in the church tower, reduced to the size of a pebble by the hazy blue and green expanse of Exmoor.

'Does she love you?' Bridget asked her husband.

'Yes.'

'And you love her.'

'I think so.'

'That doesn't sound very sure.'

'Yes. I love her.'

'Are you going to live together?'

'I don't know. It depends on her and she can't decide.'

'Do you think she's the ultimate woman? The light of your life? The one you can't do without?'

She did not know this was the wrong approach. Had she been wiser, she would not have made any observation, or asked questions which directed him into making definite responses, whether he was certain of his own feelings or not.

'Yes,' he answered, and she believed him.

'I'm sorry. You know I'm sorry,' he blurted out. 'She thinks I'm so glamorous, you see.'

'I think you're glamorous,' Bridget told him, openly. 'The most glamorous man I've ever met.'

'Yes, but I'm a personality in the town, everyone knows me. She thinks I'm absolutely wonderful.'

Of course. Tom had always felt the writing of plays and movie scripts was more of an achievement than being a good journalist, although she did not agree. But, too often, when they were out together, people paid more attention to her. Tom was treated as her husband, rather than she being treated as Tom's wife. He had always said he did not mind, that he was so proud of her. Perhaps he cared a lot more than he admitted.

'I can't help it,' he repeated. 'I think she's the one for me. I don't know. It's probably some sort of aberration really, the male menopause.'

That was more like it.

'I've just got to go through with it,' he continued.

There was a long pause. Too often in her life Bridget had delivered body blows to herself by acting on impulse and she was not going to do that now. The shock of learning of his affair had been such that her emotions were deadened, leaving her distanced and objective, as though she and her husband were simply trying to deal with a straightforward practical problem together.

'Well, go through with it, Tom. Get it out of your system,' she said. 'You haven't burnt your boats. I still stand by what I said this morning. It is not the end of our marriage for me at the moment. That position obviously won't last for ever and I obviously can't give you a time limit, because I simply haven't a clue. I've no idea how long I'll feel this way.'

'I don't really know what to do,' he confessed.

'Why don't you go and see Gareth, talk to him. You could do with a man to talk to,' she suggested. Gareth was his oldest friend, who had been best man at their wedding.

'I thought I might spend tomorrow night there,' he said, and she felt relieved. He obviously wasn't very keen to move into the new flat and Gareth would help. He would be on her side.

Years before, when she had been at her wits' end with their relationship, Bridget had been given the key to Tom by Sophie.

'He is a very complex man, but he's a man who wants to do the right thing,' the older woman had said, sagely. 'All his life he's been told he's no good, by his mother, by his sister, by every woman he's ever had and often he has behaved extremely badly. But he wants to be a good man and, if you're to get the best out of him, you must appeal to that side of him.'

Bridget had absorbed this and found that the advice worked. He was, indeed, hyper-sensitive to criticism and it had taken a very long time to persuade him that the mildest comment or discussion of a minor difficulty was not necessarily directed against him. Tom was a good man, caring and kind, when he allowed himself to be, a man to whom integrity mattered and who sincerely despised dishonesty and dishonour in others.

'I don't know this friend of yours.' She began talking again with extreme care. 'I only know what you've told me about her . . . and she does not sound a very nice lady

72

to me. For nine months she has been living a double life, very successfully. So, either she's giving her husband the sort of miserable existence I've had this year, or she's a very good actress. You say he doesn't know about your affair. If she loves you so much, why hasn't she told him?'

'I think she's frightened of him,' Tom sounded defensive.

'But not so frightened that she's not prepared to take big risks with you.' Bridget made the point, flatly. 'You're moving into a place of your own tomorrow. Why isn't she packing her bags and moving in, too? That's what I would do, if I were so madly in love.'

'I know you would,' he said.

It was not the moment to push any further. Bridget went upstairs and brought down the suitcases.

'Everything is clean and I've put in some books.'

It was time for him to go. They went to the front door together.

'I love you, Tom,' she said. 'And the dogs love you. We need you.'

He stood very close and she kissed him tenderly on the cheek.

'You're my angel,' she whispered.

He clung to her, briefly.

'I think you're my angel, too,' he murmured and, when he turned away, he was crying.

Bridget closed the door and leant against the wall, hollow-eyed.

The dusty pink T-shirt he had been wearing the day they met in Portugal had been in the bottom of his shirt drawer and she had not packed it. Putting it on, she climbed wearily into bed. Although it was clean, it smelt of him and made him seem nearer. She was still crying silently when she fell asleep.

Gareth was a grey-haired and grey-bearded reporter. He and Tom had known each other since starting together on the same local newspaper. Tom had soared off to Fleet Street and Gareth had stayed on in the same small town, about thirty miles from their home.

'I used to envy him,' he told Bridget, when she turned up at his house the following afternoon to confide the crisis and warn him of Tom's intended visit that evening. 'There he was jetting round the world and pulling all the birds and here was me, married and still stuck in the same old routine.'

Gareth had divorced, eventually, but never remarried, although he lived for several years at a time with extraordinarily young women, intense, hippy-like girls in long, ethnic skirts, who seemed to be devoted to him. The current one was a sweet, young actress and he had loved her for three years. He loved them all.

'I know she'll go soon. She's got to spread her wings and it will hurt, but it's right for her. She's got to see the world,' he said, while spooning instant coffee into a couple of mugs. 'When Tom comes over here sometimes and we go to the pub, all the women flock round him and I know he can have any one he wants; but now I think, hey, you silly bugger, when are you going to grow up?

'You see, I'm not very attractive and it takes me a long time to get the first date, but I know when a girl eventually agrees to go out with me once, she'll go out with me a second time.'

'That's because you are genuine. You don't hide yourself,' Bridget told him, wondering why she had never had the sense to fall for someone like Gareth. 'When they go out with you, you don't put on an act and you don't hold anything back. They discover you're a really lovely guy, so, of course, they want to see you again.'

He sat down on the sofa beside her and they sipped their coffee while she waited for him to think over Tom's latest escapade.

'I'll try to talk to Tom,' he decided, at last. 'But he never lets up on his performance even with me, Bridget.'

'Tom knows you're his friend. He loves you,' she said. 'He really wants to talk this time.'

'Well, I sort of believe that, er, whatever we do, we do for what's in it for ourselves. We do what we want to do.'

'What about loving someone more than you do yourself?' asked Bridget, slightly alarmed by this view. This would not persuade Tom to come home.

'You do that, um, because you choose to. It may not be best for the person you love. You do it because it's best for you,' he maintained.

Gareth was a sixties man. His philosophy was that everyone should do his own thing. Nothing ever ruffled him and he was far more 'laid-back' than Tom. Bridget began to realize there were disadvantages to that.

'I hope you won't say too much along those lines tomorrow.' She began to wonder if she had made a mistake in urging her husband to come to him for advice.

Throughout the long conversation, he had only sat down for a few minutes, then got up to put the kettle on again, answered the telephone, taken washing out of the machine, pinned notes to himself on the cork board and wandered in and out of the kitchen until Bridget was jagged with nerves at the interruptions.

'Whatever you do, don't start any divorce action,' he said, with sudden and unexpected firmness. 'I had this affair when I was married and went off for a weekend with the girl. She was, er, a really nice girl. I really liked her, but, I found myself in this hotel wondering what I was doing there with her and, by the time I came back, I wanted to make up with my wife. I went to the office and was about to phone home, when, um, this solicitor guy phoned me and said my wife had started divorce proceedings and didn't want to see me again. So I thought, um, that's it, she's made the decision. Don't make Tom's decision for him.'

Bridget was glad she had not sent off the completed divorce papers.

He gave her a clumsy little pat on the shoulder. 'Well, you'd better go now, in case you bump into him on the doorstep.'

He was such a sincere person and he meant well, but his thinking was so different. He approached life from an angle that was a mystery to Bridget and, although she hoped she could depend on him, she was not at all sure of that.

She paced around the drawing-room and then around the house, chain-smoking late into the night. Her spirits rose and fell to extremes, alternately full of hope that Gareth was managing to persuade Tom that he was losing all he really cared about, and then in despair over their friend's circumlocutory way of expressing himself and his tolerant, easy-going views.

At dawn, to use up time she took the dogs through the woods and up the hill. From the ridge, the moor unfolded silken in first light, its combes soft as swansdown, the river silver as a snail's trail along the valley below. The dogs skimmed over the heather. Their coats were the colour of wet bracken and they looked like great red birds. A buzzard hung like an echo overhead, its eyes seeing every hair on her head.

She walked until her legs ached and then turned for home. Somewhere, a long way off near the road, she heard voices and the two dogs plunged down the steep drop between the trees towards them. She sat on a mound of moss and waited.

After a while, the bitch appeared, but the young dog was not with her. Bridget began to whistle and call and, in answer to her worried inquiry, two booted walkers reported that he had galloped past, heading towards the ridge. She began labouring back up the way she had come, shouting at every few steps. An hour later, with the older dog flagging, she returned home flustered and sweating.

Rake belonged to Tom, who adored him, often growing misty-eyed with sentiment while extolling his virtues at boring length to all who would listen. He would never forgive her for losing him.

She started up the car and drove recklessly out of the village towards the foot of the far end of the hill, where she found the pup meandering happily along in the middle of the road. Two cars coming the other way had to swerve to avoid him as she approached. She stopped and bundled him in the back of her estate.

Gareth was still in bed when she telephoned.

'How did it go?'

'Well, er, Tom said everything you said, but he seems to turn it round somehow. He says he's coming home every weekend.'

77

'Yes, to do the garden,' she replied.

'Er, it's just that doesn't seem a good idea to me. I mean, Bridget, hey, he's going to have it all ways, you know, the girlfriend during the week and then, um, instead of being alone kicking his heels, he can come home at the weekend. He says you've told him to get on with his scene and that you don't mind.'

Bridget bit her lip to stop herself bursting into tears, but her voice became shrill with dismay. 'Oh God, of course I mind and I need him.'

'I know that,' said Gareth. 'But he thinks you're so capable, so good at everything that you don't need him.'

She wailed.

'Look, for what it's worth, er, I don't think this woman means so much,' Gareth offered, hastily. 'He doesn't talk about her as though she's the wonder of the world. He also says she's got her own house and she's not likely to leave that for a penniless reporter. He really doesn't seem, er, very sure of anything.'

But Bridget had heard only the fact that Tom believed she did not care about the affair.

'I can't talk to you. I can't talk to you any more, Gareth,' she quavered and rang off.

How could Tom imagine she did not need him? she thought, frantically dialling his direct line at the office with trembling fingers.

'I lost Rake. He couldn't hear my voice. It doesn't carry like yours and the dogs aren't used to being out alone with me,' she sobbed.

'It's all right. It's all right.' Tom's voice was comforting.

'It's all so hopeless without you. The garden's going to pieces. The house isn't a home any more. I can't work and I feel so useless. I can't even take the bloody dogs out for a walk without losing them.' She was crying, bitterly. 'I know I shouldn't bother you. It's nothing to do with you, really, but I was so terrified. It's all disintegrating here without you.'

'Oh, my pet, don't cry. It's all right now. You've got him back.' He was gentle and she could hear the concern. 'Now, make yourself a cup of coffee and you'll feel better. I'll ring you later.'

'No. Don't,' she answered, still waif-like, but beginning to remember Gareth's warning about Tom being offered the best of both worlds, mistress during the week and home at the weekend. 'It's better you don't. I've got to learn to manage on my own. And I can't expect to run to you and have you coming out here gardening and working on the house. It's not fair to you. I've got to make myself handle my own problems. I know you want to do it for me, but it would be better if you did not come out on Saturdays. I'm sorry I've put all this on you this morning. I shall go out, now, so don't ring. I'll be all right.'

Since returning from Greece, Bridget had not analysed her reactions. Nothing had been worked out. Her responses had been intuitive. Now, she began to wonder with some surprise if she were being devious. The loss of the pup that morning had left her distraught, but in calling Tom she had also wanted to rouse his protectiveness. She realized, after she put down the receiver, that she had created the impression of being far more helpless than was true.

It would not be particularly hard to cope with the practicalities of living without him. If they were ultimately to divorce, she had already decided to sell the house and buy a smaller one, although she would not move out of the area. Her emotional dependence on him was a different matter, but that was the one aspect she could not stress for fear of making him feel guilty and, therefore, alienated. Instinctively, she wanted to hurl abuse at him, to weep and screech at him, to find the woman and scratch her face to ribbons, but that would only drive him further away.

They say all is fair in love and war. This was certainly love. Suddenly, Bridget understood that it was also war and that it was time she found out the identity of the enemy. Sitting down, she lit a cigarette and began to ponder, carefully, about everything that had happened from the very beginning. She tried to recall every hint, every conversation with Tom and with friends.

Gareth had told her the woman owned a house. Not many married women owned their own house. All at once, she remembered Tom talking about poor Jane, the office typist, about a year earlier, how Jane's husband was so mean, taking home a big wage, but only giving her a few pounds a week and expecting her to pay all the bills because she had inherited the house and there was no mortgage.

'Don't get involved in ladies' domestic hard-luck stories,' Bridget had warned Tom. 'They're the same as men who bleat that their wives don't understand them.'

Surely, he could not be having an affair with Jane, whom anyone could recognize at a hundred yards as mutton dressed as lamb: all bleached hair, frilly polyester blouses and too-tight skirts. Tom, who could take his pick of women from eighteen to sixty, could not possibly have been so stupid as to have fallen for her.

Bridget opened the Yellow Pages and looked up the entry for Detective Agencies.

Chapter Five

A WOMAN, who seemed to be busy cooking, answered the number of the imposing-sounding detective agency.

Her husband was extremely busy, snowed under, in fact, she informed Bridget, who wondered if he were involved in high-powered industrial espionage, or employed by the secret service.

She was relieved when the woman recommended another investigator, a Mr Gates, 'very reliable, discreet and an ex-policeman'.

In answer to her next telephone call, this paragon gave his rates as ten pounds an hour and asked her to bring a photograph of Tom to his house the following morning.

Feeling quite excited, as though her life was on the move again, Bridget decided to have a day out and drove to Exeter. The summer sales were on and she browsed around the shops. For the past two years she had wistfully turned away from clothes she liked and bought only those which disguised her weight. Now she went into a boutique and picked out a white cotton skirt in the largest size they sold.

'I think that'll be too big for you,' the girl advised. 'Try this.'

'I'll never get into a twelve,' she protested.

'Try it,' urged the girl.

The skirt fitted perfectly. Bridget could not believe her own eyes as she gazed in the glass at her flat stomach and smooth hips. She bought a light green skirt, too, and then, in a nearby department store, she tried on two men's shirts with the skirts, rolling up the sleeves, leaving the top two buttons open and tying the tails in a knot at the waist. Still tanned from her week in the sun, she looked a different woman.

The orgy of spending continued on smaller bras, two sexy teddies, pure silk camiknickers, a wisp of a suspender belt and *stockings*.

Wearing the white skirt with a lemon and white shirt, gold sandals and a pair of flashy Ted Lapidus sunglasses, she greeted Sue at the door later that day and had the satisfaction of seeing her mouth drop open.

'My God, I wouldn't have recognized you,' exclaimed her friend. 'You look absolutely terrific.'

Sue talked about her next two weddings, her unreliable cook and waitresses who failed to turn up, or, in one case, appeared in bare feet expecting to serve a dinner party. The two women drank their way through a bottle of chilled Sancerre and opened another.

'Tom's been having an affair since last November,' she forced herself to say at last.

'I can't believe it. He worships you!' Her friend was genuinely amazed.

'Not so,' commented Bridget.

'Oh, they're all the same. Aren't they all the same?'

Sue's own experiences with her ex-husband began spilling out, the hotel bills made out to Mr and Mrs Smith, the ringing phone going dead when she answered, billets-doux in his pockets, anonymous Christmas presents arriving for him.

'It went on for twenty-five years, one woman after another, yet he was so insanely jealous that I was hardly allowed out the door. He was always accusing me of looking at other men, hitting me if we went out and a man so much as spoke to me,' she recounted.

'Tom's not like that,' Bridget protested weakly.

'They're all like that,' her friend replied, bitterly. 'Obsessed with proving their virility. They've got such shaky egos that they have to keep stuffing their pricks into one woman after another to prove they exist.'

She was glad when Sue left. Her fragile remission of the afternoon was over. She took two sleeping pills.

The doorbell rang and rang and rang and she reeled awake before realizing it was the telephone.

'Darling, I've been trying to get you all day. I've been worried sick.' Tom's voice sounded slurred.

Bridget fumbled for her glasses, her head spinning. It was three a.m.

'Where have you been? Are you all right?' he was asking.

'I ... I went to Exeter,' she replied. 'What's the matter?'

'I thought something had happened to you. You sounded so awful this morning.'

She shook her head and tried to sit up. 'I told you I was going out.'

'You are all right, aren't you? You sound very strange.'

'I'm fine. I took some sleeping pills, that's all.'

'What? How many?' he demanded in instantly sober tones. 'You haven't done anything silly?'

'Of course not, Tom. I just couldn't sleep.'

'How many pills? How many?'

'Look, I couldn't sleep and I took two pills, that's all,' she said and summoned up a hazy dignity. 'I haven't the slightest intention of doing myself in, so don't worry.'

'Well, don't give me frights like that,' he said unreasonably. 'I love you, darling. When I saw you yesterday, I knew I loved you. I'm behaving so badly and I can't stop, but I love you.'

He rambled on about the dogs and the house and she slipped out of mental focus and back in the struggle against the drug. She felt as drunk as he was.

'Where are you?' she asked, at last.

'In the office. There isn't a phone in the flat. It isn't the way you think, darling. I'm lonely and there's nothing to do except wander round the pubs and there's always somewhere to drink all night.'

'Where is your friend?' she wondered.

'With her sodding husband, of course. She won't make up her mind. I don't know what's going on. One minute she's going to leave him and the next minute it's off.'

It was absurd to feel sorry for him, but she did.

'I miss you and you're right. We have so much going for us. We like the same things and laugh at the same things. I don't know what's the matter with me and I'm hating all this.'

He stumbled over the words. He was very drunk indeed and she knew how easily drunks forget. It could all be very different tomorrow, yet her hopes rose.

'Angel, I'm sorry I'm so sleepy, it's the wretched pills. Ring me in the morning, early, and I'll be more able to talk,' she explained, apologetically.

'Oh, I love you so much, pet,' he told her. 'It's just that I have ... I have this amazing sexual relationship with her. I lust after her.'

Bridget froze. 'What? What did you say?'

'Lust. It's lust,' he repeated to her horror.

This was a nightmare. All the years she had wanted

84

him, all the rejections, the half-hearted, five-minute roll-
ings on and off her body tumbled through her mind. He
could not mean what he was saying. Tom did not lust.
He would not know how to. Sex did not interest him at
all. He did not know what he was saying. He was drunk.

She managed to end the colloquy with controlled politeness. A headache needled behind her temples and routed
the effects of the sleeping pills. She lay back against the
pillows, stunned.

Bridget had made love to few men, but she liked sex.
Had she been asked, she would have described herself as
a very randy lady and it had been harrowing to douse her
appetite in order to match her husband's lack of enthusiasm. Admittedly, when they had had a particularly good
night out and he had drunk enough brandy, though not
too much, there were times when he had pounded away
at her unimaginatively, but for long enough to exhaust
her and she had been grateful. But such an occasion had
not happened for a couple of years, at least.

What was this other woman doing to excite him so?
she wondered, mortified, and regretted, not for the first
time, her own ignorance.

People whipped each other, tied each other up, dressed
in silly clothes, were turned on by leather and silk, she had
heard. None of that was Tom. Physical violence appalled
him and his pain threshold was so low it was subterra-
nean. A scratch from a rose thorn sent him rushing for
plasters and Germolene. No jack-booted female would get
within striking distance of giving him a good hiding. He
might flirt, but he never so much as glanced at little girls
in school uniform, however pubescent. Nurses? French
maids? No. Underwear? He did not seem to notice that.
And Tom in high-heels was not a convincing image.

She tried to recall Jane's figure, but could only remember pale, lifeless eyes – and the polyester. Pushing back the covers and taking off the pink T-shirt, she looked down at herself. At the angle at which she was sitting, her breasts flopped towards her stomach. She was fooling no one with her new clothes. She was gross. Tom must always have loathed being in bed with her. Yet, she had been much slimmer when they met and it had made no difference, which was probably why she had grown fat.

Her face was wet and the sobs familiar. How she had wanted him, craved for him. Bridget knew what lust was, that it had eaten at her whenever he was there. She wanted him to push his tongue into her mouth, to suck her breasts, to kiss her belly and between her legs, to screw her, to love her as a man should love his woman.

She stumbled across the room to the mirror and howled at the sight, twisting away to fall back on the bed, beating at the pillows, tearing at them, shrieking in frustration and anguish, clawing at her body until long, red weals rose in lines across it, pulling at her own nipples regardless of the pain, wanting the pain, wanting him to hurt her, do anything to her, wanting him, wanting Tom.

She hurled the sweaters on to the floor and, spread-eagled on the mattress, attacked herself, working frenziedly, ululating his name, panting and whimpering, and then imagining, believing, knowing it was him, huge and demanding inside her, that he was taking her, fucking her, mad for her, loving her at last.

The orgasm exploded in a mighty convulsion, shuddering from the depths of her vagina through every single muscle, her legs pressed together; her body arched and rocked, on and on, until her head seemed to split in half, on and on, heat flaming across her skin, tumescence swelling her clitoris and nipples and lips. Moaning, she bit into the bedclothes and dug her nails deep into her thighs and let the agonizing ecstasy burn out at last. But it was not over. Within a minute, she came again, and again. She was powerless to stop. The pent-up deprivation of six years released in orgasm after orgasm, each only slightly less brutal than the one before. She must have come six or seven times until one final, tiny spasm freed her to utter weariness. It had not been pleasure. It had been a savage attack. Bridget had raped herself.

'He says it's sex, that they're having this amazing sexual relationship and he lusts after her. It's incredible,' Bridget told Sophie brokenly the next morning. 'He's never really wanted me. I've had to make all the physical approaches, all the moves, getting him going, getting myself going. He just lies on his side until he's ready.' She blurted out her most intimate secret.

'How extraordinary.' Sophie expressed the clinical interest of a professional sex therapist.

'It's been very difficult for me, but I just presumed he was a bit under-sexed and that he flirted so much as a kind of compensation. When he first told me he was having an affair, I thought at least she'd be disappointed by the performance. And now he tells me this and I can't bear it. I've wanted him so much all these years.'

'You know, Bridget, in Tom's eyes you have always been a very powerful figure.' There was a soothing coolness in Sophie's voice during such conversations. It expressed just the right distancing of them as personal friends to make Bridget feel that any confidence, however humiliating, would be safe. 'And men who believe their wives are stronger than they are often find it very difficult to make love to them.'

'But I'm not powerful. I'm hysterical and muddled and so dependent on him,' she protested.

'You don't appear so to Tom. He sees a successful woman, who achieves in a field he envies and who runs her life superbly. You own the property, you pay the bills, you're a super hostess, a superb cook, you're making money and people pay attention to you,' Sophie said.

'But he always seemed so proud of me.'

'He is proud of you, but it's having to be proud of your achievements that may well be creating the problem.'

'What can I do about that?' Bridget was at a loss. 'I can't stop writing scripts and sell up the house and become a different person.'

'Of course you can't. It's Tom who has to come to terms with the situation. Perhaps you should let him do more, give him more responsibility,' suggested Sophie. 'It is most important that you let Tom reach his own conclusions in this. Don't make the moves for him.'

'But I must fight for him,' she protested.

'Yes, fight, but don't force. Tom must come back of his own accord. Tom must make his own decision.'

'This woman apparently thinks he's so glamorous.' Bridget returned to the main subject. 'And Tom says he's a personality in the town.'

'Well, there you are. He's his own man there, respected for what he does and who he is, not an appendage to you. And he's infatuated with this woman very possibly because she is so much his inferior.'

It was not a particularly cheering conversation and gave

no immediate answers. The comments were apposite, but Bridget was left unsure of how to proceed.

As much to avoid thinking about her conversation with Tom as in expectation of any positive result, Bridget drove towards the coastal town where the private investigator lived.

Bridget had nursed hopes of a sparse, downtown establishment full of smoke and dead beer cans, and Humphrey Bogart wearing a fedora and with a cigarette hanging out of the side of his mouth. The woman who came to the door was a disappointment, as round as she was tall and wheezing with asthma. She led the way to an immaculately clean living-room full of small tables, sideboards and radiator shelves, the surfaces of which were covered with dozens of brass ornaments and dolls in frilly dresses. It could have been a souvenir shop.

'The dusting must take you hours,' Bridget commented in awe.

'The housework takes all day, dear. There's hardly time to cook,' the woman confirmed. 'And of course, dear, I'm so allergic to dust.'

Her husband, the detective, had had to go out, she explained, but Bridget's problem would be quite safe with her. If she needed someone to talk to at any time, she only had to pick up the phone.

'Any time of the day or night, dear. Don't hesitate. I'm always here and, if you want a little cry, you just let it all come out with me, dear.'

Bridget had no intention of doing any such thing and tried hastily to put the matter on a more business-like footing.

'Here are two recent photographs of my husband. His

name and place of work are on the back,' she said, briskly. 'I should like him watched from between five-thirty and six p.m. when he leaves the office. He usually goes to the Horse and Groom first and then I want to know what he does after that and who he meets.'

'Have you any idea who it is your husband's seeing?' Mrs Gates asked on the way to the front door.

Jane's name was insistent. 'I . . . I think it's someone in his office,' she said, hesitantly.

'It usually is, dear.'

'I'll mention it to your husband when I telephone,' Bridget called over her shoulder as she escaped towards the car.

She had to tell Fiona about this, she thought, making straight for her friend's boutique when she reached the local town. The two friends smoked and drank cans of Marks & Spencer white wine as girls idly flipped through the clothes on the rails in the shop and occasionally bore a pair of jeans or a top off to the fitting-room to the accompaniment of Billie Holiday.

Fiona's china-blue eyes widened and she shook her blonde curls, suitably impressed by the idea of hiring a private eye.

'Supposing Tom finds out?' she asked, ever practical.

'God, I hope not.' Bridget had stressed the importance of total discretion to Mrs Gates. 'I'll never get him back if that happens. That's something he wouldn't forgive.'

'George says he's probably having it off with someone in the office,' Fiona said, surprising Bridget, who had never thought of George as being particularly perceptive.

'Oh, it's been going wrong between us for ages.' She was past prudence. 'Whatever I said irritated him and he became dead boring. Then he was always down the pub and he was absolutely hopeless in bed.'

'Well, if he's never at home, boring and no good in the cot, what do you want him back for?' Fiona laughed.

'Christ knows.' Bridget laughed, too. 'I love the silly sod, I suppose.'

It was one of the pleasures of this friendship that Fiona made her laugh, unlike Sue, who could be quite depressing.

'I just can't imagine what he and this woman get up to together that's so riveting,' she said and they both giggled at the unintentional double entendre. 'In fact, I called at the newsagent's on the way here and bought this to see if I could learn anything. I had to hide it under a *Gardening Weekly*. I felt really shifty.'

She drew a girlie magazine from her bag and Fiona squealed and flung a T-shirt over it as one or two of her customers looked round.

They peered under the cover, flicking the pages to reveal girls with their legs open and their tongues out.

'Oh, that's no use, Bridget,' said Fiona, disappointed. 'My boys have those under their beds. That's not porn.'

'How do you get hold of porn?' Bridget asked.

'I'm not sure. I think you have to send off for that. But I saw a porn movie once . . . well, part of one. George had been watching in secret and I switched it on. There was this great pile of women all writhing on top of each other. Honestly, Bridget, they were like a heap of maggots.'

'Then what?'

'I don't know. I heard George coming and had to turn off.' She wrinkled her nose, ruefully. 'Oo, and there was another. It was supposed to be a sex educational film and there was this bloke in a white coat, but he didn't look like any doctor you ever saw. They must have picked him off the streets in Soho. He talked on and on and I kept pressing the fast-forward button and he was still talking. In the end, there was this man and woman. She was rolling about and groaning, but I can't imagine why, because he was as limp as a slug.'

They fell against each other, shrieking with mirth.

'Are you working?' Fiona asked when they finally managed to control themselves.

'Fat chance.' She shrugged.

'You've got to keep your days full, otherwise you'll brood,' Fiona spoke from experience. 'I'm going to London one day soon, why not come?'

'I'll think about it. You know, I do ridiculous things just now. I even wear Tom's old pink T-shirt in bed,' she confessed.

'Oh, I used to wear George's clothes when we split up – and smell his underpants,' Fiona told her, unconcerned. 'They were clean, of course.'

'I should hope so,' sniggered Bridget.

Deirdre had admitted that she wore her husband's underwear, too, when he went away on business. It must be a trait peculiar to women, she thought. Men would imagine they were going kinky if they were tempted to wear their wives' smalls.

The following morning the doorbell rang and the postman asked her to sign for a recorded delivery. It was addressed to Tom, but she opened it and found that the London stranger had returned his wallet. She took it back to bed, lit a cigarette, poured a coffee and allowed herself to grow angry at last and her brain went into overdrive.

Tom needed a thorough shock and she would give him one.

Paul was answering three other telephones as usual. He was an old friend, the director of a thriving advertising agency, a Londoner who had begun adult life in the army and had been something sinister in Northern Ireland before ending his service.

'Of course, darling. It'd be great to see you.' His voice was exactly like Tom's. In fact, they were alike in every way – same charm, same streetwise humour, same casual manner – and they had the same effect on women. He was younger, but they could have been brothers. 'How is the old bastard?'

She told him.

'I'll have him hospitalized,' he responded, outraged.

'No, for God's sake leave him alone. I want him back.' She knew enough about Paul to be only half-amused.

'You're mad! Get rid of him.' He had sentimental ideas about his friends and their marriages.

The two of them had played a harmless flirtatious game with each other since long before Bridget met Tom, knowing that nothing would come of it. At every party Paul had always chosen the prettiest woman in the room and given her all his attention, while his wife, Lisa, used to sit watching and rarely speaking.

For years Lisa had been a skinny, pallid girl, as noticeable as wallpaper. Then, suddenly, she had had her hair cut in a gamine style, started using make-up and wearing daring clothes, and emerged as a beauty.

Paul had carried on with his public philandering, seemingly blind to the change in his wife. When Lisa finally left him, he was devastated. Now they were divorced.

'Come to London. What about tomorrow? Make it early. Seven-thirty at Langan's?' he invited over the telephone.

She had already made an appointment with her hairdresser so now booked a beautician, too; soon she was watching, unworried, as Desmond cut her shoulder-length hair short and then Debbie stuck a cap on her head and began to pull fine strands of hair through it with a crochet hook. A thick cream was pasted on and, as there was no way of wearing her glasses to read, she sat gazing at the apparition of herself in the mirror. She felt slightly high with the promise of her idea.

An hour later, she was lying on the pink sofa in the pink room lit by pink-shaded wall lights. The place even smelt pink. Her facial muscles were deliberately relaxed in order not to destroy the paste pack and, when it was washed off, her skin felt clean and toned.

'What's that?' she asked.

'Concealer,' replied the beautician, smoothing it under her eyes.

She certainly needed plenty of that.

By the time Bridget returned home, there was just time to feed the dogs and dress.

The black, silk jump suit with padded shoulders had been an extravagant gesture to herself in Greece, when she had discovered a talented young designer in Athens. It had been slimming then, but now it made her appear positively svelte. She fastened on the gold necklace, which had been Tom's wedding present to her, a gold bracelet and earrings, and gold high-heeled sandals. Her hair, now streaked as though exposed to the sun, feathered against her cheeks. Hardly a line showed under the professionally applied make-up, which still managed to look natural, except round her eyes, which shone huge and blue, and her mouth, always too small and Irish, which was prettily pink. She looked dramatic and rich. There was no more she could do.

I'll give him glamorous, she thought, taking the wallet which had arrived that morning and easing into her car with care.

The address was not difficult to find, a run-down terrace house on a busy main road. The letterbox was broken and there was no bell, so she knocked loudly, hoping he was in – and hoping the Jezebel was not.

He was wearing a pair of jeans, an old T-shirt and no shoes when he opened the door. A shell-shocked expression crossed his face as his eyes took her in. There was no doubt her effort was effective.

'This arrived yesterday morning,' she said, holding out the wallet after a suitable pause. 'I thought I'd drop it in on my way past.'

'Where are you going all dressed up like that?' he asked, dazed.

'Out to dinner tonight and I can't stop.'

'Come in for a minute.'

She followed him out of curiosity as he led the way into the sitting-room. It was not the cheapness of the place, but the atmosphere which chilled her. She hunched her shoulders as he showed her the well-equipped kitchen, and the bedroom. It was a sufficiently furnished, taste-lessly finicky and foul flat. She stared at the bed where he and the woman screwed together and the invasion of pubic images made her feel ill. She turned and almost ran for the street.

'What's the hurry?' Tom asked.

'I'm late,' she snapped and darted to where she had parked the car.

He had lost a lot of weight. He was one of those men who could eat and drink anything without putting on an ounce, but now he looked haggard and lined. His had not been the face of a man who was having the time of his life with the mistress of his dreams. He had aged ten years.

The purpose of the day was over, as far as Bridget was concerned. Returning the wallet had been the whole point and she did not really look forward to the long drive to London, or to dinner.

She drove so fast that she arrived before Paul and ordered a Bloody Mary while she waited. As she had expected he had secured a table downstairs by the window and, when he arrived, the waiter greeted him as a familiar customer.

'I'll drive down and see Tom tomorrow, darling,' Paul said. 'And, if he doesn't listen, I'll thump some sense into him.'

'For heaven's sake, Paul!' she protested. 'He'll be no use sent back to me in bits.'

'OK. But just say the word, darling, and I'll have him trussed up and delivered to the marital bed before this goes any further.'

Then he began talking about his ex-wife. From the day she left, telling him that she was going to visit her mother, Lisa had refused all contact, other than leaving a note saying they had grown apart and she wanted to be a free spirit. He could not understand it. He'd sent money and she'd returned it. He knew she had been a bit down and he'd thought, if he ignored this, she would perk up. It was a complete mystery to him and Bridget did not have the heart to explain.

So many men seemed incapable of understanding women, she was discovering. It did not seem to occur to them that, if their wives flirted incessantly in front of them, ignored their depressions, dismissed their views, cut through their conversations, did not listen to them, or sympathize with their troubles, then the men, too, would probably go in search of pastures new. It was no accident that more wives divorced husbands, than husbands divorced wives. The popular opinion that the reverse was true was a myth.

Men seemed to see women as a separate species, not requiring the same treatment as they needed themselves. Some women grew to hate them for this insensitivity, but most others spoke among themselves with affectionate contempt, as though these grown human beings were children to be tolerated and, occasionally, smacked. Bridget felt sorry for men. They missed out on a lot. A real and equal partnership between a man and a woman was far more difficult to achieve than the old master-servant relationship, but so much more rewarding.

'It was the lack of communication which was worst,' Paul was saying. 'If we could only have kept in touch. I wanted to meet her, talk to her, but she wouldn't.'

Because he had been too late.

It was well after eleven o'clock when he saw her to her car and she set off on the four-hour journey. Time and the motorway miles passed effortlessly, so that she was quite surprised to find herself on the moor so soon. A sheep strayed across the road down to the river. Bridget stopped the car on the narrow, stone bridge and listened to the water gurgling below. Tom and she had paddled there once and she had tripped over a stone and soaked her skirt. They had lain back on the bank and, by the time they stood up to leave, it had been dry. It was one of their favourite spots.

Poor Paul, she thought. It had been unfair, almost cruel of Lisa not to explain in detail exactly why she had left him. She had owed him that, at least. If he did not understand, how could he avoid making the same mistake in future?

'Whatever happens, keep the contact going between you,' he had urged, several times. 'There's no hope when there's no contact.'

Bridget remembered how relieved she had felt just to learn the truth from Tom and then she realized that it was Saturday. He would have been coming to the house that day to do the garden. They would have had another chance to be with each other, to stay in touch, if she had not put him off and, by doing so, shut the door on opportunities to meet without having to make special and perhaps negative arrangements. Gareth's advice was wrong. She had made a mistake.

Tom had looked so miserable. She looked at her watch. It was after three a.m., but it was not too late to put everything right.

Reversing the car off the bridge, she started the long detour towards the town.

Chapter Six

TOM opened the door. He had obviously not been in bed as he was dressed.

'I knew you'd fucking turn up. I even moved my car so that you'd think I was out,' he shouted. 'What the fuck do you want?'

His face was chiselled granite, craggy and seamed. A complete stranger stared down at her through eyes of stone.

'Tom, I . . .' she began.

'You've been driving round all night just waiting to come here,' he snarled. 'I know it.'

'You're out of your mind!' This goaded her into speech. 'Why on earth should I do that? I've been out to dinner.'

'And just happened to be passing this flat at half past three in the morning, I suppose.'

'No. I came because I wanted to say something, something helpful.' She tried to placate him.

'Well, I don't want you here. I knew if I gave you the address you'd come creeping round. I don't want you here. I don't want you here, ever.'

He turned and stalked off down the corridor. Bridget stood at the door for a moment and then ran back to her car. She turned the key and the engine turned over slowly, but did not fire. She tried again and, to her consternation, the engine died. She tried several times more and then sat, helplessly, wondering what to do.

Eventually, because there was no alternative, she

returned to the house. The front door was still open. Tom was in the bedroom lying on top of the bed. The television was on.

'There's something wrong with the car. It won't start.' She was diffident.

'Yes, I expect you've fixed that, too, so that you can stay the night here.'

'I wouldn't stay the night in your disgusting brothel, if it was the last place in the universe.' She was very angry now. 'It's probably the battery and, if you give me the keys, I'll fetch the jump leads from your car.'

'That's another trick. Just a way to take my car. Well, you're not having it.'

He was insane. She looked at him with supreme contempt.

'I'm not like you, Tom O'Dare. You are a greedy, selfish, little man and you're welcome to your pathetic car, even though I did buy it,' she spat and left the room.

The kitchen seemed to close in on her and she wandered restlessly to the sitting-room. There was a smell about the flat which seemed to cling to her skin and hair, an atmosphere which made her blood crawl. It was evil and rotten. She sat on the edge of a chair and immediately stood up again. It was impossible to stay still. The place revolted her. She wanted to go home.

Tom appeared against the light in the hall, a menacing, black streak.

'I hope you're enjoying having a good nose about,' he said.

'Oh fuck off!'

'Don't you swear at me!' he screamed.

She rounded on him.

'Fuck off, you cunt!'

He hit her. He hit her so hard that the room went dark and then lights flashed and she found herself lying on the sofa.

He stood over her. Someone she had never seen before. A terrible man. A man she did not know at all.

'Take the keys and get out!' the man said and she heard them jingle as he threw them on the floor.

The town was known for the drunkenness of its men and their brawling violence. Unemployment and crime rates were high. Bridget, scurrying through the dim streets dressed in her black silk and gold, was frightened. She had brought no coat and felt exposed. Every shadow seemed ready to pounce.

Hoping that Tom's car was in the firm's car-park, she clicked down the alley and felt dizzy with relief when she saw the familiar number plate. She drove back to her own car, parked head to head and opened the bonnets. Without a torch, she had to feel about on the oily batteries to find the raised positive and negative signs to attach the jump leads. Then she tried her own starter again. It failed and failed. Tom, who must have known she was outside, did not appear. Finally, she lost patience.

A notebook was always kept in the glove compartment. Tearing off a sheet, she wrote: *You have a new car. It does not start. That is your problem. I hope you and your cheating, lying slut give each other everything you deserve. I never want to set eyes on you again.*

Wrapping this round her keys, she stuffed them through the gap where the letterbox should have been and drove home in his car.

When she looked in the dressing-table mirror the next

morning, there was a bright purple, hard lump on her cheekbone and her tongue could feel that the inside of her cheek was cut, where it had been smashed against her teeth.

The telephone rang.

'I just want to say . . .' he began.

'Forget it!' she cut in. 'It's finished between us. I saw you properly for the first time last night, Tom. I want nothing more to do with you . . . ever.'

Sophie listened as she spilled out her report of the night.

'I never want to see him again,' she ended.

'I don't often say this, but I think you're right,' said Sophie. 'Tom is a man out of control and men out of control are very dangerous. I honestly do think you should give him up now.'

'So do I,' agreed Bridget.

'He was like a monster. Someone I'd never seen before. Even his face was unrecognizable,' she ranted to her daughter next. 'I don't want him back. It was the worst day of my life when I met him. He's vicious and completely self-obsessed and he's never considered me for a single second. Everything I've offered has been taken for granted. He's just used me.'

She paused for breath and Deirdre said nothing.

'I'm certain I know who the cow is and she's nothing but a downmarket tart. By the time her husband has taken his share of the precious marital home, there'll hardly be a pot to piss in. They'll finish up in some tin-pot terrace house and Tom won't be Lord of the Manor any more,' she carried on. 'And I'll make damned sure he doesn't get a penny out of this marriage. I'm ringing John in a minute. His sister warned me he'd try to screw everything he could out of me and I didn't believe her, but I believe her now and I'll fight him all the way. He's never given me a second's happiness and I'm going to pay him back.'

'Now, Mummy, you know that's not true,' Deirdre said, in a voice too full of reason. 'You have been happy with him.'

Bridget was not going to listen to this.

'Well, I'm not now. The bastard! What's he ever done for me?'

'I know he's inconsiderate and difficult and what he did last night was unforgivable, but if something like this had happened six years ago, you wouldn't have been able to handle it. Tom has let you develop – grow up, if you like. The fact that you're not having a nervous break-down, or worse, you owe to Tom and your life together.'

'You don't even like him,' Bridget said, accusingly.

'I wouldn't like him for me. I don't know how you stand him,' Deirdre agreed, honestly. 'But you suit each other. You're both impossible.'

'I don't care. I don't care. I'm going to divorce him, anyway.'

'Well, don't rush it.'

Her solicitor, John, must have taken her file home in readiness, she consulted him so frequently these days. He was remarkably amiable about having his weekend disturbed.

It was unlikely that Tom would be awarded more than a token amount in any divorce settlement, he advised. The marriage had not lasted long and he had brought no material assets to it, nor contributed financially to the payment or maintenance of the house since.

'The pre-marital agreement you both signed to protect

your property for your daughter cannot be legally enforced in this country, as you know,' he went on. 'But I
feel sure it would carry weight should Tom decide to
cross-petition.'

Bridget, highly satisfied by this, agreed to go to his
office as soon as the detective had completed his job and
made a report.

'Presuming the report substantiates the fact of Tom's
adultery,' John said with a solicitor's caution.

'It will,' she retorted, grimly.

Mr Gates, the private investigator, was at home, too.

'I suspect it's a typist in Tom's office,' she told him.

'Do you know her name?'

'Only her Christian name, I'm afraid. Jane.'

'And you don't know where she lives?'

'I could try to find out.'

'That would be useful. Can you give me a description
of her?'

Bridget could only picture the tight skirt and frothy
blouse and pale eyes.

'Not really. I can't remember what she looks like. She's
very insignificant, wears a lot of make-up and has
bleached hair. And, of course, it might not be her at all.
It's just that I have a feeling it is.'

Mr Gates did not comment on women's intuition,
though he probably heard plenty about it at home. They
agreed that he should start work on Monday evening.

This was the first morning since the start of the nightmare that Bridget had not cried. Her hate and fury
against her husband were so powerful they were almost
glee. She would destroy him, she vowed. She would
destroy them both.

There were going to be no more whispered plans, no

more titillating, secret meetings in country pubs, no more spicy drives. There was going to be no more cosy love nest. That woman's husband knew nothing, but he was going to know everything within days. She was going to blow the affair sky-high.

It was time Tom felt the frosty bite of reality. It was time there were divorces and quarrels over money and fights over property and floods and floods of tears. The shit was going to hit the fan, and how.

Mixing herself a suitably Bloody Mary, Bridget sat down at last and pondered her revenge.

Monday came at last. A sleepy voice answered the phone. Harold was one of Tom's colleagues and a friend to both, who had been a guest at their wedding.

'It's Bridget. Tom's Bridget,' she said, conscious that she was taking a chance. Men stuck together.

'Oh, hello, m'dear.'

She wondered if he knew the situation, then guessed that he must. Everyone would know that her husband was living away from home by now.

'This is going to be a slightly peculiar conversation,' she began. 'And I don't want Tom to know I've rung.'

'Word of honour, m'dear.'

He was a darling man, round and comfortable, a man of habit, who liked to stand in the same place at the bar at the same time during every lunch hour and who walked his dog on the hills every Sunday morning and who had loved the same woman all his life. Bridget knew she could trust him.

She took a deep breath. 'Can you tell me the surname of Jane, the typist in the office?'

'Scott,' he answered, without hesitation.

'You won't say anything?' She could not help pressing the point.

'Not a word, m'dear.'

And he never did.

Tom's Bridget, she had said. She mused on this over her coffee. What did she want? Did she want him back? Right now, she did not. But she might in future. Perhaps Deirdre and Gareth were right. She should not rush into divorce. Perhaps she should get him back – and then decide what to do about him. One thing was certain, that slag was not having him.

Leaving the coffee half-finished, she went out into the fresh air. The garden, which had always given her so much pleasure, might just as well have been invisible now because Bridget walked round it unseeing. Before her life had been thrown in turmoil, she would have noticed the little bunches of grapes, like jade beads, on the vine, stopped to pull up any weed daring to sully a flower bed and registered that the hedge needed trimming and the lawn should be mown. She would have stood at the top of the orchard and looked out past the church spire and over the village to the sea and drawn in breaths of peace and renewed wonder at the beauty of the place in which she lived. Now that Tom was no longer there, the darkness of her thoughts left her blind.

She sat down on the grass under a tree and tried to separate her anger and her desire to retaliate from her true feelings.

However galling the admission in her present mood, she had to accept that she needed Tom and she wanted him back and she could not live without him. To save her marriage required control and thought.

Bridget began to imagine she was writing a play with

herself and Tom and Jane Scott as the principal characters. The dilemma to be resolved was already clear. What
was now needed was a plot; a plot far more subtle than
Old Panstick's game, a plan that would appeal to the
protectiveness in Tom's nature, that would keep the door
to his home invitingly open, that would give the impression that she, Bridget, was neither rejecting nor pursuing
him.

Mentally, just as she would have prepared a play, she
worked out the salient points and gradually a plot
emerged, The Plan to save her marriage.

First she would write a letter to Tom, then she would
bring Jane Scott's husband into the scene. She would let
the situation develop before writing another letter, then
wait for the result of that before writing again. Each
letter would adopt a different approach, but all would
have the same purpose, to bring her husband home.

Bridget returned to the house and dialled another
number, long distance, this time.

Sam, her ex-husband, was still in bed.

'Sam, I need your help. Will you do me a favour?' she
asked without preliminaries.

'Anything,' he said, at once. 'Deirdre's told me.' He
saved her from having to explain. 'I'd like to kill the bastard.'

'So would I at the moment,' she agreed. 'Sam, I think I
know who the woman is. It's hard to believe, but I've got
this gut feeling.'

'Always trust a gut feeling,' he said. 'Now, what do
you want me to do?'

'Her name's Scott and I need to know where she lives.
I've listed all the Scotts in the town and I want you to
ring each number and ask for her. She should be at work

but, in case she hasn't gone in for some reason, I daren't do it myself as she might recognize my voice. I don't want her tipped off that I suspect.'

'Supposing she answers?'

Bridget had thought of this. 'Say you live nearby and want to put an advertisement in the paper and ask who you should contact. You're an actor. Busk it!'

Half an hour later, he came back to her.

'There was no answer from one number and another line was continually engaged, but women answered all the others,' he reported. 'None of them was her.'

'OK. Well, you'll just have to phone the office to check whether she's there, but ring off before you're put through,' she instructed.

Jane Scott was at work.

Bridget rang the number which had been engaged and on her fifth attempt a young girl answered.

'Oh, it's my auntie you want,' she said.

'The Jane Scott who works on the newspaper?' Bridget was careful.

'That's right. Her number is 419.'

That was the number to which there had been no reply. Bridget checked the address alongside – 18, Harlow Road – and felt triumphant. Not all her training as a reporter had been wasted.

The detective agreed to follow Tom that evening and she passed on the information, together with her husband's new address.

'I've got a plan,' she told Sam, when she rang him back.

'I thought you might have.' After living with her since her girlhood, he knew her very well indeed.

'Tom's just had a weekend to kick his heels on his

own. He loathes being on his own and he must be feeling guilty about the way he behaved on Friday night,' she said. 'I'm going to send him a letter offering to return his car, a very nice letter.'

'What do you want to do that for? I'd keep his car and anything else you can lay your hands on,' said Sam.

At least their divorce had been free of battles over such matters. They had not allowed lawyers to goad them into an acrimonious war over possessions. Sam was the most undemanding man regarding material goods and happiest when able to pack everything he possessed into a small suitcase. Each had been aware of the pain of the other and they had worked hard to behave with consideration and loyalty towards each other until the shabby process was over, with the result that they had remained very close.

'Give me a minute and I'll explain,' she said. 'First, the letter, which will put me in the right and leave him in the wrong. Then he'll have another weekend alone and on the Monday I'll find a way of letting this woman's husband know exactly what's going on. There will be a week of chaos after which I'm going to advertise in the paper for a good home for his dog and send another letter, a very pathetic one, telling him how I can't manage.

'By that time, it's my guess that, if the lady is the cow I think she is and with a maelstrom of trouble battering him to pieces, Tom's going to want out.'

'Clever bitch,' her ex-husband commented.

'I've got to be,' she retorted.

They had always liked each other. When he was sober, he was the most generous-hearted man she knew. Their marriage had been doomed from the start by her youth and naïvety and their incompatibility – Bridget wanting roots and a home and Sam a real nomad, content with one room or just to drift. She had never regretted leaving him, but they were still each other's best friend.

The Start of Day disc purred and clicked in the word processor as it fed in the programme. She changed the disc, opened a new file and typed in the first letter.

My dear Tom,
As you know, I don't believe in bitterness and hatred. (They give one lines!) The car was always intended for your use and, in fact, had I been able to start my own last week, I should have driven home in it, of course.

If you wish to exchange the cars, I can leave yours in the firm's car-park, if you leave the keys in mine. There is no need for us to meet, or for any unpleasantness at all. I shall have had your car serviced and I certainly had no intention of keeping the Volvo – besides, the dogs get fed up when they hear it arrive and you do not walk in.

Shall we arrange the exchange for next Friday around sixish? If this is not suitable, or if you prefer to leave the car situation as it is, you will have to let me know, somehow. Otherwise, I shall go ahead as above.

I hope everything goes well with you. I remain your friend always, Tom, if you should ever need one. Meanwhile, 'be lucky'.
Yours,
Bridget
P.S. Pat thinks she's pregnant!

It was a cunning letter, cool and friendly on the surface, but planted with reminders of his home and a slight touch of humour. Nor was it the open-ended offer it seemed. Both cars were registered in her name and, when she rang the garage to book the service, she asked for spare keys to be cut. If Tom did decide to stay with Jane Scott, or whoever the woman was, Bridget had every intention of removing his car from the firm's car-park and locking it securely in her garage, along with her own. All was fair in war.

Posting the letter in time to catch the village collection, she returned to start work on the second.

Dear Tom,

I am writing because I don't want you to see the advertisement in the paper first and be upset without my explaining that I am having to look for a new home for the puppy.

I am really unable to cope here now. He has killed three hens since you left and I cannot fix the bolt on the dogs' run. Even by jamming breeze blocks in front of the gate at night, they still break out. He takes no notice of my voice and keeps running away on the main road.

Also, the old one has been ill. I was up all night with her. The vet says he thinks it was some kind of food poisoning and she nearly died.

The lad has stopped coming to help on Saturdays and the neighbours have blocked the right-of-way. They know you are not here and probably think that they can do what they like.

I am sorry that I am not managing to hold everything together and I am really heartbroken to lose Rake.

Love as ever,
Bridget

The facts were true but the letter was pure sophistry. The bitch had been ill, the neighbours were being bolshie and Rake was maddeningly unruly, but she would never have parted with him and she was perfectly able to handle any practical problem. Lies, lies, but she did not care. Jane Scott was using every wile with her hard-luck stories and adulation and unimaginable bedroom technique. There was no room for ethics here.

The biggest difficulty was going to be sticking to The Plan. Her mistakes so far had been made through acting on impulse, telephoning Tom on the spur of the moment, turning up at his flat. This had only made their conflict worse each time. She had to control herself, wait out the necessary number of days between each stage and refuse to act precipitately. Time was the strength of The Plan.

Chapter Seven

MAKE-UP did not cover the bruise on her cheek completely, but it did provide enough disguise for her not to appear like a defeated prize fighter. Bridget put on sunglasses and drove into town.

She called in at Fiona's boutique. For all her resolution, Bridget was not without guilt over The Plan, which she confessed as they sat over glasses of wine watching the customers browse.

'Don't be stupid. You use every trick. Pull every stroke.' Her friend said what she wanted to hear. 'I did when George decided on home games. Conscience is for kids and, if you pussyfoot around this, a good conscience is all you'll be left with.

'Mind you, Bridget, I've got to say it. I just can't believe Tom's tied up with that Scott woman. Her husband's a real sweetie. Everyone likes him.'

'Tom seems to be under the impression that Jane Scott is the virgin bride who is badly treated.'

'Well, Ron Scott's a friend of ours. Jane Scott had three small children when he married her, and he's been a real father to them. Actually, he's a quiet, rather gentle man. I don't believe he'd hurt a fly.'

The information filled Bridget with optimism. Tom might give all the signals of a man with liberal opinions, but he was a traditional male chauvinist at heart. If Jane Scott had played on his sympathy with a hard-luck story that did not stand up, he would not be impressed.

Bridget drove home quite elated; it was as she was lifting out her shopping that she discovered the balloons, burst balloons scattered about the back of Tom's car. And they were not in one piece, like ordinary burst balloons. They were in shreds.

Bridget gathered up the pieces and took them to her study and stared at them. What did people do with balloons?

As early as possible the following morning, she telephoned Mr Gates.

'I observed your husband's flat from five o'clock until nine o'clock last night,' he told her in the ponderous tones of a retired member of the force. 'However, the suspect did not appear.'

'What suspect?' she asked.

'Mr O'Dare, madam.'

'But what about when he left the office? Where did he go then?'

'I am afraid I did not ascertain that, madam. I thought the best course of action was to watch the flat, which was not easy, it being in a very open position.'

Bridget took a deep breath and somehow managed to restrain herself from telling him he was a fool.

'Mr Gates, I asked you to follow my husband from the office,' she reminded him grimly. 'Of course there was no guarantee that he would go to the flat. I have told you that he and this woman frequently meet away from the town and they probably did so last night.'

'Don't worry, Mrs Flynn. We'll get there in the end. You leave it with me.'

At ten pounds an hour for his inefficient services, she was certainly not going to do that.

'Will you please watch the office this evening? Wait until my husband leaves and do not let him out of your sight, Mr Gates,' she instructed with edgy firmness. 'I want to know exactly who he is having an affair with as quickly as possible.'

'Leave it with me, madam.'

'Just watch the office,' she emphasized and rang off angrily.

She stood on the scales and saw that she had lost two stone in less than three weeks.

This was to be her day of positive thinking. Sitting cross-legged on the tattered Victorian *chaise-longue* in her study, she pressed the first finger and thumb of each hand together, as she had read somewhere was the way to increase the power of meditation, and began to whisper.

'You're going to come home. You miss your home. You want to come home. You will come home.'

Hour after hour, while tidying her room, 'You're going to come home. You want to come home'; while feeding the dogs, 'You miss your home. You're going to come home'; while hand washing out a few clothes, 'You're going to come home. You're coming home. You will come home.'

She walked round the garden, 'You'll soon be here'. She cleaned out the freezer, 'You want to come home'; lying on the bed, 'You're going to come home. You are coming home.'

All day and all evening, sometimes weeping, sometimes stern, always determined, Bridget Flynn willed Tom O'Dare to return.

She awoke deeply depressed, as though unrealistically she had expected that her massive concentration of the previous day would have conjured up her husband like a genie, but he had not appeared, or even telephoned.

At nine o'clock that night she gave in and dialled the detective's number. To her disappointment, he answered.

'Yes, Mrs O'Dare. I have some news for you,' he said.

She twitched nervously and lit a cigarette.

'I parked my car in a suitable position from which to observe your husband's office at four forty-five,' he began. 'At five-thirty precisely your husband, whom I identified from the photographs you provided, left the building and walked to the car-park. Entering his car, he then drove it to the address given as his flat, parked in front of this address and entered by way of a key.'

Had he discovered the identity of the woman? Bridget bit her lip and wished he would come to the point.

'At seven-thirty a woman, wearing a black skirt and white blouse and black high-heeled shoes and carrying a handbag of the same colour, walked from the direction of the town and let herself into the flat with a key.'

She had been right. He had fallen for that old tart.

'I waited until a short time ago. No one left the premises and I returned home,' concluded Mr Gates.

'You did what?' Bridget could not believe her ears. 'Why didn't you stay until the woman came out?'

'There was no way of knowing that would happen, madam,' he replied, huffily. 'And, besides, I had not had any supper.'

'You know she's a married woman. You know she has to return to her husband each night,' she stormed. 'You should have waited outside that flat until she left.'

'Madam, if you will leave this matter with me, I can assure you we shall have a result very soon, very soon indeed.'

Furiously, Bridget rang off and dialled Jane Scott's number at Harlow Road. There was no answer.

Calling her inept investigator again, she said, with undisguised anger, 'There is no reply to Mrs Scott's telephone number. She is out. Kindly go to her address and wait outside until she returns and then verify that she is the same woman you saw entering my husband's flat.'

'If you think it necessary, madam.' He was very reluctant. 'I shall finish my meal and do as you ask.'

'Look, Mr Gates, I don't care if you starve from now until next month. If you want to be paid a penny, you had better forget your bloody supper and get back to this job at once.'

'Very well, madam. I shall do as you wish, but I must tell you that I am not accustomed to this kind of interference.'

Bridget sat, chain-smoking and rocking in a frenzy of agitation. The man was bound to be too late, now. He was like a Peter Sellers character. She wished she had thought of hiring a beard and men's clothing and carrying out the surveillance herself only, of course, Tom would have been bound to recognize his car.

When the telephone rang an hour later, she snatched up the receiver, reaching for her cigarettes at the same time with shaking hands.

'As instructed, I drove to the address given as that of Mrs Scott and parked outside,' he reported, stiffly. 'There is a telephone box nearby and I telephoned the house and, receiving no reply, concluded that the woman was not at home. A few minutes after I returned to my car, a Ford saloon drew up. The woman, who had been seen entering your husband's flat, got out, walked up the path to the house, entered using a key, and went to the front room, where she drew the curtains. I then left and returned home.'

'Oh, thank you, Mr Gates, thank you.' In her relief, Bridget forgot her annoyance.

Her reactions frequently took her by surprise. Now, as she sat, lighting one cigarette after another, she realized that she was not destroyed, or outraged, or even hurt. She was insulted.

Tom could have had anyone; instead, he was screwing this non-event.

She wished she could remember more about the typist and wondered if she had overlooked something. Thinking carefully, she itemized everything she knew; about fifty years old, short and rather overweight, thick pink and white make-up, nondescript looks, but quite good legs. The woman was a dull conversationalist with a 'genteel' voice, married. She had some money of her own and her only known hobby was playing darts, according to her lover. Even allowing for natural bias, the affair made no sense.

Painfully, Bridget forced herself to consider what had happened between them during the terrible scene a few days before. In the beginning, she had thought of him as a monster and hated him for what had happened. Yet people did do horrific things when they were distraught. Did one terrible, atypical act wipe out five years of happiness with him? she asked herself. Or did the five years wipe out the act? She knew the answer and wished he were home beside her.

Outlining the reasons for her change of view to Sophie, she added, 'I know you feel I should give him up now, but I can't. Not just because of the other night, especially when I remember some of the things I've done to him in the past.'

'Other people can only advise, Bridget. No outsider can ever know the complete truth of any relationship between two people and, in the end, you must always listen to your own heart and trust your own judgement,' Sophie said. 'But keep in mind that Tom is very confused and very unstable at the moment, so be careful.'

'What I can't understand, no matter how hard I try, is how he can be so besotted with a woman like Jane Scott.' Bridget voiced the question that kept recurring. 'He could have practically any woman he wanted, so why on earth is he prepared to give up everything for one who is middle-aged, well-used and neither beautiful nor bright?'

'I suspect the situation crept up on him, almost without his being aware of what was happening,' Sophie replied. 'You see, Tom is very conscious of the dangers of obviously attractive women and so, although he flirts, he is also guarded with them, always keeping them at a safe distance.

'But this woman is, as you say, older, a very familiar figure whom he sees every day. He would not have been at all wary of her. They probably began by having an occasional drink together and discussing the day's work and the newspaper, and then he may have felt a little sorry for her, because of the pathetic tales she was spinning about her home life. Men are extremely vulnerable in such situations. I don't imagine he saw her as a sexual threat in any way in the beginning.'

Suddenly, Bridget thought of her own mother, whose act of 'brave little widow smiling through' combined with huge, blue, admiring and helpless eyes could still reduce brawny young men to the level of devoted dogs, although she was over seventy and about as fragile and gentle as a nuclear weapon.

It was not necessary to be young or pretty to pluck a man like a chicken. All that was required was to press the buttons marked 'Protective Instinct', 'Ego' and 'Sex', in that order.

So, there was old Jane, loyal and suitably subservient worker, always neat and tidy, not hiding her admiration for him, no arguments or intellectual competition here, restful, with a hand giving his a sympathetic squeeze at the end of a hard day.

What a nice woman Jane Scott is, Tom would have thought at first. Then, so relaxing to be with, so entertaining, laughing at all his jokes, marvelling open-mouthed at his experience, his travels, his successes, the scoops and herograms of Fleet Street days, Israel, Cambodia, famous wars, famous trials, famous names, the Queen's Jubilee Year, the Royal Yacht.

So easy to put an arm round her and drop the first little kiss on to that raised, star-struck face.

Jane Scott, smiling too brightly while dropping hints of her private struggles under a tyrant of a husband, shaking her head in commiseration when he confided about his demanding wife. Jane Scott whispering, with perhaps just the glistening of a tear, of how she had tried for so many years to be faithful and keep her marriage going, of how lonely she was, of how she had never met anyone as kind and considerate and generous. How could Tom's wife not appreciate him? If she had a husband like Tom, well . . .

So easy to pull her close in the car and arrange to meet the next night away from town, where they could talk undisturbed by people who might recognize them and misinterpret the situation, which was, of course, perfectly innocent.

Bridget saw it all. Old Panstick, playing Tom's game and turning the tables on him, remaining just a fingertip out of reach, with excuses of husband, time and conscience, playing right to the edge and then pulling away, just as every teenage girl has teased every boy since being allowed out alone; spinning her web with infinite care and patience from November to April, when Tom had spent two nights away from home, officially 'on a course'. He had telephoned home at regular intervals and left the address of the hotel. But Bridget was convinced now that that was when he had finally and frenziedly and blindly fucked Jane Scott for the first time.

The private investigator's report arrived within a couple of days and repeated in writing his observations.

Bridget read it carefully, clicking her tongue in irritation over the description of Jane Scott as a lady aged between thirty-eight and forty. Apart from a brain transplant, the man apparently needed glasses as well.

Then she opened the bill. It was for well over one hundred pounds. He was not so stupid after all.

Thoroughly annoyed, she telephoned the firm which had originally recommended him. 'I had to spoonfeed him, find out the woman's name and address myself and even send him back on the job after he gave up and went home,' she complained.

'I'm sorry he's been so unsatisfactory,' said a man's voice. 'But I'm afraid I can't discuss it just now. You see, we've just been burgled.'

Chapter Eight

THERE were good days and bad days. She knew the bad days before she opened her eyes, almost before she awoke. There would be this sluggishness about her body, no thoughts in her mind, only a wad of depression, like black cotton wool. The day was going to be a bad day all day.

Sometimes, she would cry soundlessly, the tears flowing down her face, one after the other, as accurately spaced as the ticking of a metronome, wetting her skin down to her breasts, soaking through Tom's dusty pink T-shirt in which she always slept now. Sometimes, she would just sit staring into space and smoking. Tranquillizers were of no use on bad days. They only pushed her down further.

Usually, she stayed in bed, rising only briefly to feed the dogs and let them into the garden. Then she would curl, foetus-like, under the bedclothes and sleep short, dismal naps. The hours passed curiously quickly. There was no need to look at the clock. This was to be a bad day all day.

Occasionally, on bad days, she would try to visualize life without Tom and could not see the point of continuing. Life was meant to be shared. Success was empty without another human being for whom to achieve. Without a partner, work and money and possessions meant nothing at all. Tom was her chosen partner, the only man she had ever truly loved. She wanted only to create for him, to lie with him every night, to give all to him and, at last, to be buried beside him.

The Plan to which she had hitched her star of the future was not going to work. It was too obvious. Tom would see through it. He was too intelligent to be taken in. Yet, he was being taken in by Jane Scott, and there could not be anyone more obvious than she.

Unlike Gareth and Sam, he had no women friends, women whose company he simply enjoyed without any sexual overtones. These men would have recognized Jane Scott for what she was immediately. But, for women, Tom always put on the performance of charm and physical promise. Bridget realized he had probably never actually talked to a woman with whom he was not living. He probably did not know how to. In fact, for all his experience, he did not understand women at all.

As she stared blankly at the bruise on her face in the looking-glass, the telephone rang.

'How's it going, darling?' Paul asked. 'Are you all right?'

'As right as can be expected.'

'You don't sound it.'

Bridget told him everything that had happened since they had had dinner together and then, ignoring his renewed threats to dismember her husband, she told him about The Plan.

'Seems pretty shrewd to me,' he commented. 'I'm convinced the old bastard will come back to you, darling. He's having his last fling, that's all, male menopause.'

'That's exactly what he said.'

'There you are then. Last flings usually end with the husband going back to his cuddly wife.'

'Not always,' she pointed out. 'Anyway, The Plan's not going to work. I'm stuck.'

'What's wrong with it. It sounds OK to me.'

She explained that if a woman's voice telephoned Jane Scott's husband about her affair with Tom, the couple would guess that it was Bridget and then Tom would never come home.

'No problem, darling,' he laughed. 'I'll do it.'

'You? Why should you do such a thing for me?' The idea that he might had crept in only a second before.

'Let me tell you something, darling.' She could hear him light a cigarette at the other end of the line. 'I came to your wedding and it really was a lovely experience. No bullshit. There was that old dog Tom, looking as though he'd just beaten all Botham's records, and you all dewy-eyed. It gave me a bloody lump in my throat. I began to worry that I wasn't such a hard man after all. So I'll do it for you and Tom, darling. I want to do it.'

Bridget tried not to cry as she gave him Jane Scott's telephone number and told him all she knew.

'Next Monday then,' he confirmed. 'It's a long time since I blew up anything and I think I'm going to enjoy this.'

Other telephones were ringing in the background of his office.

'Got to go now,' he said. 'Don't worry and take care, darling. Leave everything to little Paul.'

She slept through the rest of the morning and most of the afternoon after that and realized, in the evening, that it had not been such a bad day in the end.

Filling in the time was difficult. It took only so long to walk the dogs and she could weigh herself only so many times a day. The garden, having been neglected since before she went to Greece, was overgrown beyond recovery for this year and, in any case, there was no incentive to garden, or cook, or look after the house. Had Pat not whizzed in and out occasionally, the dirt would simply have piled up and been ignored. She did not eat, so there was no reason to shop. She could not write, because all her concentration was used up by Tom's affair.

'I wait for him to call me and he doesn't. Then I want to call him,' she told her daughter.

'Well, you mustn't. You've decided on The Plan and it's a good one. Whatever you do, don't ruin it.'

Having a daughter was a joy and a privilege, yet they had not always been so close. Bridget remembered Deirdre's childhood with guilt. Their circumstances had been so fraught with financial insecurity and Sam had been so temperamental and demanding, that she had had little left to give the child. And she had been jealous.

She had been no more than a child herself, with too many needs of her own which were not being met, when Deirdre was born. Sam adored children and he had monopolized their daughter from the beginning. He was at home all day, while Bridget worked, and their hours together were full of games and jokes, from which she was excluded. Daddy was always fun. Mummy was always tired and cross. Bridget felt that Sam had stolen Deirdre from her, that they had been a couple and she the outsider. She had not been a good mother.

In adolescence, Deirdre, after an angelic childhood, had rebelled, growing sullen and resentful. There was no bond of understanding between them. They were opposite in every way, the girl bottling up her emotions, bearing grudges, remembering every slight for weeks and months, the mother in a tantrum one minute and having forgotten why the next.

As adults, they had circled each other warily after Deirdre left home. Each visit was spiky. Deirdre could be so prim and disapproving and something of a know-all. Bridget sometimes suspected she was tolerated only because of their undeniable relationship. She thought of her daughter as hard and unrelenting, far the stronger character, and she was slightly frightened of her.

Yet they had always confided in each other to a remarkable degree, even about sex. Perhaps because her mother was so much younger than the mothers of her friends and very open-minded, Deirdre had no reservations about discussing her private life, nor Bridget about her own. They were like rival sisters.

Curious little pointers had been overlooked. Bridget had framed a photograph of Deirdre and put it on her dressing-table and the girl had been blushingly surprised. Then she had dedicated a play to her daughter and had been amazed at the touched response. It was almost as though Deirdre had not been able to believe that she loved her until then.

Then the previous autumn they had had their first and only blazing row. A dinner party at a nearby restaurant had gone wrong when one of the men had been boorishly drunk. Bridget, hypersensitive to such scenes after years of social embarrassment with Sam, had overreacted. The evening had gone from bad to worse, until she and Deirdre were screaming at each other at home and Deirdre had walked out of the house.

Each had been convinced she was in the right and neither would contact the other. The quarrel, which had seemed superficially to be about an unimportant episode, deepened into a culmination of the misunderstandings of years. Christmas came and went. Neither would give way.

While Tom had been unhappily struggling under the

new regime at work and already drifting towards Jane Scott, Bridget was completely preoccupied by the crisis with her daughter. The profoundness of her reaction took her aback. She, too, had not thought she cared so much. She felt ill and hurt. Her birthday came in March and passed without a greeting: Deirdre's birthday, likewise. The longer the estrangement continued, the more impossible it became to resolve. She wanted to telephone, but was physically unable to do so. When Sam tried to put matters right and failed, she knew they would never speak again as long as they lived. She grew fatter and cried a lot.

Tom had been patient, at least about this. It was not easy for him to comprehend, because there was no comparable relationship in his own life, but he had tried. He had even written to her daughter.

Then, one day, Deirdre had telephoned.

'Daddy says you're not too well,' she said.

Bridget could remember little of the conversation except her daughter telling her that during the months of their quarrel one of Deirdre's closest friends, a homosexual, had died. He had had Aids.

'He was all alone in his flat and we would call him every night. No one else cared. Then, one night, I thought how ridiculous it was to spend all these hours on the telephone, so we asked him to stay here. We decided to look after him till the end.'

The disease was new and the public knew little about it. All sorts of wild and terrifying rumours circulated – that it could be contracted from cups and lavatory seats, almost by breathing the same air as a sufferer. Bridget had been absolutely appalled by her daughter's action.

'You did what? My God, Deirdre, you may have caught Aids, too!'

'He was our friend, Mummy,' her daughter had replied, with a simplicity which left her humbled. Bridget could never have done such a thing for a friend.

Finally, the boy had had to go into hospital. When Deirdre and her husband called to see him one evening, they were told he had thrown himself out of a fourth-floor window. They had arranged the funeral, cared for his ageing parents and disposed of his flat and possessions.

The story shook Bridget's views of her daughter to their foundations. She realized her judgement had been totally wrong. The tough, self-centred image the girl projected was replaced by the truth, that Deirdre was a far more caring and selfless and courageous woman than she would ever be. Love and respect filled her at last.

Now, in this time of waiting, she talked to her daughter every day. Deirdre comforted and supported and was eminently realistic, wise beyond her years. She never said her mother should give up Tom, always encouraged her to keep fighting. They were still completely opposite in character, but they accepted each other and Bridget had learnt to admire and trust Deirdre implicitly.

Three days had passed since the first letter had been delivered to Tom and he had not responded. Bridget grew more and more incensed. After all, as far as he knew she was handing over a brand new car. She fulminated over his lack of recognition of her apparent generosity and was no longer plagued by the need to telephone him.

Why was she sitting around waiting for Tom O'Dare, she asked herself? It was time she tore up The Plan and told him, in strident and irreversible terms, exactly what a bastard she thought him. She began to think of ways to humiliate him.

If only she could find a really handsome toy boy, she could dress up to the nines and parade around the town with him, visiting the bar of the top hotel where she knew Tom lunched daily with leading businessmen.

'Where did you hire the male models for your fashion show?' she asked Fiona, and disclosed the idea.

'Oh, Bridget, you can't go out with one of those. They're all gay, and very obviously gay,' Fiona laughed.

'What about an escort agency then?' she persisted.

'I don't know any and, anyway, they'd probably think you want servicing.'

'That, too,' retorted Bridget, recklessly.

'Honestly, it doesn't seem a very good idea to me. I think Tom would see through it. He wouldn't be impressed.'

Crestfallen, she was casting around for another scheme when she had the brainwave.

Hurrying to the chemist, she bought a dozen packets of condoms. They were extraordinarily expensive. No wonder there were so many unmarried mothers. At the drapers, she bought yards of red ribbon. Back home, she blew up the French letters until she had no breath left, tied them to the ribbon and festooned Tom's car with them.

Tomorrow was Friday, the day of the exchange. She would drive Tom's car to town and leave it parked in front of his office. He was into balloons, so he could have balloons.

She was startled when the telephone rang quite early in the morning.

'Hello,' he said.

'Who's that?' she asked, knowing perfectly well who it was.

'Me,' he replied in an aggrieved little voice.

'Who's me?' She was paying him back for the time he had told her to identify herself.

'Tom.'

'Oh.'

'About the car . . . I was thinking,' he ventured. 'I could drive it out there after work and save you coming into town.'

'I have to come in anyway,' she replied. 'Your car's being serviced today and I have a hairdressing appointment.'

'Oh.' He paused and then tried again. 'I'm not keen to leave the keys in your car. It might be stolen. So I could wait with it. We could meet in the car-park.'

'I haven't the slightest wish to meet you in the car-park, Tom,' she countered with dignity.

'No.' He accepted it was not such a good suggestion. 'What time are you finished at the hairdresser?'

'About three o'clock.'

'Well, it doesn't seem fair to keep you hanging around for three hours after that,' he said.

'I can go shopping and see Fiona. It's no problem.' She was deliberately unhelpful.

There was another pause and then he said, 'Why don't I bring the car out tomorrow morning? I'd like to see you and there are bound to be a few jobs I could do about the place.'

'OK,' she agreed casually, and rang off.

He had called just in time. She took the garlands of inflated French letters off the car and burst them one by one with some regret. The gesture might have been fun.

Tom looked even worse than before, if that were possible.

He was ashen and his narrow eyes had black smudges under them. His clothes were hanging on him and his fingers were stained with nicotine. He arrived at about midday.

Bridget, who had been up since dawn bathing, washing her hair, doing her face and changing from one outfit to another, was immaculate. She had also spent half an hour spraying a whole bottle of Worth's Je Reviens perfume over the upholstery of his car. A month of scrubbing would not get rid of the smell, which would cling to Jane Scott's clothes and body as a cloying reminder of Tom O'Dare's wife.

She watched as the dogs destroyed him even more by planting muddy paws all over his shirt and then she offered him a coffee. She sat easily on the sofa while he slumped in the chair opposite.

As he did not appear to know how to start, she prodded.

'How's it going?'

'Terrible.'

'Surely not.' She was only mildly sarcastic and he did not seem to notice.

He stared at the floor. 'I don't know what's happening. I've been on my own for a week.'

'What? Without your friend?'

'Yes.'

'Oh dear.'

This sounded promising. She waited and drank her coffee, and carefully avoided patting her hair into place, or fiddling with her clothes. She was aware of him studying her when he thought she was not watching.

He looked around him. 'This room could do with painting.'

At that moment Bridget knew he would come home and decorate the drawing-room. But there was a long way to go before then.

She helped him out. 'Is your friend on holiday then?'

'No.' He looked shifty. 'As a matter of fact, the shit has hit the fan.'

'You mean her husband has found out?'

'Yes.'

Her arrangements with Paul were instantly cancelled.

'Oh my God, that's awful. I warned you it would happen.' She tried not to show how pleased she was. 'How did it happen?'

'It was silly really,' said Tom. 'He was driving home from work and saw her dropping me off at the flat.'

'Then what?'

'I don't know. He's been keeping her locked up. You've no idea what a bastard he is.'

This was too much. 'Oh, come on, Tom. This isn't the Third World. No grown woman is kept locked up for a week.' She was scathing.

'Well, her old man won't let her out of his sight, so we've only been able to see each other for the odd lunch and at the office. I've been sitting in that poxy flat not knowing where I am, just waiting.'

That makes two of us, she thought to herself, but this was not the time for jibes.

Bridget forced herself to face the issue head on. 'What do you actually want to happen, Tom?'

'I want to live with her . . . I think.'

Her stomach heaved, but she kept her face expressionless.

'Look, you've got a flat, so why the hell hasn't she packed up and moved in with you?'

'She owns her own house and she won't leave it for me,' he said, pathetically.

Their home smelt of the roses she had picked that morning and placed in crystal rose bowls on the tables. Children ran along the road below and called to each other. The dogs barked in the garden. The cat jumped in through the open window and neither of them noticed.

Then he said, 'I know I'm a cunt. I've always been a cunt. I've always let everyone down. I'm no good.'

'Tom, I know that is not true. I know because you've looked after me, put up with my temperamental out-bursts, my family upheavals, my bossy ways, even my ex-husband and all his problems. You've kissed everything and made it better. You've made a home with me, made me happy and loved my dogs,' she told him, earnestly. 'Don't believe all that rubbish about yourself. You are a good man and worth loving.'

'I suppose it's because she's the first woman I've never been able to have as soon as I wanted her.' He hit the wrong note and annoyed her.

'She didn't waste much time in that direction, as I recall.'

'I mean she didn't do things my way and in my time,' he explained.

'I didn't do things your way very quickly,' she reminded him. 'It took you over a year to persuade me to marry you.'

'Mm.' That was not the same to him.

Then he announced, without any warning, 'I've ar-ranged a mortgage with the Abbey National.'

Bridget's cup and saucer clattered as she put them down abruptly to avoid dropping them. This was cata-

ticket on his own. The idea of him being inspired enough to fix up a mortgage was devastating. She forced herself not to react.

'How did you do that? You've no money in the bank.'

'I can have up to a third of my salary as a hundred-per-cent mortgage over twenty-five years,' he explained. 'I worked out that, if I buy a small terrace house, the repayments will be about seventy pounds a week.'

Country journalists, even editors, earned less than London shorthand-typists. Bridget did some more rapid mental arithmetic.

'Then there are rates and water rates and electricity and gas and maintenance, the car to run, clothes to buy,' she reminded him. 'Good God, Tom, how are you going to eat? I can't see you going without a beer for a quarter of a century.'

He was a babe in arms when it came to such matters, she thought.

'We'll just have to live simply. Do without all this sort of thing.' He gestured to the large, elegant room. 'If I buy a house, she'll sell hers.'

'Oh, has she agreed to that?'

'Not exactly.'

'And, even if she does, that house does not belong to her in the eyes of the law. The husband will be entitled to at least half the value, in view of the length of their marriage, and I don't suppose it's a mansion,' she went on, ruthlessly.

'It's quite a nice house.' He was defensive.

'You've been there then, behind the old man's back.'

'Only for a coffee.'

'And I suppose you've invited her back here, too, for a coffee.'

'No.'

'Well, some woman was here. She drank half a bottle of Sauternes and you were careless enough to leave the remainder in the fridge.'

'I opened that when I was alone here on my birthday,' he said.

That was a lie. With a cupboard full of booze, Tom would never have opened a bottle of sweet wine, but she let it go.

'So, what's it worth, this "nice" house? Sixty thousand? Fifty thousand?'

He shook his head. Even large houses in that remote part of England sold for little.

'Forty thousand then?'

'Maybe.'

'So she gets twenty thousand, if she's lucky, less estate agents' and solicitors' fees and removal costs and the costs of the divorce. Maybe fifteen thousand in her pocket.' Bridget pressed on relentlessly. He was going to be given the economic facts of this dreamy scheme, whether he liked it or not. 'Do you think she's going to hand that over to you?'

He shook his head again, as though surfacing from water. 'I don't know. I don't know.'

'Tom, I'm biased, obviously, but I'm going to sum up your friend as I see her. She's a married woman. For ten months, she's been leading a double life, never having the guts, or the inclination, to tell her wretched husband she is in love with you. You have left home and you're living in a flat, but she hasn't joined you. She knows you have arranged a mortgage, but she has made absolutely no commitment to come in on it financially. I think she's a lady who wants to have her cake and eat it and I think

135

she's a first-class actress. She's fooling her husband and she's fooling you.'

Bridget sensed that all these sentiments had already occurred to him and been pushed aside. He looked like a tormented man and, if he were so certain that he wanted to make the new life he described, he would not have come home to see her. He would not have listened so passively and he would have rejected every hint of criticism of Jane Scott instantly. Tom was in a state of emotional turmoil and might jump either way, but her instincts told her that the odds were in her favour.

'I'm going for a beer,' he said and stood up.

'Yes, we could do with a break.' She gave a little smile.

'I'll be back,' he assured her, reading her thoughts.

As the front door closed behind him, she leant back on the sofa, spent.

Chapter Nine

I T HAD been a cold summer with temperatures well below average and biting winds sweeping the moor, but the sun was shining as she went out to clear her head. The overgrown lawn and weeds were depressing. She wished the garden could have been as enticing as the house, but perhaps it was better this way, with that air of neglect illustrating that, without him, everything was disintegrating. The leaves were already turning. She did not stay there long.

Returning to the drawing-room, she put a record on the turntable and, accepting that it was unwise, she poured herself a large gin and tonic. It gave her a buzz immediately. Strolling into the hall, she studied herself in the mirror. She had put on the white linen skirt and a lemon and white striped shirt, small gold ear-rings and sandals. Sunlight shone on her through the south-facing door catching the subtle highlights in her hair. She was not at all bad, a very different lady from three weeks before.

The music followed as she finished her drink and went to pour another.

Since the formation of The Plan, there had been no opportunity to analyse her own feelings or desires in the matter. This was a battle, a battle she had to win and, as such, all her mental energy had been concentrated on it. In a way, she was grateful for this as, without such a challenge, she knew she would have broken down. But

the end of the battle would not be the end of the problem.

She had wondered if she could accept him back at any
price, but now she knew that this would not be possible.
The differences between them, which had driven her to
Greece, had not been the results of his affair and they
would have to be resolved before they could live together
again.

High on music and gin, Bridget was not going to
concern herself with that. She danced a little and, hearing
him return up the drive, went to the open window to
stand with her back to the door, still keeping time. She
did not turn round until he had walked across the room
and sat on the sofa and then she joined him.

'I've done a lot of thinking about what you said this
morning and I realize the situation cannot go on,' he
said. 'You expressed a lot of ideas, put it all in a way I
hadn't considered before and, for everyone's sake, I've
got to make a definite move to sort it out. She's got to
make up her mind once and for all.'

'Tom, I'm not prepared to be second best,' she stated,
firmly. 'I'm not going to be the woman you decide to live
with because you can't get the other one.'

'Of course not.'

'And even if you do come to the conclusion that she's
not the one for you, it doesn't mean you can just walk
back in here,' she went on. 'There was a lot wrong
between us before I went away and I have needs and
certain qualities I want in a partner which were definitely
missing.'

'Yes. I've always been a selfish bastard. I've been
thinking about that, too, how I've just bowled along,
demanding everything my own way, doing what I wanted,

without any consideration for anyone else. I know we couldn't go on as before. I would have to change.'

'Now's the time to break the pattern, if you're ever going to break it,' she said.

'What do you mean?'

'Well, you've always lived to a pattern: meet a woman, fall in love, live with her, maybe marry her, meet another woman, fall in love, leave the one before, live with the new one and so on. It's been the same with jobs. As soon as the going gets tough, you up and move on. In fact, I think, when you saw through all the problems at work this year, that was probably the first time you've ever stuck out anything.'

'It was,' he agreed, grimly.

'Well, that was an achievement,' she emphasized. 'If you leave me now and go to this woman, I promise you exactly the same is going to happen in that relationship as has happened to all the others. In a year or two, she'll be familiar and commonplace to you, as everyone becomes to their partner after a time, then you'll meet another and go through this all over again. There are always available, lonely ladies, Tom, especially for someone like you.

'If we survive this, we'll be closer and stronger. Our love will be deeper. We'll be invulnerable,' she promised and concluded, 'but if you don't break the pattern of the past now, you never will, because if you can't make it with me, you won't make it with anyone.'

'That's true. I know we have everything in common. I've been thinking about that, too. I've always loved your intellect and all the discussions and ideas. I know we like the same things and laugh at the same things. There's always something surprising and new going on with you. You're never, ever boring.'

'What about with her?' she asked.

'We don't talk much,' he answered.

'I can imagine.' She was cutting.

'No, I don't mean that. I mean she hasn't much to say. She doesn't read. She's not interested in the news, or in anything much, apart from darts.'

'So how do you pass all that time, when you're not screwing?'

He grimaced. 'There hasn't even been a lot of that. We go out for the odd drink together.'

'And you do your act,' she guessed. 'Tell all the stories, be a laugh a minute and give nothing away.'

He grinned in admission.

'So she doesn't know you at all,' she surmised.

'Nobody knows me,' he said.

'I know you,' she corrected.

'Yes, you're the only one.'

Suddenly, Bridget realized there was no point in hiding anything. If they were to come together again, they had to do so without secrets. It was the time to be straight, regardless of the consequences.

'There's something I have to tell you, Tom,' she said. 'I know the identity of this woman. Jane Scott. I made it my business to find out.'

'I thought you might.' He was not at all surprised. 'You weren't a reporter for nothing.'

The gin was making her head reel. She was no longer high, but sick.

'I'm aware that you may very well walk out when you hear this, but you have to know because we must be honest with each other.' She clenched her fists and sat rigidly trying to control the nausea. 'I hired a detective and had you both watched. The report is with John, in his safe. And, if you don't like it, I don't blame you, but that's the way it is.'

'Why shouldn't I like it?' he asked, unmoved.

'No one likes being spied on.'

'Bridget, I've spent my life spying on people and tracking down stories, so why should I kick when someone spies on me?'

He really was a remarkable man. He had this ability to deflect extreme unpleasantness as though it did not exist.

'Excuse me,' she said with strained formality, and tried not to run from the room.

In the downstairs cloakroom, she knelt on the floor and vomited into the lavatory bowl. The gin spewed out, both sweet and burning with bile. After retching several more times, she put her finger down her throat and finished the job. She pulled the chain, washed her hands and rinsed out her mouth, straightened her hair and her skirt and returned to the drawing-room, hoping he would not notice that her eyes were watering.

'Are you OK?' He did notice.

'It's the gin. I haven't eaten much recently,' she confessed and poured herself another.

'You look splendid. I've been looking at you and I know I must be mad to even think of giving you up, and the dogs, and the house. Everything that goes with you. You look the way you did when we first met. You haven't changed a bit.'

She smiled, weakly, gulped at the drink and immediately felt queasy again.

'You know that this is Jane Scott's second marriage,' she said.

'No. She's never been married before.' He was adamant. 'She's told me so.'

'Not true.' She raised her eyebrows blandly.

'How do you know?'

'George and Fiona are friends of her husband. He is her second husband and, apparently, he is not some sort of ogre. He is a quiet and home-loving man, and they are very fond of him.'

Tom shifted uncomfortably and looked away. 'Well, I suppose no one knows what goes on behind closed doors.'

'No, but they do know that he took on her children when they were very young and has been a marvellous father to them. Their own boys went to the same school, and they all practically grew up together. Don't you think this is an odd way for Jane Scott to repay a man like that?'

He did not answer. He looked worn out.

'Let's leave all this for a while,' she said. 'I'm knackered.'

'Me, too,' he agreed, thankfully.

He came up and touched her face. The bruise still showed, a lilac smudge under her make-up.

'Did I do that? Did I do that to you?' He shook his head in bewilderment. 'I keep looking at it and I can't believe I really did that. What a cunt I am, what a prize cunt.'

'Don't start that again. Yes, it was a bloody horrible thing to do, but everyone can behave like that in bad times. We all have evil depths to our natures, but this does not mean you are intrinsically evil. Look at what we've made together, think of everything you've put into the marriage, until recently, and your job. You're successful, so build on that.'

She decided to make them both some coffee.

On the way back from the kitchen, she heard him on the telephone in the study. The temptation to eavesdrop was overpowering, but, as she laid the mugs on his smoking table, he returned to the drawing-room.

'I've been talking to the intermediary,' he said.

'What intermediary?'

He looked embarrassed. 'Well, we've had to have someone to pass messages. Her friend, Rose, actually. You know, the one who works with her. I've told her to tell Jane that, if she does not meet me at nine o'clock tonight, it's all over between us.'

Bridget gripped the edge of the sofa, rigid with fear.

He must mean that if Jane Scott did turn up, they would move in together, they would live together. He would never come home again. Their marriage would be finished.

'This can't go on,' Tom was saying. 'It's not fair to you. She's got to make up her mind, one way or the other, now.'

With stiff muscles and a face like a mask, she said, 'You . . . you've made it very easy for her.'

'How? It's Saturday. She'll have to make some excuse to her husband to get out of the house. That won't be easy.'

'I'm sure she'll manage to do that without making any commitment,' Bridget said. 'If you'd asked her to pack her bags and bring them with her, she would be forced to make the choice between him or you.'

'She won't come anyway,' he said. 'I know she won't come.'

'She'll find a way.' Bridget was convinced and full of horror.

'It has to be like this. I know what I'm going to do. I've made my decision.' He was determined.

'Well, you had better leave and get on with it. There's nothing more to say.'

He stood up and walked to the door.

'I'll ring you at ten,' he said.

After he had gone, Bridget was overwhelmed by pain of such exquisite intensity that light pierced and sound wounded and even the hairs on her head were raw. Her veins became wires, the blood burning them red hot and, foundered at the nadir of her being, her soul lay colder than Antarctica, harder than carbon. Jane Scott, no longer insignificant, loomed over her, like a monstrous gold bird, with snakes for feathers and a beak full of fangs and talons dripping blood, flexed to tear the heart out of her life. She had never experienced such utter terror.

It was half past seven. In less than two hours it would all be over. Knocking over the table with its half-full mugs of coffee, she stumbled to the telephone.

'Paul! Paul! You've got to help me. I'm losing him. She's taking him from me. You've got to stop it.' She was gibbering with fear.

'Bridget, darling, stay cool.'

His voice was so like Tom's that she burst into shuddering sobs.

'Listen! Listen to me!' He was almost hypnotic. 'Take several deep breaths. I want to hear them. Breathe!'

She gasped and gulped loudly into the receiver.

'Now, light a cigarette and take a bloody great drag,' he ordered.

The matches dropped on the floor and, as she tried to pick them up, she dropped the phone. The flame flared. The smoke scorched the back of her throat. A paroxysm of coughing replaced the sobs.

'That's better,' commented her friend in London. 'Now tell little Paul all about it.'

'He's been here. We've been talking all day and now he's told her to meet him at nine o'clock. She'll be there. I know it. If they meet tonight, I'm finished, Paul. He'll leave me for good. I'll never get him back. Oh God! You've got to stop it!'

'What do you want me to do?' he asked.

'Phone the husband. Tell him what's happening. He won't listen to me. Tell him not to let her out. Please, Paul, help me!'

The receiver wavered in her hand and tears poured down her face.

'OK, darling. Now, what I want you to do is tell me everything about this as calmly as you can and then I'll sort it out. Don't worry.'

She told him about Rose Giles acting as the go-between and about the message Tom had left with her to be passed on.

'Right, leave it with me and I'll get back to you,' Paul said.

'I can't bear this, Paul. I can't bear it.'

'Yes you can. You're tough. Pour yourself a stiff drink.'

'I can't drink. It makes me throw up,' she said, miserably.

'Then make a cup of coffee you can stand a spoon in. I promise I'll make sure that old cow doesn't get anywhere near Tom tonight. I promise.'

He rang off.

Bridget dithered around the house, wringing her hands, pressing her thumbs and forefingers together and gabbling to herself, 'You will not see Tom. You will not go. Your husband won't allow it. You will not see him.' And then, 'Oh Tom, don't leave me, don't leave me.'

She fell over one of the dogs on the way upstairs and finished up in the bedroom, hunched on the bed, muttering and moaning. Eight o'clock came. She knew Paul had failed. She knew her marriage was ended.

The telephone rang, such a shrill shriek that she physically jumped before grabbing it to her.

'It's Paul and it's OK. I've spoken to the husband and I can guarantee Jane Scott will not meet Tom tonight,' he said.

Bridget felt giddy with relief. 'What happened?'

Jane Scott had been out when Paul called. The husband had talked so freely to this complete stranger, he had been like a man possessed. He felt shattered, cut off at the knees, he said, by the knowledge that his wife was having an affair. When he had found out, he had packed up to leave and she had literally knelt on the floor, weeping and begging him to stay. He had her word she had told Tom everything was over between them the following day.

'That's a lie,' Bridget stormed. 'I know she did not do that. I know they've been snatching conversations and lunches and she's been keeping him dangling since then.'

'Hold on! Let me finish,' Paul said. 'I asked the husband if Jane Scott had gone to the house of a woman friend this evening and he said she had. So I told him this friend was the intermediary between Tom and Jane Scott and that they were arranging to meet. I tell you, the man was devastated. He assured me she was due home shortly and that she would not go out again.'

'She won't go home. She'll go straight to Tom. I know it.' The panic rose again. She could feel it swelling up from her stomach and ringing in her ears and running like fire down her arms and through her hands. 'I've got to talk to him. I've got to tell him to go to Rose Giles's house and fetch her back before it's too late.'

'I don't think that's wise,' Paul said. 'I think you should leave it.'

'I can't. I can't risk it.'

Jane Scott would rush to Tom and wind the tentacles of her sex around him and he would forget everything. He would forget Bridget and their home and their years of love together. Jane Scott would seize him in her claws and carry him away.

She rang off and immediately dialled Jane Scott's number. A man answered.

'Mr Scott?'

'Yes.'

'I'm Tom O'Dare's wife, Bridget. I must talk to you. You're wrong in thinking your wife's affair with my husband is finished.'

'I'm glad you've phoned. I wanted to speak to you. I've got to tell you I'm crushed by this. When I found out, I couldn't believe it. I sort of suspected something was up, because since I went on late shift, I haven't known where she was, but it's destroyed me.'

He sounded a nice man. Bridget knew exactly what hell he was in. She felt sorry for him and sorry for herself.

'You must not let this meeting take place for both our sakes,' she urged. 'If she does not go, Tom is going to give up. Please don't just sit and wait for her to come home. Go and fetch her back from Rose Giles's house. I worship Tom, Mr Scott. I want him back.'

'I assure you my wife will not meet your husband

tonight,' he said. 'The affair has been over since I found out about it.'

'That is simply not true,' she said. 'They've had lunch together and discussed all sorts of things about the future since then, how they're going to meet and what they're going to do.'

'I have my wife's word that she has told your husband to leave her alone, but he won't give up.' He spoke with the desperation of a man unable to face what she was telling him.

The cow! Bridget was outraged.

'Can you hold on?' Mr Scott asked and she heard him talk for several minutes to someone in the background. Then he spoke to her again.

'Actually, my wife came in just now. She can tell you herself. Do you want to speak to her?'

'Yes.'

'Hello, Bridget.' Jane Scott's voice was like treacle. 'Honestly, Bridget, I can assure you I told Tom it was over between us days ago. I've been telling him to go back to you, Bridget, but he's said he'll never do that because he was going to leave you, anyway. It was nothing to do with me.'

She was unspeakable. Bridget wanted to drive straight to her grotty house and tear her eyes out.

'My marriage will be wrecked if you meet Tom tonight and for no other reason,' she said.

'Oh, I would not do that. I haven't any intention of meeting him. I have told Tom the best thing for him to do is to go back to you, Bridget, and I am definitely not meeting him tonight, Bridget.'

If she repeated her Christian name once more, Bridget knew she would scream.

'If Tom finds out I've telephoned you, it will cause even more trouble and I shall know exactly who told him, and I'm sure your husband will want to know why, Mrs Scott,' she said, frigidly.

'I won't tell Tom,' Jane oozed. 'I wouldn't betray your confidence, Bridget, and I do hope you two can get together again.'

Bridget went to the bathroom and was sick for the fourth time that day, her empty stomach heaving until she was limp and feeble.

Nine o'clock came. She lay quite still on the bed as cold as a glacier, waiting, waiting. She seemed to have spent years waiting and yet only ten days had passed since Tom had moved into that flat.

He rang.

'She didn't turn up,' he said. 'I told you she wouldn't.'

'Oh.'

'You might like to know that I telephoned her, anyway.'

'Oh.'

'I told her, among other things, that she was a lying slut and it was all over between us. I'll come out tomorrow and we'll talk,' he said. 'I want to be with you.'

'Tom, don't imagine for a moment that just because this woman did not meet you tonight you can walk straight back in here,' she said. 'There's a great deal to sort out before that happens, if it happens at all.'

'I realize that,' he replied unconvincingly.

'Anyway, I shall be away all tomorrow,' she replied truthfully, having taken the precaution of arranging to visit her friend, Beverley, who lived a suitably long distance from Devon.

'Well I'll come out to the village anyway. I can't stand

this sodding town. I'd rather drink with my mates in the local. I'll phone you in the evening.'

'I'll be late.'

'That doesn't matter. I'll keep phoning till you're home.'

Bridget flopped back on the pillows, like a discarded scarf. The emotional battering of the day had robbed her of all thought. She lost consciousness almost at once.

The telephone rang again. She felt drugged as she reached for it. It was two a.m.

'Bridget. I just want you to know that I didn't go to meet Tom tonight.' It was Jane Scott, honey stirred in acid. 'I kept my word to you, Bridget.'

'Well, you listen to me, Mrs Scott,' Bridget was wide awake now. 'I've had you watched by a private detective. I know exactly when you have been at Tom's flat, what you were wearing, what car you drive. You have even been watched at your house.'

'My house?' The woman gasped in a very different voice, one full of alarm.

'Yes, Mrs Scott. You have been followed home, watched going into Tom's flat, watched as you drove home and parked your car and watched in your own front room. It is all itemized and the report is with my solicitor. When I divorce my husband, which I now have every intention of doing, you are going to be named as co-respondent in that divorce and everyone will know exactly what sort of woman you are, Mrs Scott.' Bridget rang off in triumph. That would give her something to think about. She lit a cigarette and inhaled, letting the euphoric satisfaction wash over her for a while.

The short, deep sleep and the confrontation had invigorated her. Her mind was in overdrive once more. She considered the whole day and the events of the evening. The immediate crisis had been averted, but she knew the matter was not finished. Jane Scott's husband had been standing beside the telephone when they had spoken earlier. The woman had had no alternative but to repeat the lies she had told him. But Bridget knew she had not given Tom up. She would try again. Tom had said she was going on holiday the following Monday. Bridget had one week, while she was away, in which to turn whatever love he had left for her into hate.

Chapter Ten

EVEN in ordinary circumstances, Bridget could not manage to leave the house without returning at least twice to collect items she had forgotten. On this Sunday, she must have re-entered the house half a dozen times, having forgotten to leave the dogs water, forgotten to let out the hens, forgotten the potted plant, forgotten her door key, her handbag and lost the car keys.

Although it was a long distance to Beverley's flat, the three-hour drive was straight up the motorway. Bridget managed to make it four hours by doing the impossible and losing her way. She lit a cigarette somewhere along the route and threw her lighter out the window. It was pouring with rain and she missed hitting another car by inches when coming out of a junction. The plant, intended as a gift for her friend, fell out of its pot and was finally presented with half its leaves and all its flowers missing.

Beverley was a young reporter, who had recently landed herself a highly paid position as public relations officer for a large company. Tom had thought this a waste of a first-class journalist and, within weeks, Beverley agreed with him.

'They're all such wimps here,' she told Bridget. 'And the crap I have to turn out is incredible. I'd rather earn less money and work on a newspaper again. I've written off for a few jobs already. By the way, you look awful.'

'Thanks.'

'Are you ill?'

Bridget told her about the past few weeks and added, 'Don't say it. Just don't say it's unbelievable and that he adores me.'

'Well, it is and he does,' Beverley insisted. 'But, at least, he's coming back now.'

'That is not a foregone conclusion,' Bridget said, stiffly. 'I'm not having all that snapping and snarling, and a man who comes in the door each evening and walks straight out again to the boozer. Besides, he can't pick me up again just because Old Panstick's dropped him.'

'It won't be for that reason and you know it.' Beverley was emphatic. 'Tom can get any woman. There's no need for him to be with a woman he doesn't really want. If he starts trying to return to you, it's because he loves you and I'm sure he always has loved you.'

Bridget felt comforted by this. She followed Beverley round the flat, which comprised the top floor of a large and delapidated Queen Anne house set in unkempt gardens overlooking wide, wet meadows and a river. The girl was almost twenty years younger than she, but the age difference did not seem to matter.

They had come together when Beverley had fallen for a wild reporter in Tom's office. The affair had been an unsatisfactory one. Beverley had been hurt and turned to Bridget, perhaps because she was outside her circle of young friends. The rapport between them had been instant and, long after the wayward lad was replaced and forgotten, the friendship had continued.

Bridget slumped back in the chair and closed her eyes, while the girl made coffee.

'You really don't look well,' repeated Beverley, returning with the cups. 'Why don't you lie down?'

There was nothing she wanted more.

'Would you think it very rude of me?' she asked wretchedly.

Her friend bustled her into a bedroom and appeared minutes later with a hot-water bottle.

'Have a rest and don't worry. I'll wake you later.'

She was always cold these days, sleeping badly at home, even with the aid of sleeping pills. The continental quilt enclosed her, a delicious warmth suffused her. In this small, dark, unfamiliar room, she slept a tranquil and dreamless hour for the first time in weeks.

'That's better,' commented Beverley, when she awoke and returned to the sitting-room. 'You look great now. You've lost so much weight. It's terrific. I'm quite jealous.'

'Marry an unfaithful husband and have a model figure,' smiled Bridget wryly. 'It beats dieting any day. Perhaps I should write to a slimmers' magazine.'

After the previous day's experience with gin, she had no trouble in refusing white wine, but picked politely at the casseroled chicken. They did not talk again about her crisis, which was a relief, and the evening passed enjoyably. She was glad of the break and sorry to go out into the rain again at about eleven.

On the way through the town, she deliberately drove past Tom's flat. It was in darkness and his car was not parked outside. He was probably still drinking after hours.

Letting herself back into the house, she checked all the bedrooms and the drawing-room and study, just in case. Tom was obsessed with the idea of burglars and they made a habit of securing all the interior doors when they went out and when they went to bed at night. Bridget opened the door to the kitchen and switched on the light.

Then she unlocked the door to the utility room, where the dogs slept.

Tom was lying on top of the washing machine with his feet in the sink. He was snoring. Rage took hold of her, that he should have come despite her telling him not to, that he should think it was going to be so easy to return.

'What the hell are you doing here?' She shook him awake. 'How dare you think you can just walk back into this house!'

He stumbled to his feet, clearly drunk. His white cricket sweater was covered with mud where the dogs had jumped up on him. The remains of a pair of chewed spectacles lay on the floor.

'I've waited hours. You're bloody late.' He stared at her blearily.

'You've no right to be here,' she stormed.

'I want to talk to you.'

'Well, I don't want to talk to you.'

'It's my home,' he protested.

'Well, you should have thought of that before you gave it up for that slut. It's not your home any more, so you get out of here.' Bridget was livid.

Suddenly, she understood exactly his reaction the night she had appeared at his flat. She felt as enraged as he had. This was an invasion. He was cornering her.

'Get out! Just get out!' she shouted.

'But, darling . . .' He caught her arm.

'Don't touch me!' She twisted away. 'I don't want you here. I don't want you.'

'I love you. I've never stopped loving you,' he mumbled. 'I want you.'

'*You* want me! *You* wanted to come here. It's always what *you* want. It's never what *I* want.' She lost all control at last. All the anguish and tension of the past weeks and months were in her vicious screech. 'You never do what I want. You don't even screw me the way I want. And I'll tell you why. Because you can't. You can't screw a normal woman like me. You're only capable of screwing whores.'

She ripped open the bowels of their life.

Tom slapped her across the face with the flat of his hand.

'Oh yes. You're great at hitting women,' she ranted, so rabid that she did not even feel the sting. 'You're a real man when it comes to knocking women about. But you're fucking useless in bed.'

'You bitch! You foul-mouthed bitch!' He lunged towards her again and she ran behind the breakfast bar. 'I'll fucking kill you, you cow. You've been out all day screwing with some bastard.' Spittle had gathered in the corners of his mouth and he was crimson with temper.

He reached over the division.

'Oh no! Oh no, Tom O'Dare! You're not beating me up.' She snatched up the walking stick he kept in the corner and brought it down hard on his wrist. 'You're going to get out of here and you're never coming back.'

As he tried to grab the stick from her, she veered away and hit him with it again. He backed off, screaming at her, and she followed, swinging the weapon insanely before her. It whistled against the air.

'Get out! Get out!'

He had his back to the door and, with an unexpected move, seized the stick and wrenched it from her hand. Bridget fled across the room and up the backstairs, stopping just long enough to lock that door behind her. Running across the bedroom, she locked the door from there to the landing. Below, she could hear him crashing against the wood.

'I'll break this fucking door down and then I'll fucking kill you!' he was shrieking. She believed him. There was the sound of splintering below. Frantically, she scrambled through the pages of the telephone directory and dialled the number.

'Police,' said a man's voice.

She had the presence of mind to give her name and address first and then said, as calmly as possible, 'My husband and I are separated and I've been out today. When I returned I found him in the house very drunk. He says he's going to kill me and, right now, he's breaking down the door to the room. I think you'd better come.'

Tom gave up on the solid oak below, ran shouting through the house and up the main stairs to batter on the bedroom door to the landing, which was more flimsy. As it began to give way, Bridget rushed down the backstairs again, through the kitchen, across the hall and out of the front door. Quaking, she hid behind the garage for the long minutes before the police car turned into the drive.

'Now, what's going on here?' asked one of the two policemen.

She told them and agreed when they suggested going indoors. The noise upstairs had stopped and, as she took them towards the drawing-room, Tom appeared. He was the classic drunk, unshaven, dirty and staggering. The young officers looked at her sympathetically.

'This is a domestic matter.' Tom tipsily tried to appear sober. 'I know the police do not involve themselves in domestic matters and I'm sorry your time's been wasted.'

'I understand you are separated from your wife, sir.'

One of the policemen addressed him with some severity. 'You do not live on these premises.'

'It's my house.'

'No, it is not,' Bridget put in, quickly. 'It is my house, I bought it and I pay for it and it is in my sole name.'

'You are not required here, officers.' Tom tried again, visibly pulling himself together.

'Well, sir, I am afraid we cannot leave until we are sure there is going to be no more trouble.'

'There will be no more trouble,' he said, solemnly.

'Then you are prepared to leave the premises.'

'I suppose so.'

'I think that would be wise, sir.'

Tom was trying to stand without swaying.

'Now, you are quite sure there will be no more disturbance, sir?' the first asked in more of a heavy statement than a query.

'Quite sure, officer,' Tom was subdued.

Bridget accompanied them back to their car.

She returned to the drawing-room to find Tom sitting on the edge of his chair with his head in his hands. She sat, gingerly, on the sofa. It was very, very quiet.

'How has this happened to us?' he wondered, almost to himself, at last. 'How, in God's name, has this happened?'

She did not answer. Waves of weariness washed over her.

'I came here tonight because I wanted to make things right again. I wanted us to talk.' He was not drunk now, just spent, like she was.

'It's not so simple, Tom,' she said, gently. 'Since you went off with that woman, all my thoughts and all my efforts have been concentrated on you and her. I haven't had time to think about myself. I'm unhappy and I'm confused and I need to be left alone for a while to sort myself out now. You cannot just walk back in here as though nothing has happened.'

'I didn't expect to. I wanted to make a start, that's all,' he muttered. 'I want to come home.'

'Well, you can't. At least, not yet.' Bridget was positive about this. 'Look, less than twenty-four hours ago, you were sitting in that chair telling me you wanted to live with Jane Scott.'

'I love you. I've always loved you. I know I've made a terrible mistake. Don't ask me to explain it, because I can't. But all the time it was going on, I knew I was behaving like a madman and I didn't know how to stop.'

There were long pauses between their conversation and they spoke with hesitation. He lit a cigarette and offered her one, which she took. The ashtray lay on the table between them.

'You had this wonderful sex life with her, you lusted after her,' she said sadly. 'You've certainly never lusted for me.'

He shook his head. 'It wasn't wonderful.'

'Tom, you told me. The night you rang up drunk, you told me. She was certainly very inventive.'

'No, she wasn't,' he denied. 'The fact of the matter is that it was ordinary to the point of being dull; missionary position and she had a rather boring body. I don't know why I thought she was something special in the beginning, but she wasn't.'

'OK. You explain this.' She stalked out of the room to the study and returned with an envelope. Opening it, she tipped on to the table the scraps of burst balloons. He stared at them, uncomprehending.

159

'Explain these.'

'They're balloons,' he said stupidly.

'Yes. I found them in your car. You and she must have had some amazing antics with balloons.'

He grinned for the first time. 'If you want to know, they were hung round my car on my birthday by the office,' he said.

She felt guilty and silly, at the same time.

'Tom, if that woman had turned up to meet you last night, you would not be here. You would be with her.' She voiced her deepest suspicion.

'You gave her the choice and she rejected you, so now you think you can have me, instead,' she insisted.

'You don't understand. I wasn't giving her any choice. I had already decided to ditch her. I kept looking at you yesterday, so pretty, and wondering why the fuck I'd ever thought of giving you up. All the way back to town, I wanted her to arrive at the flat, just so that I could kick her out.'

They looked at each other through red-rimmed eyes, each face haggard.

'There's no point in talking any more. We're both exhausted. I've had it and you're in no condition to drive back to town,' she said. 'You'd better sleep in one of the spare bedrooms.'

They went upstairs together and he touched her hand lightly as they separated on the landing.

She washed slowly and cleaned her teeth, put on the old pink T-shirt and climbed into bed, wishing he were not in the house. That they would come together again was almost certain, but now that the battle was almost over she wanted to be left alone for some time. It was necessary to come to terms within herself over what had happened. She needed time to start developing a more realistic, less child-like, love and to try to restore some kind of faith.

There was a gentle tap on the door.

'Come in, Tom,' she sighed.

He was shivering as he sat on the opposite end of the bed and pulled his feet up.

'I want to come home,' he said.

She tried to explain her own thoughts. 'If you bully me into letting you return now, it won't work. I'll resent it, because I really must have the time. If you move in immediately, we'll drift on for a week or two and then everything will fall to pieces because I won't have had the chance to put my head into some sort of order.'

'How long?' he asked.

'I don't know, honestly. If I did, I would tell you. I'm not saying we can't meet, Tom. In fact, I want us to meet and go out together, but there must be a gap of at least a couple of weeks in which you do not live here.'

'I know what I've done was terrible and there has to be a punishment, but I couldn't stand it going on too long,' he said, unhappily.

This irritated her. 'Why do you always have to turn everything round to yourself?' she demanded. 'This is not a punishment. Can't you understand, it has hardly anything to do with you at all? It is for me, what *I* need for myself. I want to think about myself, not you – well, only indirectly about you. But I'm not going to be dwelling on how you feel and whether the situation suits you or not, I need to concentrate on myself, what I want, my future and how I can accept what has happened and make something positive out of it, if possible.'

'OK.' He pushed his feet under the covers, still shaking.

'Why are you wearing that old T-shirt?' he wondered.

She felt herself go pink. 'I've been wearing it at night, because I was lonely,' she confessed.

'Oh, sweetheart.' He looked frozen.

'You're cold,' she observed, but did not tell him to go back to the other room. She did not want him to leave.

He slid under the covers and put out the light. They lay apart without saying anything.

Bridget was still and wanted him to reach out and come to her. The big bed had been so empty and now his warmth was creeping towards her. She wanted him to hold her again.

Then his hand brushed her arm and she stirred and then they were lying side by side, their bodies touching and he turned her face to him and kissed her, tentatively. The bolt of desire frightened her. She could not want him, because he did not want her. Physically, she knew now that she had never attracted him: but he was still kissing her, not with stiff, tight lips as before, but with open mouth, pushing hers open to meet her tongue with his. A hand fondled her breast and the other moved down to stroke her thighs.

'Put the light on,' she whispered.

She was afraid and needed to see him, to see his face, to be sure. The shaded bedside lamp cast a soft glow. He caressed her, slowly removing the pink T-shirt, and bent to take a nipple in his mouth. It was the first time he had ever done such a thing and she clutched at him, terrified by the ecstacy. He kissed her stomach. His fingers were urgently tender. She let her body go, arching and writhing as he pushed her legs apart and gazed at her. He looked like Pan, goatish and golden eyed. Oh, there was no mistake. He wanted her. He wanted her, at last. He wanted her now. He licked. He sucked. He took her. She climaxed in seconds, stretching her arms above her head, shuddering and shouting.

Tom lay heavily on her and fucked her. He fucked her kneeling and on her side. He pulled her on top of him and fucked her again. They muttered and murmured to each other, everything they had never dared say before. He watched as she climaxed again and again.

And then she sprawled on his chest, kissing her way down to his flat, smooth belly, holding his buttocks in her hands and drawing him towards her, taking him in her mouth.

Tom lifted her back into his arms, cradling her and stroking her hair, running his hands down her back, loving her, and then he made love to her so gently, so sweetly, that they both cried.

'Tom, oh Tom. Why did you never do this before?' She wrapped her arms about him and buried her head in his shoulder.

'I don't know. I couldn't. I don't know why not.'

They lay back, close together.

'I always thought you weren't bothered about sex. In fact, I was sure you were undersexed,' she blurted out.

'I'm mad about sex. I always have been,' he said, then, 'Christ! You're a sexy woman. For someone who's not been around, you've got the most experienced body.'

'Instinct,' she grinned. 'I always told you I adored making love, but you didn't believe it. Why not? Why not with me?'

He drew on his cigarette and exhaled the smoke slowly.

'I was always embarrassed with you,' he admitted. 'You were a bit shy when we met. I suppose I thought you might be shocked.'

'You're crazy!' she exclaimed, pressing passionately against his mouth.

'Yes. Hmm.' It was the deep, contented, macho grunt of a man well pleased with himself.

'It must be a record – taking six years to pull your own husband,' she murmured, still dazed, just before they fell asleep.

She woke up to him playing with her and was instantly roused again, reaching down.

'Am I as good as Jane?' she wondered, wistfully.

'Forget Jane. There's no comparison. She was mundane.'

'So why did she seem so good to you?'

He stopped kissing and looked down at her, seriously. 'Anyone would seem good after six years of frustration.'

It was a fair answer.

'Have you always been frustrated with me?'

'Yes,' he admitted.

'So have I with you and yet I always loved your body. Just watching you walking about the room turned me on – handling your clothes, looking at your photograph, thinking about you – everything turned me on. It's awful. All this time, all these years.'

'We'll make up for them,' he promised. 'We've got it right now. We're going to have the sexiest sex life ever.'

He began straight away.

'Mmm. Yes please.'

'Mmm. More.'

'I want to move out of that flat,' he said, while dressing before leaving for the office. 'I can't stand the place.'

'Why don't you stay with Gareth?' she suggested.

'Why can't I come home? It will all be different now. We've beaten it.'

164

She kept her distance, deliberately. 'I really need to have this time to myself, otherwise all the resentments and anger will surface before long. I don't want to find myself going on and on at you about what's happened and, in order to avoid that, I want to lick my own wounds.'

'All right. But, don't leave it too long, Bridget,' he urged. 'I want to put this behind us soon.'

'We will,' she promised. 'Ring me today.'

'All day. I'll probably get no work done at all.'

Total bewilderment took over after he had left and doubts began to creep back. Perhaps his ardour had been simulated. She wondered if a man could fake such a performance. It did seem unlikely, but she could not convince herself.

'Tom's turned into a sex maniac,' she told Sophie. 'I can't believe my luck. All these years, I've wanted him so much, and now this. You don't think there's something wrong? I mean, he couldn't be pretending, could he?'

'No. I'm sure he wasn't.' Sophie was reassuring. 'Whatever block he had in relation to you seems to have been removed by this emotional trauma. He's discovered you. It does happen sometimes, you know.'

After their conversation, Bridget sat in bed smiling to herself. Sex had been the hang-up all along and they had been too stupid to realize it. She would still take the few days on her own, to rest and put the whole business into perspective. Their marriage would not be the same as before, but already good had come out of the mess. They would be united. Everything was going to be all right.

Fiona's boutique was a haven, with the kettle on and trad jazz in the background and an almost total absence of men, although occasionally one would lurk self-consciously behind his girlfriend while she searched for clothes.

'So he's moved back in then?' Fiona assumed, after hearing about the weekend.

'Not exactly,' Bridget admitted. 'I want to wait a while. I need the time and I suppose I also feel it shouldn't be made so easy for him.'

'Well, don't leave it long,' Fiona warned. 'And, when he does come back, don't keep quarrelling about what happened.'

'I don't intend to.'

'I did. George has always refused to talk about that trollopy au pair, but I used to go on and on at him in the beginning and he would not answer. It wasn't right of me.'

'Understandable though,' commented Bridget.

'Maybe. But, you know, they do feel bad about what they've done and they can't undo it. All a man wants to do is put the whole business out of his head and forget about it. He never wants it mentioned again,' Fiona said. 'I know it doesn't seem fair that the woman should be left trying to resolve all her unhappiness on her own, but that's the way it is. So don't keep punishing him.'

Bridget felt that, if she were allowed the time on her own, she could restrain herself. She was convinced she had no wish to punish Tom. He had behaved badly, but he had been misled. She was surprised at her own lack of rancour.

She picked up some steaks and drove home, her mind full of images of their night together. These caused frissons of pleasurable anticipation and, when Tom arrived, she fell into his arms and he responded passionately.

He looked less drawn already, a much more relaxed man than on the previous day.

'How was the office?' she asked, eventually.

'Back to normal,' he replied. 'Everyone seems delighted that we're getting together again, except Rose Giles, of course. She's not speaking.'

'That must cut you to the quick.'

'Oh, it does. It does,' he grinned.

A warning had been nagging insistently at the back of her mind. She had left herself open to blackmail and Jane Scott was ruthless enough to take advantage of that. She poured Tom a drink and took it to where he was sitting.

Standing over him, she said without preliminary, 'I telephoned Jane Scott on Saturday night to stop her meeting you.'

'Good girl,' he replied.

'Tom!' How could he accept everything so reasonably? 'Tom, I've lied and had you followed and laid traps and plotted. I've done dreadful things over the past few weeks. You must hate me for them underneath.'

'Darling, everything you've done, you've done to bring us together again,' he said, pulling her on to his lap. 'I'm proud of you and that's a fact. I'm proud that you love me so much. Everything you do is right by me.'

There were no secrets left between them.

'I never stopped loving you,' he murmured, later.

'Yes, you did,' she stressed.

'No. Almost from the minute I left here, I wanted to come back,' he insisted.

'So, why didn't you?' She was not prepared to let him off with everything.

'I thought you wouldn't have me. I'd dived in and I suppose I didn't know how to get out.'

'You only had to pack and move.'

'It seems simple now, but it wasn't at the time. I've always walked away from situations and never even looked back, let alone tried to go back. I really did not know how to go about it, but it was always going to be you and me in the end.'

If she was sceptical, she would not admit it. Making love with Tom was too much fun. She wanted to eat him and keep him for later. It was like having a brand new husband, with all the best qualities of the old.

'You'll stay with Gareth tomorrow?'

He looked downcast. 'If you say so.'

'I need the time, Tom,' she emphasized.

'So, when can I see you?'

'You could invite me out on Wednesday evening,' she flirted.

Gratefully, Bridget spent the whole of the next day in bed, ignoring the telephone, knowing that he would not contact her until evening. It was the first time she had been able to examine her own feelings without the threat of a bitter ending hanging over them.

She had forced herself to be understanding and calm for so long that it was difficult to stop. Yet, this was an unnatural response. Now that the spell had been broken, the affair would have no meaning for Tom. It would be incomprehensible and unimportant to him in retrospect, but she knew herself well enough to realize she would suffer a major reaction eventually, perhaps in a few weeks, or a few months, or maybe even a year and that would do neither of them any good.

She wished the reaction would set in quickly, so that it could be dealt with and then shelved, but at the moment she felt nothing.

At six o'clock, she poured herself a gin and tonic and played Fauré's *Élégie* and then the cello concerto by Saint-Saëns, content now to be emptied of emotion at last. This was the way to heal herself.

Their cars drew up at the same moment outside the pub they had chosen in a picturesque village some miles from the town, after he had assured her it was not one of his illicit meeting places. They found a quiet table and ordered a meal.

'There are going to be changes. I know I haven't carried my share of the responsibilities and the bills and I've worked out that I can contribute a lot more,' he told her and then outlined the figures. He had obviously worked them out with care and they were generous. Bridget was immensely pleased.

'And I'm not going down the pub any more.'

'Oh, come now. There's no need to go into a decline,' she teased.

'Well, not often.'

'Darling Tom. I don't want a tame man,' she said. 'The pub is part of you, an important part. You need to be with the lads. You love all that rubbish about football and cricket, and all the gossip. You're a man's man and I don't want to change that.'

'What then?'

'Well, I suppose I'd like you to come home three or four nights a week and pour us both a drink and sit down and tell me about your day and listen to mine, but there's no reason why you shouldn't have a couple of nights with your mates, play cricket in the summer and pool in the winter, or whatever. I'll wash my hair. Isn't that what girls do on their blokes' nights out?' She giggled.

'That's a deal,' he said, looking happy. 'And we're going to go out together more, have fun, do the things we used to do.'

'I'd like that.'

'I've got to move from that flat whatever happens,' he said. 'Gareth will put me up. I'm going back now to clean the whole place and pack my stuff and get out as soon as I've finished.

'When I look back over everything, I can't believe what I let myself into, I can't understand it. Every day I realize more and more what an utter prat I've been, what a fool. I was deranged, certifiable. I must have been.'

He looked stricken and she tucked her hand under his arm.

'You're not now though.'

'No, and never will be again.'

That was what nagged at her. In a few years, there might be another Old Panstick.

'There will always be women around you,' she observed sadly. 'Always chasing after you.'

'Yes, but I won't want them. I will only want you. You're my lady and you always have been.'

He kissed her as the waitress took the plates away.

It was the early hours of the morning when he telephoned. 'My cases are in the car and I've left the sodding place for good,' he exclaimed triumphantly.

Bridget simmered over Jane Scott. She had never hated anyone before and discovered that the emotion was as ferocious and consuming as love. Her stomach churned and her hands trembled and she ached with hatred. When she took the dogs walking, the moors turned purple with flowering heather and the woods speckled gold with changing leaves could not outshine the flame of her hatred. When she went swimming, the water in the pool could not cool it. The owls at night and the robins by day could not stifle the other woman's voice with their song.

Those pale, lifeless eyes mocked Bridget as she went about the house. They were the only image she had of the woman who had so nearly destroyed her life.

Another week had gone by and, at last, Tom was coming home. He had not seen Jane since before the final crisis, when Paul had prevented their meeting, and she would be returning to work in just two days. Bridget wondered what they had whispered and what they had done when they were last together, and then she could visualize the scene all too well.

'I'll cook for you,' Tom promised when he rang her from the office.

'You? Cook?'

In their six years together, he had produced two unremarkable meals and a few breakfasts.

'I've turned into a bloody good cook, I'll have you know,' he replied, proudly.

'What are we going to eat?' she asked, suspiciously.

'Surprise. I can't wait to see you, darling.' He sounded as though he really meant it.

Yet he had been so besotted with the woman, so dominated by her, how would he be able to resist once he saw her again? Surely such intense adulation could not be extinguished so instantaneously.

On Monday they would meet again and it was vital that the next two days were absolutely perfect. Bridget awaited them in fear.

Chapter Eleven

'PRESENTS!' he announced when she opened the door, and he loaded her with flowers and books and a gift-wrapped box. The torn shreds of the colourful paper fell to the floor and inside was a set of crystal glasses and a note. 'To help you back on the gin!'

'Now!' she said.

He poured them each a drink in the big new tumblers and held his up.

'To us,' he said.

'To us,' she echoed happily, and they clinked their glasses and drank.

There was a card, too. It read, 'To the one I love . . . and love . . . and love . . . and love for ever. Your Tom XXX.'

'I haven't given you anything,' she said, downcast.

'You've given me you,' he replied, putting his arms round her.

She leant against him and closed her eyes in bliss.

A few minutes later, he started towards the kitchen and she made to follow.

'Sit!' he ordered.

'Can't I help?'

'Certainly not.'

The gin and tonic was clean and pleasantly bitter. Bridget put an Eric Clapton record on the turntable and sat back. The room, the whole house felt completely different when Tom was there. The walls were thick and protective around them and they were safe inside.

The meal was a revelation, loin of pork in an orange and ginger sauce, new potatoes and French beans from the garden, and a chilled bottle of good white wine.

They listened to music and grew a little drunk. Tom talked of the fool he had been, of their years together, of everything they shared and held in common. He grew misty-eyed, holding her hand and telling her how much he loved her, had always loved her.

'But when you see her again, you might still love her, too,' Bridget was forced to murmur.

'No. No. Never,' he vowed.

'How can you say that when only days ago you were so mad for her?'

'It's over. I can't stand even thinking about her. Just the idea of her disgusts me.' He became agitated. 'You don't understand.'

She did not really understand. Love to her was something that endured, went on for years. It could not simply end in a second.

'It wasn't love,' he protested. 'I don't know what it was, but it was not love, nothing like my feelings for you, not what you and I have.'

He would have had to be a superlative actor to have played such a role and she knew he was not. It went against reason, but she believed him.

That night, they made love fiercely and gently, bawdily and exhaustedly until dawn.

'All these years,' she murmured. 'It was so lonely, Tom.'

'I was lonely, too, but we won't be lonely any more. We're closer and stronger than ever already and we'll become even more so. It's you and me, and the rest don't matter.'

In the morning he went outside and worked. The border by the drive and the rose bed were cleared, the lawns were mown, the shrubs on the terrace pruned. The little east garden, with its weeping crab-apple trees and thyme-covered path, emerged from beneath the weeds to delightful order.

On Sunday morning the sun shone brilliantly again and she prepared a picnic. Tom returned from the village with an armful of Sunday papers and opened the bottle of Dom Perignon champagne they had been keeping for a special occasion.

There was no occasion more special. They lounged on the terrace, eating and drinking, reading papers and talking until the sun went down.

He lit a log fire, for its light and flames rather than for warmth. They played more music and danced and talked through the evening. The house gathered closer about them in the soft light of the table lamps, a secure and private place, exclusively their own. Bridget relaxed against him, half-dreaming.

They sat in easy silence for a while and then Tom moved away. 'We're being straight with each other. No more secrets,' he said. 'So you might as well know that she's been here. Once.'

Bridget's whole body tensed as though he had hit her. Her mind fled back over the weeks to the day she had returned from Greece. Rage and despair engulfed her.

'You bastard! I knew some fucking woman had been in this house! I knew it! The sweet wine, the bloody Springsteen record lying about – the clean sheets on the bed! You bastard! You fucking bastard! You screwed that filthy old slag in my bed!'

'No. No. I did not. She never went near the bedroom.'

He had jumped to his feet and was standing in front of her, waving his arms.

'You liar! You screwed that whore in my bed!'

'I didn't! I didn't!' He was close to tears. 'I'm not a liar. I'm telling the truth. You said we were to be honest and I'm being honest. I brought her here for coffee, that's all.'

'You expect me to believe you brought her all this way to drink a couple of glasses of sweet white wine and then go home again? You must take me for the biggest fool in the world.'

'Well I did. I would never have gone to bed with her here. Never.'

Bitterness drenched her corrosively. 'You brought her here to show off your big house and then you screwed her in my bed.'

'I didn't. No! No! We didn't go near the bedroom. She was only here for half an hour.'

'It takes longer than half an hour to play a Bruce Springsteen record,' she spat. 'And what about the sheets? You were changing the sheets when I came home, because you knew I'd see someone else had been in our bed.'

'I changed them because I knew you'd be tired after the journey and I wanted everything to be nice for you,' he said desperately.

'I don't believe you and I'll never believe you,' she screamed. 'You've contaminated my home, my home! I'm never coming back to you. I don't want to see you ever again!'

'Don't! Don't, Bridget!' He staggered towards her with his arms out.

'You scum! Don't come near me! Nothing is more important than my home. You're expendable, but this isn't. This is my life's work. All my struggles have been for this.' She gestured wildly round the room. 'You've polluted my home! You've fucked some stinking tramp in my bed and destroyed everything.'

'I did not take Jane Scott to our bedroom. I vow and swear to you I did not.' Tom was standing rigidly, staring at her with frenzied eyes.

'It makes no difference,' she shouted. 'You took her everywhere else, I bet. Showed her all over the place, let the dogs run round her, took her into my garden. She even sat her festering, prolapsed vagina on my sofa.'

She leapt off, screeching at the thought. 'I'll burn it! I'll burn the whole place to the ground!'

'Bridget, darling, please!' He was so distraught that he was reeling.

'Well, I don't want you any more. I wish I'd never set eyes on you.' She could not even register his distress, her own was so cataclysmic. 'You've defiled my home and I'll never forgive you!'

It was as though he and the woman had violated her soul. Nothing he could say or do could console her. She rushed to the bedroom and locked herself in. She dithered by the edge of the bed plagued with images of what had taken place there. There was nowhere else she could go. Frigidly, she sat on the floor and hunched her knees to her chest. He knocked and called and begged and wept. At last, he drove away.

Anger, dark and brown and clinging as quicksand, sucked her down all night as she lay on the floor covered by a coat. She brooded over Jane Scott trailing her sex all over the house, coveting the possessions, lips licked with greed, already planning the changes she would make, the nasty little ornaments with which she would litter the surfaces, the flock paper with which she would paste the walls, the fitted carpets that would cover the polished oak floors and replace those worn old Turkish rugs, glass-topped coffee tables and a modern, veneered dining-room suite instead of the battered refectory table: smarming up to Tom all over Bridget's home, fornicating with him in Bridget's bed, establishing herself.

After such a rejection, Tom would probably fall straight back into her clutches and dive lustily into that sticky crotch again.

Bridget sat up, suddenly full of venom. That was one thing he was not going to get the chance to do. It was 7.30 a.m. She made a telephone call and was only half-surprised to receive an official answer.

'Fridays, between two and four,' the woman told her.

Bridget dialled the next number. He would seem a lot less attractive after this and Jane would find herself tinkered with more than she had bargained.

'Mrs Scott?'

'Yes.'

'I think you ought to know that Tom attended a clinic on Friday and he appears to have VD,' Bridget said sweetly. 'There is a clinic at the hospital next Friday between two and four. Perhaps you should run along there.'

May you both be very happy, she thought viciously, picturing Old Panstick's next five days of agitation.

When Fiona telephoned, she was grateful for the opportunity to let her revulsion spill out.

'He brought her here to my home,' she replied to her friend's inquiry about the weekend. 'He fucked her in my bed. He says he didn't, but I know he did.'

'Bridget, leave it,' Fiona advised briskly. 'Put it right

out of your head. It doesn't matter whether she was in your bed or not.'

'It does. It does,' she wailed. 'This is my *home*.'

'George took that bloody au pair to my bed often enough,' Fiona reminded her. 'Just don't think about it.'

'I had such faith in Tom. I was so stupid,' she said miserably. 'Fiona, it will never be the same again.'

'No, it won't be the same. It's four years since our crisis and I don't suppose a day passes when something doesn't remind me of what happened, not necessarily in a big way, but for a second or two. You don't forget, because you can't, but you do recover. You must force yourself. After all, it's not worth losing Tom, is it?'

'She sat her obscene vagina on my sofa. I'm going to burn it.' Bridget was still too outraged to listen.

'Oh, Bridget, not that gorgeous antique sofa! You can't burn that.' Fiona sounded aghast. 'For God's sake give it to me. I don't care about her vagina.'

Bridget couldn't help laughing and the laughter made her feel slightly better.

Deirdre repeated Fiona's advice.

'Mummy, I know Tom's inconsiderate and often moody, but he loves you and you love him. I'm not sticking up for him, but he must be feeling awful about what he's done and he wants to put it right. You must give him the chance. You've got to make the effort, too.'

'Supposing he meets another woman in a few years?' said Bridget. 'I'd never go through all this again.'

'Neither would he. He's not a man who's slept around, despite all your nooky hang-ups, and he won't do this again.' She spoke with certainty. 'If it's any help, I don't think he did screw her in your bed either. This affair doesn't mean he's not the same man and he's always had strong ideas about morality – quite the old stick-in-the-mud really. The marital bed would matter to him.'

Bridget wanted to believe. Tom had an almost boyish admiration for heroes, men who spoke out, who stood up to oppressive regimes, upright men of traditional valour and old-fashioned virtues. Earlier in the evening, before this latest catastrophe, he had held her hand.

'You did not take off your wedding ring,' he had observed with pleasure.

'No. I would not have done that,' she had replied.

'I did not take mine off either.'

She needed to believe.

By the time he rang in the afternoon, she had accepted.

'Are you all right?' he asked cautiously.

'Yes.'

'I'm sorry, little pet lamb. I can't tell you how sorry.'

'Don't, Tom. It's all right,' she assured him. 'I'm over it now.'

'I don't want us ever to quarrel again.'

'That's an impossibility.' She shook her head ruefully.

'Oh, we'll always bicker and fight over politics and that sort of thing,' he agreed. 'But no more quarrels.'

'There's something I'd better tell you.' She paused, wondering how he would react. 'I was so angry that I went mad and told Jane Scott you've got VD.'

'I know.' To her amazement, his voice smiled. 'She sent in a note requesting a private meeting and I replied that she was free to see me at any time when our respective spouses were present. So she went out and called me from a phone box and announced the news.'

'What did you say?'

'If you're worried about that, dear, you'd better have a test.'

'Oh Tom! You're unique!'

They both laughed. They were colluding against Jane Scott.

'How is she, apart from that?'

'Looks rough,' he replied.

'And how do you feel?' She was apprehensive once more.

'Nothing – except that I've been a fool. I took a good look at her this morning and I don't know what could have possessed me. There's nothing there. Nothing at all.'

'Honestly?'

'No worries,' he drawled.

'She might come after you again.'

'I think you've effectively put a stop to that,' he pointed out with amusement.

'Don't be too sure.'

'Wasting her time anyway, pet. It's you and me.'

They arranged to meet for lunch the next day.

On completion of each play Bridget bought herself a piece of jewellery, as both a reward and a memento. Each was related to its story, pearls which had featured in one, a Celtic design in gold to symbolize another. During their last holiday together in Greece, she had cheated by anticipating the end of her work on the latest script and a goldsmith in Rhodes had made her a gold bracelet in the shape of a snake with emerald eyes. It seemed a most suitable piece to wear for her first public appearance since the start of the scandal.

Her green skirt was freshly ironed and the white silk

shirt was soft and new. She took two of the old dog's tranquillizers and drove into town with the car radio blaring.

In the car-park she checked her make-up and hair. Then, putting on sunglasses and swinging her Louis Vuitton bag over her shoulder, she entered the office building.

As usual, Jane Scott was taking her turn at the reception desk during the lunch hour. Her eyes flicked away as Bridget walked unhurriedly towards her.

'Tell my husband I'm here, please,' she said distantly.

'You can go through,' mumbled Jane, just as expected.

'Kindly telephone my husband and tell him I am waiting here.' Bridget laced the request with edge.

The woman muttered into the switchboard and then bent her head over some papers. Bridget took off her sunglasses and stared down, not without curiosity. She wondered if she had failed to notice something special about the typist in the past. This was the first time she had really looked at her.

Bleached hair and heavy make-up, the black skirt stretched too tightly over fleshy hips. She had remembered the good legs but, no, she had missed nothing else before. Old Panstick did not look up and Bridget did not take her eyes from her. Tom appeared and kissed his wife firmly on the mouth, then took her hand and led her out into the street.

'She looked like a mouse beside you,' he grinned. 'Well done.'

As they walked along the pavement she put her face close to his ear.

'I think you'd better collect your bags from Gareth and come home for good tomorrow,' she whispered.

Chapter Twelve

TOM dropped his suitcases on the floor of the hall and hugged her, a hearty, happy, bear-like hug. She watched as the dogs attacked him with frantic love.

Darling Tom. Darling Tom, she thought.

They spent the next few hours quietly with their arms around each other and soft music in the background. They said little and were content to be together, at last.

They undressed and climbed into bed, naked, and sat reading.

How changed they were already, easy and comfortable with each other for the first time since they met. She slept with her head in the hollow of his shoulder to the sound of his breath and, some time in the night, they turned over murmuring endearments to sleep on with their backs and the soles of their feet pressed together.

He did not want to leave in the morning and lingered over the coffee and lit another cigarette and returned for an extra kiss.

The rest of the week passed quickly. Bridget cooked and gardened and sunbathed. Tom hurried home from work each night. They watched films on the video, *Casablanca* again, *The Killing Fields* and *Local Hero*. They went to the pub together and people she hardly knew greeted her and were friendly. The village was well aware of what had being going on. Villages always are. Now, it was welcoming them back as a couple.

Then they were invited to a charity barbecue. All the leading townsfolk would be there. Bridget changed half a dozen times in her concern to look right. She did not like crowds and had never entirely shaken off her adolescent shyness when confronted by new faces.

Everyone at the barbecue would know about the affair. She held tightly to his hand as they arrived, keeping on her dark glasses for protection. But people shook their hands and the women made a point of talking to her, drawing her into their circles.

Harold, the old reporter, came up and put his arm round her. 'Glad to see you looking so well, m'dear,' he said. 'Glad to see you *both* looking so well.'

'Oh, Harold, thank you. I owe you,' she responded in a low voice.

'Don't owe me a thing, m'dear.'

Tall, wax terrace candles were stuck flaring in the lawn; steaks and sausages sizzled over the charcoal. Dusk obscured the garden, leaving only a haze of scents: pine and apples, smoke and autumn. Their host glowed red and damp and earnest in the light from the embers. Bridget rediscovered her appetite.

They joined a local accountant and his wife, a couple with a dry wit and a fund of gossip. The four drank too much wine together and the women quickly became intimate.

'Oh, I'm not his wife,' the other told Bridget. 'We're both divorced and we've been living together for a couple of years.'

'We lived together for three,' Bridget said.

The woman asked, 'Why did you marry?'

It was such an unexpected question. Bridget was completely unprepared and sat with her mouth open.

'You see, we've talked about it and Henry's very keen, but I'm not sure,' the woman was explaining. She must have been the only person there who was unaware of the scandal. 'So, I wondered what made you decide?'

A few weeks before, Bridget would have answered immediately and without doubt. Her mind went back to how Tom had said marrying would make them exclusive. Now, the events of the past month rushed at her; the fights, the scheming, detectives, police, the haunting figure of Jane Scott, the tears, the pain, the ugliness.

'I suppose we felt it was time we made our commitment,' she said lamely, at last.

'So you think it's a good thing?' the other woman pressed. 'You'd do it again?'

Bridget hesitated too long.

'Yes,' she said. But she knew she did not sound convincing.

Tom and Bridget won a bottle of wine and a box of chocolates in the raffle. The rain stayed off until most people were leaving and then fell as softly as mist. She could hear it through the open French windows, dripping from the leaves, as they sat with other friends of their hosts in the large, well-furnished drawing-room. A group of reasonably affluent, small-town people, middle-aged professional and businessmen with their wives talking of VAT and central-heating bills.

Bridget looked around them and saw a façade covering turmoil. Tom knew them all. The Bonds were going bankrupt. Charles Eyton had another woman. John Grifson was wondering whether to leave his wife. Audrey Collins was sleeping with Andrew Wells. The oldest Williams son was up on a drugs charge. Jean Levin had cancer. Rivalry, debt, illness, struggles for trade and promotion, fear of redundancy, illicit love – all were seething in this civilized room.

'It doesn't grow easier as you grow older then?' Beverley had asked. 'Love is just as agonizing?'

'Just as agonizing,' she had confirmed. 'You see, one only looks older, but inside one feels the same as at twenty.'

Tom drove them home over the moor, stopping on the way at Lanacre. They sat on the wet bank and paddled their feet in the freezing water. Sheep bleated to each other, like old men. The river gargled throatily and somewhere a small creature screamed a tiny scream as a night bird dropped from the sky. They returned to the warmth of the car and kissed like kids on a date.

'Lovely evening,' she murmured, growing sleepy.

'And we'll have lots more, a lifetime of lovely evenings,' he promised.

They made love gently in the stillness of their bedroom and then lay back. It had been a lovely evening, yet not the same as before, before he had left her. Then, she would have been so confident, so certain of themselves as they moved among others. She remembered the accountant's lady asking why they had married. Then, there would have been no hesitation. She would have had no doubts. She tried not to let him know she was crying.

'Darling Bridget. Don't be unhappy.' He drew her against him and wiped away the tears. 'It was a lovely evening, wasn't it?'

'Yes,' she whispered, pathetically. 'That was the trouble. It was marvellous. Everyone was so sweet, the garden was so beautiful and the food was delicious. We even won on the raffle.'

'What's upset you then?'

'It wasn't the same as before. It won't ever be the same again.'

'No,' he agreed. 'It will be better.'

'I know.' Her voice wavered. 'But, you see, Tom, I've lost my innocence.'

There was nothing he could say.

She had expected there to be bad times when they would row and she would fling the affair back in his face, no matter how hard she tried to stop herself. Now she understood that those were not the moments to guard against. It was the good times which would be dangerous, times when they ate out at familiar restaurants and remembered their last visit, when they went to parties and remembered earlier parties, special occasions no longer like their previous celebrations. She had to learn to believe in him again and wondered if that would ever be possible.

They were tired the next day and moved lethargically about doing only the necessary chores and denying the dogs a walk. They slumped in the drawing-room and were bored by the Sunday newspapers.

'This business has worn me out,' Tom said, coming to sit beside her. 'I'm not just tired as though I've been playing cricket or working hard. I'm done for. Everything's a slog, going to work, driving the car, gardening, talking, even having a pint.'

She studied his face. Some of the colour had returned, but the lines were deep with strain and there was a hunted look in his eyes. She knew it reflected her own. They were weary and had aged.

'I've a fortnight's holiday owing,' he said. 'Let's take it soon.'

They planned for three weeks ahead and counted the days.

When he hauled himself off to the office next day, Bridget stayed in bed, still overcome with lassitude. Having talked so much to so many friends, now she wanted to talk to no one. She had listened to all the advice, sometimes conflicting, always well intentioned, but it was time to shut them all out. Time for Tom and her to be alone, to rebuild in the ways only they knew. It was time at last for them to be exclusive.

For the rest of the week she ignored the post and the telephone, except for when he arranged to call. She pottered about in the garden, sometimes not consciously thinking, but always aware. The ripe onions were collected from the kitchen garden and strung together to store in an outhouse, the vegetables they had not used were gathered with the weeds and spread on the compost, the seedheads of fennel and lovage, teasles and cow parsley were hung with hydrangea flowers from the pulley in the laundry room to dry for winter arrangements. She wrapped the green tomatoes in individual squares of newspaper and placed them in baskets to ripen. She sliced the aubergines and chopped the green peppers to freeze and left a few pimentos to sweeten and turn red on the plants in the greenhouse. The potatoes would be ready to dig up and bag before they went on holiday. The vine which Tom had trained over the courtyard was heavy with bunches of grapes just beginning to change colour and the hens were already flying up the trellis to eat them, but there were so many this year that it did not matter.

To be so close to the earth was healing, to sweat over the bonfire and rest under the laden apple trees. The bees had made a surprising amount of honey for such a bad year. She carried the heavy supers full of frames to the larder, uncapped the combs with a heated serrated knife and turned the handle of the extractor. The honey filled the white plastic buckets placed under the tap and searching bees flew through the open windows of the house as the flower-rich scent escaped.

Her mind roamed unhurriedly over the year. The earliest seedlings had died and they had had to plant more. That could happen in a cold spring. She remembered how she and Tom had lived unspeaking for so long. They might have been a continent apart for all they had known about each other. Then the rain storms and the gales had come to the garden, just as they had come for them. Now the fruit had ripened. The plum trees were barren this autumn, but the branches of the pear trees were breaking under their load. There were always rewards. It was a cliché to say that good came out of evil, but clichés were born of truth.

She would try to be more gentle and caring. She would share more with him, not leave him to walk the dogs alone, not be too lazy to join him for a drink when he wanted her company, keep herself slim and pretty. Why not? She would loathe making love to a fat man, so why should he be expected to enjoy a fat woman? She would try to leave more decisions to him, to step back a little and give him more space.

When his key turned in the front door at the end of each day, her heart met him before her steps took her to him, just as it had always done. He was able to discuss his feelings in a way he had not been capable of doing before. He no longer fell asleep as soon as he sat down. They were immensely kind to each other.

*

The tickets arrived for their holiday. The next few days went by quickly. Bridget made lists, checked their passports, prepared their clothes, and bought a bikini. The house resounded with music. She sang all day.

Tom was always with her, like an aura, and she was filled with love. She loved his tuneless songs, his Presley mime, his quotes from *Private Eye*, his silly jokes.

She loved the sex of him, the smell, the silk of his skin, his fine soft hair, his narrow eyes, his white, even teeth, the boniness of him, the cigarette in his mouth, the pints of beer. She loved the macho man.

She loved his knowledge of architecture and history and racing and that he knew the answers to *Mastermind*, that he could complete *The Times* crossword and yet still sounded like an East End navvy with the lads; his wit, his bitchiness, his gossip. She loved him for being a good reporter.

She loved his hard work, his striving to be honourable, his boyishness, the generosity with which he dismissed her most outrageous acts, his forgiveness for the humiliations she inflicted, his ego for being tough enough to withstand her, his affection and his need for love.

She loved the untranslatable; the expressions on his face, the looks in his eyes, the shifts of his body which told her, and only her, the truth. She loved the faithfulness, yes, the faithfulness of him. He was part of her and she was part of him once more.

They loaded the car and drove to Gatwick chattering and planning all the way. Two weeks of escape.

The plane took off for Portugal, dear Portugal, where they had met and where they had spent so many holidays. England dropped away, became a few spots of light and then vanished. They were going to a part of the country they had never visited before. Everywhere would be new and yet familiar, like their life to come. It was a fitting end to the affair.

PART TWO

Chapter Thirteen

'IS Thomas there?'
Hubert, Tom's uncle, had spent the last weekend with them and was telephoning from London.

'How was the journey back?' Bridget asked. 'I hope you weren't too tired.'

They had invited friends for dinner with him during his stay and the evening had been rowdy with howls of glee over his non-stop supply of slanderous gossip about old and famous lovers. Everyone adored Hubert, who was remarkably good value for a man of seventy; it was a long time since she had laughed so much. The few days since his departure had seemed flat in comparison.

'It was so lovely seeing you again,' she went on, full of affection. 'You must come back soon.'

His numerous chins would be quivering with the effort of sucking on a cigarette as he sat like Humpty Dumpty by the telephone in his London flat.

'Tom's mother's dead,' he said.

Bridget's heart wilted. Another problem. Would they never end? It was an instinctive response for which she felt instantly ashamed.

'Oh . . . I'm so sorry.'

'I'd better speak to Tom.' His usual drawl sounded clipped short.

Tom! He had not been reconciled to his mother and now she had died. It was what Bridget had always been afraid would happen. Tom would disintegrate.

'I'll tell him,' she said, her mind rushing protectively ahead.

They had both asked after the old woman's health the previous weekend and had been assured by Hubert that she was all right.

'How . . .? When . . .?'

'She died on Thursday. Angela managed to arrive in time.'

The name jarred. Angela was Tom's second sister, who lived in America. An ugly suspicion began to form and Bridget tried to banish it by concentrating on practicalities. She asked about the funeral arrangements, her fingers pulling nervously at the coils of the receiver flex through the silence which greeted her question.

'I don't know,' he answered, at last, his voice now undeniably hostile.

It was Saturday. They must have made some arrangement. The suspicion burst open inside her head like a boil.

'When is the funeral, Hubert?' she repeated with edge.

'They don't want him there. Neither Dorothy nor Angela wants him at the funeral.' The words gabbled out over each other.

All the family had known. Both his sisters had known and, even while he was staying with them last weekend, Hubert had known that Tom's mother was dying and he had said nothing. Angela had managed to fly over from America to be at her bedside, but no one had told Tom, who was only fifty miles away. Bridget hated them all as she put down the telephone.

Tom was feeding the dogs in the kitchen, scolding them as though they were naughty children as they jostled and barked. Bridget waited until he had put the two bowls in their respective places on the floor and the dogs were settled. Then she told him and put her arms around him.

'I'd better phone Hubert,' he said, after a few minutes.

'Tom ... there's something wrong ...' She did not know how to warn him. '... a problem ... with the family ...'

'Oh?' He looked at her uncomprehending as he was dialling the number.

She could not bear to stay and listen. She could not bear to see his face and, from the dining-room to where she escaped, she heard only the murmur of him talking, but not the words. And then there was silence.

He appeared in the doorway, grey-skinned, with lines as dark as make-up.

'He won't tell me,' he mumbled. 'Hubert won't tell me where she's to be buried.'

Implacability spread through Bridget. 'Oh yes he will.'

She sat him down and left him hunched with his head in his hands.

'He didn't bother to go and see her for three years. We don't want him at the funeral,' Hubert responded bitterly to her demand after she had redialled.

'You were the one who always advised him not to visit her, because you said it would upset her and upset him,' Bridget accused.

'He never went to see her.'

'Hubert, this is not your decision to make and it isn't up to Dorothy or Angela. This is between Tom and his mother. Tom wants to go to his mother's funeral and no one on earth has the right to stop him,' Bridget said icily.

'I don't know where it is. They're picking me up from Exeter station.'

He was lying, of course.

'When?'

'Next Thursday . . .'

'Look, I don't want to be hurtful, Hubert,' Bridget said. It was impossible to be unconcerned by the grief in his tone. 'But I have to defend Tom. He must be there to make his peace.'

'Oh, everyone's always had to defend Tom,' Hubert said, with a sudden coagulation of venom. 'He's never been any good and *she* wouldn't have wanted him there.'

'That's a wicked thing to say.' Bridget was jolted into retaliation. 'All I know is that Tom has a thoroughly evil family.'

Hubert burst into tears and rang off.

She did not know what to do first, return to Tom and comfort him or start making the necessary inquiries. It was an obscenely beautiful day for such terrible news. The sun was blooming through the open windows. The May birds were in full song. The first flame of summer was kindling into the blaze that would burn down spring and Tom was somewhere alone in the house thinking of the dead woman he had loved, but who had now rejected him for ever. Perhaps he needed to be alone for a while. This was one heartache she could not carry for him.

From Directory Enquiries she found there was only one crematorium in Exeter; contacting it, she was given the time of the funeral and the name and address of the undertaker. Her inquiries used up about twenty minutes.

She took Tom's hand in hers and gave him the information. 'Your mother's body is at the undertaker's,' she said and hesitated. 'You . . . you could go and see her there, if you like.'

She did not think he would, but he nodded and she

wondered if Hubert had told him that Angela had arrived from America in time to see their mother while she was still alive.

At lunchtime Tom went to the pub, to the impersonal atmosphere and emotionless camaraderie of other men.

Bridget sat down and drew in a long breath. The sympathy, which had fanned open inside her, snapped closed and she felt only anger, anger at Hubert, anger at the two sisters, anger at the old bag for dying – and anger at Tom.

The struggle had been unrelenting for the past three years, ever since he had left the newspaper. Even to herself, she did not date the time as being since the affair. Financial, professional and emotional turmoil had engulfed them both. As she had managed to extract them from one predicament, another had taken its place and now, when they had reached stability at last, yet another woman, his mother, was battering their foundations. The prospect of the abject weeks lying ahead already left her drained.

It was the wrong reaction and Bridget felt guilty, but somehow she always seemed to be in the position of feeling guilty.

Involuntarily, she found herself defending her position. If he had never met Jane Scott, he would not have left his job and started the news service, which had been so disastrous. Normally, she did not look back at the affair which had unravelled their marriage to a fragile thread, but today was different.

An affair was such a trivial matter, the butt of jokes since long before Chaucer: the old man and the young girl, the housewife and the milkman, the bishop and the actress. That such a commonplace event should be so destructive, that the circles from its falling into a life should spread out so far over the years that followed, was the mystery.

One of her friends had said that her naïve faith had really been arrogance, yet she had not been aware of arrogance. In fact, she had been so astonished that a man as handsome as Tom should have taken an interest in her in the first place that, for a long time, she had simply not believed it. The eventual persuasion of his love had created the faith, which had been coupled with amazement at her own good fortune. That could not be arrogance.

Perhaps the arrogance had lain in her possessiveness, which she did not deny.

'Love is not about ownership,' Deirdre maintained. 'If Barney fell in love with someone else, I would be very unhappy. But, if he felt that person was better for him, then I wouldn't try to stop him going to her. I want his happiness more than my own.'

Bridget could not lay claim to such unselfishness. If each partner were to remain free, there seemed little point in marrying. They might just as well live together. For marriage was a commitment and it was Tom who had summed it up.

'We shall be exclusive,' he had said.

From three years away, Bridget consciously looked back for the first time and remembered everything she had done to keep her husband – she remembered it all with some revulsion. It was true that one could not know how one would react to any crisis until it happened, but it was as though she had turned into someone else during those few weeks.

Faced with the fact that her predisposition to make

scenes and become hysterical would only have driven Tom further away, she had metamorphosed. She had lied and schemed, spun the web and sat in its centre, calculating and waiting.

Had she not done so, she would have lost him, but, equally, had he genuinely loved Jane Scott, all Bridget's plotting and deceit could not have won him back. Did that justify the way she had behaved? She did not know the answer, nor had she known since then who she really was, only that, in the same circumstances, she would have done the same again. But it would never happen again.

Yet, within a relatively short time after the affair, their behaviour towards each other had returned to the old pattern.

The wild and ravenous passion with which they had consumed each other had given way to tentative occasions; their sex life had become a comfort rather than a fulfilment, then dulled and diminished under the stress of practical pressures and, in the last few months, had stopped altogether. She did not especially miss it.

There were still areas she could not visit where Tom and Jane had been together, and pubs she would not enter, in case they had met there. Certain words acted as triggers to that shiver in the mind: mistress, typist, love nest. When she drove past, she did not look at the exterior of the flat where he had stayed, yet every detail of its interior was photographically imprinted in her head. But Jane Scott had become so small and distant and featureless, it was almost as though she had never existed; although all their subsequent misfortunes had stemmed from her.

Tom, himself, had aged. It was as though on his

fiftieth birthday he had decided he was an old man, no longer wanting to do much except sink a couple of pints, come home, eat a meal and fall asleep on the sofa. On Sundays he watched sport on television and read the newspapers and anything else seemed to be an effort. Even his stance and walk had changed, his shoulders had rounded and his neck had started to sink between them in the manner of the elderly. His face had become deeply grooved. Occasionally Bridget would notice these signs with shock, because she still carried the image of the slim, golden man she had met ten years before in Portugal.

The business, launched with such high hopes, had failed. The room in the house which Bridget had decorated and furnished as an office now stood empty, the separate telephone line was no longer used, the proudly headed paper was yellowing in the desk drawer, the computer and the fax machine were idle. Neither Tom nor she had appreciated how many of the staff reporters covering their rural area were also freelancing and Tom, who had been accustomed to information automatically flowing into his newspaper, had grown despondent.

The affair had made him enemies in the group which owned all the local papers and, as Bridget remortgaged the house to service their business debts, he had discovered that he could not get another good job. The small independent weekly where he did find an underpaid post folded and another publication some distance away had used his talent without the recompense of a living wage.

Yet their lifestyle had not changed. His beer and brandy and cigarette quotas had not been reduced. They continued entertaining a lot and going to the races and the theatre and travelling abroad two or three times a year.

Bridget had gone on buying him expensive clothes and presents and her indebtedness had increased far beyond the income with which to service it.

Then, nine months ago, Tom had been offered the position in Bristol, well-paid and back in mainstream journalism for the first time since they had met in Portugal. Their troubles seemed to be over.

After an ecstatic celebration and a nervous few weeks while he settled in, Bridget had suffered a strange reaction. She had completely withdrawn into herself.

At first she was not aware of this, but gradually she realized that Tom's living away from home during the week was a relief. Her writing improved and progressed faster, because there were no interruptions and there was more time to think. The persistent ache of dread, which had clenched the pit of her stomach since the affair, lessened and finally was no longer there. She did not want to hear about Tom's work, almost because she was afraid that he might return home with more problems.

He was happy. The house and garden were peaceful. That was all she wanted and she had almost stopped talking altogether. It was as though all her supportive resources, mental and emotional, had been used up and, even though it meant shutting him out, she had needed this respite.

Now, just when she had begun to feel stronger and to believe in their security at last, his wretched mother decided to die. She heard the front door open as he returned from the pub and that old sick feeling was back.

'I'll go to see her on Monday,' he said quietly. 'I want to.'

Yes, she thought, if he were alone with his mother's body, he could say in his soul all he needed to say.

Perhaps he could even be reconciled with her, or perhaps he would finally be able to free himself from her hold. At least, he would have the chance to come to terms with the fact that her life was over.

'Shall I drive you there?' she asked tenderly. 'I could wait somewhere nearby.'

'No,' he replied. 'I'll go by myself.'

'She just looked like a very old lady,' was all he said when he came home from the funeral parlour. He did not mention how he had felt, or what he had thought, and Bridget did not ask.

The Nuits de Young rose was in full flower, its arching branches encrusted with rosettes as dark as bruises and so potently scented that she felt dizzy as she picked them and wired them into a wreath. Flowers from his garden for his mother. He had said he would like that, but he did not take them with him to the funeral the next day.

Bridget kept restlessly busy while he was away, clumsily crashing the vacuum cleaner into furniture and dropping things, preoccupied by the ostracism she knew the family was subjecting him to in Exeter and frustration that, once again, their lives were in upheaval.

She thought about her own mother. Some months earlier they had seen each other at Deirdre's house for the first time in several years; to Bridget, it had been as though she were meeting a woman whom she had known for a long time, but had never liked. Now they talked occasionally and distantly on the telephone.

She wondered how she would react when her mother died and supposed it would be with regret at what their relationship should have been, but she could not imagine being grief-stricken. Unlike Tom, who had never ceased to react with fear and longing to his mother's repudiation of him, Bridget had no feelings left.

Tom was due a week's holiday and she had been looking forward to their spending time together, sharing the garden and lunchtime outings, a visit to the cinema and dinner at a good restaurant. She had pictured it as a tranquil break away from the pressures of both their jobs when they could be naturally close again. Now it was ruined.

He was very quiet that evening. His sisters and Hubert had ignored him throughout the ceremony and there had been no one else there. The image of him standing in isolation at the graveside squeezed her heart and she embraced him, but he did not respond.

The next day he went to work as usual and the next night he did not come home.

There were often evening meetings which he had to report and after which he stayed the night in Bristol. When he telephoned about this one, she felt no surprise.

Calling the dogs, she set off up the hill, hoping the steep climb would use up her energy and put the idea out of her head.

In the nine months since he had joined the company she had only been to the city two or three times to pick him up on her way back from seeing Deirdre or her agent in London. They had met in a pub where she noted that apparently no one knew him.

He had never offered to introduce her to any of his colleagues, who were mainly much younger than he. She could guess how he held court in the office local, impressing them with the exploits of his Fleet Street past and she sometimes wondered if he were ashamed of having a wife of her age and of the fact that she had put on weight again. Just as she had not asked about his life away from home, so he had not offered to tell her about it.

Occasionally, just before Christmas and earlier in the year and again quite recently, he had been edgy and bad-tempered for a week or two and then he had seemed to return to normal. She had deliberately ignored her qualms.

That was the legacy of an affair, the capillaries of insecurity running hardly perceived under the skin of their affinity, but filling with presentiment when they were at their happiest, in case a door should open and someone should walk through and the delicate restoration of their marriage be destroyed.

Now all this was running through her mind despite the effort of the climb up through the woods and, when she reached the top, she sat down panting on the bench placed there for the aged and for large breathless women like herself.

A pheasant sounded like a rusty wheel rolling through the grass and the dogs bolted after it. She saw it rise like a hat blowing away in the wind and heard the dogs barking with disappointment as they charged about in the undergrowth.

It was Friday. Businessmen and councillors and even charity workers were all anxious to leave their offices promptly to start the weekend. The knowledge she had been trying to suppress surfaced against her will. No one held meetings on Friday nights.

The path was so sheer in places that she had to grasp on to saplings and bushes to stop herself from slithering down out of control. Other village dogs greeted hers with beating tails and noses twitching with curiosity and were followed by their owners who exchanged comments with her on the beauty of the day. Bridget liked that, being a familiar face in the country, even though she led such a solitary life at her desk.

As she walked towards the front door of the house and passed her parked car, she had an impulse to get into it and drive to Bristol. The impulse was instantly and vehemently rejected.

Bristol was Tom's space, she thought. What mattered was their life here in their home, in their village. She did not want to know what happened elsewhere and, besides, the dogs needed feeding and the greenhouse plants should be watered and she was tired after the walk.

Pouring herself a large gin and tonic and turning on the television each evening meant that the intrusion of uncomfortable thoughts was dammed.

The village started up its lawn mowers, which purred through the afternoons as sprinklers scattered glittering rainbows through the hot air. Racemes of laburnum dripped from the tunnel of their trained trees like wild honey combs, and the countryside trembled in the heat, as though mirrored in a lake.

While the animals stretched like corpses on the grass, they worked on the garden, Tom at his vegetables and she at her flowers. They lay in the sun, she on the hammock and he on the garden bed, reading novels. She took photographs of Tom with Quinky, Tom with Erin and Rake, and Tom sleeping. She thought about how much she loved him.

Sometimes he looked tense; Bridget knew he was thinking about his mother and of the time when he was a boy, but he did not disintegrate as she had been afraid he would. Although he kept to his custom of going down to the pub at lunchtime and again while she cooked the evening meal, he did not get roaring drunk or threaten to leave his job.

Yet Bridget felt his suffering. He had never been any good at expressing his deepest feelings and she wondered once or twice if she should broach the subject, but was afraid of seeming insensitive. These quiet few days seemed to be what he needed and she believed he would talk about everything when he was ready.

He went back to work the following Monday without either of them having mentioned the death of his mother only two weeks earlier. It was as though they had spent the holiday side by side, but not together.

Bridget dug into her new play and thankfully let it take her over.

Chapter Fourteen

THE advertisement in the Sunday newspaper inspired the brainwave. Bridget was so excited that she almost blurted it out to Tom straight away but then she could not wait for him to go out so that she could make the telephone call.

When he had gone, she re-read the few lines again, convinced she must have been wrong. Yet there it was, the lease of a studio apartment for sale on the Algarve, where they had met in Portugal, and so cheap that there surely must have been a misprint.

A man answered her call with the assurance that there was no mistake.

'My business has folded,' he said, bitterly. 'I need the money.'

He answered all her questions in the same flat tone.

He had owned the apartment for five years and there were still twenty years of the lease to run.

'We've got two kids now,' he went on. 'So it's too small for us anyway.'

Bridget quickly did her sums and offered him £1,500 less.

'OK. If it's a serious offer,' he replied. 'But I've got to have the money by next week.'

They exchanged the names of their solicitors.

Of course, it was madness. There would be no time to fly out and inspect the apartment, but, on the other hand, the price was so good that, even if it turned out to be a dump, it would pay for itself in a few cheap holidays and they might even be able to let it at other times of the year.

Listening out for Tom's return, she phoned John, their solicitor, at his home.

'Bridget, you haven't even seen the place,' he protested.

'It's for Tom's Christmas present,' she said. 'And I'm sure the owner's genuine.'

'Yes, sells seriously clapped-out cars to unsuspecting housewives for a living,' John retorted.

'No. He was a greengrocer, but the business went bust.'

'For heaven's sake!' he said.

Bridget was in no mood to listen. Tom loved Portugal, but there was more to her crazy plan than that. Tom owned nothing. The house and its land and all the furniture had belonged to her when they met. The situation had always been a source of underlying disharmony, which surfaced every now and again during quarrels. Now that his mother had died, she wanted to give him something meaningful. She wanted to give him something which would be all his own. However, she could hardly explain the imbalance in her marriage to her solicitor.

'I want to give Tom the orchard behind the garden as well, so you could draw up the necessary papers at the same time.' She had been considering this way out of her dilemma for some time. 'That land might be developed one day and could be worth a lot of money.'

'As your solicitor I must advise you even more strongly against doing this.' John became heavily pompous. 'I like Tom, as you know, but it would be most unwise to start giving away your assets. You've worked very hard for them, Bridget.'

She thought she heard the front door open.

'Just check on the deeds of the apartment for me, please,' she said, hastily.

'But I know absolutely nothing about Portuguese law,' he demurred.

Tom's footsteps sounded in the hall.

'I'm sure you'll sort it all out in your usual brilliant way, John.' She was almost whispering. 'Look, I must ring off now. He's coming.'

As he came into the room, Bridget flung her arms around her husband, kissing him all over his face while jumping up and down and ruffling his hair.

'Get off, woman,' he said, grinning and shaking himself free.

Bridget plumped herself down on the sofa and beamed up at him.

'What are you looking so pleased with yourself about?' he asked.

'It's my cunning plot,' she said.

He looked slightly wary. 'Not another.'

'It's wonderful. A surprise. You'll love it.'

Tom shrugged and smiled and picked up his newspaper.

She knew she would never be able to keep the secret until Christmas. She was hopeless at keeping secrets. When everything was signed, she would tell him, she thought, and tried to picture the expression on his face.

The next day they had a row. It was over nothing at all.

Tom had had a tax rebate and they thought they would celebrate by going out for a meal. During the day they worked too long in the garden. The sun beat down and Bridget's back ached and then Tom took the dogs for a walk.

When he returned, she asked him where he wanted to go for dinner and he replied that he did not mind. He kept asking what she wanted to do and she kept replying that they would do whatever he wanted – because it was his tax rebate.

Eventually, he decided they would go to the pub and, feeling disappointed because she had hoped for somewhere more festive, Bridget washed her hair, bathed and dressed. When she was ready, Tom was still watching cricket on the television. He did not look as though he wanted to go anywhere. He looked tired and she was tired.

'Let's not bother going out,' she offered.

'Why not?'

'Because you don't really want to.'

'You mean you don't want to go to the pub,' he replied, angrily.

'Well, it would have been nice to go for a proper meal,' she admitted. 'But it doesn't matter.'

'You should have said what you wanted then!'

'I wanted to do what *you* wanted. But I don't think you really want to do anything.' She began to feel sulky, annoyed at having taken the trouble to dress, annoyed that the only idea he could come up with was going to the pub, annoyed at being tired and annoyed with herself for being unreasonable. She had said they would do what he wanted and he wanted to go to the pub.

They sat on opposite sides of the room without speaking. Wherever they went now, the evening would be fraught with tension.

'Let's forget it and go next week.' There was still time to make peace. 'We shouldn't be so cross.'

'I'm not cross,' he yelled. 'I'm fed up!'

The resentment she had been trying to quell flared up again.

'Well, I'm fed up, too,' she shouted back. 'Fed up with the sodding pub. You never organize anything for us. It's always me who gets theatre tickets and thinks of outings and plans the holidays and all you can come up with is the sodding pub.'

And then they were both screaming at each other and he stormed out of the room.

Bridget sat stony-faced, her whole body clenched, waiting for him to return and start again.

Within minutes, he stalked back in and said furiously, 'All right. I'm sorry.'

But she knew this was just a ploy. If she lowered her guard, he would strike. They had played the game countless times before.

Sure enough, a few minutes later the quarrel reactivated. It was a pattern set in concrete.

'If you didn't . . . If you hadn't . . . You always have to be right.'

Bridget knew his words by heart, but never failed to be goaded by this one.

'That's not true!'

'You're such a big deal and it's always my fault. Everything I do is wrong. I always get the blame.' He was pacing up and down, his face screwed up with exasperation.

'Ballocks! Stop bloody whinging. I'm sick of having to tart up everything I say and tell you you're wonderful, even when you're not.'

He was so infantile, she thought, throwing tantrums whenever he didn't get his own way. She knew she was being unreasonable, but she was never allowed to be unreasonable, although he could be as unreasonable as he liked.

'You dominate everything. I just do what I'm told. I can never do anything I want to do,' he was whining.

'You never do anything else but please yourself and God help anyone who tries to interfere with Tom O'Dare's boring routine.'

'You make all the decisions.'

'Only because you refuse to make any. You can't even decide which you want between two tins of soup.'

'Well I decided I wanted to go to the pub this evening.'

'Oh yes, that's the one decision you can be depended on to reach. Well, go to the fucking pub. You're far happier there than here.'

So he went.

How did it happen? she wondered to herself. Why did it happen? It could start over feeding the dogs, or over one of them wanting a cup of coffee, or just switching on the dishwasher and suddenly they would be shrieking at each other and rushing about the house and slamming doors.

Each time she felt drained, as though they were back at square one, as though they would have to start their relationship all over again.

Of course, they made it up.

'I'm sorry.' 'I'm sorry,' they mumbled to each other in bed, but they did not make love. They had not made love for months. She told herself again that she did not mind.

Money only seemed important when there was none to pay the bills. After her mother's meanness and years of frugality with Sam, Bridget had been easily infected by Tom's happy-go-lucky attitude to finance and, as the nation continued its spending spree, the value of her house had risen dramatically and she had happily borrowed on the increased equity. There was still enough money left to buy the Portuguese apartment from the third remortgage of the property since their marriage, which had also financed a long safari in Kenya.

The negotiations actually took several weeks, during which, whenever Tom came home, they seemed to have little to say to each other. Over and over again, as he sat morosely apart from her in the drawing-room, Bridget asked herself whether she should encourage him to talk about his mother's death, but each time she drew back, afraid that he would shut her out and recoil from her attempts to console him.

Then John rang one morning.

'Well, everything *seems* to be all right with this apartment,' he said, reluctantly. 'But I shall have to write to you pointing out that there has been no time to go into the necessary aspects of Portuguese property law and that I advised you against this purchase.'

'You mean we've completed?' she asked, overjoyed.

'I've paid over the money and I have the documents here,' he confirmed. 'So you can't go back on it now.'

John the solicitor was a stark contrast to John the man, who made such a play for women at their parties that he was known to her friends as The Groper. No wonder his wife always looked so sour. He really was a wet blanket, she thought, as she took out the snapshots sent by the previous owner and gazed at the modern block of apartments with a cross marking the balcony of the one she had bought. The architecture was pure Costa Brava, but she did not care. Mental images of the hot, narrow streets and the sandy coves of Lagos were so clear that she might have been physically transported there.

After choosing *My Gastronomy* by the chef Nico Lad-
enis and *At Home With The Roux Brothers* from the
shelf of cookery books in her study, putting a bottle of
Pouilly-Fumé in the fridge to chill, she hurried to the
shops. Then she spent the rest of the day preparing
Terrine de Saumon aux Epinards to be followed by Fillet
of Beef with Anchovies.

Cooking has a lot in common with gardening, a celebration of smell and colour and texture and timing, combined
with the satisfying anticipation of sensual gratification
and watching other people's pleasure. Bridget, who de-
tested all forms of domesticity, including the day-to-day
providing of ordinary meals, seized on the chance to cater
for a special dinner or a party as though invited to an
orgy. If she had had her way, she would have created
feasts for every saint's day and banquets for every bank
holiday.

That Tom would have been just as happy with sardines
on toast that evening was unimportant. Shaping and
cutting up pretty little vegetables, fussing over the sauce
to the background of the radio in the large, light kitchen,
she passed the hours humming contentedly.

The bottle of 1976 Château La Tour St-Bonnet was
dusty from years on the bottom row of the wine rack. By
the time she opened it to breathe, the crystal glasses were
sparkling on the table and there were fresh flowers in the
Victorian epergne and she had put on a shoulder-reveal-
ing, full-skirted frock and a pair of long, ornate African
ear-rings.

'It's not your birthday, is it?' Tom looked alarmed as
he saw the table.

'No, angel. You're quite safe,' she replied, smiling. 'But
it *is* an occasion.'

While they ate the terrine, she managed to contain herself, although she had no idea how it tasted and she gulped down the white wine so quickly that its shock waves ran through her veins, making her serve the main course with a certain recklessness.

'I'll tell you when we've finished eating. I've got to. I can't keep it to myself any longer,' she said to him, aware that already her speech had that careful precision which comes just before the words start slurring.

'You've finished the play?' he guessed.

She shook her head and beamed, wriggling on her seat.

'You've been offered a new commission?'

'No. You might as well give in. You'll never guess.'

The bottle of red wine disappeared without the swirling round the glass and nosing it deserved and they finished the cheese.

At last she gave him the photographs of the building in Lagos. He looked at them and then at her and raised his eyebrows questioningly.

'It's supposed to be for Christmas, but I just can't hold out that long,' she giggled. 'I've bought that apartment for you for Christmas.'

He sat back in his chair and looked at her without expression for a second.

'I know how much you love the Algarve and I saw this advertised for sale in Lagos and it really wasn't expensive, so I bought it,' she rattled on.

'It's . . . it's . . .' Tom was lost for words.

'Darling, you work so hard on the garden and put so much into making this place beautiful,' she tried to explain. 'And I want you to have something of your own because . . . well, I know it's sort of made things difficult between us sometimes and it's not right. So this will be all yours.'

'Lagos.' His face was beginning to brighten. 'Lagos . . . Darling, it's a marvellous present.'

She left him staring at the photographs and went to make the coffee.

Afterwards she could not even remember how the quarrel started, although she tried. It just stormed in out of nowhere and he was shouting and she was sitting on the sofa wondering what had happened. He was so enraged that there were tears running down his cheeks. He was dashing around and running in and out and she was being swept along. She did not even know what terrible things were said.

'But Tom . . . why are you so angry?' Later, she was to recall her own bewilderment. 'No one's ever given me anything like an apartment. Why aren't you thrilled? Why are we doing this?'

'Because you won't leave me alone. You never leave me alone.'

And once again he was raving on about being dominated and restricted, and then she heard the word 'freedom'. And she knew when she had heard it before.

For the next few days Bridget tried to tell herself that she was wrong. After all they had been through, all the emotional distress, all the reconstructing of their marriage, all the worries about work and money, she had to be wrong. But then she picked up the telephone to John anyway. That night she would know the truth.

Tom returned from the office, kissed her on the cheek and went for his beer. Then they ate and settled for the evening as usual.

'There's a bit of a hiccup.' She was watchful. 'Something to do with the fact our surnames are different because I kept my maiden name. Something to do with Portuguese law. Apparently they can't handle the fact that your name's O'Dare and mine's Flynn.'

'Oh?' he said.

'John seems to think the apartment should be put in both our names,' she lied, her eyes reflected in his eyes. 'He's discovered some complication to do with inheritance.'

Tom looked thoughtful and then he said, 'Well, I'm not about to drop off the perch.'

'Of course not, but John feels that it would be best in the long term.' She studied his face and he stared across the room.

There was a very long pause and, at last, he met her gaze again.

'All right,' he said. 'Have it put in both our names and then we can go to another solicitor and you can sign the apartment over to me by Deed of Gift.'

Bridget felt a fine icy needle go right through her brain.

In all their years together Tom had never asked for anything and she had believed that, although he certainly enjoyed the status symbols and the good things of life, he would have been equally happy with her without them. Had he replied that it didn't matter a damn if the apartment were in both their names, she would gladly have gone ahead and given it to him. Now she saw that the only reason he had never asked for anything was because she had always anticipated all his wants. He had never had to ask – until now.

Just before they went to sleep she said to him, 'When are we ever going to make love again?'

In the morning, for the first time in a long time, she awoke aware of hunger for him. As always the urge was immediately intimidated by the fact that she could not run her hands over his body and kiss him with the ardour she felt, because he might not want her. She turned over to face him with her eyes shut. He knew at once. He always knew.

He put a hand on her shoulder. The hand was heavy and bored. It lay on her shoulder without moving and she knew this was the only signal he was going to make. A knot of rancour marred her desire.

'You don't have to do that, just because I mentioned making love last night,' she said slowly.

She wanted him to reassure her, to tell her not to be so silly, to take her in his arms, to love her and prove that she was wrong.

He leapt out of bed.

'That would turn anyone off,' he snarled, frantically pulling on his clothes. 'No wonder I'm turned off by you. What do you expect when you say something like that? That would turn anyone off.'

His voice was rising and she knew he was dressing fast so that there was no way he would have to come back to bed. It was Saturday. The thought of the wrecked week-end lying ahead was unendurable.

He charged into the bathroom and Bridget sat up and took three sleeping pills. Then she curled up and drew the duvet over her head. Quite quickly his contemptuous words grew faint and the warmth from the feathers lapped around her and she was asleep.

Some hours later, not long after she surfaced, he came into the room again. He was raging and pleading and accusing and repentant in turn, but all she wanted was to escape from him. She took another pill.

'He can't hurt me while I'm asleep,' she thought drowsily. 'He's not here while I'm asleep.'

Each time she regained consciousness, she took another pill and obliterated the whole of that day and night.

The following morning they looked at each other through eyes dead with dislike.

'I think we should have a month's separation,' he said.

'You're having an affair,' she said.

'No, I'm not. There's no other woman, but there's no point in telling you that because you won't believe me.' He was noisily rooting about in the chest of drawers. 'I feel completely suffocated. Our life is intolerable. I need some space for myself. I need freedom.'

It was the same script he had used three years before. He hadn't even bothered to change it, she thought. Or perhaps he wasn't even aware that he was repeating himself.

'All right,' she said. 'Have your month's separation.'

Tom packed a couple of bags and left.

It was not the same as before. If he thought a few nice words and some good intentions were going to bring them together again this time, he was mistaken. Bridget was sick of the strain and quarrels and sick of being treated like a doormat.

He thinks of me as that fat woman indoors who is too stupid to know what is going on, she fumed to herself. But she knew perfectly well what was going on and, as the days went by, she finally admitted that she had always known what had been happening in Bristol. He had been playing the field.

Months ago, she had made an almost conscious decision that, for as long as his activities in the city did not interfere with their life together at home, she was going to be blind to them, but now they had spilled over and were spreading across their marriage like acid.

They spoke to each other daily over the telephone and were friendly. He was fine, he told her. He would soon be home.

Home to dear old Bridget, who would put up with anything, she thought to herself. He really believed he could leave her for the second time to get the latest Sharon or Tracy out of his system and then come home. He was sure she loved him so much that she would put up with anything.

But twice might as well be three times. Bridget could not tell herself again that this was a mistake, or an aberration. Twice was a habit. Nor could she blame the other woman as she had Jane Scott. This was just the latest woman. She could have been any woman.

Living alone was like a religious retreat. She spent the evenings quietly, pottering about in the garden for a while, deadheading roses, tidying the herbaceous border, picking a few runner beans. Then she ate a light supper on her knee, watched television and worked at her tapestry. Some mornings she awoke feeling quite euphoric at the prospect of the peaceful and undisturbed day stretching ahead.

It was easy to concentrate on her latest play and the hours passed quickly as she worked on the research. Then, while going through some old files one day, she came across a letter, a letter she had written to Tom within twelve months of their meeting, when she had fled from him to stay with Deirdre ten years earlier. Now she read it with growing horror.

Dear Tom,
Last night's call from you really was the last straw. One minute you're saying you love me and want me

and the next you tell me you've written off for a job in Australia 'to keep your options open'. Is it to be 'For my next trick, I shall simply disappear'?

How do you expect me to feel? You are a kind of cuckoo. You arrived as a beautiful, big, warm, peaceful egg, which I couldn't believe was mine and which I fussed round and fretted over. Then, about three months ago, you hatched, pecking and thrashing about and now the nest is being destroyed.

You've spent a lot of time persuading me to believe in your promises. Then, when I am persuaded, you always do exactly the opposite.

I know I try to do the things you want and be the way you want. I listen to your troubles and attempt to be constructive. Your work always takes priority over mine. I've given up my writing for weeks until you were settled and I act as your chauffeur and try to be charming to people who make me feel awkward. But I miss my music and it would be nice if you cooked for me once a week and if we went to a movie, or did something I enjoy sometimes.

I've spent all my life in conflict, worrying over how to please mother and then Sam and trying to assert my own needs. I've failed dismally. I feel myself being drawn into the same situation all over again because I've reached the stage of being afraid to mention all sorts of ordinary, daily, minor problems in case I am shouted and ranted at, or in case you just drive off. I am even afraid of saying I'm afraid.

Sexually, I never know how I am expected to respond. I do not know whether you want me. Sometimes I approach (which you don't make easy) and you aren't interested, but, if I turn away, you ask me why.

You use sex as a weapon instead of for love and fun.

I translate your distance with me and flirting with other women as rejection and criticism – meaning that they are prettier, more sexually attractive and worth responding to than I am. But I am not prepared to compete with other women. You must accept me as I am.

You accuse me of trying to change you, but surely I am also having to change. Two people half-way through their lives could not possibly settle together without each adapting, unless one were totally dominated by the other. I don't think there's any fear of your being dominated by me, but there is a real fear of my being repressed by you.

When Sam and I parted, I did not imagine for a moment that I would meet anyone else I could share my whole life with. Meeting you was extraordinary – unbelievable. We have so much mentally in common and, on an unemotional level, we make such good companions that it's tempting to pretend this is a sound enough basis on which to build everything.

No one really wants to be alone, but, last night, I realized that I would rather be alone, unloved but content than spend most of my time in agitated distress for the sake of occasional nervous and unstable happiness. On balance, it looks as though you are basically quite happy (so long as I don't bother you with all this) and I am basically not happy.

Anyway, I can't think of any other way of expressing it all. I love you very much and I want it to work out more than anything else, but at the moment it isn't working out and I don't know what to do about it.

It was all there. Bridget read the letter several times, unable to believe that ten years earlier she had put her finger on everything that was wrong between them and that nothing had really changed. And she had been so right in her prediction that she would be overwhelmed by him. She had loved him so completely that her life had finished up revolving entirely around him and yet, ten years ago, she had written down in black and white the timebomb of their failure.

Why had she stuck it out for so long? Because she loved him. But why did she love him? What did she love about him? She did not know.

The letter was lying beside her when he telephoned. He needed some more clothes, he told her, and thought he would drive over the following evening. They had been apart for a fortnight.

Chapter Fifteen

IT WAS their seventh wedding anniversary. Tom arrived home with a card. It was a picture of two puppies and some fluffy yellow chicks.

Inside it he had written: 'What can I say? Seems a funny way to spend a wedding anniversary. Tom.'

'Thank you,' Bridget said.

It was autumn. She had lit the log fire as she did every evening. The house was clean and tidy, but not especially so. She was wearing a jumper and skirt and no make-up. She remembered how she had spring-cleaned and decorated the house with vases of flowers and cooked an expensive meal and tarted herself up for him when he was having the affair with Jane Scott, but not this time. This time she had made no preparation for his coming, and she had not bought an anniversary card.

They talked about her script and his work and discussed her intended business trip to London in a few days when Tom agreed to return home in the evenings to look after the animals and the poultry. She felt at ease. In fact, they were both unusually serene with each other.

As he sat in his armchair, he fondled and played with his dog, just as he always did. Rake had grown into a big, scruffy creature and when Bridget sometimes commented that Tom loved the animal more than he did her, she was only half joking. Her husband was like a doting father, producing photographs of his dog from his wallet to total strangers and once, when Rake had disappeared for two days, Tom had put reward notices in every pub for miles and spent hours tramping the moor to find him. Believing the dog was dead, they had both cried together and cried again when he was discovered, reproachful and unhurt at the bottom of a quarry.

Eventually, Tom glanced over at her. 'Well, when you come back from London, we'll see how we feel.'

'I know how I feel, Tom,' she said quietly. 'I want a divorce.'

A look of utter bemusement passed over his face. He looked so stunned that, unexpectedly, she had difficulty in not smiling.

After a few moments he began walking up and down the room.

'Right.' He began grinning in a desperate attempt to hide his shock. 'Right.'

'There is no reason why we shouldn't remain friends.' She was quite sincere. 'Because we are friends and I'm still friendly with Sam.'

'Right,' he repeated.

His mental adjustment was visible, the cogs clicking into ratchets of his mind as he grappled with the situation and then took up a position. A few minutes later he went out for a beer. Bridget poured herself a very large gin and tonic.

She had not even thought of a divorce until she said it, but, as soon as the words were spoken, she knew it was what she wanted.

When he returned within an uncommonly short time, she was already pouring herself another drink.

'Nothing's irrevocable,' he said to her.

'You're having an affair.'

'I'm not. I'm not. I've told you there's nobody else.' His voice rose.

She looked at him steadily as he sat down and lit a cigarette with the care of a man taking control of himself.

'You might feel differently in London.' He studied his glass.

'Nothing's going to happen in London to make me feel different,' she replied.

Then she saw him look at her left hand. For the first time since their wedding day she had taken off her wedding ring.

They both got slightly drunk. They talked of the divorce as though it concerned other people and agreed on the grounds of two years' separation. They even joked with each other. Irrationally, it was one of the most relaxed evenings they had spent together for a long time.

Because he had had too much to drink to drive back to Bristol, they went to bed at last, in separate rooms. Bridget slept fitfully, fragmented images, unidentifiable and menacing, rasping against her need to rest until she came fully awake at 4.30 a.m. She made a cup of cocoa and sat back in bed thinking about the night before.

Had she said the word 'divorce' to test him? Did she *really* mean it? Did she? She did not know. The trouble was, she thought, that if she wanted a divorce he would go along with that and, if she didn't, he would go along with that, too. He would not fight for her, or for their home. He would not fight for their marriage. He was too insecure to fight for anyone. Women had to chase after him.

An hour later Tom came into the room looking haggard. He looked down at her and there were tears in his eyes. But still she could not put out her arms and hold him to her.

'Goodbye,' he said.

'Goodbye, Tom.'

Even if he had refused to go back to Bristol, even if he had insisted on staying, she could not have changed her mind. He had left her twice for other women and Bridget knew that she could never live with that. It was over for her and Tom.

Unable to stay in bed any longer, she dressed and went into the garden. The sun was just rising over the south hill and the hedges glistened with spiders' nets. The leaves had not yet turned red and gold, but the cotoneaster and holly were thick with red berries. If she cut the holly branches and stuck them in soil now, the berries would still be there for Christmas, she thought, but knew she would forget and the birds would take them all.

Walking quietly under the laburnum tunnel, she went through the wooden gate and into the orchard. There were so many apples this year that their weight had broken large branches on some of the old trees. The little roebuck was nibbling at the leaves of one of these. Bridget stopped and stood completely still.

He had begun coming down into the garden when he was very young and crowned with just the shafts of his antlers, but now he had two tines. Each spring he ate the bluebells and stripped the camellias bare of leaves; but there were always plenty more bluebells and the alkaline soil did not suit camellias anyway. Bridget would have been happy to let him eat all her flowers just for the enchantment of those times when he was bold enough to appear on the terrace in front of the window where she worked.

The stag looked straight at her, grazed on unconcerned for a few minutes and then, with a saucy flick of his scut, he bounded across the grass. As he jumped the wall, a hind appeared from under one of the fruit trees and then, to Bridget's surprise, a second hind.

'You randy old thing!' she silently accused the departing buck, recalling the folklore that roe deer are monogamous, remaining with their chosen mate for life. 'You blokes are all the same.'

The hinds trotted straight towards her on legs so slim and fine that they appeared to be on tiptoe. With their sensitive tapering ears and huge eyes, they did not seem like flesh-and-blood creatures. As they floated through the September mist, the rays of the dawn buffed their copper coats, still silky from summer, and lit their eyes with the lambency of candles, making them as ethereal as a fantasy.

'Oh Tom,' thought Bridget, sadly. 'What have you thrown away?'

The two does saw her and stopped, testing the air, then they turned and sprang away.

The scene cast a spell over Bridget, leaving her feeling hopeful and blithe. It was as though she had unsealed a corner of the future and been given something to hold on to in the dark winter that lay ahead, a hint that there would be redemption.

She dreamt that he was dead and that she began to dig a hole in which to bury him, but, although she lifted shovels full of earth until her arms and back became feeble and she was groaning with exhaustion, the hole grew no deeper than a shallow trough. When she stopped, unable to continue, and looked at him, his body had changed into a massive boulder. Then, as she tried to roll the boulder into the hole, it turned into rubble spread all around her and she was beating at it with a lump hammer.

Every piece of stone had to be pulverized to make sure he was dead, but the rubble spread deeper and wider over the surface of the ground and, although she dementedly smashed and smashed, she knew she was never going to be able to destroy it all.

When the alarm went off she awoke as though she had just come out of the shower. Her hair was drenched with sweat. Water was running down her whole body and her nightdress was so wet that it clung to her. The sheets and even the mattress were soaking and she lay on them gasping and trying to free her mind from the tentacles of the nightmare.

Holding her morning mug of coffee in unsteady hands, she felt the cinder of anger which had been smouldering under the cortex of her life for so long grow hot and begin to burn through the embers of suppressed resentment.

Tom had been a bottomless pit. The more she had poured of herself into him, the more work crises and financial spasms and emotional turbulence he had managed to initiate. Here she was lying stinking and shaking from another nightmare ten years after they had met simply because some woman had gazed at him open-mouthed and assured him that he was the most glamorous and irresistible man who had ever walked the earth and he had fallen for it. Again.

Bridget drew on her cigarette and wondered what this latest one was like; younger probably, because the newspaper was used by journalists, apart from Tom, as a rung on the way up their career ladders.

The coffee spilt over the duvet as she awkwardly shifted her position.

Thank God I'm alone, she thought automatically, or

the accident would have caused another song and dance, and at least it was a cream-coloured cover. The stain would not show too much.

Two hours later she drove defiantly past Bristol on her way to London, glad that her imagination was still full of riling memories from the past.

As long as I can remain angry I'll be all right, she thought. As long as I don't let myself get depressed, I'll be fine. She was not going to go through the torment caused by Jane Scott again. This time was different. This time she was going to divorce him and never look back. This time she was in control.

London was fast and thrilling after the country. Carter Blake, her agent, took her to a fashionable Soho restaurant where two famous politicians renowned for their mutual animosity sat at tables one on either side of them. When the elder statesman of the two had finished his lunch, he walked over to greet his erstwhile protégé, now a cabinet minister. The two men grimaced at each other like wolves then, as the older man turned away to leave, their smiles pursed shut as though they had just farted.

'You're looking very well,' Carter commented.

'I'm getting divorced,' she replied, by way of explanation.

'Oh my dear, how do you feel about that?' He tasted the wine and gestured to the waiter to fill her glass.

'Right,' she answered.

Boozy lunches were obviously a thing of the past, she noted. All around them people were ordering salads and drinking Perrier water, although the selection of food was fit to die for to someone who lived far beyond the reach of gastronomy in an area where gammon and pineapple still ruled. It was a source of irritation to

Bridget that she was always too excited to feel hungry in London, but she was certainly not going to give in to that.

She ordered pâté de poisson aux asperges to be followed by carré d'agneau en croûte with glazed chicory and mushrooms and new potatoes, then offered Carter a cigarette.

'I've given up,' he responded, mournfully.

'All the most fascinating people smoke,' she told him and lit her own. 'What on earth do you want to live until you're over seventy for anyway? It's all downhill after that.'

He was a slim, good-looking man, with alert, amused eyes and a slight tension about his mouth which hinted at an underlying conflict always attractive to women; a man who had had to train himself to be cautious where, Bridget suspected, passion burned.

He gave her the latest gossip on the machinations and throat-cutting in the media and then got down to the purpose of their meeting. 'The Americans are dragging their feet about the script. It's the usual story of endless producers' meetings and no one making decisions.'

'They will commission it though, won't they?' she pressed anxiously.

'I'm sure they will in the end.' He sounded confident.

'But when will they pay up?' she asked. 'I'm virtually broke.'

'Well, don't expect anything for a few months,' he warned. 'We've got to ensure a really good deal and that takes time.'

He was not known in the business as Cardiac Blake for nothing and Bridget knew he would strike a very hard bargain for her. But, until this moment, she had not considered her financial position – and she realized it was dire.

Tom and she had both known this was going to be a lean winter and, for the first time since their marriage, they had agreed to live on his salary until the American contract came through. Now there was no Tom, which meant no salary.

A strobe light of pessimism played over her self-confidence. Tom would just have to help her, she thought, and instantly recoiled from the prospect of asking him for money. She had never asked anyone for money.

Carter was watching her shrewdly. He had been her agent for years and had seen her through her divorce from Sam, the first euphoric months with Tom and their wedding, the abject misery of that first affair and the painstaking resuscitation of her marriage. He knew her very well.

'Why don't you keep working on that idea for the TV play in the meantime?' he suggested. 'Small cast, straightforward setting, plenty of suspense. It would be very inexpensive to make and nothing appeals to a producer more.'

'It'll still take time,' she pointed out, dolefully.

'All the more money to come in the end,' he grinned.

The energy generated by all the hurrying people and the taxis swooping on their prey like sharks and a million businesses serviced by clattering typewriters and tills was infectious. Bridget tripped through the streets slightly high from what had turned out to be a satisfyingly boozy lunch after all. Furtive men slid into cinemas showing soft-porn movies just as they had when she had run away from home to live here with Sam so long ago.

She used to have coffee with the Italian family who

had run the grocery shop on the corner. The shop was now a wine bar, but the faded brown front door of the Frith Street house in which she and Sam had rented a room did not look as though it had been painted since then. What a sweet, idealistic little soul she had been, she thought with a pang and looked quickly away from her youth into a shop window.

Denied the pleasure of buying flattering clothes, over-weight women treat themselves to scent, handbags or shoes and, despite her insolvency, Bridget bought a very expensive pair of shoes to add to her considerable collection. At least, she still had slim ankles.

I'm becoming another Imelda Marcos, she gloated as she wore them from the shop. Come the revolution, my shoe cupboard will be held up as an example of rich-bitch profligacy.

Deirdre would not be returning home from the ante-natal clinic for another two hours, so Bridget headed for the writers' club tucked away down a Soho lane. There she would have another glass of chilled white wine and sit talking to interesting people with her new shoes in view.

Before she had joined the club that year, she had been asked if she were a poet.

'Not really,' she had confessed, thinking her application for membership was about to be rejected. 'I mean I have had some poetry published, but I couldn't honestly call myself a poet.'

'Does your poetry rhyme?' she was asked.

'Actually, I'm afraid so,' she had apologized. Her poems were very old-fashioned. She was definitely going to be blackballed.

'That's all right then,' came the cheerful reply from a

man renowned for the acid eccentricity of his opinions. 'We don't accept poets whose work doesn't rhyme.'

The entrance to the club reminded her of the old song, 'Behind the green door'. When the bell was rung a disembodied voice answered through an electronic grille; when she gave her name, the latch was remotely released and she stepped from daylight into blackness and found her way blinking down a narrow staircase to the basement.

There were a few couples sitting together at tables. She ordered her drink and some olives, fiercely spiked with garlic and red pepper seeds, and looked admiringly at her new shoes. More people began to arrive as the publishing houses and features departments of the newspaper offices closed early because it was Friday. The men wore long coats and long hair and the women wore long jackets and short skirts. They all looked very assured and successful and they all knew each other.

Bridget began to be aware of her outdated frock and her locally cut hair and her age and, above all, of her weight. There were magazines laid out on a table and she took one to hide behind. She could overhear snatches of their conversations about the books they had just completed and the high-powered jobs they did. They were going on to dinner, or to friends in the country for the weekend, or home to smart Hampstead houses, achieving husbands or wives and clever children.

As they sat all around her, she knew they did not even see her. She was exactly what Tom thought she was, a fat, frumpy, middle-aged woman, invisible because she was such a stereotype. When she had visited the club before, she had been going home to him. Now she was going nowhere.

She checked her watch and smoked another cigarette, turning the stem of her empty glass between her fingers and staring, unseeing, at a page of the magazine. She thought of trying to talk to the two women who had sat down at her table because the others were full, but they might look at her blankly and, in any case, she did not have a clue what to say.

As a young reporter, she had been so shy that she had had to write down all her questions before every interview and there had been one excruciating meeting with a duchess during which she had come to the end of her list over tea and had been unable to say another word. The poor woman must have thought her very peculiar.

Tom had finally drawn her out of herself, his easy sociability bringing her into company. With him beside her, she had felt shielded and had been surprised to discover that occasionally she could be quite quick-witted and funny. But he was not there any more and that old paralysing fear of strangers was back. Bridget knew that a timidity which might have been beguiling in a young girl was ridiculous in a woman of her age. But still she could not speak.

She checked her watch again and, although it was still too early, she slunk from the crowded room unnoticed into the night.

The rush-hour traffic was still lurching out of the city, bonnet to boot, stopping every few yards at traffic lights and then pitching forward again. Rush was the last word to describe its progress.

The darkness was lit by a discord of lights from shop windows, buses, street lamps, cars, signs and Belisha beacons. Composite animals of human flesh pushed and scrabbled into the underground stations, or swayed wearily at bus stops. In her car surrounded by other cars, each packaging one anonymous face, Bridget felt the intensity of her exclusion. Everyone was going home to a waiting family. Next week they would all return to work and meet their colleagues again. They were travelling into known futures. Everyone else was moving towards someone else.

She longed for the freshness of her garden and her dogs. It had been a mistake coming to London, too dislocating at a time when she needed to be protected by the sanctuary of her own home.

Deirdre's and Barney's small house in the suburbs enfolded her at last, like a foil wrap at the end of a marathon, and she sank into a chair with her head throbbing to watch her bulging daughter lay the table for supper.

'London always does this to you, Mummy,' Deirdre reminded her. 'It's nothing to do with what's going on with Tom.'

She was right. On each visit Bridget arrived in the city full of exuberance and finished up collapsing into this same chair under one of her daughter's huge paintings of nudes, feeling ill.

'You think I'm doing the right thing?' she asked.

'Yes.'

'Supposing he hasn't got another woman?'

'If your instincts tell you he has, then he has.'

Deirdre went into the kitchen to check the soup and returned with a gin and tonic and pushed it into her hand.

'Look, Mummy, he's never been any good for you. Every now and again you've had a peaceful couple of weeks and then, as you keep saying yourself, it's been back to square one. He's self-obsessed and he was already far too damaged when he met you to put himself right.'

'But we've so much in common,' Bridget said, unhappily. 'And I understand why he's such a mess. We had the same childhoods.'

'Yes, but you developed along different lines. You're fairly crazy and you drive us all mad half the time, but you mean well, you try hard and you face up to things. Tom just runs away and hides behind a phony act, so no one can find him, not even himself. He's never grown up. Now, have a look at these.'

Deirdre pulled over a large box and started taking out baby clothes, absurdly small cardigans and leggings and booties in brilliant, striking colours not normally associated with newborn infants. Bridget smiled over her fondly. She was so thickly swaddled in her pregnancy that no outside vexation could touch her. There was something touching about seeing her so busy nesting. Already the room was full of toys and the nursery was waiting and there was a pram in the garden shed and the small suitcase was packed ready for the hospital.

'They showed us this awful film at the clinic. The woman having the baby was screaming and shouting.' Deirdre looked up and Bridget saw fear behind her daughter's impassive expression. 'They tell us everything that can go wrong.'

'Darling, all young mothers are afraid the first time.' Aware that her daughter did not like demonstration, Bridget gave her a quick hug and a kiss. 'Honestly, you arrived with no trouble at all. The contractions are no worse than curse pains. I don't know what people make so much fuss about and those idiots at the clinic have no right to tell you all that rubbish.'

Her daughter did not look convinced and Bridget wished she could have knocked the heads of the medical profession together. Either they terrified patients by giving them no information, or they terrified them by giving them too much.

'It's because of the miscarriage,' Deirdre said. 'It might happen again.'

'That great lump doesn't look like a miscarriage to me,' Bridget laughed. 'Just don't do too much, darling. Take care of yourself and you'll have a marvellous baby within a few more weeks.'

'I can't imagine you as a grannie.' Her daughter began to perk up. 'Going drippy all over the cot.'

'Neither can I,' agreed Bridget, whose avoidance of the company of young children was a family joke. 'But I expect I'll get used to whoever arrives. By the time he or she is about seven we'll probably have formed quite an acceptable relationship.'

They went shopping the next morning and Bridget found herself gazing at banks of fluffy playthings for the first time in twenty-seven years. In the end, she bought a ferocious-looking bear, because he seemed to be the only toy with any personality.

Then they had lunch in a cheap and cheerful Italian restaurant, full of young families and smelling richly of tomatoes and olive oil. Deirdre looked at her across the table with her head on one side.

She has such a sweet face, Bridget thought, admiring the way her daughter's shining hair rippled over her shoulders to her breasts. It was a strong, unusually wise face for someone so young, with the large observant eyes of an artist and a full, sensuous mouth.

Deirdre was only five feet tall, but she had always

despised the way so many small women played on their lack of height, talking in childish voices and pretending to be helpless. The word petite would probably have made her throw up.

'I'm not little,' she had once stated firmly. 'I'm just short.'

But, to Bridget, her daughter was still little. She remembered how, when Deirdre laughed as a child, the sound had been so natural and spontaneous that people had turned and smiled or laughed, too. It hardly seemed possible that she was now expecting her own child.

'The trouble with you, Mummy, is that you don't seem to know how to set the limits.' Deirdre's voice broke into her reverie.

'What limits?'

'Everyone sets limits in all their relationships. I do; lines which no one – not even Barney – can cross without invading *me*. But you never seem to have learnt how to protect yourself, not even with your friends. No one knows where to stop with you and people will always see how far they can go. It's human nature.

'That's what happened with you and Tom. He just went on doing his own thing at your expense and, although you sometimes protested or quarrelled, you never stuck to your guns. So he thought there were no limits to how he could behave with you.'

'Well, he knows differently now,' Bridget said grimly.

'Yes, Mummy, but you need to lay down your terms with people long before it gets to this, before everything explodes.'

'If you love someone, you want to fit in with them and do things for them. You want them to be happy.' Bridget stopped eating to explain what was a very deep-seated conviction. 'Surely, if they love you, they will do the same for you.'

'No, they won't.' Deirdre smiled tolerantly and shook her head at the same time. 'If you adapt too much, people see that as weakness and they take advantage of you.'

'That's very cynical, darling.' She turned the spaghetti round her fork and brooded.

'Maybe, but it's also a fact.'

Bridget had to admit that her own experiences with her mother and Sam and Tom certainly appeared to indicate that there must be something to this opinion. Where had her daughter learnt so much, she wondered, when she herself knew so little?

'If you're right, it's very sad,' was all she said.

'It doesn't have to be.' Deirdre patted her hand. 'It can be better and it makes sense, because people can only relate fully to you if they know where they stand.'

In the afternoon Bridget went to see Zoe, who had invited her to stay overnight. She found her friend togging up her two young sons to play football, trying to deal with a hysterical telephone call from her mother and snapping at her husband, David, for forgetting to collect the cleaning.

'Help yourself to a glass of wine, babe, and park yourself somewhere,' she threw at Bridget and galloped across the hall with a pile of anoraks.

'It's been a hellish week. We've been taken over,' she went on, pushing a heap of newspapers into her husband's arms. 'No, James, you can't go to McDonald's after the game. You're to bring Edward straight home.

'I thought they'd appoint a completely new board of directors and I might lose my job, but I've just signed up GRT so they've kept me on and given me a mega-rise.'

The children were seen out the door and David thankfully disappeared into his study and she flung herself on to the sofa at last.

'You look great, babe. You've lost weight.'

Zoe could always be depended on to give her a boost. She was the most positive woman Bridget knew.

'I'm divorcing Tom,' she told her.

'About time, too.' Zoe tossed her straight blonde hair. 'I suppose he's screwing around again.'

'I think so.'

Bridget was taken aback by the general enthusiasm with which everyone was greeting the end of her marriage. It made her feel disloyal. Tom would be at home now, looking after the dogs until she returned. Supposing she were completely mistaken and that all he needed was time to himself for a while? His mother had died and they had never even discussed that. Suddenly, she desperately wanted to talk to him.

The doorknocker banged and, as her friend went to answer it, Bridget asked if she could use the phone.

She dialled her own number and listened as it rang out at the other end and went on ringing unanswered. Then she dialled the local pub, to be told that Tom had not been seen there for days. But Tom always went to the pub.

She began to feel nervous and looked up Sue's number in her filofax.

'Could you just go up and see if Tom's in the garden? If not, let yourself into the house with the spare key and make sure the dogs are OK.'

'I'll ring you back,' Sue promised.

Tom would cross the Arctic for Rake, Bridget reassured herself, trying to quell the jitters in her stomach. He would never neglect the dogs.

When Zoe returned to the room, she could not concentrate on all her news about the company with its massive budgets and international plans and, when the telephone bell rang, she literally jumped.

'You'd better come home, Bridget.' Sue sounded distressed. 'I found the dogs shut in the back with no food or water. I've fed them, but they're in a dreadful state with shit all over the place and there's no sign of Tom. No one's seen him in the village and it's obvious he hasn't been home at all.'

Chapter Sixteen

'DON'T you feel angry? You must feel angry,' Zoe stormed. 'I'd kill him. I'd cut him into pieces and grind him through the mincer. My God! You've got to feel *angry*.'

But all Bridget felt was pain; the most all-encompassing physical pain she had ever experienced. It was as though all her organs had been removed – lungs, heart, stomach, bowels – and her empty skeleton had been filled with molten lead. She could feel it burning behind her eyeballs and eardrums and making her head huge and misshapen where her brain had been and massively weighing down her body. Even her fingers felt too swollen and heavy to move. And the pain hardened into an unassailable density.

There was no question now that there was another woman, and that she and Tom were finished for ever.

She curled up into a ball of anguish, hugging her knees and sobbing.

'Why aren't you angry? Why don't you hate him?' Zoe was demanding, standing before her, arms outstretched in incomprehension.

'I hurt. I hurt,' was all Bridget could weep.

'Babe, you're worth so much more than this. You're a great lady. We've all seen what was going on between you two for years and someone's got to say it to you. The man is a worthless bastard. He's not fit to be on the same planet as you. He's used you and taken you for everything he could get.'

'No!' Bridget writhed and buried her head in her arms.

'Yes!' Zoe shouted at her. 'Face it! You picked him up with nothing and stood by him through everything. You've given him a fabulous home and a lifestyle he couldn't even have dreamed of. You've practically wiped his arse for him for ten years and he's treated you like a lavatory – and you've let him. You're a talented, successful, hard-working, attractive woman. You've got everything going for you and it makes me pig-sick to stand here and see what the conniving bloodsucker has done to you.'

'I've got to go home,' Bridget mumbled and stumbled from the house.

All she remembered of the journey was hours of speeding black cars and blaring headlights and, at the end, Rake and Erin jumping all over her with their excrement-covered paws and yelping hysterically.

When she let them out, they hurtled up the dark garden baying and then, as she disinfected the utility room, they kept returning anxiously to see if she was still there.

At last she put on rubber gloves and sponged them clean and washed herself and took them with her into the drawing-room to dry. It was midnight.

They stood in front of her, as if wondering whether she wanted anything of them; she looked down at them, so helpless and totally dependent: creatures who gave nothing but unqualified love. If Tom walked in tomorrow, they would not know he had left them thirsty and starving and they would greet him with the same ecstatic adoration. Their clear, trusting eyes looked back at her and their tails waved gently and, just as they always did when she was upset, they laid their muzzles gently on her lap, and she cried.

He hadn't been expecting her to return home for another twenty-four hours. Supposing she had not telephoned? They would have been left for three whole days. How could he have done something so wicked, something which just thinking about made her insides churn?

Without warning, the drawing-room door opened and a man walked in. The dogs bounded forward growling and Bridget started to her feet.

'I'm sorry, love. I thought there was no one here.' It was Steve, one of Tom's friends from the pub. 'I've just had a call from your husband.'

'He's had an accident! He's ill!' With a leaping heart Bridget knew there must have been a good explanation.

'No, love. He's paralytically drunk,' Steve said, obviously embarrassed. 'He just asked me to shut your dogs up and, when I asked if anyone had fed them, he didn't answer.'

'Shut the dogs up!' Bridget screamed. 'He's left them shut up for the past two days.'

'Well, he did phone a couple of days ago and ask me to look after them if he couldn't get down,' Steve told her. 'He was going to let me know, but he never rang back, so I thought everything was all right.'

'They've been locked in without food or water for two days,' Bridget told him.

'I don't believe it! Tom worships that dog of his. Sit down, love.' He sat down beside her. 'Now, what's going on here?'

'Another woman, what else?' Bridget said, bitterly.

'For Christ's sake, not again.'

Tom's affair with Jane Scott had been common knowledge in the village.

245

'I'm divorcing him,' she said, not caring any longer who knew.

'Well, I'd like to get my hands on the bugger. I got two dogs of my own and I don't hold with mistreating animals.' Steve was furious. 'You're well rid of him, Bridget, my dear. Any man who can do that to his dogs shouldn't be allowed near a woman.'

She smiled wanly. He had a countryman's priorities of animals first, woman last.

It was the first time he had ever been in the house and he looked round the large room.

'Tom must be mad leaving all this,' he said slowly. 'He's got what every man dreams of, a fine house and a bit of land and a good job and plenty of money and a wife to be proud of.'

He left still shaking his head in disbelief and Bridget went to bed at last.

'Yes,' she thought. 'He must be mad.'

While Bridget had been away, one of the lavatories had leaked through the kitchen ceiling and the next morning no plumber was prepared to come out because it was Sunday.

Grass had grown up and broken the earth of the electric fence round the bottom of the orchard where the dogs were let out, so they were able to break through and run off, and she gave herself a shock the force of a cattle probe while mowing under the wires.

Then the poultry escaped into the kitchen garden and, as she chased them about, one old hen dropped dead in front of her. Finally, she returned to the house to find that the cat had thoughtfully deposited the gizzards of some unknown victim on the sofa as a present for her.

It was just a normal day, Bridget thought, and felt more positive. At least she now knew the real situation without any shadow of doubt and it was one she would not tolerate.

The pain was still there, established as an immovable block of concrete lying below her diaphram, and her breathing was quick and shallow, but, after dealing with the melodramas of the livestock, she sat at her desk and made out cheques to cover the latest bills, hoping that there was still enough in her account to honour them. Then she wrote formally to her solicitor, John, with instructions to start divorce proceedings and enclosing her birth and marriage certificates. She sealed the envelope with the feeling of competence which comes from reaching a definite and final decision.

It had been her intention to continue working on the television play, but, unable to concentrate, she treated herself to an afternoon watching an old Hollywood musical on television and reading the Sunday papers in front of the fire.

Her mind kept sloping off down forbidden paths, so that the movie reached her as a mass of meaningless pictures and the newspapers made no sense at all. Then, as she was giving the exhausted dogs their afternoon feed, she suddenly resolved to drive to Bristol to see the truth for herself.

The city was unknown to her and it was dark by the time she arrived. As she had never been to the house Tom rented with a male colleague, she finally called at a police station for directions.

Even so, she lost the way several times before eventually finding the narrow road behind a motor auction yard and drawing up outside the unlit address.

After staring at it, she re-checked the number in her Filofax and then the number on the door. There was no mistake. But the downstairs windows were boarded up and torn curtains hung upstairs and there was the transudation of emptiness which comes from a house which is uninhabited.

Nevertheless, she went up and rang the bell. It echoed tinnily in unfurnished space somewhere inside and the smell of damp through the letterbox told that it was a long time since anyone had lived there. No wonder Tom had always maintained that the house did not have a telephone.

Bridget sat in her car and lit a cigarette, trying to control her dismay and her impulse to go straight home. She did not want to uncover any more. She just wanted to run away. But she had come to look at reality and, if she did not go through with it now, she might never find the courage again.

Wondering where he was, she began to drive slowly around the strange city, holding up impatient drivers behind her as she crawled past the department stores with their enticing windows, up the long hill and round the university, along the side of a common bordered by large expensive houses, steeply down to the river and back towards the centre again. Scores of pubs and restaurants dotted the streets and she did not know where she was going, or what she was looking for.

Then she came to a set of traffic lights on green and, across the street, she saw an Indian restaurant. Without indicating, Bridget stopped the car. Ignoring the angry shouts and horn-blasts, she crossed straight through the moving traffic and looked over the half-curtain stretched across the window of the restaurant.

Tom was sitting at a table in the corner with a woman, just as she had known he would be. Bridget watched him with the strangest feeling of detachment. His suit was creased and his shoulders were hunched. He was eating stiffly, with his head down and his elbows clamped against his sides. It was the first time she had ever looked at him without his having any effect on her. There was no fluttering stomach, no jumping heart, no joy or anger. There was nothing. He looked like a downtrodden insurance salesman out for his weekly curry.

Then Bridget looked at his companion and saw a whey-faced young woman with long lank dark hair picking at her food. A mousetrap. There was no more to see. They ate without looking at each other and without speaking. Bridget looked from one to the other and her mouth compressed with exasperation.

'You bloody fool!' she mouthed silently to him and walked back to her car.

When she returned home, she wrote a second letter to John telling him what she had discovered and that she wanted to divorce on the grounds of adultery.

Bridget stood on the bathroom scales and discovered she had lost a stone in weight. Encouraged, she slotted an exercise video into the machine and worked through the whole programme, then went out and bought another two hundred cigarettes.

Over the next few days she altered the draft of her television play, cleared up her garden in preparation for winter and walked her dogs. She exercised and painted her nails and set her hair and made up her face. Late into the nights she restarted her affair with Brahms, glutting herself on his symphonies after the years of musical starvation. She tried to fill up every minute of her time, both to avoid contacting Tom and to retain her anger.

Her solicitor agreed to arrange through a Bristol solicitor for a private investigator to obtain proof of Tom's adultery. She put down the telephone with a sense of *déjà vu*, but with the knowledge that at least this agent would be efficient, unlike the clown who had trailed Jane Scott. She felt able and resolute.

Then, just as she mixed a gin and tonic after switching off her word processor one evening, the telephone rang.

'Your husband's got someone else,' a voice said. 'Someone much younger than you and he's telling everyone how old and fat you are. He's going to divorce you.'

'Who is that?' Bridget's throat dried and the words croaked out.

'I just thought you should know.' It was a woman's voice.

The telephone went dead.

Bridget stood transfixed with the receiver in her hand. She was shaking violently all over.

'With someone else.' Hearing the words. 'Going to divorce you.' Spoken in her ear by a stranger. 'You're old and fat.' Over and over. 'He's telling everyone.'

Without noticing, Bridget knocked over and broke her glass as she returned to the sofa.

Who could it have been? The woman? The woman Tom was living with? But she would not have called him 'your husband'; she would have called him Tom, and surely she would have said who she was. It had to be someone in Bristol. Who else? Questions scurried through her mind and Bridget seized on and discarded answers with rising revulsion.

They were exposed, she and Tom. What had been

private between them was known to others, to outsiders. 'He's telling everyone.' She felt invaded by the unrecognized voice which had come into her home, stealthily like a robber. Who would want to make such a call? A woman with a grudge. Some woman he had rejected? Yes. Some jealous woman out to make trouble.

Bridget would have telephoned him, but she did not know where he was. Instead she went straight to bed and, unable to sleep, picked over everything that had happened in the past few weeks and composed letters to Tom on her work pad, then tore them up. She acted out meeting him in Bristol or here in the house, what she would say, what he would say. She shouted at him. She persuaded. She reasoned. Wild, impossible plots and scenarios vied with each other. All her resolve, her careful balance had been crushed by the anonymous call.

Until now, she had not looked ahead. The house and the garden and the village had cocooned her, creating the fallacy that her routine would continue exactly as before. She had always been married, first to Sam and then to Tom, and imagined there would be little change, apart from having no man around. Bridget had not considered the world beyond these boundaries. But now someone she did not know, had never seen, had broken into her seclusion and, all at once, she was confronted by the cold and empty future where she would be entirely alone. She wanted Tom to come home and tell her it was not so. She wanted him to protect her.

A couple of sleeping pills would have restored her spirit. She would have slept and awoken refreshed, ready and able to fight on. Instead Bridget made a bad mistake. In the early hours of the morning, she got up and opened the little side-drawer in the chest of drawers which had

251

belonged to her grandfather, undid the white satin ribbon which bound them and let all the cards Tom had ever sent her spill onto the bed.

Bridget, Who makes my life so happy. Merry Christmas, Tom XXX.

To wonderful Bridget, my darling. Tom.

Card after card for birthdays and anniversaries: cards with jokes and cards with pictures of times and places they had shared.

Amazing love, Tom XXX.

Everything's sure to go your way with me around. I adore you. Tom.

Each one expressing in a different way that he loved her. Each one lacerating her as bloodily as an open razor.

Our story will outrun them all. With all my love, darling. Tom.

Bridget hugged them to her breasts and sobbed until her eyes were so swollen that they could not open and, still clutching the cards, she lost consciousness – for it could not have been called sleep.

Even while still insensible, she knew that she was lost. The raven of despair which had hovered over her through the weeks, had descended with outstretched wings and dug its talons into her soul. When her raw eyelids opened against her will, the morning sun was eclipsed by the misery which had already engulfed her, as though night had clamped itself over the coming day.

She lay motionless and full of dread. This was her ancient enemy over which there was no victory. Will-power never prevailed here, nor obsessive activity, nor logic, nor work, nor changing scene. Sensible, down-to-earth people told those in the stranglehold of such desolation to pull themselves together. Friends tried kindness and then gave up. Doctors handed out pills. All were wasting their time.

Bridget knew there was no point to her existence without Tom. For ten years she had loved him with every breath she took. She knew every pore of him, every expression in his eyes, every quality, every failing. She knew him in sickness and in health. She knew him better than she knew herself. In devotion and in rage, in compassion and in disillusion, not for a second of all those years had he been out of her thoughts.

However much they quarrelled and however much she rebelled they belonged together. No one else on earth understood either of them as well as they did each other and no one ever would. They were a double-sided mirror.

To lose someone you love is described as being like losing a limb, but the prospect of losing Tom was far worse than that. She could not tell herself she had had a fulfilled and happy life. She could not pretend to know what life was supposed to be about, or what it was for. Life for her was Tom. As she lay rigid and cold, Bridget saw that she had become an extension of him and that without him there was nothing of herself left. She had been sucked dry.

There was still time. He had left the house in tears when she had demanded the divorce. He did not want to lose his home, or his dogs, or their life together. If she went to Bristol, if she were caring and careful, she could win him away from that pasty-faced young woman. They could save their marriage.

She pictured the scenes of their reconciliation, their clinging on to each other again as though washed up on the shore after a wreck, their talking, explaining, each taking the blame, their grateful return to their quiet, close habits; but she did not stir, because beneath all the mental furore there ran one damning sentence.

'Twice means three times.'

He had left her twice for other women. If she took him back, he would betray her again, and again – and she could not endure it. She was almost fifty and one day he might leave her anyway, when she was older, when it would be too late for her to salvage anything for herself. This was her last chance to make a new start. She had to divorce him.

We should never have married, she thought. I never liked being married and neither did Tom. If we had remained separate instead of becoming a unit, none of this would have happened.

Marriage pushed people into roles. Suddenly, there was the assumption that the wife washed his underpants and he had to clock in, that each party was involved in the finances and daily job of the other, that they took on joint responsibilities and concerns which they would have handled alone had they remained single. Bridget and Tom had always mutinied against institutions. No wonder they had both felt ensnared in marriage.

There were couples who came together again after divorce, she remembered. In that position they would see each other because they chose to do so and not because they were bound together. They could handle their own business without interference from the other and neither would feel restricted. The more she considered it, the more this seemed to be the answer for her and Tom.

Fleeing before dejection which she knew would drag her down and embracing this apparent solution, Bridget made her next mistake. She telephoned Tom at work.

'It's me.'

'Hello.' He did not sound unfriendly.

'Tom, we should talk.'

'Maybe.'

'Everything important is here. Everything we've both spent ten years building up. It doesn't have to be thrown away.' Just hearing his voice banished the shadow. Whatever had happened to them, she was sure they could resolve it all.

'Well, you made the decision,' he said.

'What decision?' Reflex put her on guard. She knew perfectly well what he was talking about, but she wanted to see if he would say it.

'You've decided to divorce me.'

The gall of him! No matter how conciliatory she was or how much in the wrong his own actions, in a few words he always wound them back to the imbroglio of their failure. All the old bile was there again.

'Tom, you have left me twice for other women and no one tolerates that,' she snapped.

'I've told you there is no other woman and I've never left you before,' he replied, without a second's hesitation.

She could not believe it! He had actually convinced himself, and no doubt the mousetrap, that this was his first affair.

'What about Old Panstick, the virgin bride, Tom?' she asked, and listened to his silence. He had genuinely forgotten all about Jane Scott. 'And I know there's someone else. You took her to dinner at the Taj Mahal last night and I saw you.'

The silence was now as sharp as a thorn between them.

He must think I'm a witch, Bridget thought.

'I might have guessed you'd be spying on me. Well,

you're quite wrong.' He spoke coldly at last. 'I went to dinner with a colleague last night.'

'Of course she's a colleague. Aren't they all?' Her voice was laden with sarcasm.

There was another long pause and then he said, 'I've changed, Bridget. I'm the way I used to be. I'm hard and in control.'

'Hard and in control?' she repeated, analysing the phrase. Of course, she did not know what he had been like before they met, but none of those words seemed applicable to his behaviour now.

'I'm an ace reporter again,' she heard him say. 'And I don't need you any more.'

He had kicked her, just as she had known he would. 'I don't need you any more', that was the truth of it. He finally had a half-decent job paying reasonable money and there was some pitiful woman faking it for him, so he did not need her any more.

'An *ace* reporter?' She laughed lightly, dipping the tip of her own blade into the poison between them. She knew where his soft underbelly lay, just as he knew hers.

'Don't be absurd, Tom. You're not an *ace* reporter and you never were. Blundy was an *ace* reporter. You could have been an *ace* reporter, but you always blew it and you're never going to make it now. You're far too old.'

She rose on the beats of her fury for a moment or two and then, even before she had slammed down the receiver, crashed back into the oil slick of her doomed marriage, like a gull with clogged feathers.

On Deirdre's bedroom wall there hung a small frame and behind the glass was a piece of paper on which was written:

256

Do you love me
Because you need me?
Or do you need me
Because you love me?

Bridget realized that she needed Tom because she loved him, but he had only loved her because he needed her. She had come along when he had lost his way and she had been the rock to which he had held each time he lost balance, but now, because he was doing all right for himself at last, he did not need her and so he did not love her any more.

On the surface Bridget seemed to be an organizer and a professional success, so people thought her strong and, because she had a quick, fiery temper, they thought her tough. Her apparent strength was what had attracted Tom to her in the first place, but every man who falls in love with a strong woman wants to weaken her. Lying in bed, unable to force herself to get up and cope with the day, Bridget recognized that this had been all too easy in her case because her strength was an illusion.

Everything she had ever done had been driven by fear. Fear of her mother's disapproval and Sam's violence and Tom's rejection had made her twist her own personality into contortions of adaptability, punctuated only by occasional bursts of screaming frustration.

Fear of being unable to pay the rent and later the mortgage had driven her to work and plan and become efficient. Fear had made her learn how to manipulate the system and conjure up loans, which often no bank or building society manager in his senses should have agreed. But they had.

She had learnt to disguise her crippling shyness for fear

of failure, to deal with crises, to systemize every practical aspect of life, to check and re-check all her facts for fear of the consequences of making a mistake. She had learnt to excel through sheer fear of catastrophe.

Fear had led her to believe that there was no point or value in life lived for one. There would have been no purpose in doing it all for herself. Life was about living for someone else and making him happy. It was not Tom who had been dependent upon Bridget. She was utterly dependent upon him.

Now, everything she had run ahead of in terror for so many years had happened. Tom had betrayed and rejected her. She had no income. She knew she was going to be unable to work and she was entirely alone.

Chapter Seventeen

BRIDGET returned from shutting up the chickens that evening to pick up the ringing telephone.

'He's going to marry her as soon as he's got rid of you. He told everyone in the pub at lunchtime.' It was the same voice. 'She says he can't get enough of her and he's a mega-fuck. She says . . .'

Bridget dropped the receiver as though electrocuted. They were lies. Bridget knew they were lies, but the effect of the voice was seismic. As her heart palpitated and she stood hyperventilating, transparencies of Tom and the woman were flung down on the light box of her mind. She saw him gaze at the woman with the look of love once reserved only for her. She saw them kissing and copulating. She saw him sinking upon her with his post-coital groan as clearly as though they were there in the room. Putting her hands over her ears to block out the sound and closing her eyes to shut out the sight could not intercept the vividness of what she saw. The pain across her chest was so acute that, when she found herself lying on the floor, she thought she was having a heart attack. She hoped she was dying.

Later, veering from burning heat to freezing cold, she spent the hours of the night fanatically speculating about the identity of her tormentor and why anyone should want to torture her so. All the other horrors erupted through her crumbled defences: the massive debt on the house which she did not know how to pay, the isolation which lay ahead for the rest of her days, the certainty that she was never going to be able to write again, the phobia she had never confided to a living soul that her mother had been right – that she was actually insane.

Only the needs of the dogs forced her to go downstairs in the morning. There were two letters waiting on the doormat. One had a Bristol postmark and the other was Tom's bank statement.

Too frightened of what she might read in the former, she opened the second and her eyes riveted on the debit. In four weeks Tom had spent over £2,000.

Pulling a pocket calculator from her handbag and taking a foolscap pad of paper, Bridget began what she had been avoiding for months, adding up her debts. Loans, credit cards, store cards, her overdraft, Tom's overdraft, first mortgage, second mortgage, the three-and four-figure numbers spread down the page.

Then she began pressing the buttons to add up the column without daring to glance at the soaring reckoning until she reached the end and the final total was stamped in black across the narrow green window of the calculator.

One hundred thousand pounds.

It was far, far worse than she had imagined. During her years with Tom, she had earned well and paid all the bills without thinking, borrowing on the equity of the house when she seemed to be short and believing that, if she ever found herself in difficulty, the house could be sold and there would still be plenty of money to buy another. But, during the past nine months, the property market had collapsed and the house was now worth thousands less.

Bridget slowly wrote down the appalling figure –

£100,000 — in large numerals on a new blank sheet of paper and stared at it. She was bankrupt.

This fact wiped out all the emotional havoc. Just as she had been about to flounder out of control, it had come as a lifeline. She might not be able to handle emotional chaos, but dealing with practical disaster was her forte. Automatically, her mind began coolly studying the options.

The house could be put on the market and there might be enough left over to buy a cottage with a small mortgage. But, in the current financial climate, the house would not make anything like the amount it was worth, or the value it could reach in the future. And it might not sell at all.

Besides, Bridget loved and needed her home now more than ever and she knew she would not be able psychologically to withstand being forced to move to somewhere new while her personal life was in such disarray.

The only solution was to buy time, time to reach some equilibrium, time to start earning again and time for the housing market to recover.

Eric Burnley had been her friend and insurance broker for twenty years. He had sweetened money sources and procured mortgages and bent the rules on her behalf, often without any commission for himself. She recalled their first meeting when she had been very young and needing a far larger mortgage than she could produce proof of income to cover.

'Do you have an accountant?' he had asked.

She had replied that she had.

'What's he prepared to do for you?' he had wanted to know.

It had taken her a minute to understand the question. Then she answered, 'He's an honest man.'

'Change him,' Eric instructed instantly.

She had not, in fact, followed his advice and had discovered that although her accountant had remained an honest man, his devious cleverness combined with Eric's sang-froid had never failed to yank her out of the troubles which beset anyone who is self-employed.

'You can borrow enough to pay the mortgage for a year on your insurance policies,' Eric told her, after she had explained her latest predicament. 'And you won't have to pay interest on those loans until the policies mature, unless you choose to.'

'Oh Eric, why didn't I marry you?' she wailed in mock regret.

'Because I'm too old,' he chuckled.

'Better an old man's darling,' she said, ruefully.

The exercise left Bridget feeling at least temporarily in command of her circumstances again. After working out her monthly commitments, she calculated that, if Tom agreed to give her a little help, she might just survive until the Americans bought the film script. There was no point in worrying that they might not. Anything could happen between now and then.

Much calmer and with a renewed sense of her own capabilities, she opened the letter from Bristol. It was the report from the private investigator hired by John.

'I first saw your husband, Tom O'Dare, the subject of my observation, at 6.15 p.m. on Wednesday, 26th September. He was drinking with two or three other men in the Stag and Hounds public house, Bristol, where he remained until 7.15 p.m. when he left with one of these men. They walked to the Holiday Inn and then went on to the Bird's Nest pub where he met a Female whom I later found to be a Tracy Sorex.'

Bridget paced round the room and lit a cigarette, inhaling deeply before reading on.

'Your husband, the man with whom he had been drinking earlier and Tracy Sorex all remained in the Bird's Nest until 11 p.m. when your husband and Tracy Sorex left together and walked in a very roundabout way to 28, Old City Road, where they both went in at 11.45 p.m., the woman Sorex having opened the front door with a key.

'I then saw that your husband's blue Toyota Estate car was parked on the opposite side of the road to this house. I marked the position of the car in order that I could check in the future if it had been moved. I remained in Old City Road until 1.30 a.m. but saw no one come out of the house. I then left.'

The wave of nausea that had eddied through Bridget since she and Tom had separated now threatened to make her retch. She gulped down the drink in one into her empty stomach where the shock of the alcohol seemed to stop her throwing up and left her feeling dizzy instead.

The report continued: 'I returned to Old City Road at 6.46 a.m. on Thursday, 27th September and checked my marking of the car and am able to say that it had not been moved.

'I have checked on Old City Road on several occasions since and have found that the car is parked in that road most of the time when it is not in use.

'The address you provided in Bristol is being used by your husband as a mail address. He does not live there.

'Thank you for your confidence and I am pleased to have been of assistance.'

After visiting the false address in Bristol that Tom had given her, Bridget had known in her heart that he must be living with the woman, but, in even minimal uncertainty, there is always hope. Seeing the fact in hard official type demolished her precarious self-esteem of only minutes before, and brought a glut of questions.

Biting her lip, she dialled the number of the agency.

'Alan Maxwell,' a man answered briskly.

'It's . . . Bridget Flynn, Tom O'Dare's wife.' She hoped she sounded business-like. 'I've just received your report and there are a few things I would like to ask you. Would you mind?'

'Not at all, Mrs Flynn.' He sounded pleasant and professional.

'Is my . . . Do you think my . . . husband is actually living with this person?' She could not bring herself to say the woman's name.

'I believe so,' Alan Maxwell answered.

'Has he . . . has he been there long?'

'I have a lot of contacts in this city,' the man told her, 'and I understand he has been in Miss Sorex's flat for several weeks.'

Bridget's grip on the receiver was so tight that her knuckles were white as she tried not to burst into tears.

'What is she . . . Can you tell me anything about her?'

'She is aged between eighteen and twenty-two, dark-haired, noticeably thin and wears glasses.' He reeled off the description with the fluency of long practice.

'Yes, I've seen her,' Bridget told him. 'But what does she do?'

'She works in the advertising department, selling space in the local daily newspaper.'

'What is she like . . . as a person, I mean? Is she clever?'

'I wouldn't say she was particularly intelligent but she handles your husband very cleverly,' Alan Maxwell commented.

'Oh?'

'She treats him like an overgrown schoolboy. She lets him dominate all the conversation. She never expresses an opinion and she makes it appear to him as though she defers to him in everything.'

Oh God, Bridget thought. She had never even begun to understand that type of woman, although she had observed a few and the power they exerted over men.

'Do you think . . .?' It was very difficult to formulate what she wanted to know. 'The relationship . . . is it really serious?'

'Your husband is extremely affectionate towards Miss Sorex in public.'

Bridget squeezed her eyes shut. She had asked the wrong question. She had not wanted to hear that.

'Tom . . . my husband . . . what do people . . .? How is he regarded?'

'Well, he's a hard-drinking man, Mrs Flynn.' Bridget wondered whether she heard approval there. Men always seemed to admire other men who drank. 'And, of course, he's very well-breeched.'

'What makes you think that?' She was surprised.

'He's always extremely well-dressed and he certainly spends a lot of money,' the man said. 'It's a case of "Don't buy me a drink. I'll buy you one." I believe that, before coming to Bristol, he sold his business for a good profit and that the marital home is a valuable property.'

'Appearances deceive, Mr Maxwell,' was Bridget's terse observation.

So the two thousand pounds had been blown on buying rounds and being the life and soul of the bar to impress the mousetrap. It was a replay of the other affair. Another woman lagging behind the opportunities and excitements of life being bowled over by Tom's tales of glory and flashing banknotes and references to his big house.

Bridget remembered the c.v. she had invented for him when, desperate for work, he had wanted to try for the Bristol job, but was afraid of not getting it. To obscure the fiascos of the previous three years, she had written that he had recently sold the news service as a going concern, and she had typed his letter of application on the old business-headed paper.

What goes round comes round, she thought. No wonder everyone thought he was loaded and the mouse-trap was so eager.

Yes, it was different from the last time. Although she yearned for Tom with such heartache, Bridget could not bring herself to make any gesture to try to alter the situation or stop the divorce. Nor did she feel able to talk to her friends. After all, what could they say? And Deirdre could not be upset during her pregnancy. This time she had to manage on her own.

If, as she believed, underneath everything Tom did not really want to lose their life together, he had to make the moves to save them. But he would not. He saw her decision to divorce him as rejection and he could not face rejection.

Even honesty on her part would only exacerbate the predicament. Her instinct was to go and see him and openly discuss the idea she thought could be the remedy, that they should live their separate lives, but keep in touch on friendly terms and then perhaps, in a year or two, begin to see each other again.

But Bridget knew that Tom would see such an approach from her as weakness and he would use it to knock her down, to pay her back for going through with the divorce.

In fact, they were both trapped; he by having given in to an impulse which had led to consequences he had never envisaged and which was forcing him along a route he did not fundamentally want to follow, and she by being unable to accept his behaviour, while still loving him. All she could do was try to keep the peace between them somehow.

When she told him she was in financial trouble and needed his help, he agreed immediately. It sounded too easy, but Bridget did not want to give him any reason to be aggressive. She was not going to mention the £2,000 he had spent, or the investigator's report, and she had worked out a figure he would find impossible to refuse.

'I don't want much,' she assured him. 'Now that you are living over there full-time, I realize your expenses have increased.'

'I'm discovering that money doesn't grow on trees,' he laughed.

Because the tree it grew on was me, she reflected wryly.

'I thought about £35 a week.' It sounded better as a weekly figure than a monthly total. 'And I think you can get tax relief on it.'

'That sounds very fair,' Tom agreed. 'Give me your bank account number.'

He told her a joke about some local town councillors. They had always laughed together and she laughed now.

Then she brought up the anonymous telephone calls. There had been another and she had started to leave the receiver off the hook in the evening.

'They're very upsetting, Tom, and it must be someone you know.'

'I bet it's that bastard at the next desk.' Tom sounded angry, although not as outraged as he should have been. 'He's always trying to wind me up.'

'It's a woman. Probably someone who fancied you and is jealous of your girlfriend.'

'I've told you there is no girlfriend,' he insisted with edge.

Bridget said no more. But, after their conversation, although she knew it was foolish, she felt thawed by having heard his voice.

That week she kept busy. There were documents from Eric to sign for the loans, and letters from John, and she had the deed to the Portuguese apartment made out in her name only. The mousetrap was certainly not going to have the chance to parade about there in her bikini.

Then John rang and asked her to come to his office.

The moor had swaddled itself up for winter, the green life of the heather and bracken withdrawn to hibernate underground, leaving only withered stems and dead leaves as dense protection against the coming frosts. Wild horses and deer and foxes had shed their satin summer coats and grown pelts heavily waterproofed with grease. The voucher of fat built up under their skins would buy them time during the months of austerity ahead. The combes had cast their foliage and turned into shadows of massed clouds already pregnant with snow and the valleys were mysterious with mists.

As she crossed Lanacre Bridge, she remembered the night she had been returning home after dinner with Paul and, taking his advice, she had detoured over this river to try to talk to Tom, and Tom had hit her right across the living-room of that awful flat. It seemed a very long time ago.

She walked through the small market-town and up the Dickensian stairs to John's office and sat signing the papers he put before her without reading them. The traffic rumbled by outside the open window and John gave her advice in a monotone which seemed far off. He was annoyed that she had agreed such a low maintenance payment.

'In your financial situation you should have claimed more and had the Court ratify it.' He leant back in his chair and shot her a look of disapprobation. 'I really wish you would not contact him or take any action without consulting me first.'

But she could not pay attention to what he was saying. It was as though she were not wholly present, as though the real Bridget were a long way off in Bristol, near to Tom.

Then her solicitor led her down the stairs again and across the street into the office of another solicitor, a bored stranger after whom she repeated, 'I swear by Almighty God that this is my name and handwriting . . .'

It was a grotesque parody of her wedding day, with no guests and no flowers, only herself swearing her own marriage vows into reverse in a squalid back room.

'. . . and that the contents of this my Affidavit are true.'

As she spoke the words, all her dreams were breaking into shards around her, her rainbow was turning into barbed wire and the dingy, claustrophobic room became symbolic of her life to come.

When they returned to John's office, she broke down, burying her head in her knees and curling her arms over her hair.

'I'm so sorry, Bridget,' John said. He had seen it all

before, but he had also been there when Tom and she married.

'I know,' she sobbed hopelessly. 'I know.'

He took her to a local hotel for a drink, which she accepted out of politeness before driving home, unseeing, across the moor.

It was not Tom's physical presence that she missed. She was solitary by nature and accustomed to being alone all day. It was his spirit, knowing that he was coming home, or was in the garden, or down the road at the pub.

Over the next days she bumbled around aimlessly, like a dog without a master, having no notion of what she should be doing or where she should go, without purpose or direction.

When she came in from another pointless wander round the garden one afternoon, there was a message on the answerphone. 'He took her to a party on Saturday and then they fucked for hours, all night in fact, without stopping, and he told her he'd take her on holiday. They spent yesterday choosing where to go from the Sunday papers and they're going to Tenerife. He's already bought the tickets.

'They're getting married as soon as he's got rid of you. They never stop screwing. She says . . .'

There followed obscene descriptions of where and when and how. Bridget listened, unable to help herself. That she knew Tom was unlikely to have made love in the bath, or against walls, or late at night in the deserted newspaper office, that he could not have stayed such a contorted course, did not prevent the voice from sounding convincing. Bridget sat on her study chair with her head on the desk as the tape ran on and on.

She poured herself half a tumbler of neat gin, drank it

in one gulp and poured another. By the time she went to bed that night, she was drunk.

The divorce papers would have arrived in Bristol and Tom would know by now that she had proof of his adultery and was not going to wait the obligatory two years necessary for divorce on other grounds.

As the event she had instigated took on its own momentum and carried her further and further from him, the anguish of their separation increased to the piercing shriek of an express train speeding through an endless tunnel. Bridget felt so brittle that, had a fly landed on her, she would have turned to ash.

'Tom, I can't stand what's happening to us. I can't,' she told him. What did it matter if she made the move? One of them had to try to stem the haemorrhage.

There was that silence in which she wondered anxiously what was going through his head.

He cleared his throat. 'Bridget, I care for you, but I've found a woman with whom I can come and go as I please. She's so crazy to hang on to me that I can do anything I want,' he said.

Ah Tom. Again. He had to do it, just as she had to erect the Berlin wall of self-defence instantly between them.

'That's not a woman you're describing, Tom. That's a blown-up doll.'

'It's what I want.' He cut her off.

The humiliation of their contact made Bridget view herself with loathing. She saw in the mirror a haggard, ageing, useless woman. He had spelt out that the person she was and all her achievements meant nothing. The plays she had written, the house she had worked so hard to buy, the garden she had created, the family she had maintained almost single-handed, her friends, her intelligence, everything, in fact, that amounted to her life was worthless in comparison with Tracy Sorex, simply because Tracy Sorex was half her age and servile.

Yet beneath the self-disgust there was bewilderment. Tom may usually have put his own interests first, but that did not make him any different from most men and had not cast doubt upon his love for her. Bridget knew that he had loved her for herself, for all that he was now discarding. What baffled her was why, when so many attractive and talented women of all ages had always been drawn to him, he should have chosen two such colourless women with whom to have his affairs. He had confirmed Alan Maxwell's description of Tracy Sorex as a woman who he believed deferred to him in everything, yet Tom had a very low boredom threshold, so the conundrum remained.

As so often happened, she worked out the reason during the night. The blame lay with her. By simply being herself, she had unwittingly always put pressure on him. A woman of impulse, she awoke every morning with her brain in overdrive. She was always thinking up new projects for the house and garden, bombarding him with ideas, asking people to dinner, planning holidays, suggesting changes, altering their plans. She was opinionated and her moods swung without warning. Although sedentary, somehow she generated an unremitting buzz of mental and physical activity.

When Sam and Tom and Deirdre had each at some time said that she was demanding, she had been uncomprehending, believing that because she was tolerant, she must be easy to live with. But she recalled Tom plaintively asking, 'Why can't we do nothing?'

Now Bridget saw that Jane Scott and Tracy Sorex were her complete opposite; women without drive, who did not strive, who sought no extra stimulus and made no demands, women with little or no ambition for whom Tom had been required to do nothing. Their looks did not even come into it. Naturally amusing, extraordinarily worldly in their eyes, he was the only star and neither had the intellect to challenge or surprise him. That was the real secret of their attraction.

Why couldn't I have been more sensitive? she berated herself. And why can't I bite my tongue and shut up? Beside the importance of making him happy, her own personality should have been of no consequence and she should have changed.

If she had been like Jane Scott, whose furniture had probably stayed in exactly the same position for twenty years, who went to the same pub to play the same game on the same evening every week and took her holiday during the same week at the same Spanish resort every year, if she had been docile and placating, she could have held Tom. But she had failed.

Chapter Eighteen

THE room was decorated in neutral colours, magnolia walls and a beige carpet. There were no distracting ornaments or pictures, just two beige armchairs, a very large ashtray and a box of tissues on the window-sill. Bridget walked in as she had done so often three years earlier, sat in the same chair, buried her head in her hands and wept.

Sandra Vicars sat down opposite her.

Bridget cried inconsolably and nakedly, her body shuddering and the tears washing her hands and running out of her nose into her mouth. Sandra Vicars did not move and did not speak. She just sat there quietly.

'It's happened again,' Bridget managed to say at last. 'He's gone off with another woman, and I'm divorcing him, and I can't bear it.'

Three years ago she had come here week after week, month after month, to heal the wound of Tom's affair with Jane Scott, and here she was again.

'Do you want to divorce him?' Sandra Vicars asked.

'No! . . . Yes! . . . No! I've got to. He'll do this again, and again. I can't tell myself it's a mistake this time, not twice,' Bridget spoke despairingly. 'I can't go through this over and over. He'll leave me anyway in the end. But I love him so desperately. I know you think I'm stupid. *I* think I'm stupid.'

'I don't think you're stupid,' Sandra Vicars said. 'Why do you think you're stupid?'

'Because I know he's selfish. I know he plays games with me and he hurts me. I know he doesn't make me feel good and I should write him off. But all I can do is love him and I've lost him and I'm heartbroken. I can't go on without him and there's nothing much stupider than that.'

She rocked and sobbed, clinging to herself with her own arms.

'When you met Tom, what did you feel?'

'He was my saviour,' Bridget recalled. 'After all those years with Sam, he seemed so gentle and so full of fun and so relaxed and certain. He was my saviour.'

'So you have lost your saviour,' Sandra Vicars said in her composed voice.

'Yes,' whispered Bridget, brokenly.

On her first visit to this place, the small, neat woman had seemed to her to be like an absorbent sponge, floating wherever the tide pulled. Dressed unobtrusively and sitting with her legs tidily together and her hands folded in her lap, she could have been of either gender because she gave off no sexuality. She neither liked nor disliked, neither encouraged nor rejected. She was neutral in the war and it was her deliberate effacement of her own personality which had freed Bridget from all inhibitions. Here, in this bare room without a view, there was no competition, no opposition, no criticism. It did not matter what she said. She could be herself.

The counsellor had a way of repeating and rephrasing as questions what Bridget had already said and, in that very first hour, Bridget had thought her not very bright and had become irritated. It was only later, when she thought over their session, she had realized that this was a very clever way of making her listen to herself.

In fact, she quickly appreciated that Sandra Vicars was

something rare, a very subtle and gifted counsellor, who over the months had enabled her to rebuild her shattered confidence without once insinuating her own opinions or advice into the delicate process. In finding Sandra Vicars, she knew she had been extremely lucky and now, mentally corkscrewing into chaos, she had returned to the one place where she might find deliverance.

'I don't know why I love him so. I think about it and think about it and I still don't know,' Bridget told her now. 'But, you see, we are the same. Our mothers were the same, so cold and disapproving, and we both spent so many years locked up in boarding schools and we chose the same profession. We even worked on the same newspaper and lived in the same street without knowing it and we love the same things, animals and the country, and we have the same sense of humour and the same interests. We read each other's thoughts. We're twins.'

'So you have lost your twin. You have lost your saviour and your twin.'

Sandra Vicars did not have to spell out to Bridget that it was not stupid to love her saviour and her twin.

'If I'd been different, if I'd changed, been more aware, less pushy, we would still be together.' She rubbed her eyes, not caring if mascara streaked her face.

'You've told me he was previously married and there were many women in his life before he met you. Were they all like you?'

'He always said I was not like any other woman he knew, but that was the problem.'

'What were the others like?'

Bridget knew they had all been pretty and younger than she, because Tom had once told her that he had never been in love with a woman of her age.

'Was it their intelligence that appealed to him?'

'He said not.'

'Did they have successful careers?'

'They weren't career women, apart from his last girl-friend, and she threw him out.'

'So, apart from her – and she threw him out – none of them was in the least like you?'

'I don't think so.'

'They were pretty and young and unambitious and he left them anyway.'

Bridget had to agree and she knew her counsellor was guiding her to look at the fact that, even if she had transformed herself, Tom would probably have moved on anyway.

'I need him. I really need him, but he'll do it again.' She was back twisting in the same ambush. 'He'll do it again and I can't face living with that, and I can't lose him.'

'I am quite sure that, if you really want him back, he will come back,' Sandra Vicars said.

'I really want him back.'

But she could not humble herself enough to try to win him back because he would cheat on her again, she thought as she drove home.

Each week after that she made her way to the room. Each week they started with the feelings she had as she walked in and each week she cried her eyes out and was released from the crucifixion of the previous seven days. Often, when she stared into another bleak dawn, it was the prospect of that hour to come with Sandra Vicars that persuaded her to carry on.

She learnt that losing Tom was a bereavement. That it

was the same as, and in some ways worse than, losing someone through death. Had Tom died, he would have ceased to exist; she would have known that he had not wanted to leave her and there would have been the good memories of their years together on which to build acceptance.

But Tom had not died. He was still living in a nearby city and he had chosen to betray her. She could not even look back on their time together with the certainty that any of the happy occasions she recalled had not been charades, during which he might have been having other affairs.

Her own failure left her feeling degraded and she learnt that there is no shortcut through grief.

One Friday, Sandra Vicars asked if she were angry with him.

'Sometimes. Not really. Well, never for more than a few minutes. Everyone tells me I should be. I know I should be, but I feel sad for him because he's lost everything he loves,' she replied. 'His home and his garden and his dogs and the life he loves in the village, being greeted and recognized, even watching the Sunday football game with his friends, everything he has spent ten years assembling.'

'You have missed something out,' Sandra Vicars commented.

'What?'

'You mentioned his home and his garden and his dogs and his village life and his friends, but you didn't mention you.'

'And me, I suppose,' Bridget agreed without conviction.

Her counsellor raised her eyebrows and smiled. 'Why do you think you didn't include yourself?'

'Well, I was there for him anyway.'

'And the house and the garden and the dogs and the village life?'

'They were there for him, too.'

'Where did they all come from for Tom?' Sandra Vicars asked her.

Bridget wondered what she meant. 'They were just there.'

'They were just there?'

'Yes.'

'All these things he loves? Did he just stumble across them?'

'No, of course he didn't.' Sometimes she wished Sandra Vicars would not be so obtuse.

'How did he find them?'

'Well, he met me.'

'He met you.'

'Yes.'

'If he had not met you, where would he have been?'

Bridget answered this ridiculous question impatiently. 'I don't know. Somewhere else.'

'But he met you. So where did the house and the garden and the dogs and the village life come from? Where did everything he loves come from?'

Bridget struggled against the question, looking for another answer in the long silence which widened between them.

At last she said, in a very small voice, 'Me.'

Sandra Vicars spoke in her slow level way. 'So, because he has lost *you*, he has lost everything he loves.'

'. . . Yes.'

Deirdre and Barney had once stayed in the house for a

fortnight while Tom and she had been on holiday. When she had returned Bridget had wanted to know if her daughter had enjoyed herself.

'No,' Deirdre answered. 'It wasn't the same and, when we discussed it, we both agreed that it was because you weren't there. We've always felt happy there if you were away for a few days, but this time you were away too long and the house just lost all its atmosphere. It felt deserted.'

Bridget thought over that hour with Sandra Vicars and saw that, in some way which she could not explain, Deirdre was right. Even if Tom and the mousetrap were given the house and they moved in to live there, Bridget knew he would not find what he had loved so dearly again. That had come from her.

Such tiny bonuses were not enough. She was ill. In ten weeks she had lost three and a half stones. The anti-depressants prescribed by her doctor had not worked. Depression bruised her sleep, which shivered and started each night for two or three hours, keeping her on the edge of consciousness until she was suddenly wide awake again in her bitter-smelling bed with rat's tails of hair stuck to her neck, cold sweat running down her sides from under her arms and over her stomach from the creases under her breasts, her thighs and calves slipping against each other, and the nightdress with which she tried to rub them dry already wet through.

Some mornings, with enormous effort, she tried to pick herself up. Tipping out her make-up bag on to the dressing table, she would lean both elbows on the wooden surface and hold tightly on to one wrist with her other hand and try to stop shaking enough to smear lipstick over her mouth. But the red grease always slewed off and a clown gazed back at her from the mirror.

The sight of food was enough to make her vomit and climbing the stairs sometimes made her so faint that she had to stop and hold on to the banisters. Whatever the weather, its colour was charcoal and it was as though she were the source of gravity carrying the weight of the world.

'It goes on and on, all day and all night, every day and every night. I want it to end,' she cried to Sandra Vicars. 'I'm exhausted. I want it to go away.'

'You're grieving and grieving takes time.'

'You don't understand. It's not just how I feel in my head. It's physical. I shake all the time. I sweat. I can't eat. I throw up. My hair is falling out. I can't sleep for more than a couple of hours and then there are such terrible nightmares that I wake up in pieces. Why won't it end? I don't want any more.'

Sandra Vicars said nothing.

Tom was coming home! Most of his belongings were still at the house and he was going to collect them.

Occasionally, they had communicated about the divorce in a guarded, but outwardly cordial way, as though neither wanted to risk cutting off all contact.

Once he said, 'Bridget, we have to talk. There is a lot to talk about. I'll ring you tomorrow.'

At last, she had been certain they were about to reach each other and for the next twenty-four hours she had been immobilized with nerves. But there had been no phone call.

The maintenance they had agreed did not arrive and, at first, he had sworn he'd signed a banker's order. Then he had asked for her bank account number again. She knew he would not pay it. But now he was coming home.

All week Bridget quaked and longed for him, rehearsing the scene from every different angle, swinging between abject pessimism and illogical optimism. She made lists of what she should and should not do. She must remember all his qualities and be friendly and sympathetic. She must keep the door open between them. She must buy in some beer and brandy. She must ensure the house was welcoming. At least, the dogs could be relied upon to play their adoring part.

She drew up tables of the advantages and disadvantages between herself and Tracy Sorex.

TRACY SOREX	BRIDGET
Advantages	*Advantages*
Young	Love
Vulnerable (maybe)	I know him well
Flatters him	I'm good company
Nearest influence	His home and dogs go with me
Sex – temporarily	I carry our responsibilities
Disadvantages	
No personality – boring	*Disadvantages*
He's not naturally 'paternal'	Old
He'll have to carry all the responsibilities. He doesn't like responsibilities	I know him too well
	Divorce has started
Not someone he can show-off	My expectations of him
Expensive	Poor sex life
His age	
Eventually she'll want more	

The overall picture in her favour was superficial. All her devotion and everything she brought to him could seem insignificant when set against youth and constant ego-massage. A woman in her twenties playing at being a little girl for a man as weak as Tom was a formidable opponent and, besides, Bridget could not bring herself to the abasement of making an obvious and visible effort for him.

She packed his possessions in dustbin bags and roamed the house for the whole of the night before he was due to arrive.

He did not come.

'I've got better things to do than hang around waiting for you,' she shouted at him over the telephone.

'I can't leave here.' He was icy. 'I'm on standby for Saudi. They've given me a bleeper.'

Lies. Always lies. No provincial evening paper was going to fork out the money necessary to send their own reporter to the Gulf War. But, petrified of ruining their only chance to meet, she swallowed her pride.

'Oh Tom, I hope they don't send you there. It's dangerous. Let me know what's happening.'

Afterwards, her skin crept at the way she had crawled away from confrontation, letting him think that she had been taken in by the lies. No wonder he despised her and thought she was such a mug.

They arranged that he should come the following Saturday (if, of course, he were not sent to Saudi Arabia) and Bridget went through another brutal week, paralysed half the time, and weaving to and fro, like a demented monkey trapped for research, the other half.

On Saturday morning the telephone rang and she knew he was not coming.

'I'm glad you rang,' she said, before he had time to speak. 'Because I'm going out today, so it would be better if you came next week.'

'Oh. Well, that's all right because I'm still on standby, so I couldn't have come anyway.'

'He's frightened to come home,' she said to Sandra Vicars. 'Frightened of seeing everything that matters to him.'

In the sessions, she picked over her husband's relationship with Tracy Sorex obsessively, wishing she knew more about the other woman. She might just be someone genuinely defenceless and inexperienced who was as terrified as Bridget of losing Tom, but Bridget's gut reaction was that this was not the case.

'Is it possible that he really has found the right woman for him, the person who will make him happy? I mean, if I thought that, it might not be so bad. At least one of us would have come out of all this with something,' she asked Sandra Vicars. 'Do you think he will stay with her for ever?'

'You know him best. What do you think?' Her counsellor played the professional game of turning the query back on her.

'I know you're supposed to answer every question with a question,' Bridget confronted her in return. 'But I want your opinion. You know about people and I need to understand.'

Sandra Vicars smiled. They had developed sufficient understanding over the months for the counsellor to lower her guard very occasionally.

'Children who are rejected go on expecting rejection all their lives,' she began to explain. 'It may be that Tom's mother accepted him when he was born and then rejected him when his father was killed in the war. You once said she resented him because he was not his father.'

'But I didn't reject him. I love him,' Bridget put in.

'He sees the fact that you're divorcing him as rejection.'

'What else can I do?' she asked miserably. 'I can't live with all the lies and the constant threat of other women.'

'Because he was rejected as a child, Tom expects rejection,' Sandra Vicars repeated patiently. 'Although he constantly searches for a different ending to the one he experienced in childhood, at the same time he puts himself in a position where the ending must be the same. If he is not rejected, he pushes at the limits of acceptable behaviour until he has created a situation in which he has to be rejected, because that is what he expects.'

'Supposing I hadn't rejected him?' Bridget asked. 'And what about the women he left before he left me? They didn't reject him. He rejected them.'

'Well, you have said yourself that he was treating you with contempt. Because he was rejected by his mother, subconsciously he cannot believe he is worth loving, so, if someone comes along who loves him, he will ultimately think her contemptible. If you had not rejected him, he would have behaved more and more badly towards you until you did, or he would have gone anyway.'

'So I could never have made it work.' Bridget lit a cigarette and wiped her eyes with one of the tissues from the box which always stood on the window-sill. 'No one will ever make it work with him.'

'It's unlikely. Men with his psychological background cannot be satisfied. However much love and attention are poured into them, they have too little self-esteem to believe it and so they keep demanding more and more proof, or they end up despising the person who loves them.

'From what you have told me of him, to make a relationship work, Tom would need a lot of professional help, not just to face up to his relationship with his mother, but to overcome the damage that caused within himself.'

'Perhaps he'll stay with Tracy Sorex because he's older now,' Bridget suggested.

'He's only a year older than he was last year,' her counsellor pointed out. 'When he was with you.'

Bridget had believed that she wanted Tom's new relationship to fail, but now her reaction was more complicated. If ultimately there proved to be no possibility of saving anything of their own feelings for each other and then his partnership with Tracy Sorex were to fail, the destruction of their marriage and their home and the suffering she was going through would have been for nothing.

Large, sore lumps developed on the joints of her hands. They were hard and red and they distorted her fingers. Her doctor was mystified.

'I've never seen anything like them.' He was frank about his inability to make a diagnosis. 'I can write for an appointment for you to see a specialist, but it might be a good idea to leave them alone for another couple of weeks and see if they go down. I should think they're stress related.'

He looked up from her hands which now trembled all the time.

'You're not going to marry another man like Tom, are you?' He had a benevolent, humorous face and Bridget knew he counselled alcoholics several evenings a week.

'I've no intention of ever marrying again,' she assured him stoutly.

'Ladies like you always seem to get tied up with that kind of man.' He shook his head in mild bafflement over human nature. 'Try not to do it again.

'You know, this sort of relationship breakdown does more than emotional damage. The immune system is also attacked and you become less resistant to disease. It has actually been proved that many women who go through a bad divorce are left with fewer white blood cells with which to fight cancer. You must ease up.'

He had treated Tom's cluster migraines and various aches and pains over the years and Bridget was tempted to ask him more about his opinion of her husband, but felt too embarrassed.

It was simple for him to advise her to ease up, when he did not have to tell her how to achieve this. There was nothing her friends could give, except their patience, and, although going to counselling was certainly a way of unloading herself, it offered no solutions. But, if someone Tom respected were to urge him to think about where this affair was leading and where his life was heading, she was sure he would listen.

Had Gareth, his oldest friend, been a different sort of man, she would have gone to him, but Gareth always felt the safest place to be was on the fence and would never agree to involve himself, and no one in Bristol had known Tom before his arrival at the newspaper office.

In fact, there was one person who could help her. Bridget had been aware of this all along, but the gamble was so threatening that she had shied away from the idea for weeks. If Tom ever discovered, he would never forgive

her. Now, too distraught to be prudent, she sat down and
wrote to Tom's editor.

Dear Mr Martin,
If I were not so desperate I would not be writing this
letter to you asking for your help.

As I am sure you are aware, my husband, Tom
O'Dare, is having an affair with Tracy Sorex. I
cannot describe to you the misery this is causing me,
or the desolation I feel.

My husband is twice the age of this woman.
He is roaring around the town drunk and has
spent a great deal of money on her, which we cannot
afford.

Although the affair has led to divorce proceedings
being started between us, I do not want my marriage
to end because I love Tom.

I feel that, if you could just talk to him off the
record, he would listen to you.

Therefore, I do ask you, please, to consider this
situation and to speak to him for me.

Yours sincerely,

Bridget signed her name, addressed the envelope and
went straight to the postbox with the letter in case she
changed her mind.

Even before Tom rang the doorbell, she had been sick
several times, although there was nothing but bile to
bring up. Then she had taken four Valium pills, which
left her almost catatonic, but at least they stopped her
trembling so that she was able to put on make-up to hide
the black marks under her eyes and her putty-coloured

skin. Bridget knew there was no point in trying to parrot the mousetrap's act of dependent, obedient little woman. Her strength lay in the contrast between them, that she was everything the other was not. At least Tom had to be given the impression that she was looking good and forging ahead with her life.

Afterwards, she could not remember any of the conversation, only that they reflected each other's distrustful faces laminated with bogus smiles. Then he loaded the black plastic dustbin bags into his car and they stared at each other with overbright eyes and as he started up the engine, she turned and walked inside the house.

The second she shut the front door, she knew the whole meeting had been wrong: the pretence, the lack of communication. Each had needed to say so much and neither had been able to risk revealing the slightest susceptibility which could be used by the other. Yet Tom did not want what was happening to them any more than she did. She had read it in his eyes.

By the time Bridget ran outside again, his car had disappeared. Rushing to her own car, she accelerated through the gates without pausing to check for traffic and drove through the village like a hot rod. A stream of cars prevented her from screeching straight on to the main road and she sat panting and swearing at them and finally shot between the moving vehicles to the fury of a driver who had to brake violently to avoid an accident.

There was no sight of Tom's car ahead and she drove like one possessed, overtaking on blind corners, roaring ahead and swerving to avoid last-minute collisions, taking insane chances to pass lorries and tractors, completely oblivious of danger.

At last, she saw the dark blue estate ahead; in a series

of fate-defying moves she was speeding towards it, flashing her lights and sounding her horn. He drew in at the first lay-by and she stopped behind him and ran to sit in his passenger seat.

'Tom, we shouldn't be doing this.' She spoke urgently. 'Everything important is here, everything we've both spent ten years creating. I know there are problems between us and we haven't got it right, but, don't you see, it's because we're married. We should never have married. It doesn't suit us. I've hated being married and so have you. But we have everything in common, we love each other and we like the same things. If we weren't married, we'd be able to handle our money and jobs and all that rubbish separately and we wouldn't feel trapped any more. We could have a different and better relationship. We would be together because we chose to be together and not because we were married. Tom, don't destroy everything.'

Even now, she could not simply tell him that she wanted to stop the divorce and that she needed him. He looked at her impassively and then he turned and stared back at the pile of bin bags into which she had stuffed all his possessions and which he had carried one by one to his car.

'I'll think about it.' He sounded distant. 'But, as you've just said, you hated being married to me.'

He had switched it all round. He knew that was not what she meant, but he had turned it against her.

They drove off in opposite directions. Bridget arrived home mute with misery. She knew this had been their last chance and she had bungled it. She should never have driven after him. He should have left with the image of the solidity and permanence of their home and the impression of her resilience. Instead she had revealed her dependency and he had despised her for it.

The days that followed were like quicksand and, as she was dragged under, she ceased struggling. Once, she half-heartedly thought of telephoning Sue and then remembered that her friend had gone away for a winter holiday somewhere in the sun.

Unable to read, or watch television, or even to listen to music any more, she sat dry-eyed in her room, not bothering to wash or put her clothes on. A future of segregation stared back at her, no one to eat with, to sleep beside or go on holiday with. No one with whom to drink champagne to celebrate the birth of her first grandchild. No one to love. She did not want to join the ranks of mortified lonely women. She just wanted everything to end.

Bridget thought of ways to die. She wanted to die in her bed, quietly; but she did not know the right pills to take. She could draw a bath and wash herself all clean, then run another fresh bath with lots of scented oil and lie listening to music, and just let the live end of an electric extension lead drop into the water; but she did not know if there would be enough current to kill her. She thought of a Roman death, cutting her wrists and lying in the deep hot water until her life bled away, but that would be horrible for the person who found her.

Any unhappiness Deirdre would feel if she died would be more than assuaged by the arrival of the new baby. Her friends would feel sad and come to her funeral and continue with their normal lives. Tom would shed a few crocodile tears and then pretend nothing had happened.

When that morning came, she felt so much better. She

dressed and splashed her face and brushed her hair and went to her study.

There she wrote out her Will, leaving some paintings to Zoe, and one or two keepsakes to friends and her macho gold and silver snake ring with the opals to Sam, who had always wanted it. Everything else went to Deirdre. Then she visited the couple who ran the village post office and asked them to witness the document, without showing them what it was, and she posted it to John.

Arrangements kept her busy all day. The Irish setter rescue centre agreed to take in Erin and Rake, if, as she told them, she had to go abroad. Someone in the village would no doubt want the chickens. In reply to her calm question, Eric replied that there was no suicide clause in her endowment policies and she rang off before he had time to grow concerned.

Letters were written to Zoe and Sam and her son-in-law, Barney, asking him to look after her daughter; and to the police. Then she wrote to Deirdre.

My darling Deirdre,
Try not to be too angry with me. I think I know the pain my death will cause you and I know that suicide is a selfish act.

But my own agony is too great. I know that I have loved Tom too much and I cannot live without him. His leaving has utterly destroyed me.

I have always loved you. I know our relationship has sometimes been difficult because we are so different and you have sometimes felt that I let you down. I am also aware that, being the tormented person I am, I have often put a great burden on you and, for that and for anything else I have done wrong, and for this, I can only say I am sorry.

I shall not be able to see my grandchild, but I know he or she will be wonderful and you will find more than consolation in this new little person. If I could leave my grandchild a gift, it would be self-confidence, a belief in his or her own worth, which I have never had.

In case you cannot manage to take the dogs I have made arrangements for them to be cared for, but please take Quinky. He is no trouble.

The endowment policies will pay off the house and, when it is sold, there should be enough money to be of use to you.

My darling, I cannot go on. Please forgive me. You will get over this. I love you with all my heart, yet I cannot live for you. You must only remember the love.

Try to think that I am at peace now, after such a turbulent and unhappy life. It has all been such a long struggle and I want this end. I should like to be buried in the cemetery under the wood behind the house which I love so much.

Have a happy life and care for yourself and forgive your mother, darling Deirdre.

With all my love,
Mummy

Lastly, she wrote to Tom.

Dearest Tom,
I have written you many letters over the past weeks, but sent none. Some were to beg you to come back to me. Some were lies. Some were ways in which I thought I might be able to cope with this.

But the truth is that I cannot go on living without you. The pain is unendurable, day after day and night after night and with no hope for the future.

Women do become besotted with you, but they become besotted with the image. When I met you, you were not in a position to fool anyone and I fell in love with the real you – faults and all. Yes, I knew you were damaged by the past. We both were. But I always believed you were a good man who genuinely wanted to do the right thing and I didn't expect you always to succeed. Who can always succeed?

I thought you knew that I believed you had saved me. You were my angel. I thought you knew that I have always depended on you totally. Yes, you needed me and I never failed you, but I needed you more. I thought you understood this and that was why you loved me. I am not a strong woman, although I seem so. My strength came from living for you. You were my life.

I thought you understood how helpless I am and that you would never, could never destroy me, because I am so easy to destroy.

Everything, home, work, effort, good and bad depended upon you. Now you have gone, all is gone and I cannot endure the loss of us, the future stretching pointlessly ahead and containing only struggle and isolation from you. To die is to reach my haven.

Bridget, with eternal love

Bridget put an unused cassette into her music centre and the record of Brahms' Third Symphony on the turntable and pressed the play and record buttons and left the room.

Then she carried the garden hose from the shed to the garage where she cut off a length with a kitchen knife and pushed one end into the exhaust pipe of the car, stuffing tightly compressed rags into the gap between the rubber and the metal and hoping that the heat of the exhaust would not burn them. She pulled the other end of the hose round the car and through the driver's window, which she wound up to hold it in place.

Returning to the house, she put the newly recorded Brahms cassette into her tape recorder, collected her duvet and a bottle of sleeping pills from her bedroom and placed them all in her car.

It was already evening. Her preparations had taken all day. No one would call at the house before the next morning. She would be completely undisturbed.

Serenely, she sat down with her dogs in the drawing-room, just waiting until it was time to put them to bed. Then there would be no more travail, no more weariness, no loss, no disappointment, no love, no grief, no passion. There would be nothingness. Everything would stop. Bridget was looking forward to death.

At ten o'clock she let the dogs into the garden and, fifteen minutes later, as they lay down on their rug, she gave each a cuddle and a kiss on the head and heard their tails lazily beating as she left the house.

It was not necessary to light the garage. She closed the doors behind her and switched on the car engine in the dark. Then settling down in the passenger seat, she took some pills with the aid of bottled mineral water and tucked the goosedown quilt around her. The carbon monoxide did not smell too unpleasant. As the glorious music filled her ears, soft warmth diffused through her and she relaxed into a delicious drowsiness. Nothing mattered any more. Everything was being left behind and she had no regrets. Death beckoned as a shining light ahead of her and she went towards it willingly. Finally, Bridget was happy.

Chapter Nineteen

P EOPLE were pulling at her body. Someone was shouting her name.

'Bridget! Bridget! Can you hear me?'

Fluorescent lights blazed into her eyes as they half-opened and blurred figures moved across her vision.

'Bridget! Did you take any other pills besides sleeping pills? What were they? How many pills did you take, Bridget?'

She was lifted and dumped on a flat rubber surface. Her jaws were wrenched apart and a snake was being forced into her mouth. She began to struggle, twisting her head, lashing out, panic swelling her strength, kicking and writhing.

'Hold her! Keep her steady!'

Hands gripped her arms and legs and a living weight pinned her down. She could not move or scream. The back of her throat was being scraped raw as the reptile pushed down her oesophagus. Curdled liquid was splashing into a bucket somewhere.

'Oh Christ!' someone swore as she managed to jerk her body free and the enemy fell on her again and the lights went out.

'Breakfast, Mrs Flynn?'

A cold-eyed nurse set against a high, bare window full of winter was looking down at her.

'I wanted to die. Why didn't you leave me? I want to die.'

Bridget turned her face away and felt all the anguish she thought she had left behind engulf her again. The nurse walked off.

From where she lay, Bridget could see the length of the ward, bed after bed each containing a figure with wispy grey hair and vacant eyes bled of colour and a skeletal neck draped with shrivelled skin and empty bag breasts; old women propped up with pillows, old women being spoonfed, old women clinging on to uniformed arms and shuffling by with short, laboured steps, old women sick and helpless and alone, widowed, deserted and abandoned in this clinical hangar smelling of antiseptic and their own decay, old women groaning.

Bridget shut out the sight of the future and wished they had let her die. Her head felt as though a panga had split it in half, but she must have fallen asleep again.

'If you expected me to send you flowers, you'd have been disappointed. I'd have been disgusted with you if you'd pulled it off.'

Sue's angry voice harangued her. Bridget looked up at her friend and saw that her expression did not match her tone.

'How could you do something so crass? Now get up and come home.'

They were both crying as Sue snatched her clothes from the bedside locker and threw them on the bed.

The same nurse appeared quickly.

'A psychiatrist is coming to see Mrs Flynn,' she told Sue.

'She doesn't need a psychiatrist,' Sue snapped. 'She needs her friends and her home.'

The nurse glared at Bridget and shrugged. Attempted suicide cases were an affront to her profession.

'You gave me the fright of my life,' Sue raged as she tugged a jumper roughly over her friend's head.

Bridget suddenly thought of her daughter.

'You haven't told Deirdre?' she asked fearfully.

'I haven't told anyone,' her friend replied. 'Do you want me to phone Tom?'

'No! No.' Definitely not Tom.

A harassed young doctor came up and took Sue to one side. They kept glancing at her and whispering. Her concentration ebbed so that she was startled to find him standing over her.

'How do you feel?' he asked.

'All right,' she mumbled, shamed by his irritated expression. Of course he had better things to do. He had real patients to heal.

'Do you want to see a psychiatrist?'

She shook her head and then wished she hadn't as the pain chewed at her temples.

'I hope you realize you are a very lucky woman indeed,' he said. 'If your friend had arrived any later, you could have suffered permanent brain damage.'

He obviously thought that she had known someone was going to turn up and save her. She wanted to tell him he was wrong, that it had not been some sort of attention-seeking ruse, but he nodded curtly at Sue and strode off.

Her body felt like a waterbed, her muscles swishing uncontrollably from one side to the other as her friend helped her to stand. Then, just as though she were one of the geriatric women, Sue supported her to the lift and out of the hospital and both staggered to the car-park, where Bridget slumped like a sack of grain in the car.

Sue had returned from Kenya the previous day and, after unpacking and taking a nap, had decided, although it was late in the evening, to visit Bridget to tell her she was home.

As she drove them through the lanes towards the village, her friend told how she had rung the bell of the unlit house, heard the dogs barking and decided that Bridget must have gone to bed early. She had started walking back down the drive and heard the car engine running in the garage.

'I'm not going to nag you, darling, because this is not the time,' she said. 'I felt the way you do when Phil and I split up, but it's not the solution.'

'It would have been the solution for me,' Bridget muttered as the old car rattled through the shrouded November countryside. 'It would all have been over.'

'Well, it's just beginning: a whole new life and a good one. I won't let you let that bastard win, Bridget,' her friend said firmly as they turned into the village high street and passed the thatched, white-washed cottages. 'But we're not going to talk about it any more today. You're going to rest and tomorrow you're going to start afresh.'

Bridget wished she were alone, but she was bustled into bed and, as she lay like a zombie, she could hear her friend laughing with the dogs downstairs and then, still half-drugged, she fell asleep again.

The petals of the chrysanthemums in the vase by the bed were hard and varnished, made of metal, bronze and copper, and the silver brushes on her dressing table and the brass handles of her chest of drawers glittered. The furniture in the room stood out in angular relief against blinding white walls. It was as though Bridget were seeing everything for the first time.

She lay gingerly exploring her state of mind, wondering why everything seemed altered, where all this adamantine brilliance had come from and why she felt as coiled as a spring.

A Moroccan birdcage, shaped like the onion dome of a mosque, hung from a beam in the ceiling and held a stuffed robin. His breast had turned into a ruby and, suddenly, Bridget knew that she was angry, her blood was coursing with anger, she was inhaling anger from the air, she was seeing everything through eyes irradiated with anger. For the first time in months, she was vibrantly alive again, alive with rage.

How shabby Tom had seemed in that Indian restaurant. He had looked like a loser. No wonder she had had no reaction, she thought. Ten years before he had been a clever, witty, golden man with opportunities lying ahead and so much potential. But now he was back where he had started thirty years earlier, in furnished rooms with a mousetrap and a job as a hack on a provincial evening paper. Tom was at the end of the road. And she, Bridget Flynn, had actually tried to kill herself over him.

Still wearing her nightdress, she ran downstairs and out into the garden. The frost crackling under her bare feet and the north wind biting her skin electrified her. The fangs of the laburnum tunnel arched in chevrons over her and beech leaves took flight like wasps from the hedge as she passed. Clouds like tank formations were powered by her passion across the sky and when she looked down the hill the river foamed.

Recollections of the tantrums he had engineered and the servility he had induced in her sandblasted her memory as she stood proudly taking stock of the house and garden. *She* had created all this despite Sam's alcoholism and Tom's inadequacy. Both men had been monumental burdens, but now she was free – and she had never been free before.

Her hands were bruised and icy, but she was too preoccupied to notice as she returned to the kitchen to drink strong black coffee. Freedom put a completely different perspective on everything.

Until then Bridget had believed herself imprisoned by the past, while Tom had been released. But it was he who was tied to his job because of his age, restricted to living in the same town for the rest of his life, limited by a shortage of money, which would diminish even more when he retired, and securely shackled to Tracy Sorex. After all, he could hardly publicly wreck his marriage over some woman and then turn round a few months later and say she wasn't worth it. Tom had used up all his options and was facing a future which would remain as suffocatingly dull as his present, while she had been liberated. She was the one who could now come and go as she pleased and do what she wanted.

Four letters slapped on to the floor in the hall. One was addressed to her from Avon County Council and she did not need to open that. Since he had left home, Tom had run up three hundred pounds of parking fines in her name because, although she had bought the new car for him and had never driven it herself, it still officially belonged to her.

She swore, almost choking on the picture of him cruising around with Tracy Sorex in the shiny estate and leaving it anywhere, still assuming that dear old Bridget would pick up the tab, as always.

Seeing that the second letter was addressed to him from the DVLC in Swansea, she slit the envelope automatically and was stunned to find that it contained a new document for the car, which had now been registered in her husband's name.

Recalling the way he had tried to secure the apartment in Portugal for himself, Bridget was forced to see that he must also have stolen the original registration document from her at about the same time and filled in the Notification of Sale section to have the ownership transferred.

When the DVLC insisted, in answer to her call, that a warning notice had been sent to her asking for confirmation of the transfer, it became obvious that Tom had intercepted this shortly before he left.

Despite the birth of her anger that morning, Bridget subconsciously shied away from thinking too deeply about the scale of his duplicity. Had she taken time to sit down, write out and study the bare facts of his behaviour towards her over the past months, she would have been confronted by the possibility that for ten years she had been living with a man she did not know at all.

Instead, she busied herself writing the necessary instruction to Swansea to revoke the new document. Then she quickly opened the third envelope and the news that the loan on her insurance policies had been granted directed her concentration willingly on to her own financial situation. Then it occurred to her that scrabbling about for more money was unnecessary. The car was worth money. She could take back the car and sell it.

Already, the real significance of the theft had been submerged and the whole incident had been reduced in her mind to the level of yet another minor misdemeanour for which Tom could pay by having to buy himself a fucking car.

Delighted by the shock she was about to deliver, she telephoned his office.

'Can I help you?' a man's voice asked. 'Mr O'Dare is on holiday this week.'

It was as though a custard pie had been thrown in her face. Bridget clenched her teeth and held on to the receiver speechlessly.

'Are you there? Can I help you?' the voice was asking.

'I doubt it,' she managed to answer, at last. 'I'm his wife.'

She dialled another number, her fingers slipping on the buttons, and a woman at the other end confirmed her suspicions.

'I'm afraid Miss Sorex is on holiday.'

'Sod you, you bastard! Sod you!' Bridget hurled her coffee cup and saucer against the wall and, as they smashed to the floor, the dogs shot out of the room with their tails between their legs.

The stimulating idea of taking back the car had caused her to forget the fourth letter that had arrived that morning. Now, the envelope caught her eye and, to distract herself, she opened it.

Dear Mrs Flynn,
Thank you for your letter.

Despite my sympathy with you in your predicament, I am sure you will understand that the management cannot interfere in the private lives of its employees.

I am afraid, therefore, I cannot help you in this matter.

Yours sincerely,
sgnd G. Martin
Editor

They were all in it. His editor, his colleagues, his pub mates. The whole of Bristol was egging on her husband's ridiculous Mills and Boon affair. Bridget wondered whether the wives married to the directors and managers of companies like this realized that, if their own husbands ever strayed, they too would be kicked into the cold just as she was.

So, there the men were, all being chaps together, nudging each other and laughing among themselves, thinking it a great joke, as Tom drunkenly fell all over literally the latest Tracy. And now he had taken her to Tenerife, to tacky Tenerife, for God's sake!

Bridget switched on her word processor and pushed in the disc marked 'Personal' and looked under the group heading 'Tom'. This was where she kept all his business and accounts files. The group was empty. It had been wiped clean and only he could have done that.

Yet there had been no opportunity when he had come home for his belongings and Bridget puzzled over when he could have had access. She even considered whether he might have come to the house while she had been out shopping. Then she remembered that she had gone to London just after telling him she wanted the divorce. During the time she was away, he must have returned home secretly after all, not to bother looking after his dogs, but to remove all trace of his records from the disc.

Opening the bottom drawer of her desk, she took out the back-up disc, only to find the group wiped clean on that, too.

Bridget gave a tight little smile. Since she had once lost the entire research for a play on a faulty disc, she had methodically made three copies of all her work and Tom would not have been aware of the existence of a third disc. Going to a small cupboard, she found it and, as she expected, his complete files came up on the screen.

From her metal cabinet, she drew out all the letters from Tom's bank about overdrafts which she had paid, Court Orders which she had settled, letters of dismissal from firms, evasive letters from the National Union of Journalists and solicitors avoiding being drawn into hopeless causes, and fed them through the copying machine. Then she printed out all the replies she had written for him. Lastly, she typed out the true record of his career and stapled it to a copy of the false c.v. she, herself, had invented for his application for the Bristol job.

She posted them all in reply to the letter from his editor.

'You want him, Mr Martin? You can have him!' she thought.

'I'm cured!' she told Sandra Vicars triumphantly. 'I don't love him any more. I'm furious at the way he's behaved and at myself for having let him get away with it, and I'm getting my own back.'

'Good,' commented her counsellor. 'That sounds as though you've stopped wanting to destroy yourself and turned your anger on to Tom.'

'I'm going to take my car back and I've written to Avon Council telling them that he is responsible for the fines. And I've shopped him to his editor.' Bridget was full of enthusiasm. At last she felt in a position to defend herself. 'I think I'll be all right from now on and I don't really need to come back. I know there are so many people who need your help much more than I do.'

'How are you sleeping?' Sandra Vicars wanted to know.

She did not sleep well, but was too embarrassed to confess the recurring nightmare. Night after night she dreamt of having diarrhoea in public with people all around her and of being horribly ashamed but unable to control and hide herself. She still awoke at four or five o'clock every morning sweating and shaking.

'This has to be your decision, of course, and I shall always be here if you need me,' Sandra Vicars said in her neutral way. 'Your anger is healthy. It shows you are progressing, but recovering from grief is not a steady process. Your emotions will still fluctuate and, although I'm sure you won't go as far down again, I wouldn't advise you to stop taking counselling just yet. Why don't you come at least until Christmas and New Year are over?'

Celebrating her recovery, Bridget bought a new suit with an absurdly short skirt and then went to the hairdresser and had her hair dyed red.

The rest of Britain was deep in snow, with crashed cars and lorries slewed across the motorways and tales of stranded motorists sleeping on the floors of school buildings dominating the television screens and newspapers, but in the West country it was a mild blue day.

A white sun bobbed like a moon along the tops of the hedges as Bridget drove home between the folds of the hills. Smoke rose from every farmhouse chimney and occasionally she passed a red-faced figure standing studying his sheep with a collie at his heels. Soon the earliest lambs would appear, wobbling alongside their dams on unsure legs, their immature cries calling to spring like birds.

Unexpectedly, Bridget began to imagine her coming

grandchild. The baby was due in two weeks' time but, until then, she had not considered the real significance of Deirdre's pregnancy, that a completely new person was about to arrive: someone who would be an intrinsic part of her own life until she died.

Infants had never appealed to her, but she found herself dreaming of holding this first grandchild in her arms and planning to buy a big wooden rocking horse. She visualized the toddler playing in her garden with the dogs and the picnics and treats they would share together, just the two of them.

Granddaughters were supposed to take after the maternal grandmother, she had read somewhere, and could see a naughty little girl with pigtails riding a fat pony just as she had done. She would read stories and spoil her and, as she grew up, her granddaughter would come to stay in the school holidays and then go on to university and bring boyfriends and, eventually, a husband to meet her grandmother.

As she drew up outside the house, Bridget gave an abashed grimace. This was pure escapism from the chaos of her own life. The child would probably be a horror and she was definitely not the sentimental type.

Yet, as the days passed, even her agitation over Tom was patinated by anticipation, as though a miracle was about to happen that would compensate for everything. However much she tried to ridicule herself, she could not stop looking in baby shops at bootees and frilly frocks and teddies. She had never had a real family, no father, no brothers or sisters, no nephews or nieces, but soon Deirdre and Barney and her grandchild would come down from town for weekends and there would be sticky kisses and harmless, happy secrets. There would be bonfires and fireworks on Guy Fawkes nights and Christ-mases with big woollen socks hung from the chimneypiece and birthday parties with an extra candle lit each year until the whole cake was covered with dancing flames.

Each day she telephoned her daughter who was both as jittery as a flea and as insulated as a nut kernel by her approaching maternity and Bridget would smile over this sweet tangency and hug it to herself.

'We thought it was all going to happen last night and Barney took me to hospital, but they sent me home.' Deirdre sounded thoroughly fed up. 'It was a false alarm.'

Bridget felt her own stomach muscles tense. 'I'd better come up.'

'No, honestly, Mummy.' There was a tinge of impa-tience in the reply. 'I've just got a bit of a pain in my back, but I'm fine. It'll be ages yet. There's no point in your driving all this way and having to hang around for days.'

Bridget wanted to belt up to London at the speed of light, but she knew how private her daughter was and how she hated to be fussed over.

'Are you sitting with your feet up?' she asked.

'Yes, Mummy.'

'Well, for God's sake don't do anything strenuous. I decided to start painting our flat and was at the top of a ladder two days before you were born, so don't you do anything so stupid.'

'I'm being very sensible, Mummy.' She could hear the tolerant smile. 'You've nothing to worry about.'

But she did worry, glancing at the clock every few minutes and inventing chores which would keep her near the telephone all day, but not daring to dial her daughter again.

At half past seven, she sat down with the portable phone in her lap and forced herself to watch *Coronation Street*, without the pictures or words making any connection with her brain at all. The minute the episode ended, unable to contain herself any longer, she pressed the memory button on the instrument.

The number rang out, but there was no reply and, in case she had been misrouted, Bridget tried again and waited and waited, thinking her daughter might be in the bathroom or upstairs.

Forgetting there was already a cigarette burning in the ashtray and lighting another, she telephoned the hospital.

Deirdre had been admitted. A nurse on the ward confirmed that she was there.

Bridget felt a great surge of excitement.

'Has she had the baby?'

'Yes.'

'Is she all right?'

'I cannot give out information.' The nurse sounded snippy.

An autocratic ward sister full of her own self-importance, Bridget thought to herself, but she did not care. Her first grandchild had arrived on earth.

'Has she had a boy or a girl?' She was grinning idiotically and already opening the champagne in her mind.

'I'm afraid we cannot give out any information,' the woman repeated. 'You must talk to the father.'

People in official positions seemed to come from a different mould from the rest of humanity. They took such sour enjoyment in spoiling everyone else's pleasure.

'I'm Deirdre's mother,' Bridget protested. 'Surely you can tell me whether the baby's a boy or a girl.'

'No, I can't. You must talk to her husband.'

There was an unnatural timbre in the nurse's tone and a warning frost made Bridget's skin prick.

'There's something wrong. Something's happened to my daughter. You must tell me. What's happened?'

Panic began mobilizing in her.

'I'm afraid I can tell you nothing.' The voice was harshly uncooperative.

'Where's Barney? I want to speak to him.'

'Your daughter's husband has gone home, Mrs Flynn.'

But there was no answer from Deirdre's home although she kept ringing, over and over.

She contacted the hospital again only to be funnelled into the same cul-de-sac.

Inside her head Bridget was screaming. The unthinkable refused to be dammed. The impossible, the incomprehensible invaded mercilessly. Her daughter was dying.

Frantically, she called Zoe. 'Something terrible is happening. They won't tell me anything. Something's happened to Deirdre. Nobody will tell me. Will you go to the hospital?'

The words tumbled out, meaning nothing and meaning everything.

'Stop, babe. Stop and listen,' Zoe cut through. 'If Barney's left the hospital, whatever it is can't be serious, or he'd still be there.'

Somehow the message reached Bridget, who struggled towards the raft of hope being thrown to her.

'He's probably on his way home and he'll ring you as soon as he arrives,' Zoe was saying. 'If you haven't heard in half an hour, I'll drive over to the hospital and find out what's going on.'

'No nurse would sound like that if everything was all right,' she insisted. 'Supposing . . . supposing . . .'

But primitive superstition prevented her from speaking it aloud. If she gave voice to the profane, all creation would end.

'Suppose nothing, babe, because you know nothing. It's probably hospital policy not to tell anybody anything. I mean, if they did tell all the relations about the new babies, the parents would be furious because they want to give out the news of the great event themselves.'

Although this made perfect sense, she was certain that Zoe was wrong.

'Now sit back, pour yourself a large drink, light a fag and wait for Barney's call,' her friend instructed. 'Just think, you've got a wonderful grandchild.'

Bridget did as she was told, but she did not drink the brandy. She sat hunched into her knees and staring dumbly into space. She knew that Deirdre was dead.

The telephone had not even rung out before she grabbed it and heard Barney's voice.

'Bridget.'

'What's happened to Deirdre? What's happened?'

'Deirdre's all right, but it was a very difficult birth.'

Unhappiness emanated from him and filled the room.

'Tell me,' she said.

'She's had a boy.'

Bridget was reaching out, searching down the line, trying to read his mind, bracing herself.

'The baby has Down's syndrome,' he said. 'He has major heart abnormalities and he has Down's syndrome. He is severely handicapped and he may not live.'

Chapter Twenty

BRIDGET ran dementedly through the house, howling like a she-wolf, throwing herself against furniture and battering on walls, tearing out handfuls of her hair and finally kneeling on the floor and curling into a ball with her fists crammed into her eyes, wailing for Deirdre's agony and for the child of all her hopes who had not been born.

From amidst the ruins of her own life she saw her daughter's life destroyed, the years of servitude ahead demolishing the marvellous talent as a painter and making her darling old. As she keened and clamoured, had she believed in God, she would have cursed him to her last breath. She wished that she had never been born that this child could never have come into being.

Barney had told her not to travel to London until the next day and her cries echoed up through the emptiness of the great room to its high ceiling, stressing her isolation and impotence. She wanted to absorb her daughter and change her back into a little girl again and make the nightmare disappear.

When the telephone rang, she fell on it for someone to say that nothing she had been told was true.

Tom's voice.

The telepathy between them was still working. He must have sensed that she was stricken. Weak with gratitude, she knew he would help her.

'Oh Tom. Oh darling.' She told him everything; how

she had believed that Deirdre had died, of waiting through the hours: of terror beyond description. She told him about their grandson.

He murmured soothingly as she sobbed.

'Bridget,' he said at last. 'I know I've let you down, but anything you need, anything Deirdre needs, you have only to ask and I'll do it.'

She wanted him to come home, to cradle her all night and never let her go again.

'Take a large drink,' he said. 'All you can do right now is get drunk and sleep. Call me first thing tomorrow and we'll sort everything out. Bridget, you can depend on me over this.'

She focused on the glass of brandy still sitting on the coffee table, but she could not drink it and, after he had rung off, she remained where she was until dawn, alone with her formless thoughts.

Then, as light filtered over the hill, she knew what she had to do. A baby had been born. She had to arrive at the hospital smiling and cheerful because her daughter had had a baby.

Bridget fed her chickens and dogs and the cat, then she bathed and washed her red hair and set it in heated rollers. She put moisturizer on her face and then foundation. Using a magnifying mirror to ensure perfection, she brushed on dark grey eyeshadow and then light shadow under her brows and pencilled with care along her eyelids. The mascara swept easily over her lashes. She powdered her face and brushed blusher under her cheekbones and painted her lips. Her hands did not shake at all.

She put on her best underwear, combed out her hair, dressed in her new suit and sprayed Joy scent behind her ears and on her wrists.

314

The packages at the bottom of the wardrobe were already wrapped in gift paper, a mahogany carving of an African woman breast-feeding her baby for Deirdre and a knitted woollen scarecrow with a robin on his shoulder and a mouse coming out of his hat for her grandchild. Bridget wondered whether to take them with her, before reminding herself sternly that she was not going to a funeral. Every new baby was a cause for celebration. So she put the presents in her bag and fetched a bottle of champagne from the pantry.

Then she became frightened, frightened of what she would see, frightened of her daughter's face, frightened that she would say the wrong thing or, even worse, that she would break down.

She needed to talk to someone, just for half an hour, someone to give her courage. She needed to talk to Tom.

'I have to pass Bristol on my way,' she told him. 'I wondered . . . I wondered if we could have a quick cup of coffee together.'

'I'm tied up this morning.' He sounded as remote as if he were in another galaxy.

'It would only be for a few minutes.' It was nearly a plea.

'I'm just off out on a job and I won't be back till after lunch.'

Contempt gave her the courage she needed all the way to London.

The people and the smoke in the hospital side room made Bridget blink. At first she could not see her daughter, only Barney and Sam and a number of young women. They were all talking and Sam would not meet her glance. Then she saw Deirdre sitting up against pillows, puffy-faced with black smudges under her eyes and wearing a smile more desperate than tears. There was no baby.

Bridget kissed her daughter's hair and smiled back broadly, laying on the bed the flowers and chocolates she had bought on the motorway. Unsure of what to prepare for, she had left the presents and champagne in the car at the last minute. Then she embraced her son-in-law. The baby was in the special care unit, he told her.

Cards and bouquets covered every surface. The women friends chattered and smoked and Sam cracked the occasional pointless joke and Barney sat in silence and Deirdre tried to join in normally, and Bridget was appalled.

At last she stood up. 'Deirdre is very tired,' she told them. 'And it's time we left.'

She opened the door and waited until they had all trooped out and then turned to say goodbye herself.

'Don't you want to see the baby?' Deirdre asked in a very small voice.

'Of course I do!' Bridget ran back to her. 'I didn't think I'd be allowed to.'

'We'll take you.' Deirdre began getting out of bed.

'Oh darling, don't! I can wait till tomorrow. Please don't get up!'

But Deirdre was already putting on her slippers.

On the way down in the lift, Bridget felt sick and was sure the expression fixed on her face must look more like terminal rictus than that smile she intended.

'We're calling him Patrick,' Barney told her as they entered the dimly lit unit and led her forward.

Bridget took a deep breath.

He lay inside a plastic bubble, a tiny pearl of a baby with a heart-shaped face and translucent skin and auburn hair and wide almond eyes.

Bridget stared and stared and a long forgotten sensation welled up through her body, speeding her pulse and constricting her throat. For he was not lying there sickly and dying. His arms were pumping and his back was arching and his legs were kicking and there was a familiar stubborn expression on his face. Patrick was fighting with all his strength to live. And she knew that the feeling was maternal love.

It did not matter that he was not as she had expected, that her fantasies for his future would never be more than fantasies, that he would never go to university and perhaps never marry. He was her grandson and he would give her sticky kisses and they would go on picnics and share secrets together and she would fill his stocking at Christmas.

Deirdre's eyes were searching her face.

'Do you like him?' she asked, tentatively.

'He's beautiful!' Bridget laughed with pleasure. 'And I'm a grandmama.'

It was David who put his arms around her and Zoe who sat up comforting and talking with her as reality hit her that night. When eventually she went to bed, it was as a woman now inherently troubled for her daughter, but utterly secure in her love of the child.

The idea came, as they usually did, when she woke up and she contacted Sam at once.

The baby was going to need constant medical attention for a long time, visits to doctors and clinics and hospitals, operations and check-ups, and Deirdre and Barney could not drag him round the city on public transport.

'There are some very good offers about on new small cars,' she told her first husband. 'And I'd buy them one myself, but I'm broke, so if you pay half, I'll talk mother

317

into paying the other half and I'll settle the tax and insurance.'

'I'm game,' he replied at once. 'But don't bank on your mother.'

'She can afford it,' Bridget pointed out.

'So?' was all he said.

Her mother was in tears which snuffled down the phone between the words 'tragedy' and 'dreadful, dreadful' and what were they all going to do? And what could she tell her cousin?

Bridget tried to be kind and then put her proposition.

'A car?' Her mother's voice sharpened.

Bridget explained the reasons why she felt that the biggest aid the family could offer Deirdre and Barney and Patrick would be a car.

'Well, I think we should wait and see.' All traces of martyrdom had now gone. 'I'm certainly not prepared to rush out and pay for a car at the moment.'

'Why not?' Bridget demanded. 'It's mid-winter and they're going to need one as soon as they come out of hospital.'

'They might not need one at all,' her mother retorted.

'Of course they will . . .' Bridget began, feeling her temper rising, and then she interpreted. 'What you mean is that they might not need a car because the baby might die.'

'I just think we should wait and see.' Her mother was unfazed.

'Forget it, mother, and hang on to your money,' Bridget snarled. 'I'll buy them a bloody car myself.'

Why do I always imagine that woman will give the right response when she never does and never has? she thought to herself, as bitter memories surfaced.

*

At seventeen Bridget was a virgin, as were most girls of her generation. She was invited to a party by a friend (whose name she had now forgotten) just after they left boarding school and found the house full of braying ex-public schoolboys and alarmingly confident girls. There was a big bowl of punch into which the boys kept pouring bottles. It was sweet and Bridget, who had only ever had the occasional glass of wine, drank several glasses and got drunk. And, while she was drunk, she was raped.

When her period did not come on time that month, she told her friend and her friend put her in touch with a slightly older girl, who gave her a telephone number.

There was no question of having an illegitimate baby and there were no legal abortions in those days, so Bridget rang the number and a harsh-sounding woman answered.

'Seven-thirty next Friday night. Eat a big meal before you come and bring twenty-five quid,' the woman instructed.

She did not have twenty-five pounds, but her closest friend, Liz, had a gold and amethyst necklace which she pawned for Bridget.

Then Bridget told her mother she thought she was pregnant.

Her mother had stared at her for some minutes and then asked, 'What are you going to do?'

'It's all right, Mummy. I won't have a baby. It's all arranged,' Bridget had answered quickly, dreading the tears of disappointment that habitually filled her mother's eyes.

'What do you mean, it's arranged?' her mother asked, boot-faced.

'I'm going to have an . . . an abortion,' Bridget stammered.

'When?'

And she told her the date, which her mother wrote down in her diary.

Bridget and Liz met after college and went to Choy's Chinese restaurant in the King's Road, Chelsea, and ordered an enormous meal, which Bridget ate until she felt she would burst.

Then they took the bus across the river to Battersea.

It was a back-street terrace house, smelling of stale fat. A thin, middle-aged woman, with a cigarette dangling from her mouth, took the money and Liz was left in the front room while Bridget was led into the kitchen.

'Take your knickers off, dear, and get on the table,' the woman said.

There was a black-and-white television blasting out from the corner and a large enamel basin full of bright pink liquid smelling of carbolic from which the woman filled a black rubber syringe.

''Course, you got to be careful you don't get bubbles in you,' she said, fumbling in Bridget's vagina and pushing the syringe up. 'If a bubble gets into the womb, it goes straight to the heart and kills yer.'

The woman pumped the liquid in and filled the syringe again, and then again.

'Dry yourself with this.' She handed Bridget a dirty dish towel. 'And keep walking. No staying in bed tomorrow, or you might stop it and you don't want to have to fork out another twenty-five quid, do yer?'

The two girls stumbled out into the night and walked to Clapham Junction underground station and, on the tube, the pain began and, when they reached King's

Cross, Liz managed to drag Bridget into an empty waiting room where she writhed and doubled up on the wooden bench. The pain had been like a broken glass bottle piercing her bowels and stabbing up into her stomach.

Liz, white-faced with terror, could not go for assistance because they were criminals. Giving, aiding or having an abortion was a crime for which they could be imprisoned. So she fetched some tea. 'It'll do you good. It'll do you good.'

Bridget moaned and grabbled at her stomach in agony and tried to drink the tea because it was good for you.

At last they were able to board the train for St Albans.

Liz's mother was a fat, short lady, who had always worn hats like the dome of the Blue Mosque and flowing, diaphanous garments to Speech Days and looked like a jellyfish. She allowed Liz and Bridget to stay up very late that night and, when Bridget kept disappearing up the stairs to roll silently on the bed, biting her lips in agony, she made no comment.

When Bridget insisted on walking round the garden and walking to the shops in the rain the next day, Liz's mother looked at her shrewdly and said nothing. In the afternoon, she took them both to see a film.

Bridget was wearing a turquoise blue, princess-line coat with a grey, astrakhan collar. While sitting in the cinema she felt lumps coming out of her and she was too frightened to move. When the lights came on and the audience stood up for the national anthem, her blue coat and the seat were soaked in blood. Liz's mother did not say a word, but on the Sunday she fondly kissed Bridget goodbye.

When Bridget arrived home, her mother was sitting reading in the drawing-room.

'It's all right, Mummy. You don't have to worry any more,' Bridget told her. 'I've had the abortion.'

'Really?' said Bridget's mother. 'I thought it was next weekend.'

The matter had never been mentioned again.

Patrick was sent to West Brompton Hospital, which promptly sent him back again.

'They won't treat him,' Deirdre was anguished.

'Why not?' Bridget demanded.

'They don't offer heart surgery to children brought in with Down's syndrome there. They don't think they're worth it.'

'You must be mistaken, darling.' Bridget looked down in disbelief at her grandson lying in her arms. In his sleep he made twitchy little faces, like a puppy. He had refused to die as expected, so they had opened the incubator and brought him to his mother's room. She stroked his petal-soft skin. Surely no one could refuse to give such a beautiful child a chance.

'Apparently a lot of heart surgeons aren't interested in operating on children they don't consider perfect, Mummy.' The bleak disillusion of experience was already stamped over her daughter's young face.

Outrage almost overwhelmed Bridget as she tried to assimilate what was happening to her family.

There was no reason why Patrick should not have a happy life, even though it might not conform to the normal pattern, she thought. Human beings could not be standardized. It was possible to be fulfilled without having all the attributes society took for granted and a child like this might contribute much more than one born with all his faculties who grew up cruel and selfish. How could anyone with the skill to help him turn away?

Yet she knew she had been just as guilty. Before his birth, she, too, had wondered what was the point of keeping severely handicapped babies alive only for them to face futures so lacking in what she had believed was quality. Now she recognized that this was no different from suggesting that those born in poverty should be expunged because they were not rich. In just a few days, so many of her assumptions had been proved wrong.

'West Brompton is only one hospital,' she said to Deirdre, with a stoicism she did not feel. 'There are thousands of others and they can't all be the same.'

Nurses came in and out. Booklets on Down's syndrome and special schools and the back-up services available already littered Deirdre's bed. Tea had just been served from the trolley when the paediatrician arrived.

'Great Ormond Street have agreed to take Patrick, when the time comes,' she told them as she sat down, and Bridget closed her eyes and swallowed hard and hugged the baby to her.

The grey-haired woman and Deirdre talked in low voices of the stuff of horror videos, of blood filling his lungs, holes in his heart, flooding and leaking, the odds against his life.

The baby awoke and looked steadily at his grandmother with a hint of mischief deep in the blue of his eyes. She held him against her breast and felt his light breath against her neck as she nuzzled his fine red hair.

He had given her a purpose. The months and years to come were unimaginable but, whatever they held, her role was quite clear. No matter what her own emotions, she was to provide support and reassurance and hope, to be practical and reliable, to listen, to comfort, to love. Her role was to be a mother and a grandmother.

She left London for Devon and, half-way through the long journey feeling utterly worn out, she pulled into a motorway service station. She bought some magazines in the shop and a hot chocolate in the cafe, sat down and lit a cigarette.

'This is a non-smoking area,' a *Guardian* reader at the next table told her frostily and Bridget burst into tears.

She moved to the far end of the room and sat with her face turned away, no longer able to stop the flow which had been dammed up inside her for days.

Although the place was almost empty, an elderly woman came and sat at the same table. As Bridget silently stared unblinking out of the window with the salty drops running down her cheeks, the woman talked of her family: sons and their wives, grandsons and grand-daughters, of Christmas and the presents she had bought them. She talked of being widowed eight years earlier and of how her husband was always in her thoughts.

'Have faith,' she said, as Bridget stood up to leave. 'In life.'

Reaching home was like being rescued. The wood of the polished floor of the hall was warm, the protective arm of the staircase curled over her, the brass doorhandles were like welcoming lanterns, the kettle steamed cheerily, the dogs smelt earthy and snug. She ignored the signalling answerphone and the pile of letters and that night there was no need to take her customary sleeping pills.

With only a week to go until Christmas, she went out the next morning and bought the largest tree she could find and several boxes of cards to send, although she knew they would all arrive late.

Christmas was the day of the year when most people in personal crisis felt worst through remembering earlier happy festivities. But Tom and she had always quarrelled over erecting and decorating the tree, she recalled as she climbed up and down the ladder hanging glass balls and wooden ornaments and tinsel. In fact, most of the Christmases of her marriage had not lived up to expectation, with Tom ill-at-ease over the whole business. He would be no different with the mousetrap, who would probably give him a Bruce Springsteen record.

The coloured lights went on and she put an old record on the turntable and, as the choir of Winchester Cathedral sang carols, she sat back on the sofa to enjoy the tree. The magic never failed. A fashionably decorated tree in white bows and matching baubles or sparse Scandinavian candles could not have woven the same spell. Bridget was a sentimentalist about Christmas. Each year as she gazed at her tree she was filled with the spirit of the season. Disillusion was replaced by an all-too-transient, uncritical belief in human existence as it should be.

This year she thought of her new grandson and what lay ahead for him and already she knew he would face it all with courage. Although he had been born with so few advantages, he would fight just to survive.

And she thought of Sam and Tom and herself, born with everything – talent, intelligence, good health and looks, and unlimited potential – everything Patrick needed. Yet they had each squandered their gifts, wasting their opportunities and taking for granted what had been offered to them.

She thought with a sense of disgrace of how she had valued life so little that she had tried to throw it away. Possibilities which would never be open to her grandson were still being offered to her. Sitting quietly in the soft light of the Christmas tree and listening to the piping voices of the choirboys, Bridget knew that she must make her future work for her grandson's sake. It was as though, because he had been born with so little and she had so much, she owed it to him to build a new and fulfilling life.

Although Deirdre and Barney had decided to spend Christmas Day by themselves with their son and she was to travel back to London on Boxing Day, Bridget was able to plan for her own day without stress.

Various friends had wanted her to join them, but she had refused their invitations, afraid of being surrounded by unknown members of their families and of feeling like an outsider. This was to be a few hours of peace. She would light a fire and treat the dogs to a walk over the moor and open her presents. She would eat smoked wild Scottish salmon and a pheasant and drink a bottle of fine old claret and play music she had bought specially for the occasion. As the tree filled the room with its enchantment, Bridget looked forward to Christmas.

When she answered the door, their faces were familiar but she did not know the couple standing under the porch.

'You don't know who we are,' the man said in a London accent.

'Of course I do,' Bridget lied. 'How lovely to see you. Come in.'

He was a man of about forty with thick dark hair and sleepy eyes. His wife was exquisite. Her hair had a professional sheen and, when she sat down at Bridget's invitation, she crossed her long legs with the practised elegance of a model. Her make-up was flawless, enhanc-

ing wide, hazel eyes and a classically beautiful mouth.
Her hands were slim and white and pampered, with a
perfect oval of gleaming scarlet nail varnish at the end of
each finger. The couple looked affluent and at ease in
casual designer clothes and they were both suppressing
knowing smiles.

Oh God, Bridget thought to herself. Who are they?

'Would you like a drink?' she asked, playing for time.

'Cyprus,' the man grinned.

Bridget's mind went blank.

'We met you and Tom in Cyprus.'

She vaguely recalled a couple they had met on holiday
some years before and that they had owned a weekend
cottage in a village nearby on Exmoor. Then she remembered how, later, Tom had occasionally mentioned seeing
them in the pub. She smiled back at them with relief.

'You didn't know us, did you?' There was something
very likeable about the amusement on their faces. 'And
you don't remember our names.'

'No,' she admitted, abashed. 'I'm very absent-minded.'

'So I see. I'm Nick and she's Sasha,' he said. 'I hear
Tom got caught with his fingers in the candy. What a
wally.'

They chattered about their cottage and gave her all the
latest gossip from the local.

The self-designated sage of the village had run off with
a woman, who'd only wanted him to put in a new
bathroom for her and had turned him out as soon as the
job was done. Now he was living in a tent, because his
wife would not take him back.

'Must be brass monkeys in this weather,' Nick commented laconically. 'That should shrink his violets.'

There were some very kinky goings-on between a

327

couple who'd moved down from the city and the weirdos who owned the restaurant. The village vamp had got herself a toyboy and some sex-starved moron had been taken to Court for sodomizing a goat.

'I always thought it was sheep-shagging down here. London's evangelical in comparison,' Nick commented.

They all laughed and Bridget felt as though they had known each other for years.

'You're much better value than the local rag,' she told them. 'I never hear anything much now Tom's gone.'

'We'll have to keep you posted then,' Sasha said. 'Can't have you missing out on the fun.'

Nick looked up at the curtain rail which had come partially unscrewed when Bridget pulled the curtains one evening, and despite her protestations that she had been about to repair it, he fetched a ladder.

'I just can't believe Tom,' he said as he completed the job. 'He brought us up to show us the garden in July. You were out somewhere. He and I walked up the hill and looked over that magic view and I told him what a lucky bastard he was. I asked if he could ever imagine leaving this place and he said he had everything a man could want, a wife he loved and a great home, his garden and his dogs. He even said he would stay here till he died and be buried in the village cemetery up there.'

'He left at the beginning of September,' Bridget told them.

'Well, his brain must have gone the wrong way down the motorway. That's all I can say.'

'You'll join us tonight, won't you?' Sasha asked.

It was Christmas Eve and everyone always gathered in the pub where mulled wine was served and they all sang carols until they lost their voices. Bridget and Tom had gone there every year.

'And we're expecting you for Christmas dinner tomorrow,' Nick added.

'Oh no. I couldn't,' Bridget protested, her heart sinking.

'You're not turning us down,' Nick told her.

'I . . . I've everything arranged here,' Bridget told them.

'You got family coming?' he asked.

'Not exactly.'

'What do you mean, not exactly? You mean you're going to sit here on your tod being miserable?'

'It won't be like that at all.' Bridget tried to distance herself, resenting the pressure.

'You bet it won't.' Nick was not going to be put off. 'Because we're picking you up at eight o'clock tonight and collecting you tomorrow.'

As soon as she walked into the pub Bridget knew she should have stayed at home. The brass band from the nearest town was playing and the traditional ashen faggot crackled in the medieval open fireplace and the whole village was singing.

Bridget and Sasha squeezed into a corner while Nick fought through the crowd to fetch the drinks. Last year Tom had been standing at the bar. At five foot ten, he was of average height, but he had always seemed taller than the other men around him. She pictured him in his big sheepskin coat, laughing with their friends and singing in his out-of-tune voice, and the cushioned security she had felt then hovered and mocked her.

More and more people crammed in, bumping past, spilling their beer and shouting to each other. They crushed her against the wall and their faces grew bloated and red and their bonhomie crescendoed and the heat became suffocating. Sasha and Nick yelled cheerfully at her and others she knew roared and waved and as she waved back her heart dissolved into longing for Tom and, from behind the bars of disjunction, she stared out at a party she could never join again.

It should have been enough. He had left her to live with the mousetrap. He had failed to protect her from the vicious telephone calls, which had mercifully stopped. He had neglected their beloved dogs and broken all his promises. He had left her penniless while he had taken the other woman on holiday. Patrick had been born and Tom had not even recognized his existence with a card or a telephone call; yet her daughter was facing problems which were life-consuming, unlike Bridget's tacky soap opera clichés.

It should have been enough to make her hate him unrelentingly and turn her back for ever. But she could not. Bridget had betrayed Tom to his editor and the divorce was going through inexorably, but she still loved him. Each time they talked over the phone, even in anger, she felt soothed just by the sound of his voice. Each time he promised to complete a form or carry out some detail of the divorce, she believed him, although he never kept his word. Not a second of any waking hour passed without his being in her thoughts, without his being part of her.

She supposed it was rather like being the mother of a drug addict, who lied and thieved and committed crimes to feed his addiction. Even knowing there was nothing she could do to stop him destroying himself would not stop her loving him.

Against her immutable love for her husband, all Bridget's resolutions about putting the past behind her did not stand a chance.

Chapter Twenty-One

SURPRISINGLY, Christmas had been enjoyable after all. Sasha and Nick, their parents and two friends had proved jolly and uncomplicated and the day had passed in the sort of laid-back haze produced by a good joint.

Her Boxing Day visit to London had found her grandson still astonishing the medical staff by his progress and, although her daughter had outlined all the appalling possibilities lined up against his future, Bridget had held him and gazed into his eyes and returned home full of optimism, as though she and Patrick had made each other secret promises.

It was the afternoon of New Year's Eve when Gareth appeared with a new companion whom Bridget viewed with interest. This was not one of the ethnic-garbed *ingénues* he usually had in tow. For the first time since they had met, Gareth seemed to have found himself a real woman.

Claire was in her forties, her character strongly etched in the uptilt of her chin and the confidence with which she scrutinized Bridget while they were being introduced. Bridget knew she was either going to like this woman very much or dislike her intensely.

He had been working in the area and, er, it was a long time since they'd seen each other and, um, it was New Year and, well, Tom ... Gareth floundered through his explanation of their visit in his usual vague way.

'Tom came to see us recently with Tracy,' Claire cut in.

Bridget stiffened with indignation and curiosity. Of course she had known her husband would take his new woman to meet his oldest friend, but the knowledge that the two people now in her house had made up a cosy foursome with them raised her hackles. On the other hand, she could not wait to hear their opinion of Tracy Sorex.

'What did you think?' she asked Gareth pointedly and his eyes slid away.

'Well . . . er . . . I suppose introducing a new girlfriend to, er, your friends is always . . . um, you're kind of nervous . . .' he said.

'He introduced me to you as a new girlfriend. Was it the same as that?' Bridget asked, trying to force him to the point.

'No. It was nothing like that. He was absolutely crazy about you.' For once, Gareth managed to give an unhesitating answer.

'He got drunk and she sat there with her head down all evening,' Claire said contemptuously. 'She didn't say more than two words – and girls who sell advertising space for a living are not known for their shyness.'

'Er, for what it's worth . . .' Gareth stood up and poured himself some more coffee, while Bridget sat on the edge of her seat waiting for him to continue. 'Oh, why do I always start to say things . . . and . . . yes . . . well . . . no . . . I'd give it eighteen months if he's left alone and maybe about, um, three years or four, if he's not. It's like, when your marriage breaks up you sort of want to . . . er . . . play the field and Tom's got himself trapped, you know, in another marriage-type situation . . . and, um, she's . . . well, she's boring.'

'The whole visit was awful,' Claire put in. 'The atmosphere was so bad that, in the middle of the night, I left Gareth in bed and went back to my flat because I couldn't stand the thought of seeing them in the morning.'

Bridget leant back against the cushion and felt her muscles go limp. For months there had been no one to give her an objective view of the relationship between Tom and the mousetrap, and she had been left to wonder whether her own assessment were imaginary or realistic.

Claire's opinions were not so important, perhaps, because women often take the side of the injured wife, but Gareth knew Tom very well and, although his male inclination would be to back his friend loyally, Bridget's past experience told her he would not lie to her. She latched on to his comments because they were what she wanted to hear.

Claire was giving him the meaningful look of a woman trying to push a reluctant man towards some previously agreed action and Gareth was fiddling with his beard and shifting in his seat.

'The thing is . . .' he began. 'It's like . . .'

'Bridget, there's something you ought to know,' Claire took over with unconcealed impatience. 'Tom's buying a house.'

The walls of the room clashed together like cymbals. Then Bridget laughed.

'Well, you've certainly got that wrong.' Her voice wavered with nervous incredulity. 'He's got no money.'

'He's been given a hundred per cent, twenty-year mortgage on a house in Bristol.' Claire was unsparing and, as Bridget stared at him, Gareth nodded, almost squirming with discomfort.

They had to be mistaken! She and Tom were still

333

married. He was her husband. Thoughts began scrambling over each other. He could not just go out and buy a house. He was still her husband. He was fifty-two and due to retire in ten years' time with no company pension. No financial institution would give him until he was seventy-two years old to pay off a hundred per cent mortgage.

'He deserves to lose you. You were the best thing that ever happened to him and I really thought he'd made it at last. But he's just gone and screwed up again.' Gareth was suddenly astonishingly lucid. 'You've got to stop being good old Bridget. If you can sort of get rid of him from your head, good for you. Write him off. You don't need all this hassle.'

By the time they left, Bridget was seething. She drove to the next village and knocked on the door of the cottage.

'Great!' exclaimed Sasha. 'We hoped you'd turn up.'

There seemed to be a lot of people in their sitting-room and Nick pushed a drink into her hand. She had completely forgotten it was New Year's Eve.

'I want to ask you a favour,' she said to him.

'Consider it done,' he replied.

She hardly knew them, but social niceties no longer mattered.

'When are you going back to London?' she asked.

'You can't wait to get rid of us, I know,' Sasha teased.

'Day after tomorrow's hangover,' Nick told her.

'Would you drop me off at Bristol?'

'Sounds interesting.' He tapped the side of his nose. 'Whatever it is, I wouldn't miss out on it.'

He was right about the hangover. Bridget awoke feeling like a jelly. As tentatively as a criminal on probation she tiptoed through her essential morning tasks and returned to bed. There was drunk and there was over the horizon and the previous night she had definitely been the latter. She sat, fragile with dehydration and guilt, dismally thinking back to how she had reached the stage of drinking wine straight from the bottle and then fallen over with some man who had been trying to dance with her and broken a coffee table. There was an ominous blackout of her memory after that. God knew what she had done next, but Sasha and Nick would probably never speak to her again.

She thought of telephoning them to apologize. What a way to start a new year. This was supposed to be a time of fresh beginnings and she had not even made a resolution.

As she fretted over whether a letter of apology might be better, a maggot of rebellion wriggled in her mind. George Bernard Shaw had once said, 'I never apologize', but Bridget always grovelled.

Her magnifying make-up mirror was lying on the bedside table and she picked it up and stared into it. Unhealthily yellowed and bloodshot eyes stared back. There were all the lines scored to the depth of troughs by a night of alcohol abuse, but they were her lines and that face was her face and the age she was was her age.

She began to think about who and what she was. She was hot-tempered and she was generous, impatient with fools and tolerant of failings, obsessively loving and often insensitively unobservant. She was usually too soft, but that could change into ruthlessness. She wrote, cooked and gardened well. She couldn't add up and was indiscreet. She loved gossip and she smoked. That was the package and the package was her.

It occurred to her that the people who accepted her for what she was were those who really cared and those who did not should be irrelevant because, for the very first time, Bridget discovered that she actually quite liked herself, faults and all.

This is me, she thought, slightly wary of her own boldness. And, from now on, anyone who does not accept the whole package can get stuffed.

It was a New Year's resolution.

As she looked over the past from this unfamiliar angle, the perspective of her situation gradually became clear.

Her first choice, to spend the rest of her life with Tom, was no longer on offer to her and somehow she had to accept this. She admitted her real wish to keep the door open between them and her hope that eventually they might form a new and different relationship; but she recognized that such a prospect was very far off at best and might never happen. In the meantime, vague ideas of creating another life had to be turned into practice. Only she did not know where to start when there was nothing left to build on.

No. That was wrong. *She* existed. And Deirdre and Patrick and Barney and her friends were there for her. Everything good untouched by misfortune began to reveal itself; her home, her dogs, her work; the solid foundations for the future were still in place.

Of course nothing would happen without action on her part, she thought. A new life resulted from going out more and making breaks and having adventures.

Bridget picked up her writing pad and wrote down everything she enjoyed, ranging from the countryside and travelling to churches and films. The list grew quite long and there were organizations associated with each of her interests which she could join.

Then she scribbled down interests which there had never been time to pursue: astronomy, learning to ski, learning to fly, travelling the entire length of the Rift Valley, taking the trans-Siberian train.

Finally, she printed the words 'Singles Clubs?' and immediately crossed through them. The meat market was out. Any man was not better than no man. She wanted to make new friends, not be up for grabs.

As though by telepathy the telephone rang.

'Happy New Year, babe,' Zoe said. 'We're giving a dinner party next weekend. Why don't you come up to town? There's someone we want you to meet.'

This was the start. She was pleased. Bridget had not been unattached for long enough to have learnt about the matchmaking enterprises of friends.

She had been ready for an hour when Nick and Sasha drew up at the door and she was rewarded for the care she had taken to look her best by an appreciative little whistle. Neither of them mentioned the broken coffee table.

'I'm looking forward to telling Tom what I think of him,' Nick announced as he started up the car.

'Oh no, don't do that,' Bridget stopped on the point of fastening her seat belt. 'You must promise you won't do that.'

He looked doubtful.

'Promise you won't,' she insisted. 'Or we can't go. There's not going to be a scene.'

'OK. But that's what he needs.'

Music from Radio One filled the car and the motorway flashed past as they sped up the outside lane, but Bridget was too deep in thought to notice either. As they reached

337

the outskirts of Bristol, the palms of her hands became damp and she physically braced herself, sitting up and straightening her shoulders.

Nick and Sasha refused to leave her in the city centre to take taxis to the various public houses which the private investigator had told her Tom used. Instead they drove around and Nick went into each and came out shaking his head until they came to the last on the list.

'I'll go this time,' Bridget decided.

The Bird's Nest was a run-down building on the corner of a street. As she walked in, a couple of girls with kohl-lined eyes glanced over sullenly from behind the beer handles and she just had time to register that providing comfort was obviously not the aim of this remarkably squalid establishment when she saw Tom and Tracy Sorex sitting hunched over the bar. They both seemed to be staring into their pint glasses without speaking or looking at each other, just as they had sat eating their food in the Indian restaurant.

Bridget walked up softly and stood behind Tom.

'I want my car back,' she said.

He twisted round.

'I haven't got the keys on me.' When he wished, he had always been able to control his reactions with mercurial speed.

'Then get them.'

The woman had tucked her chin into her neck, so that her long hair hid her features.

Tom decided to brazen it out. 'I'll come in a minute.'

Bridget stepped back a couple of paces. A complete silence had fallen over the seedy room.

'Now, Thomas!' she commanded, projecting her voice so that everyone's curiosity was satisfied.

Then she tapped his companion on the shoulder. 'You are very stupid,' Bridget told her. 'You don't know what sort of man you've got hold of there.'

She was rewarded with the briefest glimpse of a rabbity face, the face that had wrecked her marriage and her life.

A man, with the immaculate perfection of a gormless visage and the muscles of a professional gorilla, flexed into view. Bridget left.

Tom followed her out and, not seeing Nick and Sasha in the parked car, began striding up the hill ahead of her.

Bridget hurried behind, glaring at his back, hearing again the unknown woman's voice on the telephone describing what he and Tracy Sorex did together and remembering how she had lain on the floor after one of the calls with such a pain in her chest that she had believed it to be a heart attack. There was Tom strutting ahead, unconcerned by the anguish and mortification they had both caused her, untouched by her attempted suicide which had so nearly succeeded.

'You cunt!' she shrieked suddenly, catching up with him. 'You know I've been tormented with filthy telephone calls and you must know who's been making them and you've done nothing about it . . . nothing . . . You didn't care . . .'

The words poured out and the effort of climbing the hill made her so breathless that she gagged on some of them.

'I don't know who it is!' Tom stopped and stared at his wife, his face pulled down so tightly there could have been a tourniquet under his chin. It was not the expression of a swaggering man.

'I suppose you give the whole office a blow-by-blow account every time you have a screw?' Bridget was leaning back against a garden railing, gulping in air. 'So it could be any of them.'

'No, I don't! And I don't know who's responsible for the calls!' In the yellow street-light he looked like a tortured animal.

'You don't want to know, because you couldn't care less.' All she could think about was her own pain. 'And you couldn't care less because some stupid cow sits on your face every night and that's all you do care about.'

'I'm ill. I can't stand all this. I'm having the worst migraines I've ever had and it's all your fault,' he shouted, holding his head.

Fury and pity warred through her, and fury won.

'My fault! You haven't heard a word from me in weeks. It's not my bloody fault. If you're on a migraine cycle, you'd better look for someone else to blame, someone a lot closer.' She was half-aware of Nick's car driving slowly by and she wanted to hit Tom and shake him and pull him to her and stop screaming, but she couldn't. 'Only it's easier to blame me, isn't it? Just blame Bridget and you don't have to take a good look at your mousetrap and you don't have to see where you're going. Well, I tell you this, any woman who can do what she has done to another woman is not the poor, sweet, little Miss Clean she's play-acting at being and, when the time comes, you're not going to be able to offload this one the way you've shaken off all the others, Tom O'Dare, because you are not in control here. She is.'

They had started stumbling on while she was savaging him and now they reached the door of a terrace house. Tom opened it, walked in and stopped. He looked back at her as though he wanted her to follow, but there was an invisible, impenetrable barrier across the threshold.

This was where he lived with Tracy Sorex and, if she saw the room where they ate and read newspapers side by side and did all the simple things a couple do together, the image would never leave her.

When he returned down the stairs, they walked up the rest of the hill without speaking until they reached a car-park. Bridget took the keys and got into the car while he held the door. He opened his mouth, as though to say something, and she slammed the door out of his grasp. While she started the engine and backed out of the space, he still stood staring at her.

Nick's car passed without stopping and Bridget drove round the car-park. When she reached the exit, Tom was already waiting there. He took a step forward so that she had to brake. There was a look of utter despair on his face. Bridget jerked her head away and put her foot on the accelerator.

She drove Tom's car towards London, relieved that Nick was a driver who ignored the seventy-mile-an-hour limit and she could follow without having to pay much attention but at a speed which suited her churning emotions. If Tom had been bumptious and unaffected, her self-righteousness would have been bolstered, but he had looked ill and unhappy, more unhappy than she had ever seen him. Yet he was still forging ahead and putting himself in a position from which he would never be able to extricate himself.

Nick's car indicated at the turn off to a service station and, when they had parked, Sasha ran back to ask if she was all right.

Bridget tried to smile and nod.

'You look as though you need a drink, but a coffee will have to do,' her new friend said.

They sat down in the unflattering light and the smell of onions as a coachload of football supporters arrived, singing and shoving at each other, throwing empty beer cans on the floor and one vomiting as they jostled to the food counter.

'We are the champions!'

Timid men and women scurried out and Nick folded his arms. Sasha, cool and beautiful, went on talking as though they were having tea at the Savoy.

'Are you going to sell the car?'

'No,' Bridget answered. 'I'm giving it to Deirdre. It's a surprise. She needs it far more than Tom O'Dare, so I'm going to leave it in London and return home in a few days by train.'

The football fans had bundled to the far end of the restaurant and were brawling among themselves and Nick had relaxed.

'Well, you certainly let it all hang out back there,' he grinned. 'Are you feeling better?'

'No,' she admitted.

'You'd have him back tomorrow. You know you would.'

That sleepy look in his eyes was deceptive. Nick didn't miss a trick.

'I would, but I couldn't.' She summed up the dilemma that had set her against herself since the beginning. 'He's done this before and he would do the same again.'

'The man's on a rollercoaster he can't get off,' Nick said.

'Why can't he get off?' Bridget asked with some belligerence.

'Look, he's backed himself into a corner. He thought he was going to have a bit on the side and now you're divorcing him and he's stuck with it.' He dropped his arm over the back of his chair and stretched out his legs. 'What do you expect him to do?'

'If he's in a situation he doesn't want to be in, why the hell doesn't he just say so?' Bridget demanded.

He shook his head at her. 'You don't know much about blokes, Bridget. They don't work like that.'

'Why not?'

'All right. Supposing he turned up at the house and said he'd made a total cock-up and wanted to come back, what would you do?' he asked.

'I'd tell him to piss off.'

'Exactly.'

'He could hardly expect just to be able to walk back into my open arms. But if I really mattered to him, he'd keep trying,' she argued.

'That's not the way it goes. He wouldn't risk you telling him to piss off in the first place.'

'Why not? He knows I love him. He knows.'

'Maybe. But he knows he's blown it.' Nick took a bite out of his sandwich and ruminated while he chewed it. The football supporters began pushing their way out, jamming each other in the doorway and falling over their trainers.

'I really like Tom, you know,' Nick went on, looking at her questioningly. 'He's a mate and I'd like to see him again.'

Bridget knew he was asking her permission and her immediate impulse was to wave a hand and tell him to feel free, but she recalled her revulsion over Gareth's news of Tom's visit with Tracy Sorex and she could not.

'I know it's unreasonable. I'm being unreasonable,' she began, avoiding Nick's eyes and talking to Sasha. They

343

had adopted her over Christmas and she wanted their friendship. 'But, right now, well, I don't think I could handle you and Nick and Tom and that woman all going out for jollies together. I mean, I'll get there in the end. Eventually it won't matter. But it's too early.'

It was a cheek. They were his friends and they hardly knew her. Yet, although she did not want to offend them, she was asking them to choose between her and Tom.

'I'm sorry,' she added, miserably.

'It's OK, Bridget. Honestly,' Sasha said.

'No sweat.' Nick winked at her and she was sure he meant it.

The table was set with black octagonal plates and Scandinavian glasses of Presbyterian design and knives and forks which were of such symmetry that it was hard to tell one from the other. The central light was pulled down so low and so darkly shaded that the faces of the men seated on either side of Bridget were indistinct.

She had not been to a London dinner party for years, but it took very few minutes to realize that nothing had changed. They still talked about recalcitrant nannies, school fees and the train service. Yet there was a sophistication to which she was no longer accustomed and which she found exciting.

Country people roasted great joints of meat and provided a selection of three or four puddings when entertaining their friends and the food was piled high to satisfy Devon appetites. They discussed cattle prices and the different merits of solid fuel versus oil-fired central heating. The animated arguments over politics or current affairs which accompanied the brandy and left a London hostess feeling the evening had been a success would have been considered very bad form in the country, where differences of opinion were taken as personal affronts.

The city men dressed less formally and the women, with their understated haircuts and clothes and winter sports tans and manicured hands, had a self-possession denied their more traditional sisters. There was no division here into men's business and women's gossip.

'Come and meet Colin. He's a doctor and works in research,' Zoe had said as she relieved Bridget of her coat. 'He's a real sweetie. You'll love him.'

Opening the door to the living-room from the hall, she had added *sotto voce*, 'He's divorced.' And this had been followed by a significant look as she introduced them.

He was a rather short, overweight man who drew air up his nose in what was almost a pompous sniff when they shook hands.

As each course, arranged like a collage and occupying no more than a couple of mouthfuls, was served, Colin had ample opportunity to tell Bridget about himself. The test-tube by test-tube description of his work on female fertility had lasted through the warm chicken liver salad with yoghurt dressing, the fish course and the sorbet.

'Have you always worked in the same field?' she asked, politely, hoping for a change of subject half-way through the stuffed quail.

'Oh no. I spent ten years on contraception.'

'A contradictory career,' she observed, but her remark was lost on him.

He continued as though she had not spoken and contraception proved to be tediously similar to fertility after all. Both seemed to have a lot to do with urine samples.

Bridget tried to look interested. She nodded with slow appreciation. She fixed an intelligent expression on her face. She encouraged. She appeared impressed. She flagged.

When the German au pair and the Sloane hired to do the cooking arrived to clear the table and they all adjourned to the large sitting-room, she saw her chance to escape, but Zoe manoeuvred her firmly on to a sofa next to Colin again.

'When's your divorce coming through, babe?' her friend asked pointedly.

As the other guests focused on her, she felt like a frozen turkey being offered to a man who probably wanted a baron of beef.

'I'm not sure. Not long,' she mumbled, conscious of flushing unbecomingly.

'You must have been divorced about two years now, haven't you, Colin?' Zoe smiled with the brilliance of a cleaver.

'Two and a half, and the bitch has just applied for an increase in maintenance,' he answered savagely.

'She's living with some toyboy,' he said to Bridget as Zoe sat back looking smug. 'And I'm damned if I'm going to pay another penny towards his upkeep.'

Bridget murmured something she hoped sounded sympathetic – and an inner voice began to ask insistently, 'What about the package?'

'Mind you,' he went on. 'She regrets it. She'd have me back tomorrow, if she could.'

David's generous topping up of her wine glass throughout the meal had taken effect and she stood up to go to the lavatory.

'Turn round,' Colin said.

She looked at him, puzzled.

'Go on. Turn round,' he repeated. 'I want to see if you have a nice bum.'

Aware that everyone in the room was watching again, Bridget turned a full circle very slowly until she was facing him.

'I don't suppose there's any point in asking if you're well hung, Colin,' she said sweetly. 'Because you'd be bound to say you are and I'm quite sure you're not.'

There was a stunned silence. Then David gave a guffaw of laughter and the others joined in; all except Colin.

'If you don't curb that acerbic tongue of yours, you'll never get another man, babe,' Zoe told her, crossly, over a final drink before they went to bed.

'The last thing I want is another fucking man,' Bridget retorted. 'And, even if I did, I could do better than that.'

'Colin's seriously looking for a new wife.' Zoe wagged a finger at her. 'And he's loaded.'

'I bet he's not,' Bridget giggled. 'I hit the bull's-eye there. Did you see his face?'

'You're impossible.' Zoe was exasperated. 'You're going to have to learn to pander to them a bit.'

'No, Zoe. I'm not. Listen, I spent the entire evening flattering that bore. He didn't ask me a single question about myself. He didn't make any attempt to be entertaining. He certainly didn't try to flatter me. He was too busy being self-obsessed; and I fell right back into the simpering, wide-eyed crap we all put on for them.' Bridget was furious with herself. 'What about the package?'

'What package?'

'Me. The package that is me.'

Zoe looked at her as though it was all too obvious that she had drink taken.

'I wasn't being me,' Bridget tried to explain. 'Just because some man was sitting next to me, I put on a completely artificial performance, because he expected it.

I should have told him he was leaden enough to reduce a Porsche to a donkey cart.'

'Thank God you didn't.' Zoe's eyes went heavenwards. 'You did quite enough damage. He'll never lift his head again.'

'Or anything else, with luck.'

'There you go,' Zoe scolded. 'You've got to stop it, babe.'

'No. That's how I am.' Bridget drained her glass and looked intently at her friend, determined to make her understand. 'I've thought it all out, Zoe. I am what I am. I say what I say. I do what I do and, from now on, that's the way it is. People can either accept me as I am, or bugger off. I'm on my own terms – especially with men.'

'You're going to have a hard time, then, babe,' Zoe warned.

'Not half as hard as it's been up to now,' Bridget replied with conviction.

Patrick was allowed home and Deirdre was measuring drops of various medicines into little milk bottles. She was struggling with a combination of breast and bottle feeding and Bridget watched as the baby took tiny amounts and then stopped, gasping for breath.

'He's just not taking enough,' the new mother said worriedly. 'Sometimes I spend over an hour trying to get him to feed, but he hasn't the strength.'

Bridget looked at her daughter's exhausted face and forgot about her own troubles. Your children are always your children, she thought to herself, and although Deirdre was a grown woman, she still seemed like her little lamb and little lambs should not have to carry terrible burdens.

'Will you come with me to see the specialist this afternoon?' Deirdre asked. 'Every time I have an appointment with another expert I don't seem to remember a word I'm told. I sit there and his mouth moves and I just feel frightened.'

The waiting room in the hospital was full of tired women and pale-faced children, each one of whose lives was under threat. The children played with the toys with noisy determination, as though defying their illnesses.

'We're lucky to be here.' Deirdre was pressing her son's small nose and tickling his tummy and blowing against his cheeks. 'This consultant specializes in Down's syndrome children with heart defects. That's why there are so many here.'

Bridget had not even noticed that most of the children in the room were like her grandson and, as they enjoyed themselves all around her, she felt the same sense of outrage she had felt on first learning that so many were just abandoned to die.

The heart specialist examined the baby with a gentle affection that belied the violence of his words. Bridget glanced at Deirdre's frozen face and shut down her own feelings of horror in order to concentrate on what they were being told.

The septum separating the chambers of Patrick's heart was missing and so oxygenated and unoxygenated blood was swirling and intermingling there, he explained. Because the valves could not do their job properly, pressure built up and the blood was flowing too fast into the lungs leading to the danger of their being flooded.

There was no alternative to open-heart surgery — to construct a septum from spare tissue and repair two more holes. The only question was the timing of the operation, which should be done the later the better to give the baby time to grow bigger and stronger before undergoing such trauma.

After the consultation, Bridget and Deirdre drove into Richmond Park and drew up among the trees.

'Will you tell Barney what he said?' Deirdre asked.

'Of course.'

They sat quietly for a while looking out at the soporific winter landscape and recovering from the past two hours.

Dogs greeted each other familiarly, two old English sheepdogs, a Welsh collie and a mongrel. Their owners, men who had left their wives in the warmth of the central heating, tramped across the grass. Bridget absently wondered what they thought about: their jobs, sport, opening time? How did they work out their problems? Deal with emotion? Reach their conclusions? They were all a mystery to her.

Crows plodded about and a bald jogger laboured through the trees and a tall, elderly man, who looked just like Sophie's husband, Julian, strode by in whites, determined to play tennis despite the cold.

Deirdre and Bridget had grown very close since the baby's birth. Unspoken misunderstandings reaching back into her daughter's own childhood had been smoothed away without reference to the past. Even Barney, whose reserve had always rather alarmed his mother-in-law, was now affectionate.

'I never thought you'd react like this,' Deirdre said at last.

'Like what?' Bridget had been trying very hard not to react and worried that she had been giving the wrong signals.

'Barney and I thought you'd crack up over Patrick.'

Her daughter was looking at her with a little frown. 'I mean, you always get into such a state over crises.'

'Only over my own nonsensical relationships. Never over anything important.' Secretly she had surprised herself and questioned whether her response could be some form of retreat from her own failure.

'But you don't like children.'

'Patrick isn't children. He's part of me. He's my grandson.'

Becoming a grandparent was like becoming a parent for the first time, she thought. Until it happened, you had no idea of what it really meant. Suddenly there was this baby, who had come from her through her own child, untouched by guile, utterly pure. All the disappointments and regrets she had experienced only made this new life more miraculous.

'You do like him, don't you?' Deirdre anxiously pressed her mother for the umpteenth time.

Bridget looked at the sleeping child.

'I love him with all my heart.' It was the simple truth.

Chapter Twenty-Two

HER grandson haunted her conscience. Since his birth, Bridget had become conscious of the limits of time, that an average lifespan was the equivalent of a few seconds and that she had reached the last second. An unspoken pact had been made with him that she would not waste what was left and, however sorely she was tempted to hide herself away, she knew that could only lead to a barren existence.

When she reluctantly drove to town to join the film society, it was the first time that she had ever gone to somewhere unknown entirely on her own, without the backing of a husband and family behind her.

Twenty or thirty strangers sitting on hard wooden chairs surrounded her in the library while an out-of-focus foreign film flickered on the screen. She was still so unnerved by the events surrounding Christmas and New Year that she could not take in any of it.

When the tea interval came, the strangers mingled with each other and one or two glanced over, then looked away. In the past, Tom, just by his existence, had been imperceptibly present wherever she went, confirming her place in society and who she was. Now she was no longer part of the structure of couples introducing their partners to each other, connected through business or neighbourhood, widening their circles through meeting other couples while entertaining each other. She was flotsam and, in this room where no one spoke to her, she felt stripped naked.

Throughout the second film, she sat unseeing, too self-conscious to draw attention to herself by leaving, aware only of the stretched-out minutes.

When the end came, Bridget crept from the building, a woman on her own unnoticed by anyone, and sobbed bitterly all the way home.

But, after each session with her counsellor and as each week loomed ahead, she tried something new to break free from the cage of the past – a lecture on eighteenth-century Bath where she arrived and sat alone in a crowded room and left without exchanging a word with anyone; a meal with two acquaintances determined not to mention Tom, when he was all she could think about; and, finally, a skiing lesson with a lot of teenagers, who got the hang of it in minutes and sniggered among themselves every time she fell over.

With her legs and hands skinned from the dry ski-slope and every aching muscle proclaiming that she was a geriatric, Bridget returned home to find Beverley standing in the porch with a suitcase beside her.

Since her days as a public relations officer, Beverley had moved on, returning first to journalism, becoming woman's editor of a major provincial newspaper and rapidly progressing until now she was the features editor of a national daily.

They met frequently for lunch in London and Beverley had not changed. There was still the same freshness and honesty about her and she seemed untouched by the ruthlessness which so often accompanies a successful career. Confronted by an unethical story, she would have turned it down.

With a couple of days free, she had decided to take up the offer of a break in the country and, over an instantly opened bottle of wine, Bridget hungrily listened to the latest newspaper gossip.

A royal scandal had broken a few days earlier and Beverley recounted how her editor, realizing one of his rivals had a scoop, had telephoned their circulation department, pretending to be the managing editor just about to leave his home for the office. Asking for the expense figures for the story, her editor had given his own fax number and, when the figures had duly arrived under the heading Royal Divorce, he had been able to snatch the scoop for his own tabloid.

'The man's a monster.' There was unwilling admiration in Beverley's voice. She was probably aware that if her boss knew of her professional reservations, he would sack her.

'Ah, but great entertainment value,' Bridget laughed.

It was the stuff of countless hilarious evenings spent with other journalists in city pubs when Fleet Street had still existed and it was good to know that, despite rumours of reporters now being as deskbound as accountants, there were still a few characters around and the tricks and spoilers of competition had not died.

With a prayer of thanks to Marks & Spencer, Bridget pulled a packet of satay chicken breasts from the freezer, put them in the microwave with some rice and opened another bottle.

They sprawled about in old clothes and without make-up and talked about their work and their hang-ups and their sex lives (or, in Bridget's case, her lack of one). There was no need to score points or pussyfoot around each other's egos.

Men were so amazed when they discovered another man to whom they could reveal themselves that they had invented the mystique of male camaraderie, but women frequently reached the point of exchanging the most intimate confidences during their first meeting and, after years of friendship, there were no secrets between Bridget and Beverley.

In a circumstance where men would have started throwing back the booze, becoming noisy and showing off to each other, the two women grew undramatically befuddled together.

'I've often wished I was a lesbian,' Bridget told her friend as she luxuriated in the sheer comfortableness of the evening.

'Me, too,' agreed Beverley.

'Trouble is, I've never been turned on by women physically.'

'Me neither.'

'I just like their company better.'

'Me too.'

They staggered to the mantelpiece for refills from the bottle.

'Bridget, I'm going to do you an enormous favour,' Beverley waved her glass expansively so that half the wine fountained on to the carpet. 'I'm going to get engaged to Don.'

'You can't do that. You'd have to get married.' Bridget had decided that women should stop marrying. It never seemed to do them any good.

'Oh, I'm not going to marry him.' Beverley gave her a slurred assurance. 'I'm just going to get engaged so that I can have an engagement party so that you can meet his Uncle Barry.'

Uncle Barry, in Beverley's opinion, was just the man for her friend. He was rich and widowed and cultured and witty and kind to women, children and animals. In fact, Uncle Barry was Mother Theresa.

'He's got no hair,' Bridget challenged, sceptically.

'He has magscent . . . magni . . . magnissifent hair.'

'Then he's got a beard.' Visions of an ape-like Uncle Barry with growth from his ears to his navel made her shudder.

'No beard.' Beverley shook her head solemnly and tilted in her chair.

'And no teeth.'

'Definitely teeth, all his own,' Beverley was beginning to look peeved that her judgement of a suitable man for Bridget was being questioned. 'He's perfect for you.'

There had to be something wrong with Uncle Barry. Bridget mentally mulled over her standard requirements for a mate to see what she had missed out.

'How old is he?' she asked at last, with deep suspicion.

'Sixty-five.'

'Sixty-five!' she yelled at her friend. 'Sixty-five! How many walking sticks does he have?'

'He's very fit,' Beverley said with a look of injured dignity. 'Despite his age.'

'Despite his age! Oh yes, despite the prostate, the senility and his last stroke. My God! So you think I'm so desperate that I'm going to spend the rest of my life pushing Uncle Barry round the supermarket in a bath chair!'

'I was only trying to help.' Her friend was definitely wounded by now.

'Well, thank you very much, but if you think my only choice is between a drooling infant like Tom O'Dare and your boyfriend's Uncle Barry in his Zimmer frame, you're mistaken.'

*

Zoe's dinner party and Beverley's visit seemed to signify the start of a united conspiracy by Bridget's friends to pair her off again. It was as though they were affronted by one of their number escaping the time-honoured traditions of laughing at a husband's jokes heard countless times before, sitting with a fixed smile while the other-half gazed lecherously down other cleavages at parties, and heaving the old man fully dressed on to the bed before he had time to fall into a drunken stupor on the floor.

As she prepared to spend weekends relaxing with the newspapers in front of the fire in the totally fulfilling company of a large gin and tonic, invitations were issued that she might be introduced to yet another prospective husband.

Wayward brothers discarded by everyone else were dragged out of cupboards and suddenly society seemed overrun by single-parent males with uncontrollable children. Then there was a solicitor with halitosis like a blowtorch introduced by Sue and Zoe's second attempt, an elephantine middle-aged bachelor, who had once been rejected for the priesthood by the Jesuits. Sasha had even offered up her own father.

These unattached men were all utterly convinced of their own desirability. They were constantly being introduced to divorced women and had developed an almost coquettish game of 'catch me if you can' when confronted by the latest female sacrifice.

'The ones between forty and sixty want young flesh and the ones over sixty are looking for a woman to cook and clean for them, and nurse them when they become decrepit,' she told Sophie, wearily. And, worst of all, none of them was Tom.

357

'Well, whatever you do, before you get tied up with another man, make sure he had a good relationship with his mother,' Sophie advised. 'Men who hate their mothers take revenge on their women and men whose mothers doted on them expect the same selfless commitment from their wives.'

Bridget did not want another man. Had she felt herself attracted to any of her friend's promotions, she would have run away. Emotional damage was not all she had suffered. Ten years of believing and trusting in Tom, only to discover that she had been wrong, meant that she no longer had faith in her own judgement. Even had there been any risk of her falling in love, that would be no guarantee of having found the right man.

Betrayal is like a vulnerary physical injury. Long after the pain ceases, the limp remains. There would be no total recovery and she would never again be able to give herself completely to anyone else. When you have been shot, you don't stand in front of another gun, she thought.

Sometimes she caught sight of men on their own in the village, or in the nearby country town, wearing those green oilskins favoured by vets and Tom; thin, tall men with grey hair and that looseness of facial muscles, that defeated look in their eyes which comes with the loss of their manhood to age. That's how Tom will look soon, she would think to herself. Already the firmness of his mouth had slackened almost imperceptibly, so that at times it appeared about to tremble, just as the mouths of old men made them look as though at any moment they might weep. But old age in Tom would not have mattered, because she, too, would have been growing old alongside. They would still have been lovers and companions.

Her attempts at expanding her life on her own were failing. She had discovered that the world was comprised of couples between which single women drifted like ghosts. Each time she saw a hand caressing another, or a woman's hair brushing against the head of her lover, or a husband and wife kiss with that fleeting accuracy which comes from long intimacy, she had to turn her head away.

The more she forced herself to go out, the more cut off she felt and, returning late one night from a venture into the astronomy society, which had been completely incomprehensible and demoralizing, she poured a huge measure of Cointreau, went to her desk and took out a very old address book.

Twenty years had passed. He could not still be at the same address. She thought back to that long-ago love affair with Sean, after her return from Madeira when she had still been separated from Sam.

They had made love in more positions than the Kama Sutra and, between fucks, he had quoted Molly Bloom's soliloquy to her.

'I used to go to Father Corrigan he touched me father and what harm if he did where and I said on the canal bank like a fool but wherabouts on your person my child on the leg behind high up was it yes rather high up was it where you sit down yes O Lord couldnt he say bottom right out and be done with it.'

Then he would pull her on top of him, so that she was free to wriggle down on him so far that his cock seemed to reach her throat and she came over and over again. Oh, multiple orgasms were no myth.

359

'I wished he was here or somebody to let myself go with and come again like that I feel all fire inside me or if I could dream it when he made me spend the 2nd time tickling me behind with his finger and I was coming for about 5 minutes with my legs round him I had to hug him after O Lord I wanted to shout out all sorts of things fuck or shit or anything at all.'

Then he would turn her over and tease her unmercifully until she was backing against him moaning. He had never seemed to tire.

Once, they had holidayed together and made love in the ocean. She remembered him slipping her swimsuit down her body and the sun hot on her back and wrapping her legs round him and being impressed that the coldness of the sea did not reduce his erection. They had laughed helplessly when the weightlessness caused by the salt water had caused her to drift out of the reach of each thrust, until he had seized her shoulders and pulled her down hard on him and they had stopped laughing, only to start again on discovering that her swimsuit had floated away on the waves and was lost.

When the post had come up in America, he had wanted her to go with him. Instead she had returned with Deirdre to Sam. But she had never forgotten him. The only good sex she had ever had had been with Sean and she had been aware of what she was missing ever since.

His wife had left him before they met, but he must have married again and probably had innumerable children and grandchildren by now.

It was midnight when she dialled the New York number.

A man answered.

'Is that Sean MacMurrough?' She did not have to ask. That Belfast accent with the slight break in the tone was unmistakable.

'Yes.'

'You won't guess who this is ... a voice from the past.'

'Bridget,' he said, without a second's hesitation.

Sheer delight opened in her. He had known her instantly and recaptured in both their minds were the same images of the way they had been, pristine as though the years had not passed.

Where are you? How are you? What are you doing? He had seen one of her plays. He had not married again. She told him about her coming divorce.

'I still have "Other Men's Flowers" and the collected Dylan Thomas.' She often read the books he had given her and wore the heavy silver bracelet he had brought back from Ireland.

'*Oh as I was young and easy in the mercy of his means,*
Time held me green and dying
Though I sang in my chains like the sea,' he quoted.

Bridget closed her eyes and walked again with him through the Inns of Court and along the Thames embankment wound in each other's arms and kissing under the dolphin street lamps. She should have married him.

'It's wonderful to hear you again, darling. You sound exactly the same.' She could hear his pleasure. 'Come to the States.'

'I will.'

It was an illusion. She knew that. They were no longer the same people and there must have been a reason why she had refused to go with him, although she could not remember it. Now they were carrying the reality of each

361

other when they were young and beautiful. To meet again would destroy a shining memory encapsulated in a bubble of time. She knew she would not go to New York.

Sometimes Bridget spoke to Tom and sometimes Tom spoke to Bridget. Once, he asked her for advice about his mortgage and she gave it to him. On another occasion he told her he had searched for some indication of Tracy Sorex's financial position.

'There isn't a bank account, a building society book or even a letter relating to the divorce in the house. She's removed them all,' he told her. 'You think I'm being taken for a ride, don't you?'

'If you're paying for everything, I think she knows she's on to a good thing,' was her restrained comment.

It was as though the street quarrel between them in Bristol had not happened and, each time they made contact, Bridget went in whatever direction he led and was left in turmoil.

For hours afterwards she would sit smoking and shaking, wondering if he were playing cat and mouse, or whether he genuinely did not want to lose her completely.

Perhaps he, too, nursed the possibility of their coming together again one day, but was unable to say so, just as she could not because their surface response to each other would have been rejection.

It would have been better if he had cut her off with unshakeable hostility. Then she would have been released to the future. As it was, each time she tried to take a hesitating step forward, Tom's voice pulled her back. Decisions she had reached were revoked. Plans seemed mistaken. Her emotions were jerked from one extreme to the other, from despair to hope, from love to hate, from rage to self-pity.

Each day, the first page she turned to in the newspaper was the astrology column. Her telephone bill mounted with expensive calls to the forecast lines and she bought magazines only to read her stars. In her desperation to find some framework, she would have read signs in entrails if someone had suggested it, but all the time she became more confused and absent-minded.

On the way back from another visit to London, she found herself approaching Guildford, when she should have been on the motorway driving past Heathrow Airport, and after eventually making her way back to the correct route, she went straight past the turning to the West country and only came to her senses again half-way over the Severn Bridge. Such incidents were no longer unusual.

What she saw as her feebleness of character was mortifying. All her resolutions seemed to end in vacillation or further confirmation of her own inadequacy. The only boost to her morale since the New Year had been the conversation with Sean, but that had also exposed her to the admission that she was lonely for male company.

Deep inside, she was waiting for Tom, but, meanwhile, her friends could be right, she thought. A man to go out with, not a new partner, or a lover, but someone who shared her interests was what she needed. However, she would find him on her own, without their help.

The advertisement for the computer-dating organization showed pictures of couples smiling ecstatically into each other's eyes. There were thousands of personable men, who had immersed themselves in their careers, or lived abroad, or were in Bridget's position and wanted to meet an attractive woman, Sue pointed out enthusiastically when they discussed the idea.

Bridget could not envisage Sam or Tom or Sean joining such a scheme. None of them had ever had the slightest trouble pulling birds, but, as Sue reminded her, she was trying to give up Jack the Lads.

So, some days later, she attacked an incredibly long questionnaire and pondered over whether she was really an atheist or just an agnostic and whether she was justified in calling herself a redhead, when without the aid of her hairdresser she was really a brunette. Then she ticked off the attributes of the man of her dreams: slim, five foot ten or over, clean-shaven, blue-eyed, professional, intelligent, witty, well-dressed, sociable, likes pubs – and realized she was describing Tom. Scoring out blue eyes and replacing them with brown, then adding the word 'solvent', she sent off the form with a cheque for £90.

It seemed very unlikely that an Adonis out there could actually be looking for a woman who smoked like a bonfire, believed exercise was what a child wrote in a school notebook and who, forced to leap from a sinking ship, would probably have made saving a bottle of gin her priority.

A list of four names and telephone numbers arrived by return post and that evening Bridget sat down with a powerfully mixed drink and picked up the telephone.

'I suppose I'd better tell you, I've been made redundant and I've had to sell my car and it looks as though they're going to repossess my house,' the man said.

Bridget could feel her instincts crowding together like smurfs and squealing at her to ring off.

364

'I'm very down, you know, really depressed.' He was still talking. 'I've nothing to offer anyone. My life's in a complete mess.'

Sympathy stirred insidiously inside her and she mentally began to stamp it out. This road had brought her nothing but trouble in the past. She did not know what to say to him.

'I'd like someone who could cheer me up, but I don't suppose you're very interested,' he went on pathetically.

She swigged down the gin and took a deep breath.

'I don't want to sound uncaring,' she began. 'It's just that I am not in a good position myself at the moment and it's as much as I can do to keep upright. I don't think I've anything left over to be able to help anyone else. I really am sorry.'

'That's OK,' he replied dolefully. 'It's only what I expected.'

Deirdre's laugh was infectious and, before the end of her guilt-ridden report, Bridget was joining in and agreeing that, as she must have already landed the runt of the litter, she might as well try another number.

Within his first sentence, the next man told her he was divorced and wanted a wife. It did not seem to matter to him if the wife were old or young, fat or thin, bright or dull, as long as she was female.

Bridget's explanation that she was not looking for a husband was greeted with incredulity and her flippant comment – that she wouldn't mind having another couple of weddings, with the frocks, the parties and the honeymoons, but she wasn't prepared to sign anything – seemed to offend him. He rang off coldly.

Then there was Bob on the end of the line, lively, funny and rich, if the description of his Rolls-Royce were anything to go by. Warning bells sounded at the word 'entrepreneur'. He did 'a bit of this and a bit of that' and sounded like the Arthur Daley of Exeter, but he made her giggle.

He telephoned the next night and made her laugh again. An hour flew by like minutes. He was fifty years old, with black hair and brown eyes. He seemed to have had a lot of businesses, but that's what entrepreneurs did, and he had had a couple of wives, which could happen to anyone, she told herself. She'd had a couple of husbands. He was exactly the type of man she should avoid and they agreed to meet for dinner.

With her red hair fluffed up and another new outfit, with a long jacket and short skirt like the suits she'd seen worn by women in London, and wearing almost tarty high heels, she looked ten years younger and a completely different person from six months before. Tom would not have recognized her as she drove into the city.

Bob had arranged to be waiting outside a pub in the centre and, when she reached it, she was driving too fast and the traffic was too heavy for her to stop. There was a man standing on the pavement and her heart sank.

Manoeuvring through the one-way system, she considered driving straight home, then scolded herself sharply. It was unfair to judge by appearances. Look where Tom's instant impact had led. This man was fun to talk to and she had nothing to lose.

She left the car in a side street and walked back and involuntarily took in the badly dyed black hair, the crumpled shirt and the fact that Beverley's boyfriend's Uncle Barry had seen fifty more recently than Bob had. And, oh God, brown shoes. A resurrection of the last scene of *Death in Venice*, with Dirk Bogarde slumped on the beach with hair dye running down his face, refused to be banished from her mind.

Parking congestion in the city centre had made him leave his car at home, he explained, and she thought wistfully of the Rolls-Royce that certainly did not exist as she drove them both to the Chinese restaurant he had suggested. They passed an elegant house, which he pointed out as his own, waving a bony hand and frayed cuff in its direction. A headache jabbed Bridget between the eyes.

In the restaurant he masterfully ordered the 'Chinese Feast' and the wine without consultation. As they ate, he talked with the incessancy of an orange being rolled up and down a piano while Bridget tried to ignore the axe chopping away at her temples and wished he had brought his telephone manner with him.

Both his wives would have him back tomorrow, he assured her. Did they all say that? She was just grateful that he had the sense to order a second bottle of wine.

He had joined the dating agency because the females in Exeter were deranged. Once, he had answered an advertisement in the 'Eye Love' column of *Private Eye* and he bet Bridget could not guess who that woman turned out to be. He had taken her out and she had told him it was one of the best evenings she had ever had and he bet Bridget couldn't guess who it was!

The second bottle of wine was still half-full and her shoulders drooped as he told the waiter she did not want any more. No, she could not guess.

Bob leant back in his chair and his eyes narrowed into slits of triumph.

'Joan Collins,' he said.

The waiter brought the bill.

'We usually go halves,' Bob said and Bridget resignedly brought out her cheque book.

As they stood up to leave, he picked up the half-bottle of wine and put it in his pocket.

Deirdre howled when she told her.

'Mummy, I don't know what I'd do without you.' She could hardly get the words out.

'It wasn't bloody funny,' Bridget protested. 'It's another world out here.'

That only set her daughter off again.

'When are you going to try again? I can't wait.'

'You could be more sympathetic.' Bridget felt herself starting to smile against her will.

'I am, really I am.' Another burst of chuckles belied the words. 'Now ring off. I've simply got to tell Barney.'

Fourth time lucky. It was more enforced optimism than a vote of confidence. But with sixty-seven pounds fifty of her ninety-pound investment gone, Bridget thought she might as well complete the distance.

He was an academic, courteous and rather reserved on the telephone. Robert invited her to have tea in a picturesque village on the coast. That sounded civilized and sensible. Tea took place in the afternoon and did not last long. If they did not like each other, they were not condemned to spending several hours in each other's company.

A tall, well-built man with thick grey hair and bloodhound jowls, he was waiting with a box of chocolates and a bunch of flowers, which was a very good start.

He had been divorced, but his wife would have him back tomorrow, of course, and he mentioned the world of academe several times before she discovered that he taught town planning in the local polytechnic.

Bridget had ceased expecting to be asked about her work, or, indeed, her life and had developed the technique of appearing to listen while merely observing. However, he was amiable and she felt comfortable with him and, by the time he settled the bill for two cream teas, she had decided that it would be pleasant to see him again.

His cottage was just around the corner and, although he realized it was rather early, he wondered if she would like to come back for a drink.

As she sat down in a big, chintz-covered armchair, Robert opened a bottle of wine and filled two glasses. The room was well furnished, with a number of fine antiques; a walnut and marquetry long-case clock, a lovely Pembroke table and a pretty brass-bound wine cooler.

As she admired them, he invited her over to examine the secretaire.

'It's William and Mary,' he told her, bending down and opening one of its drawers. 'Look at this.'

He stood up, smiling, and held out a whip.

She just had time to cast an astounded glance at the tangle of leather filling the drawer before bolting into the street.

When she reached her car she realized she was still holding something in her hand.

Well, she thought, looking down at it ruefully. This is the most expensive wine glass I'll ever own.

Chapter Twenty-Three

A CAT could not have slept more peacefully and, when Bridget awoke, she thought the battery on her watch must have run out the previous night. Then she was astonished to discover that it was eleven o'clock in the morning.

This was the day she had been dreading, the day of the Decree Absolute.

The prospect of dejection had been numbing, but instead she felt a floating sense of relief. At last it was all over. Tom was yesterday's man and the future was shimmering with untried adventures. Outside the window the sun shone. Winter was over, physically and metaphorically, and tangy promises of life were rising like bubbles to the rim of the day. This was the propitious start of all her tomorrows.

Only when she went downstairs and saw all the envelopes on the mat did she remember that this was also her birthday. Fate had shown a fine sense of irony in engineering that her decision to divorce Tom had been made on their wedding anniversary and their divorce was finalized today.

There were more cards than she had received all her adult life. Her daughter and son-in-law had sent one each and another from Patrick. There were cards from Sue and Beverley, Nick and Sasha, Zoe and David, Sophie and Julian, Carter Blake and other friends, who she had not been aware knew the date of her birthday. There was even one from Gareth, who did not believe in such things, and must have been influenced by Claire.

The previous year Bridget had spent the day alone. Tom had left her a card, but no present, and he had not come home that evening. Despite an artless enjoyment of occasions, she had really tried to ignore the fact that her own day was unmarked by any celebration; but by evening she had been in tears.

Now, she set out the cards on the chimneypiece and sat back feeling cherished. They had all stood by her, listening with endless patience to her woes, comforting her, scolding her, advising her, picking her up each time she fell over the edge of despair, restoring her spirits, encouraging her to fight on. Not one of them had ever accused her of the quivering self-pity she often felt guilty of, but was unable to curb. Bridget knew she did not deserve such good friends and that, without them, she could not have survived.

The doorbell rang and two men began unloading large pieces of stone from a van with the name of a garden centre painted on its side.

'I think you've made a mistake,' she said to them. 'I haven't ordered anything.'

'Mrs Flynn?' one asked, glancing at a docket.

As she nodded, he went on, 'Ordered by Mr and Mrs Seymour. No mistake.'

Deirdre's present.

'What are they?' she asked.

'Garden seat,' he replied.

She had always wanted a stone seat by the fountain and she felt herself beaming.

'It's my birthday,' she told the men.

They carried the heavy pieces right up the hill and put them together with unusual good humour.

371

'Happy birthday, love,' they said and waved as they drove off.

It was months since she had been in the garden, but now she sat on the stone seat under the white blossoming Shirotae cherry tree and looked down through the arch of hawthorn. The earliest daffodils were already in flower and, within the protection of their rapier leaves, the sugared almonds of the crocuses opened their six silk petals into cups of purple and white around bright orange stigmas. There were primroses beside her, almost hidden by overgrown grass.

The dogs followed, panting and adoring, as she walked round her land. This year the garden was to be more beautiful than it had ever been, she resolved. When Tom had had the first affair, disease had destroyed the roses and weeds had choked the flower beds and brambles and ivy had run rampant, strangling the young trees. That was not going to happen this time. Spring was just beginning. If she worked hard she could clear the neglect of the past months in time for the firework display of colour to come.

The kitchen garden had been his pride but, after his mother died, he had not bothered with it any more. Bridget stared at the crust of dead weeds and meadow grass covering its surface and remembered how she had enjoyed filling a basket with the baby carrots and courgettes, beans and peas he had grown for her and plaiting the golden onions into long strings, some of which still hung in the pantry. In summer he had dug up the new potatoes, leaving them in clutches like big brown eggs to dry on the earth before bringing them down to the house.

Bridget contemplated the steep slope of the plot with irritation. This was the one part of the garden too heavy for her to maintain and there was little point in telling herself she could now do anything she liked, if she couldn't even have the new potatoes she wanted.

I'll damn well grow them myself, she decided stubbornly, marching to the toolshed and hauling out the Rotovator.

The loam was compacted from lack of autumn preparation and her shoulder ached from yanking the string to start up the motor. The cumbersome machine constantly threatened to tip over as the rotors dug lopsidedly into soft patches. Bridget, cursing and swearing, repeatedly wrenched it upright, the sweat running saltily into her eyes and her heart hammering. The furrows weaved out of control and her feet slipped in the wake of soil until the Rotovator suddenly bucked on a stone and fell over with its blades spinning, dragging her down with it.

'OK. So I'll never win a ploughing competition,' she retorted to the robin, which had followed her up and down. 'But you wait till I dig up the crop.'

Puce-faced and coughing, she looked back over the game of snakes and ladders she had created on the ground while the robin laughed openly

'There's no law that spuds have to grow in a straight line,' she informed him loftily and staggered to her feet to start placing the seed potatoes in the channels. Eventually, five earthed-up squiggles ran up the hill and Bridget lay flat on her stomach in the grass and tried not to think of having to dig them up again in July.

The sun flamed down and her head ached. Blisters had been rubbed and burst on her fingers and the muscles in her thighs felt as though she had just ridden the Grand National, but the challenge of the garden had become symbolic. It was as though she had to bully it into order at once to signpost this day as the beginning and not the end.

Fetching the Strimmer, she started to tidy around clusters of primulas, pulling out bramble shoots with her bare hands and clawing up dandelion roots until the bank behind her new garden seat was studded with theatrically brilliant blues and reds and yellows and pinks.

She uncovered clumps of wild, green-frilled snowdrops under the hedges and freed the white Irish heather planted for luck. She hoed the old rose garden and the herbaceous border. The witch hazel was in flower in the winter garden, its yellow filaments searching the air as sensitively as a sea anemone, and its raspberry scent showered over her like dew as she crawled on her knees to weed around its base.

As the garden began to slip away from the sun, she made her way back to the stone seat with bloodied arms and swollen joints and broken nails and a scalp full of thorns. The bands made by the rollers of the mower had accentuated the emerald sweep of the lawn and butterflies of white petals fluttered on to it from the starry magnolia. The roebuck and his hind appeared from the wood to eat the bluebell leaves and Bridget watched them with her soul at peace.

That night, as she snuggled down into her bed, bruised and sore from the unaccustomed labour, she realized that she had not thought of Tom at all for hours. She had had a lovely birthday.

With images of leather bomber-jackets and helmets and goggles and moustachioed men who talked like Biggles, Bridget pulled on a pair of jeans and a baggy sweater.

Would they shout, 'Chocks away' and 'Roger and out,' and prang their machines? She was on her way to the Flying Club for her first lesson.

'Shit!' she swore as she reached the front door and noticed a letter from her solicitor. A quick scan of its contents told her little.

'. . . application for leave . . . first Direction . . . the Respondent . . . Affidavit of Means . . . valuation of the property . . .'

It was a nuisance, but nothing to worry about, she thought as she stuffed it in her pocket. The divorce was through and the house belonged to her anyway.

The Cessna aeroplane was smaller than a Mini car on wings and, when she put on the headphones, the instructor seemed to be telephoning her from Zanzibar as he explained about roll and yaw and pitch and trim and went through the pre-flight check of more panel instruments than she would ever remember.

There were twin controls and, after showing her how to work the rudder and brakes with her feet and making her practise moving the control wheel and adjusting the throttle, he shouted, 'Relax,' with foolhardy optimism and they were rolling over the grass.

Then they were bumping along the Tarmac faster and faster and the end of the runway was rushing towards them until, suddenly, it disappeared and they were airborne.

'Oh Christ!' exclaimed Bridget, winded by excitement and terror as they rose and the countryside spread below them like a child's toy farm.

'You have control,' he said.

'What?' she squeaked. 'I can't. I don't know what to do. There's only a bit of tin between me and the ground.'

375

But his own hands were in his lap and she was flying! She was actually flying an aeroplane entirely on her own.

Her hands were like the teeth of a pit-bull terrier on the control wheel, her mouth was dry and there was a kangaroo where her stomach should have been. Had she looked round, she was convinced they would have plummeted from the sky.

'Try to keep the line of the horizon in the same position.' The instructor sounded as though he were falling asleep and the horizon immediately rose as a tidal wave ahead of them and then crashed out of view.

'Fingertip control,' he directed lazily. 'And I think we should stop climbing now.'

So that was where the horizon had gone. She must have left it thousands of miles behind as they shot vertically towards space.

'Straight and level,' he drawled. 'Move the control column forward.'

As the aeroplane dropped its nose and dived towards the earth, he roused himself sufficiently to place a hand on his control wheel.

'We usually practise stalling later in the course,' he commented as they steadied. 'Now, let's have some back pressure on the stick and right-rudder pressure.'

The machine zoomed sideways, tilting so that a village below seemed to spin past her eyes and Bridget felt her face turn into papier mâché as the blood siphoned from it.

'I'll take over now,' he said. 'You'll be good when you learn to stop worrying.'

She leant back, feeling wobbly and rubbing eyes red-veined from staring out without blinking.

'Look,' he said.

They were over Exmoor and below them a buzzard hovered, the tensile curve of his wings like a drawn longbow, patterned with black lace over gold, surfing on the thermal currents and hauling the anchor of his shadow across the land beneath.

A few minutes later they flew over the town where Tom had worked and had his affair with Jane Scott. Bridget found herself contemplating how she had been driving miles out of her way to avoid the place for years. Now it looked no bigger than a human hand, an insignificant group of buildings. England, verdant and misted with heat, flowed away from it; hills she had never climbed, woods she had never explored, roads running to the sea, to ports from where ships sailed to unknown lands, to people she had never met, roads leading to the world.

From high in the sky where the clouds sailed a new perspective was offered, and with a dip of the ailerons and a flick of the rudder the town was reduced even more, to a smudge, to a dot and then it was gone.

She forgot the presence of the instructor beside her. It was as though she were flying alone in the limitless spiritual freedom of an out-of-body experience, looking down on her life and seeing how much of it, which seemed so important, did not really matter at all.

'I'm going to take regular lessons,' she told Deirdre. 'Although it's madness, when I'm living on borrowed money.'

'Think of it as an investment,' her daughter advised.

'In what?'

'The new you. You need to break away from the past, so why not this way?'

'Flying was so terrifying that I feel like a heroine. Up

there you know you are microscopic and yet you are winging through infinity and there seems no limit to what you can do.' She tried to describe the sensation. 'The exhilaration would make the ultimate orgasm seem boring.'

'Oh well, as you've found the answer to every woman's prayer, don't let lack of money stop you,' her daughter laughed.

Her writing was going well at last and she had almost finished her play when John wrote again to say that Tom had not replied to his request for an Affidavit of Means. Bridget felt annoyed with both men. The divorce was over and she had not expected any further business.

'You have been left with massive debts and virtually no income,' John reminded her firmly. 'Tom and Miss Sorex are earning far more than you and the Court will almost certainly award you maintenance for a period to give you time to recover financially. You must allow me to look after your interests, Bridget.'

Depressed, she put down the receiver and found her concentration broken. For a couple of days she dithered over what to do and then another legal letter arrived with a copy of one sent to her ex-husband suggesting an out-of-Court settlement.

Emotions just starting to heal began to chafe and, when she finally telephoned Tom, they split wide open again. He asked how she was and said it was good to hear from her and agreed that everything could be settled amicably between them.

'I'll sort it out today. No worries,' he said, taking her back to their first days together and bleeding her heart dry.

378

Although the Court had awarded her the costs of the divorce, Bridget had had to pay all the interim invoices in advance of the final account being sent to him. These were now mounting again.

'The costs are going up all the time.' She contacted him once more. 'Why don't you reply to John's letters?'

'I have replied,' he answered testily.

But he had not.

The round raised logo of her solicitor's firm began to greet her regularly like an evil eye.

John was insistent. It was as though this were now no longer a question of her ex-husband meeting his obligations to her, but of one man being personally insulted by another man.

'. . . if you do not respond in the manner ordered by the County Court then we shall make application for a Penal Order to be fixed to the Directions Order that the Court has made. The effect of this will be that unless you comply with the Directions Order within seven days, the Court is in power to order your arrest.'

Bridget read the latest copy letter and dialled Tom's number in panic.

'This is getting out of hand. I don't want this. It's not necessary. What's the matter with you?'

'I'm fucking busy,' he snarled.

'Look, Tom, scribble what he wants on a piece of paper and fax it,' she urged.

The scribble was apparently unsatisfactory and only led to more legal threats. The situation escalated. For a few days there would be no interruptions and she would try to recreate her work routine, then another envelope would be delivered and her day would be reduced to shivering confusion. Weeks went by. The letters went backwards and forwards as the two men played cat and mouse against each other, with her as the mouse. John obtained the Penal Order, the Penal Order was served, the costs had become astronomical. By the time the necessary Affidavits were sworn three months had passed and Bridget had stopped eating and sleeping again.

Her fingernail hold on the future was weakening. Over and over she asked herself what it was about Tom that so devoured her. However much she forced herself to study their marriage, she could find no rational explanation for his devastating effect on her. The only conclusion she reached was that Tom was her addiction. The minute they had met, she had been hooked as surely as though she had injected heroin. Her physical symptoms now would have been identical had she been withdrawing from the drug and recent renewed contact with him was like another fix. At night she sweated and lay awake, then plunged into nightmares and awoke already in another anxiety attack. Her nails had become brittle, her hair had thinned and her hip bones jutted.

Although always determined to control herself when she went to counselling, each week her construction of expensive clothes and jewellery and laboriously applied make-up and the veneer of assuredness she was trying to present to the world crumbled.

'I talk to Tom all the time. I act out, sometimes for hours, what we would say to each other if he were in the room,' she told Sandra Vicars. 'I can't stop. It's become a compulsion. If I'm out somewhere, or if I go away, I become so edgy that I have to find a loo or some room where I can be alone to whisper it all. I'm frightened. I think I'm losing my mind.'

It was an aberration which haunted her and which she

had confided in Deirdre, who had looked very anxious and urged her to get advice, so greatly increasing Bridget's own fears.

'Do you act out everything?' her counsellor wanted to know. 'Relationships with other people, other things that affect your daily life?'

'No, just me and Tom,' Bridget answered.

'When someone dies, the one left behind often talks to that person,' Sandra Vicars told her. 'Some widows talk to their dead husbands for years.'

'So you think I'm all right?' Bridget was not convinced.

'If you were doing this over everything, then it might be something we should look at.' The reply was cautious. 'Would you worry if you were writing out possible scenarios with Tom rather than talking them out aloud?'

'No, but writing is how I express myself.'

'So is talking,' she said. 'And I don't think you should be perturbed. What you're doing is quite natural.'

Only the garden gave her reassurance. No longer able to write at all, she obsessively nursed seedlings into plants and filled the flowerbeds, staking up delphiniums and lupins and hollyhocks, spraying the roses, earthing up the potatoes, feeding, raking, weeding and watering. In return, the garden pledged borage leaves for glasses of Pimms and vases spangled with honesty like mother-of-pearl and beacons of giant sunflowers to light her walks and lavender seeds to fold in muslin and hang among her clothes.

The apple trees blossomed like pink and white icing, stalactites of yellow and mauve flowers dripped from the wisteria and laburnum branches and twin sprays of deep purple and white nodded on the lilac trees. Through the salad freshness of its leaves and the munificence of its blooms, the garden rewarded the hours of her time a thousandfold.

As she buried her hands in the rich texture of its soil and cut fat stems of asparagus and removed the first sideshoots from the tomatoes and picked the first sweet peas, she was able to forget the possibility, which was becoming a probability, that she and Tom and Tracy Sorex would end up confronting each other in open Court.

And while the earth confirmed the worth of faith by fulfilling all its promises, the sky kept her vision alive. No longer afraid, Bridget learnt to take off in the small aeroplane, to climb and descend, to turn smoothly, to stall and recover. Without her visits to the Flying Club, she might have buckled completely under the endless bombardment from solicitor and ex-husband, but each lesson restored her self-confidence and she landed elated from each flight, with a sense of her own capability rebuilt.

During that last hour, they had practised spins. Her instructor had turned off the power and dropped the nose of the Cessna steeply and, as they rapidly began to lose height and the pressure in her ears became drum-bursting, Bridget had squeezed her eyes tightly shut.

'We'd better try that again,' he had said with an easy grin. 'You're less likely to find your eyes closed permanently if you keep them open now.'

The next time, to her surprise, although the landscape below seemed to turn round and round them, the aeroplane did not feel as though it were moving at all.

By the end of the lesson, she was completing the exercise herself; turning off the power, maintaining height and, just before the stall, applying full rudder and holding the control column right back, counting calmly as the aeroplane spiralled downwards and their altitude rapidly decreased, then closing the throttle, applying the opposite rudder, pausing, easing the control column forward and gently lifting out of the dive.

With her adrenalin still coursing, Bridget switched on a Freddy Mercury tape at full volume and drove at speed towards home singing.

Deirdre had left the message on the answerphone.

'Patrick kept going blue. We're in Great Ormond Street. They're carrying out open-heart surgery this week.'

Chapter Twenty-Four

H E HAD been playing, shunting over the floor on his stomach to grab at toys which rattled and rang bells. He had banged them on the carpet enthusiastically and sung along with their sounds and, when Bridget picked him up, he had gurgled with laughter.

'You're lucky,' Deirdre commented. 'He doesn't like other people holding him.'

'He knows I'm his grandmama,' she had answered complacently.

She had laid him on the sofa, where he gazed with fascinated affection into the eyes of a jolly cloth caterpillar with a dozen booted feet which he kept by him all the time. Then he had fallen rosily asleep.

'Yes. He looks so good that it's hard to believe he's such a seriously ill little boy.' Her daughter had read her thoughts.

Only two weeks had passed since Bridget had seen Patrick. Now, as she drove towards London, she replayed the memories of her visit: his shout of temper when the pop-up clown was out of reach and his dogged determination to get to it, his delight when Deirdre turned up the radio and danced around the room with him, his stubborn refusal to eat more than he wanted, his irrepressible energy.

'We know he might die. We've thought about it and talked about it and tried to prepare ourselves,' Deirdre had told her.

'No,' she had said emphatically. 'He will not die.'

His natural joy, his obstinacy, his courage, his lucent spirit would defeat the louring risks and bring him through all danger. Patrick would live. Bridget had no doubts.

It was raining when she reached High Holborn and there were no parking places in the narrow streets. The nearer she had drawn to the hospital, the more tense she had become. The operation had taken place twenty-four hours earlier and Patrick was in intensive care. It had not been possible to get an update on his condition during the five-hour journey from Devon. Then the city traffic had been even worse than usual and she had arrived much later than planned. Cold with anxiety, she left the car on a double yellow line and ran into the huge building.

The corridors were endless and somewhere she lost the signs to the cardiac unit. The few people she passed looked drawn and preoccupied, young parents holding each other's hands, speechless. Her footsteps clattered intrusively past them on the polished vinyl floors. Once she took the wrong lift and was quickly turned back. At last she found the correct floor and rang the bell.

A nurse showed her where to hang her coat and gave her a large plastic apron and tied a mask over her mouth. And she walked into the small room, to a sight beyond any atrocity she could ever have imagined.

A massive bank of machines rose above her. Constantly moving coloured graphs and changing numbers filled a huge electronic screen and needles quivered and swung inside a battery of dials. Scores of plastic tubes tangled over each other and bags of fluid hung suspended from steel poles.

Taking up such a little space, her grandson lay on a white sheepskin in the middle of the bed. His head was almost hidden by a plastic helmet. There was some sort of cap clamped across his nose. His mouth was open and all the tubes led to him; all the tubes were running into his body, into his neck and his wrists and his feet and his chest and his anus, and into his heart.

The walls of the room moved and the bright lights dimmed as, totally unprepared for what was before her, Bridget started to faint. She wrenched back her consciousness and stood swaying and blinking.

Deirdre and a doctor were staring at the screen. They had not even seen her. A nurse pushed her to one side and suddenly the door opened and people hurried in. Deirdre turned and grabbed her arm. Her eyes were without expression.

'We've got to go,' she said.

Bridget just caught sight of the team of surgeons crowding round her grandson before the door shut.

Then she was standing beside her daughter in the corridor, unable to speak, too frightened to ask.

'His blood pressure's dropped. They're going to open him up again,' Deirdre said in a flat voice. 'There's no time to get him to the operating theatre.'

Bridget kissed her fiercely on the head and gave her a brief hard hug.

They found the canteen and carried their polystyrene cups of coffee to a stale-smelling empty room and, as Deirdre went over every detail of the operation and Bridget listened and chain-smoked, Barney arrived and sat close to his wife; somehow the hours must have passed.

The swelling of the heart after the operation had caused the blood pressure to fall, a doctor was to tell them eventually. Now Patrick's sternum had been splinted open to create more space and allow time for the swelling to reduce.

Bridget stood by his bedside, forcing herself to look as Deirdre compulsively explained the wires running into her son's chest in case he had a cardiac arrest, the two drainage tubes taking blood from the wound to a tank, the urinary catheter, the ventilator, the nose cap from which metal prongs were pushed through his nostrils to just below his throat for air to be pumped in and out of his lungs, the temperature and oxygen lines, and the machines monitoring the fourteen different drugs being administered through necklines into his main arteries and peripheral lines into his wrists and feet.

But all she could see were the dark hollows under his eyes and the delicate violet tissue of his closed eyelids, the transparency of his skin and the piteous vulnerability of his tiny body.

Two nurses monitored Patrick's progress round the clock and, as she sat beside him all day, they were always occupied, checking the dials and graphs on the machines, topping up the medication through the peripheral lines, turning and washing him, protecting his limbs from cold and sores with fleece and water-filled balloons, writing up endless notes.

Her daughter watched them like a lioness. She had learnt all the correct medical terms and the names of every drug and the amounts he should be given to the exact millimetre and second. She was the first to be aware of minute changes in his condition and to point them out. She questioned and discussed each new aspect of his treatment. Bridget saw the respect with which the doctors behaved towards her and marvelled that, during the months of preparation, Deirdre had made herself an expert.

'Everyone, no matter how experienced, can make mistakes. A nurse might forget to make a note of what has been administered, then when the next one comes on duty, she won't know what is due,' Deirdre told her. 'So I make sure that I know.'

Her daughter was staying in the basement of the hospital, crawling off at 1 a.m. to snatch some sleep in a small room with four bunk beds for herself and three other mothers and returning to the intensive care unit five hours later. She would be living like this for many weeks. Fathers were only allowed to stay during their children's life-or-death crises and Barney was sharing a similar room with three other fathers. Bridget had spent the past two nights with Zoe.

Sometimes they all went to the large canteen and queued for food which they could not eat, but mostly they sat mesmerized by the changing numbers on the huge screen and alternately talking hopefully or falling silent as these went up or down.

'The surgeons are very pleased with the surgery,' Deirdre said. 'But he has to come off the ventilator within the next twenty-four hours. Some babies forget how to breathe on their own.'

'What happens then?' Bridget asked.

'They have to switch the ventilator off,' her daughter answered bluntly. She went to the other side of the room to wash and disinfect herself again, as they all had to do each time they returned to the intensive care unit from outside.

'Patrick, it's your grandmama.' Bridget took his hand deep in her own. 'I know you're very busy and you have lots to do, but I want to tell you that I love you and you're doing very well.' She talked to him in a low, secret voice that only the two of them could hear. 'Mummy and Daddy are here watching over you, and Caterpillar and Scarecrow. We are all waiting for you.'

She stroked his arm and drew his cover up over his tummy and told him of all the things they were going to do together and of Erin and Rake and Quinky and the garden. She talked of flowers and snow and boats and honey and bonfires and stars.

'The world is lovely, Patrick, with so much for you to see and you'll have so much fun. Very soon you will start to breathe on your own. I know it seems such a big effort, but I promise it will all be worth while. I'm very proud of you. You are my little hero, Patrick, and heroes always win.'

It did not matter that he did not understand the words. They were reaching each other and she believed he understood their meaning.

The next afternoon Deirdre and Barney stood together by one side of the bed as Patrick was taken off the ventilator. From behind the medical staff, Bridget saw the flutter of shock across his body and then her grandson's chest began to rise and fall.

'I can't pay this! I haven't that sort of money.' Tom had received the account for the divorce costs and was bawling down the telephone.

'You've known it was coming for months and I've borrowed to pay the interim accounts on the strength of your paying me back.' Bridget was too tired to sound angry. 'You'll just have to borrow, too.'

'I'm already in debt up to the hilt,' he snapped. 'I had

to take out a loan when we split up, and I've agreed to pay you thirty-five quid a week.'

It was an invasion when all her thoughts were with Patrick. Mentally she searched for some way out of the dilemma which would not cause more hostility between them.

'Tracy Sorex is responsible for half the costs,' she reminded him.

'She hasn't any money either.'

The holidays they had been on and every night spent in the pub had seen to that, Bridget thought.

She wanted to tell him that it was none of her business how he paid the money he owed. She wanted to shout at him to leave her alone, but she could not face the months of anger, solicitors' letters and the inevitable court case which would follow.

'You don't have to pay it all at once,' she offered. 'But I've got to have something. I'm sure we can work this out.'

'I'm free on Thursday,' he said suddenly. 'I'll come over and we can talk about it.'

Deirdre sometimes commented on how much she had changed since Tom had left, that she was more calm and self-assured, that she joked and relaxed in a way she had never done before and perhaps the more she adopted this persona, the more ingrained it became. But Tom could undo all with a word. The knowledge that he was coming to the house instantly replaced all her intentions for the time ahead with that other tarnished dream.

Bridget reflected on her longing for him. It was a longing which now ran so deep that, although it might not seem to disturb the surface of her life, it had become established, a permanency, a hidden part of herself, as intrinsic as a gene.

She had not looked for a perfect physical mating. She had looked for more. She had craved union and, because this need had never been assuaged, it would never release her. Maybe what she had wanted was impossible. Perhaps man and woman, following their parallel paths, eternally side by side, eternally separated by their different thoughts and ambitions and drives, could not achieve what she so desired. But she had heard that some do. She had read of it in books.

To love as she did, so totally, was unfair; unfair to the recipient and unfair to herself, and it was unhealthy. Yet she could not help it. If she could have stopped such a devouring passion, she would have done so, gladly.

When she picked him up from the nearest station, her demeanour was so independent that he could not have guessed all this was going through her mind.

'I have an idea.'

As they sat down in the drawing-room she did not waste time. The practical complexities between them were going to be settled once and for all and they were not going to quarrel.

'If Tracy Sorex pays her share of the costs now, so that I can at least reduce my own debt, you can pay your share later.'

'I told you she hasn't any money,' he said, his face closing.

'Then she'll have to go to the bank and beg like the rest of us,' Bridget answered. 'She's a big girl who's been earning her own living for years, Tom. I'm aware that you are paying a mortgage and that you've agreed the maintenance and I'm trying to be fair. Her financial commitments are minimal and yours are not.'

He shrugged, but did not argue.

'We'll work out a reasonable figure which you can afford to pay monthly until the balance of the costs are settled,' she went on. 'And, if we can make a deal on this in a friendly way today, I'm prepared to give you my car.'

He was taken by surprise, as she had known he would be.

I've gone through life with a notice pinned to me reading 'Wally', she thought to herself, ruefully, but it was the only way to wrap up the whole squalid business and still keep the peace.

'What about you?' he asked. 'Living in the sticks, you've got to have a car.'

'I have to keep travelling to London because of Patrick and the old car is not going to be up to that sort of mileage for much longer,' she replied. 'I've arranged to buy another on credit over the next three years and, as you'll only need it for local jobs, this one should last you for quite a while.'

'You could sell it,' he pointed out. 'This seems very generous.'

'I've never been mean,' she reminded him. 'I don't want any more hassle, Tom. I want us to agree. As far as I'm concerned, we spent ten years together and, although we're divorced, those ten years matter. I want us to retain some warmth for each other. I want us to be civilized and to be able to move on without bitterness.'

He leant back in his chair, looking as enervated as she felt. Why on earth had they done this to each other? she thought.

'OK,' he said. Then he lit a cigarette. 'It's been appalling.'

'And bloody expensive. John's come out of it laughing.'

'You don't have to tell me.'

They looked at each other, thinking of the thousands of pounds that had been squandered and the benefits they had jettisoned so impulsively. Then Tom went for a walk with the dogs round the garden.

When he returned, he seemed almost his old jaunty self. 'The bees are flying well,' he said. 'You must have a glut of honey.'

'I can't lift the supers,' she shrugged. As a super containing eleven full combs of honey could weigh sixty pounds, Bridget had not harvested the honey that year. 'The bees will be so fat by next spring, they probably won't even manage lift-off.'

'Let's do it now,' Tom suggested. 'I can carry them down for you while I'm here.'

They changed into their bee suits and tramped up the hill looking like spacemen. The bees were landing and taking off in a constant stream as Bridget puffed some smoke into the entrance to the hive, although they needed little pacifying.

She and Tom worked together with practised smoothness, covering each wooden frame with a cloth and easing it off from the one below, twisting it gently to break any connecting comb and then Tom lifting it on to a flat board where she could take out each comb and shake it free of bees. Beekeeping is a quiet hobby. They talked without raising their voices and were careful not to cross the entrance or jolt the hive and the bees responded to their calm, unhurried movements by flying around them with curiosity, but without aggression.

'I really enjoyed this afternoon,' Tom said, before he drove away in the old car.

Everything about their meeting had gone right. She had

seen Tom taking stock of the life they had had together, and contemplating her.

'You're looking amazing,' he had said. 'It's hard to believe.'

It was true. The fat woman indoors he had left no longer existed. Red-haired and slim, Bridget was a different being.

He had given every indication that he, too, was still uncertain about the path he had taken and that he wanted to keep the door open between them. Bridget felt light and gay, she was so happy. She went to her desk and, for the first time in weeks, her writing flowed.

A couple of days later the news from London was that Patrick was out of danger and astonishing the doctors with his rapid recovery. Then her first maintenance cheque arrived.

Everything was coming right. The months of tears and grief had not been wasted. The humiliations she had endured in order to avoid irreparable confrontation between them had been worth while. He still cared and, although their situation was heartstoppingly fragile, if she continued living her life with patience, one day they might find each other again.

When Claire and Gareth arrived for the day, she was bubbling over with optimism and, learning that they were going on to spend the night with Tom, her only concern was that Gareth might inadvertently drive him off.

'I know you feel I'm better off without him, but that's not how I feel,' she told him as they sat at the bar of the local. 'And you're also his friend, so you must want what's best for him. If you had been here when he came, you would have seen that he's in two minds about me

394

and about his home. Please be careful what you say. And, for God's sake, be nice to that woman.' She turned to Claire.

'Oh, come on.' Claire gave her a look of unconcealed disgust.

'You can think what you like, Claire, but this is my life and my choice and, if you can't help, at least don't hinder.' When they first met, Bridget was not sure about Claire, but they had become friends and she could speak directly. 'If you cross Tracy Sorex, Tom will only be put in the position of having to stick up for her.'

'No, I don't approve,' Claire admitted. The expression on her face clearly indicated that any man who pissed her about would get short shrift. 'You're crazy.'

Which Bridget took to mean that they would not rock the boat.

When they left, promising to telephone her the next day, she did not know what to do with herself. For some reason, she had become convinced that her fate hung on this night. She tried to watch television and to read and then she returned to the old pattern of smoking and shaking, grateful that she was due to go to counselling in the morning.

As the hour for her appointment drew nearer, she sat by the telephone, checking her watch. Twice she dialled Gareth's number and got no reply. Their stay with Tom and the mousetrap would have been unimportant to her friends, who certainly had no idea of how much significance she had placed on it.

Already late for Sandra Vicars, she picked up her handbag at last and was leaving the room with a backward glance at the telephone when it rang.

'Bridget, you've got it all wrong. It's not the way you

think.' Claire sounded angry, as though she did not want to be making the call.

Bridget gripped the receiver.

'Tom and Tracy Sorex aren't good with each other, but you've got trouble coming.'

It was a conflicting message and Bridget apprehensively waited for her to continue.

'I'm not going to make a meal of this.' Claire's voice sounded like metal crumpling against metal. 'He did not behave towards her like the great lover. In fact, he put her down quite viciously, but it's not Tom you should be worrying about. It's her.'

But Bridget had already dismissed the end of her last sentence and was fixed only on the information that Tom's relationship with Tracy Sorex was showing cracks.

'Are you listening?' Claire was asking.

It was five past eleven. She was going to be very late for counselling and she had heard all she needed to know.

'I've got to go in a second,' she said.

'Bridget, that woman hardly spoke all evening, until we were all fairly drunk. Then, while the men were going on about football, or something, she suddenly told me that she was not going to pay a penny of the costs and she is sick of Tom defending you. She wants him to go to court. Bridget, is there any sort of ancillary claim he could make against you?'

Bridget felt the back of her neck and her scalp creep and a clammy sweat literally break over her skin.

'The only thing he could claim an interest in is the house and he would never do that, never,' she declared categorically.

'Tom is a very weak man and you've got to realize that you aren't the influence in his life any more. You aren't there. *She's* there.'

'But you've just said they don't get on,' Bridget pointed out desperately.

'No, I didn't say that. I watched them very carefully and, OK, Tom makes superficial gestures of being the boss, but I bet you didn't know he also does the shopping and the cooking and the cleaning,' Claire replied.

Bridget blenched. 'What?'

'This woman isn't like us. She's close. Sure, Tom can do what he likes, as long as he's handcuffed to her arm, because she never lets him out of her sight. Honestly, that man doesn't know what's going on. He's met his match and I'm not sorry. But she is the dominating factor, Bridget, and he will go along with whatever she wants. So you'd better prepare for a major battle in court, because I think your house is at risk.'

Chapter Twenty-Five

B RIDGET stumbled blindly up the stairs in front of Sandra Vicars, her hair and blouse already plastered against her skin with tears. She hunched into the chair and pulled her feet up on to its rim and banged against the back of the seat, pressing her head into her knees.

Sandra Vicars waited, but Bridget was oblivious of her. She had driven there in utter despair for counselling, but as soon as she had arrived in the room she had realized there had been no point in coming. The place to which she had run for strength and succour for so many months could no longer supply either.

After a few minutes, the counsellor asked, 'Why are you crying?'

Bridget went on beating against the chair and sobbing.

'Why are you crying, Bridget?'

'You can't help me. You can't help me any more.' Her voice was muffled in her skirt.

Repeatedly the other asked what had happened, but Bridget only wrapped her arms over her head and curled further into herself and went on crying.

Half an hour passed. Sometimes Sandra Vicars sat silently and sometimes she asked Bridget what had made her so unhappy.

'Try and tell me about it,' she said, patiently. 'Try to talk to me.'

'She's going to take my home.' At last Bridget raised

her swollen face. 'She's going to push Tom into going to court to take my house and everything he can get.'

'You think Tracy Sorex is going to try to take your house.'

But Bridget did not hear how Sandra Vicars had subtly introduced less certainty into what she had said.

'It's all I have left. I can't face a court case. I thought it was over. I gave him the car. I thought we'd agreed.'

Her voice was harsh from weeping.

'Have you talked to Tom?' the counsellor asked.

Bridget had dropped her head again and clamped her arms around it. Saliva was running out of her mouth and her body was juddering as though she was epileptic.

'How can I help you, if you don't talk to me?' Sandra Vicars asked.

The hands moved silently round the clock and there was only the sound of Bridget drawing in raucous breaths and retching.

'How do you think I feel, sitting here unable to help you?' Sandra Vicars asked.

Bridget flung back her head. 'I don't care how you feel,' she brayed, covered in tears and mucous. 'I only know how I feel. I want to die, but I'm not allowed to any more.' She was tugging at her hair and scratching her cheeks. The spittle had frothed round her lips. Inside her head was crackling like Cellophane on fire. 'I can't escape. There's nothing left. I can't die and I can't go on. No one can help me.'

She gripped her knees and jammed them against her chest and pushed her chin into her neck and locked her head against them.

Sandra Vicars looked at her for a while and then left the room. She returned a short time later with a man.

'Bridget, this is Doctor Brown.' He put a hand on her shoulder and she shuddered.

'Bridget, I think you should go into hospital,' he said. 'You need a complete break. You need to rest.'

She did not react.

'I'm going to send you to The Vale.' The Vale was the local mental hospital. 'It will only be for two or three days, but I think it's best for you,' he went on. 'Do you agree, Bridget?'

Her teeth were chattering. 'I don't care. I don't care what you do.'

She was sitting in a small office, wondering why she was wearing a candlewick dressing-gown that smelt of someone else. A man in a short white coat was writing at a desk.

'Name?' he demanded without looking up.

'Bridget Flynn,' she replied automatically.

'Address?'

And she gave it.

'Age?'

She wondered who he was.

'Who are you?' she asked.

He raised his eyebrows while still writing. 'Mark Miller.'

'And . . . and what do you do here?'

This time he shot her a look of unmistakable dislike. 'I'm the charge nurse.'

She answered the rest of his questions and he went out, leaving her alone. There was not a lot to see; a wall opposite the exterior window and an interior window on to the corridor. The board was pinned with notices, some of the drawers of the filing cabinet were open and the desk was untidy. She looked around for something to do because she could not remember how she had arrived here. She was shaking uncontrollably.

Another man in a longer white coat came in, sat down and began writing.

'How much do you drink?' he asked without preamble.

Middle-aged woman, husband left her, must be hitting the bottle: Bridget read his thoughts.

'I usually have one or two gin and tonics each evening when I finish work and I drink socially,' she replied truthfully.

'How many bottles of gin do you buy a week?'

'I've told you, I drink one or two gin and tonics most days and I'd be surprised if I buy a bottle of gin a fortnight.' She spoke with emphatic irritation.

'Why are you defensive if you have nothing to hide?' His expression was deadpan, but she saw the smugness in his eyes.

'I'm not defensive. I'm annoyed,' she snapped. 'Because I gave you an honest answer and you asked a stupid question.'

'Why are you shaking?' He was unimpressed. 'You know that shaking is a sign of alcoholism.'

'Shaking is also a sign of acute distress,' she shouted, shaking even more. 'I'm shaking because my marriage has broken up. I'm shaking because I've lost my husband. I'm shaking because my grandson is fighting for his life. I'm shaking because I'm going bankrupt. I'm shaking because my home is going to be taken from me. I'm shaking because I've nothing left. I'm shaking because I can't take any more. And who the hell are you anyway?'

'I'm Doctor Wilson, a psychiatrist here,' he replied impassively.

'Well, alcoholism is about the only problem I haven't got and, if that's the best cliché you can come up with, you're fucking useless,' she yelled.

'You can go now,' he said, indicating the door.

Go where? It felt wrong to be wearing her shoes and carrying her handbag with someone else's dressing-gown. She should have been wearing slippers. Suddenly, she felt dazed again.

There was a door at one end of the empty corridor and, when she tried it, it was locked. She wandered the other way and passed a small kitchen with a large tea urn and a lot of dirty cups. Through an open door she saw rows of people watching television. It was Friday and outside the sun was shining in the middle of the afternoon. The next room was vast and empty. It contained a lot of plastic bucket chairs and three low tables. No Smoking signs were hung on the walls. Bridget sat in a chair and lit a cigarette.

Some time later, someone asked her if she wanted supper, but she just shook her head; later still, a male nurse took her to a dormitory of cubicles and showed her a bed. A woman was moaning and talking to herself somewhere behind one of the curtains. There was only a sheet and a single cellular cotton blanket on the bed. The night was very cold, too cold to sleep and Bridget lay not thinking of anything except that she was so cold.

People began to stir around her in the morning, mumbling and coughing and clicking their teeth and farting. There did not seem to be any set time for getting up and, had she been warm, she would have stayed in bed.

As she did not know where her clothes were, she put on the candlewick dressing-gown and went into the corridor. Women with vacant faces shuffled past her and one was facing the wall deep in conversation on her own. Bridget returned to sit in the same plastic chair in the huge room. There was a smell of breakfast, but she was not hungry. It did not seem to matter. No one told her where to go.

Women wandered aimlessly in and out. Some were in night-clothes and some were dressed. They all looked disoriented and unhappy. There were no nurses and no one spoke. Eventually, at about midday, a young woman came and sat near her and lit a cigarette.

'I'm glad you did that,' Bridget said with a glance at the No Smoking signs.

'No one takes any notice of those,' the other replied. 'Are you new?'

She nodded.

They did not speak for a while and then she asked, 'What happens here?'

'Nothing.'

'What does everyone do?' she persisted.

'Watch television. I don't like television.'

'Is there anything to read?'

'No.'

They smoked and gazed into space and Bridget began to wonder what was the purpose of all these women being here with nothing to do.

'There's basketwork,' the other said as though she wanted to offer something.

Bridget looked around the room. There were no pictures on the walls. The windows were all open several inches at the bottom and it was draughty. She went to close one.

'You're wasting your time. They're fixed,' the young woman told her. 'Just enough to keep you fucking freezing and not enough to throw yourself out of.'

Bridget began to feel agitated. The parkland outside was empty. Although her eyes searched the great expanse of grass, no one walked there. There did not even seem to be birds in the mature old trees. She had read in the local paper of the number of suicides in this hospital. The atmosphere of misery was like paint covering everything. She remembered the locked door at the end of the corridor and that neither Deirdre nor any of her friends knew where she was.

'I haven't seen a doctor or a nurse since I was admitted,' she said to her companion. 'Who talks to you?'

'No one. You take your drugs and that's it.'

'But someone must see you . . . to discuss things, you know.' She did not want to appear nosy by questioning why the girl was there. Perhaps that was something you did not do.

'If you want to talk to somebody, you can ask, but you'll be lucky if they have time.'

Dr Brown had told her she should rest, but this did not seem like resting.

'How . . . have you been here long?' she asked.

'Two years.'

Bridget stared at the fixed windows. A winged insect of panic began fluttering in the pit of her mind. She was reminded of the film, *One Flew over the Cuckoo's Nest*. This place was the same as that mental hospital. Every fibre of her body recoiled from it. The women patients were too quiet, they moved like sleepwalkers and their bleak eyes were robbed of life. The uncontrollable shaking started again as she thought of the dogs. Someone had to be told where she was, but not Deirdre.

The two nurses in the office sighed as she explained that she must make a telephone call. She was taken grudgingly to a small room, bare except for a table and the instrument. The nurse asked for the number she wanted to contact and she rifled through her Filofax, inexplicably unable to recall her friend's surname. Then the operator was given the number by the nurse.

'Sue,' she said. 'I'm in The Vale.'

'Aren't we all, dear.' At any other time it would have been funny.

'No. I mean it. They've put me in The Vale.' She was whispering, although she knew the operator would be listening. 'I haven't any clothes and I want to go home.'

'Give me half an hour to get organized and I'll be right there,' Sue said at once.

Time no longer seemed to have any precision. Since the session with Sandra Vicars, hours on end had been lost while her mind was blank, but sometimes she was sure she had been sitting in the bucket chair for the whole day, only to realize that just a few minutes had passed since she last looked at the clock. She had no idea when they had brought her in. It might have been several days earlier. By the time Sue arrived, she thought she had been forgotten.

Suddenly they were conspirators. Bridget pressed a warning finger to her lips and hurried her friend into the ward cubicle.

'I've got to get away. This place is evil,' she said in a low urgent voice as she pulled on her clothes. Then she peered paranoically round the curtains for eavesdroppers before asking, 'How did you get in?'

'Through the main door in the corridor,' Sue replied.

'It's not locked then?'

Sue shook her head. 'Bridget, why are you here? What's happened?' She held Bridget's shoulders to make her stand still.

'It doesn't matter.'

Footsteps sounded down the centre of the ward and Bridget clutched at her friend. The steps returned, slapping on the wooden floor, approaching the cubicle and then there was the sound of the door shutting. 'I should never have agreed to come. No one gets better here. I've seen them. I've got to get out.'

The two friends hurried down the corridor, past the office with the interior window where the nurses were sitting and through the unlocked door. They moved swiftly down the stairs and through a foyer and out into the grounds.

Bridget was filled with premonition and, as they reached the car-park, she looked over her shoulder. A man in a short white coat was running after them. She let out a little cry and Sue grabbed hold of her.

'Wait,' she said. 'Let's sort this out.'

The man caught up with them and took Sue to one side where what they said was out of hearing. Then he came up to Bridget.

'I'm going home,' she insisted, before he had time to speak.

He was the nurse who had asked if she would like some supper and who had shown her to her bed.

'You're very upset, Bridget.' There was plenty of space between them, enough for her to be able to run away if she wanted to. 'It really would not be a good idea if you went home now. We want you to stay for a few days. Come in and we'll talk about it.'

'Nobody's spoken to me. You're the only one.' She clasped her hands together so that he should not see them trembling.

'It's usual to give people a couple of days to settle in,' he explained.

'How can I settle in when I don't know where to go, or what to do? How am I going to find answers by just wandering around here?' she demanded.

'Don't you think you're too frightened and distressed to be thinking about answers at the moment?' he asked.

'Nothing's going to go away just because I can't look at it,' she said, miserably. 'Everything will only get worse.'

'Please come back and talk to the doctor. You do need help, so give us a chance.'

He met her searching eyes steadily. His expression was open. She wondered whether to trust him.

Sue, who had been standing apart, joined them and gave the nurse her assurance that she would bring Bridget back, if he left them alone for a few minutes. Bridget stared at her friend mutinously, suspicious of betrayal. But the man walked some distance along the gravel drive before stopping. He was far enough away for them to reach Sue's car and drive off.

'Listen, Bridget, I think you should agree to see the psychiatrist,' Sue told her. 'But there's something far more important you must do. The game with Tom has got to stop *now*. I don't believe for a moment he would dream of trying to take your house, but you have got to stop wondering what he wants and what he's going to do and what will happen in the end. You have got to stop squirming about thinking up ways to keep the connection between you without ever knowing where it's leading. You have got to stop wishing and hoping. It is literally driving you insane and it's time to come right out in the open. Tell Tom you need his help and tell him how you really feel about him. Tell him you miss him. Tell him you love him and tell him you want him back.'

No one had said anything so sensible to her since their

initial separation. All the months and months of guarding herself against the possibility of Tom's final total repudiation had only caused a mental chaos far worse than any clear-cut rejection. Whatever his response, to know her position, once and for all, had to be better than this. To Bridget it was as though she had emerged from the jungle on to a wide clear road.

As they returned into the building all her concentration was bent on what to say to Tom. For nearly a year she had been acting against her own nature. As a straightforward woman, the strain of living in the shadows had finally become dangerous. Now there would be no pretence and no ambiguity. She would speak the plain truth that there could be no more misunderstanding.

The man in the office introduced himself as Dr Patel and, as Sue was about to leave, Bridget took her hand.

'I want her to stay,' she said to him and he nodded.

As he studied some notes, she sat down and her friend stood beside her.

'I see you have an alcohol problem,' he said.

Bridget leant back and closed her eyes. She might have known.

Then, ignoring him, she turned to Sue. 'How long have you known me?' she asked.

'Ten years,' Sue said.

'How often have you seen me drunk?'

'Twice.'

'How much do I drink?'

'She drinks a couple of gin and tonics, or sometimes we've shared a bottle of wine or occasionally, over a meal, two bottles of wine,' Sue told Dr Patel. 'Bridget is not an alcoholic.'

'If you want to know why I don't have a drink problem,

I'll tell you,' Bridget cut in. 'It's because, if I drink too much, I'm ill for days. I've never been able to drink heavily and get away with it. It doesn't make me feel good. It just makes me sick as a dog.'

The only time she had ever been drunk and surfaced clear-headed and bursting with energy had been the night Sue had filled her with brandy when Tom had run off with Old Panstick and Bridget had woken at 5 a.m. and driven to town to find him.

'Why don't you ask Sandra Vicars?' she demanded.

'We have spoken to your counsellor,' he admitted.

'And?'

He frowned.

'And?' she insisted.

'Well, she does not feel you have a problem with alcohol abuse.'

'I see.' Bridget glared at him with contempt. 'But because some wanker made an instant and uninformed diagnosis and scribbled it down on that bit of paper, it's written on tablets of stone as far as you're concerned. Well, take a blood test. Do anything you like. But I am telling you that you are completely wrong.'

'All right,' he said, but she knew his mind had been set before he had even seen her and, as he went on talking, she made it obvious that she was not listening. What a preposterous twist of fate that she should have landed with a bunch of psychiatrists determined to treat her for the one aspect of her life she had under control.

'You know, Bridget, there are people on your level here,' he said at last.

'Are there? Well, I haven't met any yet,' she answered rudely. 'I've only met imbeciles and they aren't the patients. They're the psychiatrists.'

Before she left, Sue arranged for her to telephone Tom and agreed to return the next day.

It was half past five and Tom was at the Bird's Nest.

'That'll be Tracy checking up on you,' someone said in the background as he was called to the phone.

The smell of the patients' supper made Bridget feel sick. Tears were already welling before she heard his voice.

'Tom.' She tried to sound steady. 'Tom, I'm in The Vale. Tom, I need your help.' She had never once asked his help for herself. 'I need your help.'

'You're in The Vale? The mental hospital?' He sounded confused, almost as though he doubted her. 'Why? What are you doing there?'

She fought against the tears and tried not to sniff.

'Tom, please listen to me. Ever since we split up we've never talked and I can't go on with all the evasion.' She stopped and wiped her nose with the back of her hand and inhaled deeply. 'I want you to know that I love you and I miss you. There is a way we could work everything out. I know it may take time, but the truth is that I want us to be together in the end, however long it takes.'

There was silence at the other end of the line as the water from her eyes coursed soundlessly down her face.

'Whatever you decide, I desperately need your help now, Tom. Please phone the hospital and talk to them. This is a terrible, terrible place. I'm frightened and I want to go home.' She was crying openly now. 'Please, please help me, Tom.'

'Darling, don't worry,' he said, at last. 'I'll deal with it. I'll phone them and get you home first and we can talk about everything else after that.'

'Tom . . .' There was something else she had to ask

him. 'I've been told Tracy Sorex is going to get you to claim the house.'

'That's a lie! I don't know who told you that, but it's a fucking lie!' He sounded livid. 'That is your house, Bridget, and I know what it means to you. I would never put any claim on it. I would never do anything so despicable.'

She felt as though she would disintegrate with relief. How could she have been persuaded to believe such a thing of him?

'Tom, I'm so frightened. You will telephone the hospital, won't you?'

'Yes.'

'You won't leave me here?'

'No, Bridget, I'll make sure you go home.'

Bridget went back to her place in the large room suffused in peace. Her mind drifted off into nothingness and she chain-smoked without noticing the saucer on the table overflowing with dog-ends. She spoke to no one and no one spoke to her. Tom would organize everything. Tom would look after her. She did not have to think any more. Tom would save her.

Several times during the next morning Bridget went to the office to ask if her husband had telephoned.

'Well, he's my ex-husband really,' she said nervously, to make sure they understood, but their reply was still negative.

'Tom contacted me last night,' Sue said when she arrived. 'He seemed to want to check that you were really in here.'

'They will have confirmed that by now.' Bridget jerked her head in the direction of the office. 'He's promised to get me home. I don't think they're telling me that he's phoned.'

Sue looked uncomfortable. A couple of women came into the room and pulled two chairs together and sat very closely side by side. Bridget shrugged at her friend to ignore them.

Sue brought out a box of chocolates from her bag and gave it to her. Then she walked over to the window and stood staring out. She was behaving very oddly. She lit a cigarette and then, as though she had reached a decision, turned round abruptly.

'That doctor caught me on my way out yesterday and I'm not supposed to tell you this,' she said. 'But all that stuff about you being here for a few days is rubbish. They're going to have you committed under some section of the Mental Health Act as being at serious risk to yourself. In fact, he told me I needn't bother coming back for a month because you're going to be in here for a long time. They aren't going to let you leave.'

Bridget leapt to her feet, the blood rushing in her head.

'Sit down,' Sue hissed. 'For Christ's sake don't go off half-cocked in a place like this or they'll drug you to the eyeballs and you'll never get out.'

'But I'm not mad. I'm just upset. What am I going to do?' Her voice was shrill as the ague, which always attacked in times of stress, took over again. 'What am I going to do?'

'Ssshh! I don't know.' Sue glanced over at the two patients, who stared woodenly ahead apparently unaware of their existence. 'Sit still!'

Bridget became rigid immediately.

'Think,' Sue instructed. 'You've got to think.'

'But Tom . . .'

'Will you forget Tom! Forget everything else. This is far more important. For God's sake, nothing worse than this can ever happen to you. This is deep trouble and I can't do much, because I'm only a friend and they're not going to listen to me. Bridget, you have a very good brain and the only way you're going to get out of this mess is by using it. You have got to think your way out of here.'

But Bridget's brain was in a state of pandemonium and, long after Sue had gone, she remained transfixed. Three days had passed since she had eaten and she felt giddy and faint and terror-stricken. What thoughts she had went round and round the same wheel in the cage her life had become, getting nowhere.

Most of the patients went to bed, but still she did not move. A tall, blond young man came into the room and sat opposite her at the table.

'Can't you sleep either?' he asked.

He was not wearing a uniform and she realized he must be a patient, although she had not seen any male patients before. She looked up and saw that it was only ten o'clock.

'I suppose not.'

He was leaving in a week, he told her, having been in the hospital for six months because of drug abuse. But his father had found him a good job and he was going to be all right. He wasn't coming back.

He was well-built and handsome, with an easy, likeable manner. As she half-listened to him, she began to relax. He told her about his home and his girlfriend and his dog and how he had been bloody stupid and how he was going to make a go of everything from now on.

He was in the middle of a sentence when the door opened and the charge nurse, Mark Miller, walked in.

'Go to bed,' he ordered.

The young man stood up without finishing what he was saying and walked meekly from the room.

Bridget was jolted. She had seen the women sitting inanimately before the television set and meandering sadly about the corridor. She had watched the psychiatrists scuttling after their text books down the wrong track, but nothing had shocked her as much as the sight of this powerful young man behaving like an obedient child.

This is going to happen to me, she thought. They were going to take away her willpower and her options. They were going to reduce her to a docile automaton.

'And you.' Mark Miller stared coldly at her.

'No,' she replied calmly. 'I am not ready to go to bed yet.'

At eleven o'clock Bridget decided to test out what Sue had told her. After tidying her hair and rubbing on some lipstick, she picked up her handbag and went to the office where Mark Miller and a boot-faced female nurse were drinking tea together.

'I have decided to leave,' she said. 'I am going home.'

'No, you're not,' the charge nurse replied and the other sneered.

'You have no right to keep me here against my will.' Bridget kept her voice level. 'I am a voluntary patient.'

'Not any more,' he said.

'My case has not been properly discussed with any doctor and no documents or orders could have been signed relating to me,' she said.

'It's only a matter of time,' he replied, with satisfaction. 'If you want discussions, you'll have to wait until the morning. There's no way any patient would be allowed to leave at this time of night.'

'Very well,' she agreed. 'I shall wait in the day room until morning and then I shall leave.'

Already she had made the plastic bucket seat near the window her own. Had she walked into the room to find someone else sitting in it, she would have felt her territory had been invaded. It disturbed her that this was the last tiny space to which she could lay claim and even that was not secure.

Sue had told her to think. If she went to bed, she might sleep and tomorrow would come before she had had a chance to collect herself. But, although she tried to be rational and constructive, the strands of her predicament tangled in her head; the dozens of solicitor's letters, the words of her counsellor, Patrick's condition, the prospect of bankruptcy, her age and the impossible struggle ahead. Tom.

The hours passed as she tried to find some explanation for what had become of her until, at last, she was so tired that her mind shut down altogether and she sat unfocused and no longer aware of herself or her surroundings.

The night reached its nadir, that point at which the dying close their eyes for the last time and the desperate fill their mouths with pills and hope is lost.

Bridget straightened up and looked round the vast room as though coming out of a trance.

'What is a woman like me doing in a place like this?' she asked herself. 'And how have I allowed that man to do this to me?'

Then, at last, the truth unfolded before her.

And the truth was so simple that she could not believe she had not seen it in ten long years.

It did not matter if Tom's mother had spurned him. It did not matter if he had been unhappy as a child and frustrated as an adult. All the excuses and motives she had always given herself to explain his behaviour did not matter. What he had done in the past and what he might do in the future did not matter. What she felt about him did not matter.

All that mattered was that Tom O'Dare was the man he was and he was no good for her. He was destroying her and she had to put a stop to it. This was the truth of the affair.

It was Monday morning. Soon the patients would be waking up and the nurses would be standing over them while they took their drugs.

Bridget stiffened. That was why she had not been interviewed by a psychiatrist and why she had been given no medication, for the same reason that the documentation necessary to commit her had not been drawn up. She had been admitted on a Friday afternoon, when the staff would have been reduced to a minimum for the weekend and the whole place had just been ticking over. But now it was Monday morning.

With icy clarity, she realized that today her case would be decided and today her drugs programme would be prescribed. Once she was forced to take their drugs, she would have no further control over her life. Months or even years could pass before she was released from this place. She would lose her home and her beloved dogs and her friends and her work. She would lose everything.

When she had tried to commit suicide, death had not frightened her, but the prospect of total strangers regulating her brain, subduing and deadening her emotions and turning her into another of the withdrawn, defeated women who peopled the ward, was the ultimate spectre. She had to escape before this happened.

Laying her hands on her knees, Bridget deliberately

relaxed her body muscle by muscle from the toes up until even the tense corners of her mouth softened. Then she began to tease out her thoughts methodically and very carefully, refusing to allow extraneous ideas to interrupt, or to be diverted from her objective.

To open the doors of this hospital was going to require tunnel vision. Here, she was not a free individual with ordinary rights. She was a mental patient and any sign of perturbation, however natural, would be interpreted as mental instability. Whatever happened, anger, tears, trembling or any other evidence of emotion could not be displayed. She had to be implacably in control of herself.

She breathed deeply and rhythmically. Each time a muscle tightened she loosed it. As the hours passed she exerted her will over every atom of her mind and body and centred her spirit on the goal of reaching home.

At six o'clock Bridget went to the cloakroom and washed. She combed her hair and used her cosmetics, not too much, just enough to make her look like a normal, well-presented woman. She checked her shoulders for stray hairs and straightened her clothes. Then she went to the office.

'I am going to leave here now,' she told the two nurses.

Their hostility was spiced by the spite in their eyes.

'If you try to leave, you will be restrained,' Mark Miller said, looking as though he could not wait for the opportunity.

'I am going to leave,' she repeated.

The female nurse spoke for the first time. 'You cannot leave here without seeing a doctor and there are no doctors available.'

'There is always a doctor on duty at night,' Bridget pointed out. 'I want to see him.'

'Well, you can't. He's in bed.'

Bridget leant forward and fixed stony eyes on them.

'Then get him out of bed.' Her voice grated with authority.

The woman picked up the telephone and pressed a few buttons. Bridget sat down composedly as someone was told that they were having trouble with a patient.

A few minutes later, following the female nurse, she was taken to another office where a man was sitting at a desk. He had dark, curly hair and alert, intelligent eyes and he was not wearing a white coat over his suit.

'I am Doctor Andrews,' he said, holding out his hand for her to shake. This was an improvement on the other two, she thought, and he was Irish.

'I hear you want to leave. Would you like to tell me why, Bridget?'

'Ms Flynn,' she said firmly. He was not going to get away with the trick of reserving his own title while demoting his patient to a Christian name. The discussion was going to be on equal terms.

He inclined his head. 'Ms Flynn.'

'I have been here for two and a half days, Doctor Andrews, and that has been long enough to observe the patients and the staff. Frankly, it is hard to credit that a place like this can exist when we're almost in the twenty-first century. It is soulless, cold and barren. How you can imagine any of the women here have a hope of recovering from their wretchedness when all that happens is that they are given drugs and left to wander about with nothing to do, I do not know, but I do know there are no solutions here for me.'

The hatchet-faced nurse glared at her and the thought of coming under her unsupervised control and that of Mark Miller only strengthened Bridget's resolve.

'You haven't given us much time,' Dr Andrews said amiably.

'I sat up all last night considering my position. It was my choice to do so, but neither that woman, nor the charge nurse checked on me once,' she told him. 'Supposing I had not known what I was doing? Supposing I had been as desperate as I was when I arrived here? Supposing I had found a way to kill myself last night, as so many other patients have done? Those two would not have known or cared. I came here distraught because of unmanageable personal problems and was immediately diagnosed as an alcoholic, which I am not. I have given you time enough.'

'As you say, you were very distressed when you were brought here, Ms Flynn,' he said, avoiding her accusations. He leant back and put his hands behind his head, a man giving an impression of neutrality, creating a casual atmosphere, portraying himself as someone dependable, someone in whom she could confide. 'Would you like to talk about that?'

'No, doctor, I would not.' Bridget smiled openly at him. She had anticipated this. 'I haven't the slightest intention of discussing anything with any of you. I am going home and if you prevent me, I am simply not going to co-operate in any way while I am here. Without my co-operation there can be no psychiatric assessment and, without an assessment, you cannot prescribe medication. I shall just sit it out until you let me go.'

'All right, then tell me how you feel you would benefit if I allow you to leave?'

It was a fair question.

'My home is where I feel secure. I shall have my friends around me and that is what I need most,' she explained, honestly. 'In a way, coming here has been the best thing that could have happened to me, because this place is so horrifying and the possibility of being forced to remain here is so dreadful. Being confronted by such a fate would galvanize anyone into concentrating their mind, assuming they had a mind left, and it's certainly brought me to my senses. Whatever problems I have are never going to be resolved here.'

She could see him weighing her up, checking for body language that might give her away. She sat with her legs neatly together and her hands loosely in her lap, the way Sandra Vicars sat. He was almost persuaded, but not quite.

'You know, one of my plays will be on television in a couple of weeks and it's likely to cause quite a stir.' This was a barefaced lie. She did not even know if her play would be accepted. 'Not only my family and friends are going to want to know why I am being kept here against my will then.'

Next she brought out her only weapon.

'The press is going to be asking questions, too.'

She looked him coolly in the eye. He leant forward and clasped his hands together on the desk.

'Will you agree to continue going to counselling if I let you go home?' he asked.

She was free! She did not alter her expression by a flicker.

They shook hands again and the nurse went ahead of her and unlocked the ward door. Bridget walked unhurriedly down the stairs to the foyer. There was a payphone in the corner. She pushed in a few coins and called a taxi.

Chapter Twenty-Six

IN THE wardrobe looking-glass by the bed her reflection was immediately recognizable, but altered. The expression on the face that looked back at her was quizzical and even slightly amused.

The morning after her return from The Vale, she lay quietly, aware that an inherent part of herself had been mislaid. It was nothing to worry about, rather like looking down and finding that an unsightly mole on her body had suddenly disappeared.

Her hands, when she stretched them out, were steady, her stomach ulcer was not complaining, there was a proper anticipation of breakfast and even the passing thought that it seemed a nice day to take the dogs for a walk. Everything was obviously in good order physically.

Yet there had been a mutation somewhere within her. With the detached interest of a scientist she thumbed deliberately through her problems to see what would happen and they were certainly brain-teasers, but eventually, she concluded, every single one of them would be dissolved by the future – and no doubt be replaced by others equally transient.

Full of curiosity, she prodded at heartstopping memories and images and discovered that they did not disturb her. Growing more daring, she crossed boundaries so exquisitely sensitive that she had previously refused to admit their existence, but now she found nothing there that could not be assimilated after all.

Then it became clear what it was that was missing. Fear was missing. Her fear had gone. It had vaporized and vanished as though it had never been. For the first time in her life Bridget was not afraid.

The sensation was peculiar. The fluttering and twittering, the darting and starting, the electric stabs of nervousness, the jolts of her pulse, that bloody trembling, the acute alertness and unsleeping vigilance which had accompanied her since childhood were no longer there.

She rested back on the pillows, still wary enough to wonder if a bogeyman was about to jump out at her. But none did. There was just this pleasant feeling of philosophical assurance. She wondered where it had come from and gradually deduced that it had been born of her experience in the mental hospital.

Bankruptcy, homelessness, suicide or isolation; no imaginable nightmare would ever compare with the abyss of her own mental destruction that had opened before her in the psychiatric unit. She had been confronted by the worst catastrophe that could ever befall her and she had defeated it entirely on her own. Now, quite simply, there was nothing more to fear. She had survived.

She knew implicitly that this transformation was not ephemeral. Never again would she be the neurotic, defensive woman of the past. Come joys and sorrows, victory or failure, this solid inner sense of impregnability would be her companion for the rest of her life. It was as though Bridget had arrived at the place within herself for which she had always searched.

There was just one loose end left.

She picked up the telephone and dialled Tom's number. 'You were going to telephone the hospital,' she said.

'Well I didn't,' he replied.

His confirmation of what she had known caused her no emotion, for, with the vanquishing of her fear, Bridget had finally reached understanding – understanding of everything that had happened to her since that holiday in Portugal, why it had happened and that it had now ended.

The man she had just spoken to had not suddenly become a monster. Nor had he gradually turned into some heartless unknown being. Middle-aged men do not change. Tom O'Dare was the man he had always been. But he was not the man who had been her husband.

What Bridget understood at last was that Tom, her Tom, had never existed.

In Portugal she had met a man, a man with such a powerful chemical attraction that he had been irresistible and, before she knew anything about him, she had read into this man all the qualities she wanted to find. She had invented the person she believed him to be and, over the years, whenever he had behaved in ways that did not fit in with her creation, she had conjured up excuses and reasons and explanations and justifications and, when she could think of nothing better, she had blamed herself.

But Tom O'Dare had never been the man she thought he was. He had always been a complete stranger.

As a playwright, she of all people knew that make-believe can be far more powerful than reality. The characters in her plays had always seemed alive to her and Tom, in the guise of a living, breathing man, had been the most totally compelling character of all.

There could never have been an answer to her obsessive question of why she loved Tom O'Dare so much, because she had never loved Tom O'Dare. At last Bridget saw that for ten years she had been besottedly in love with her own fantasy.

What a lifting of the scales from the eyes, moment of truth, light on the road to Damascus, open Sesame, and abracadabra, she thought, looking back over the past four days, suitably stunned. The Book of Revelations had nothing on this.

'I know this is going to sound absolutely bizarre, but I've realized that Tom was a figment of my imagination. He was never there at all.' That evening she outlined her momentous conclusion to Deirdre. 'Do you think that's bizarre?'

'It's bizarre.'

Deirdre was spending the night at home for a well-earned break from Great Ormond Street Hospital, where Patrick was now making cheering, steady progress and her mother's latest crackpot idea was a diversion from her own worries.

'Yes, but it's possible, isn't it? I mean it's not completely crazy?' Bridget pressed.

'It's completely crazy, Mummy,' Deirdre replied. 'And entirely probable. Although you're very practical in lots of ways, most of the time you're on another planet. It seems perfectly feasible to me that you could dream up a mirage and then spend ten years demolishing yourself over it.'

'Thanks,' Bridget responded acidly, accepting that once again her daughter's assessment of her was accurate, although it showed a marked lack of respect for a woman who was now a grandmother.

'Look, despite everything, I basically liked Tom and I've even missed him being part of the family,' Deirdre continued, with a little smile in her voice. 'But he was always a total fuck-up and it was obvious that you weren't seeing him as he is. You were seeing something else.'

'Well, I'm seeing him now,' Bridget giggled. 'As the man who never was.'

For all Tom O'Dare knew, she was still in the psychiatric unit, she thought more soberly to herself. And he was prepared to let her rot there. At least her daughter knew nothing about that.

There were still a few of his belongings in the house. She packed them in a cardboard box: a miniature television she had given him one Christmas, some sweaters, a framed set of cricket cartoons, his cricket bat wedding present signed by the Kent team. She signed the vehicle registration document for the old car over to him and put it in an envelope and placed her wedding and eternity rings into the box with his gold cufflinks.

When Nick and Sasha came down to their cottage that weekend, she gave the box to them.

'Would you drop this off on your way back to London?' she asked. 'I don't mind any more if you visit Tom and Tracy Sorex.'

When they left she switched on the radio and the Polka by Strauss came romping into the room and bounced her through the house and whistling into the kitchen. The dogs, who had decided since she came home from The Vale that every day was their birthday, took hooligan liberties, jumping up on her and stealing a packet of biscuits and fighting over their food, sensing that they could now get away with anything.

Everything had finally fallen into place. Her new car was delivered and parked before the house like a television advertisement. It might have been a new lover, the way Bridget could not stop going out to delight in its big, powerful body and metallic skin and the masculine leather smell of its interior.

After midnight she sidled into the driving seat just to open and close the electronic windows and sunroof, and adjust the exterior mirrors through the rubber pad on the dashboard, and centrally lock and unlock the doors, and swing the sound of the radio round each of the four speakers. Of course she should have bought a Robin Reliant, but why look down? If she was going to sink financially, she was going to sink in Janet Reger knickers and a large car, having had a bloody good time. If she survived, she promised herself, while pressing the buttons with glee, one day she would buy a Rolls-Royce on principle.

The heat of high season was softening towards autumn. The garden was healthy with polished leaves and weed-free beds and trim edges. She abandoned her word processor and took her notebook with her to the hammock and there the play, with which she had fiddled about off and on for nearly a year, virtually wrote itself to the end in a week.

Sue and Sasha and Nick brought over bottles of champagne to celebrate with her and they all lolled about on the lawn eating stuffed vine leaves and olives and feta cheese and pitta bread, food Bridget thought in keeping with the Mediterranean languor of the day.

They took silly photographs of each other, Nick striking the macho pose of a successful hunter with his foot on Quinky, who was stretched on the grass like a corpse; Sasha as Society beauty with a glass of champagne and a wide-brimmed hat; Sue balancing a precarious column of plates and Bridget spreadeagled in the hammock with her eyes closed in mock exhaustion and the completed manuscript festooned in ribbons on her chest.

They were joined in the evening by Fiona and George. The men grilled sausages and kebabs on the barbecue and Bridget lit wax torches on sticks and they teased each other, started earnest discussions, expressed vehement opinions and finished up laughing helplessly over nothing. A group of friends on a summer evening.

With her play finished, Bridget decided to take her purring new car to London and spoil herself.

At the hospital she found Patrick released from the tubes and machines, with colour in his face and eating and breathing well. As she smothered him with kisses and played very gently with him, he chuckled and pulled her glasses off and she felt as though she had been born just for this moment.

Then she met Zoe for lunch, strolled round Covent Garden, had tea at the Savoy and went to a concert at the Festival Hall.

The next day, she bought new clothes she did not need and a floppy black velvet hat and several pairs of ear-rings, so long that they trailed below her shoulders, and a frivolous pure silk camisole for Deirdre and a selection of pungent cheeses and continental sausages for Barney, who loved his stomach; she filled the back of the car with carrier bags and they all went out to dinner.

Happier than she had been in years, Bridget returned home just in time to take delivery of a cornucopian bouquet of fifty lilies from Carter Blake, who telephoned a few minutes later.

The Americans had finally accepted her film script. The contract was signed and a ravishing, buttery cheque was on its way to her.

She awoke next day knowing she had reached Paradise. Her grandson was recovering, her immediate financial future was assured, already an idea was forming for a new play and the past had been laid to rest at last. Singing, she skipped downstairs into the scent of the lilies and through the sunlit hall.

There was a letter on the doormat, a long, white envelope with a black circular logo.

Bridget stopped and stared at it. She picked it up as though it was a dead cockroach. She opened it and her eyes flashed over its contents.

Six months after their divorce Tom O'Dare had gone to a solicitor to raise the question of 'ancillary matters generally and his entitlement to a share in the former matrimonial home'.

Letting out a shout, Bridget ran from the house, dived into the car and drove off down the drive, leaving the front door wide open behind her.

Intent only on reaching Bristol, she seemed to be speeding up the motorway within minutes, a ball of rage expanding in her head as though about to explode. Without plans, without knowing what she would say, she was going to confront Tom O'Dare and Tracy Sorex, once and for all.

He had wrecked their marriage and cut off her daughter and ignored her grandson and almost ruined her. With broken promises and sham he had reduced her first to trying to kill herself and then to near madness. The more she had tried to be conciliatory, the more of a fool he had thought her. He had got away with everything and, now, when he believed she was helpless in a mental hospital, he was trying to take her house.

All her life Bridget had worked for her home, opening the first cottage door when she and Sam had been young and poor, going without all but necessities to hold on to it through the years of his unemployment as an actor and alcoholism, repairing it, decorating it, pouring the money from her plays into it, creating a garden to enhance it and the dark, velvet warmth of its spirit.

She had laid this home before Tom, gladly inviting him to share and love it as she did. But he was not going to take it from her. She would burn it to the ground before letting Tom O'Dare force her out.

Looking for his address, she backed and shunted and reversed the big car through the city s eets, growing more and more virulent, until, at last, she came to a one-way road so narrow that she had to park on the pavement.

She banged the knocker on the door and banged again, and again, and then stood back. They had a house. They were both working and earning and this house was theirs. They had everything they needed, everything they had taken at her expense and still they wanted more.

The house of her ex-husband and his mistress branded its image on her mind. She wanted to dynamite it, blitz it to dust, just as they were trying to annihilate her.

They were inside. She knew they were. She peered through the net curtains of the downstairs window. There was no one in the small furnished room, but she knew they were somewhere in the house, hiding from her, and she stood choking with impotence.

Then she saw the ladder, left against a neighbouring wall by builders who had gone for a tea-break. Her wrath had become a cauldron, bubbling and spitting inside her. She grabbed the ladder and dragged it along the terrace gutters until it was propped against Tom O'Dare's house, then she climbed it until she was level with the first-floor window.

The double bed was unmade, a tangle of grubby sheets and blankets and crumpled pillows. There were clothes lying about, discarded on the carpet. Bridget squeezed her eyes shut and clung to the sides of the ladder, gulping in air to counteract the wave of nausea. Tilting her head back to avoid looking into the room again, when she opened her eyes they were focused on the open rafters of the neighbouring house that was being re-roofed.

Reaching up, she grasped a tile above her and, to her surprise, it came off easily in her hands. She hurled it to the ground.

As it smashed on the pavement below, the most fabulous sense of liberation spread through her. It was as though she were physically breaking free from steel chains. Euphoric with rage, she climbed higher and pulled off more tiles. They spun away, shattering like china as they landed. Twelve months of pain and humiliation were being avenged, a lifetime of frustration was being exploded and left behind. She was magically flying, high and free, away from her mother's beggarly spirit, away from Sam's turbulence and far beyond Tom O'Dare's insatiable demands, soaring out of the reach of her past and into serenity.

A gap opened in the roof; sunlight fell over the accumulated cobwebs and dust of years. She was like a dog furiously digging to bury a bone, she thought. This jogged her sense of humour and she began to grin as the tiles arced faster through the air, the more expert she became.

'Hey! That's my ladder!' A workman was standing on the road staring up. 'What are you doing that for?'

'Fun,' she replied, reaching dangerously across the ever-widening hole to dislodge more tiles. Nothing would have stopped her now. 'You'll have to wait for your ladder and you can fetch the police if you like.'

'Oh no, love. I'm having fun, too,' he said, folding his arms and watching.

The English have an incomparable sense of the ridiculous. In any other country there would have been a local riot, she thought.

'They're not going to like you,' he commented laconically after a few minutes.

'They don't like me anyway.' She leant back and surveyed her handiwork. An area of about six feet by four feet had been exposed to the sky.

Bridget descended the ladder and returned coolly to her car. As she began to drive home, she was humming and hoping for rain.

The second she saw Tom's car – the car she had bought – parked outside an Italian restaurant, fury poured through her again like boiling tar. He had never taken *her* out for meals. Jamming on the brakes and catapulting from the driver's seat through the door of the restaurant, she was no longer calm.

There were two untouched plates of spaghetti on the table in front of Tom O'Dare and Tracy Sorex. At the sight of these, Bridget went rampantly out of control again. She threw a plateful over him and the second plateful over her. As Tom leapt to his feet and ran behind her, she flung herself on the woman, pinning her to her seat and shouting everything she knew about Tom's past. Tom and another man were trying to pull her back, but Bridget was dimly aware of having incredible strength. They had as much effect as a pair of puppies.

'You've ruined my life,' she shrieked at the woman.

Tracy Sorex looked up with spaghetti dangling in

worms from her hair and smirked. She put her head on one side and let her eyelids droop and she smirked.

This was the first time Bridget had had the chance to look the other woman full in the face; in that instant, she realized that her idea, never quite relinquished, that this might just conceivably be a desperate, inexperienced girl had always been nonsense. Whatever had happened in her life had already made this a bitter woman. Everything was written there.

'I can see your face,' she gasped triumphantly, and immediately lost all interest in Tracy Sorex. She was nobody and nothing.

As soon as she released her hold, Bridget was hauled backwards so violently that she fell. Scrabbling to try and stand up, she held on to a small fire extinguisher, which came away from its mounting on the wall, and she looked up to see Tom O'Dare and Tracy Sorex standing over her. Screeching, she pulled out the safety clip and squeezed the handle. Foam streamed over her ex-husband's chest and, as she struggled upright, he turned and fled through the door. But Tracy Sorex stood her ground.

'Fuck off!' she swore.

Oh no, thought Bridget, almost bursting arteries with savagery. That slut is not going to swear at me and get away with it.

Grabbing the woman's arm, she ruthlessly turned the extinguisher on her until she was smothered from head to foot in foam and the container was empty. Tracy Sorex was not swearing and smirking now. She was screaming her head off.

Two waiters, who had been keeping well back from the spray, at last took courage and frogmarched Bridget past other diners, sitting frozen in their seats, and out to the street where, while they were still restraining her, Tom O'Dare appeared and hit her hard round the head.

Then she was walking into her kitchen and wondering how she had arrived there. The last thing she remembered was yelling at Tom. After that, everything was blank. She must have driven for over two hours to reach home, but she could recall nothing of the journey.

She felt absolutely magnificent, effervescent and ecstatically uninhibited. She went into the garden and lay flat on her back and gazed up into the sky and floated off into the blue.

She was still high two days later, when the first newspaper reporter telephoned.

'I hear you've had a bit of a battle with your ex-husband in Bristol,' he said. 'Do you want to talk about it?'

Why not? she thought. I've escaped. I can do what I like and say what I like, and what other people think doesn't matter a damn. She was certainly not going to cover her head in ashes now. So she told him all about it.

'Why did you do it?'

'It made a diversion on what might otherwise have been a dull day,' she replied lightly.

'How do you feel?'

'Wonderful!'

'What about the consequences?'

If she ended up in prison, it would still have been worth it, she thought to herself. After allowing Tom O'Dare to walk over her for months, for years, she had finally stood up for herself and slapped him back – hard.

'One always has to face the consequences of one's actions,' she replied.

'Any regrets?' the reporter wanted to know.

'I ruined my Gucci handbag.'

The tabloids splashed the story across their front page and centre page spreads and, at a time of general gloom, the nation held its sides and laughed.

The document had arrived, just an ordinary piece of paper, but irreplaceable: Bridget had passed her flight test and gained her Private Pilot's Licence. She had framed it and hung it on her study wall.

The weather forecast was excellent. She selected her route, checking it for controlled airspace, prohibited areas and air traffic zones, and entered the check points on the flight log. She booked out with Air Traffic Service and carefully made her walk-around inspection of the aeroplane. Now she was taxiing to the take-off position. This was her first flight as a qualified pilot, but she was not going very far.

The Cessna skimmed from the ground into the air, like a swan rising from water and, as she set the heading, she saw the motorway below jammed with holiday traffic and she smiled.

The day was cloudless. Even the forbidding tracts of Dartmoor to the south looked as inviting as a Greek island in the sun. Bridget drew in a deep breath of pure pleasure.

The Court case was over. She had stood in the dock listening to her solicitor defend her. Then she had made her own plea in mitigation. The three magistrates had adjourned through a door behind the bench and returned a few minutes later to give her a conditional discharge.

She had wanted to fight Tom O'Dare to the end, but John warned that, not only could he legally claim an interest in her house, but he could also claim on her future earnings.

'He's on the way down and you are on the way up,' her solicitor had said and, eventually, his advice had prevailed.

She had agreed to shoulder the £100,000 debt, to waive maintenance and to pay all the costs for the divorce. Gaining her liberty had been expensive, but ever since the moment of hurling the first tile from her ex-husband's roof, she had needed no more psychotherapy, taken no more tranquillizers or anti-depressants. Her hands no longer shook. She slept each night through as blissfully as a baby.

Bridget looked down at the farms and hamlets of Devon from the aeroplane. The corn was cut and the fields were the colour of shortbread. She reached into her travel bag for one of the ripe figs she had picked in her garden only that morning and bit into its carmine heart. Changing course, she set the verdant curves of Exmoor as her horizon and listened to the voices of other pilots reporting their positions to ATS through her headphones. High and unimpeded in the sky, she was not alone.

Checking the directional indicator against the magnetic compass, she looked through the cockpit window and found she was exactly on target. Dunkery Beacon, the highest point on the moor, was her sign to descend gradually until the village came into view. And then, on the side of the hill, she saw her house, gleaming white in the sunlight.

There had only been horse-drawn transport when it was first built and now she was dipping over its slate roofs in a modern flying machine, yet it stood solid and unchanged.

For two hundred years the people who had lived there had performed the same cycle of tasks. Open fires had been lit in the grates during every one of those winters; every summer the windows had been opened to the sun. The cobwebs had been brushed from the high ceilings and the chimneys had been swept. The woodwork had been painted against the weather, the grass had been cut and the fruit had been picked. An intrinsic continuity had been created that imbued everything.

Bridget circled so low that she could see the rose hedge hung with hips as big as cherries. The boundaries of walls and paths, the speckled silver of the ancient birch tree, the laburnum tunnel, the soft contours of the cherry wood and the orchard were all composed into the garden of her dreams that she had made come true. The garden symbolized her achievement.

Despite the destruction and trauma of the past eighteen months, she had retained everything of importance and permanence: her family, her friends, her work and her home. Yet her fulfilment no longer depended upon anyone else, or upon how other people saw her. She had finally been liberated, freed to be her own woman, freed to be at ease with herself, freed to look forward to the future. Circling over her home for one last time, Bridget realized she had never been happier.

When Tom had arrived in her life, she had seen him as her saviour. Now, as she looked down on her lovely house and garden, she knew she had been right. He had not saved her by carrying and supporting her in the way she had envisaged. By leaving her to drown, he had taught her to fly.